CAN'T HELP FALLING IN LOVE

ERIKA KELLY

CAN'T HELP FALLING IN LOVE

Erika Kelly

ISBN-13: 978-0-9992585-3-8

Copyright 2020 EK Publishing, LLC

Cover design and formatting by Serendipity Formatting

Editing by Kristy deBoer

Titles by Erika Kelly

The Calamity Falls series

KEEP ON LOVING YOU

WE BELONG TOGETHER

THE VERY THOUGHT OF YOU

JUST THE WAY YOU ARE

IT WAS ALWAYS YOU

CAN'T HELP FALLING IN LOVE

COME AWAY WITH ME

WHOLE LOTTA LOVE

Rock Star Romance series

YOU REALLY GOT ME

I WANT YOU TO WANT ME

TAKE ME HOME TONIGHT

MORE THAN A FEELING

Wild Love series

MINE FOR NOW

MINE FOR THE WEEK

Sign up for my newsletter to find out when COME AWAY
WITH ME and WHOLE LOTTA LOVE go live and get
PLANES, TRAINS, AND HEAD OVER HEELS for free! I
hope you'll come hang out with me on Facebook, Twitter,

Instagram, Goodreads, and Pinterest or in my private reader group.

Keep On Loving You

"I adored this book! It is exactly what I love in a second-chance romance. The characters are so vibrant and real, I was rooting for them with every page." --- *USA Today* Bestseller Devney Perry

"KEEP ON LOVING YOU is such a fun and sexy second-chance romance that I didn't want it to end. Their connection is a swoony blend of tender first love and sizzling heat, and Erika Kelly delivers a highly entertaining and sigh-worthy romance that shouldn't be missed." – Mary Dube, USA Today

We Belong Together

"I loved every sweet, heart-wrenching, crazy, mixed-up minute of this book. It was an emotional journey from the first chapter to the last. This is Erika Kelly at her best, and this is not-to-be-missed book!" – Sharon Slick Reads, Guilty Pleasures Book Reviews

"Erika Kelly damn near pulled my heart from my chest with Delilah and Will's story. It's so well-written that you feel everything. My heart got tugged so hard! I honestly cried at a few moments in the book. I fell all the way in love with "Wooby." It's hard not to, really." – Ree Cee's Books

The Very Thought Of You

"Wow, THE VERY THOUGHT OF YOU was simply OUTSTANDING! This second chance, friends to lovers romance is enchanting and entertaining." – Spellbound Stories

"I just finished this story, and I want to start all over again. Or maybe at the start of series. To once again feel the events, the emotions, that brought these amazing characters together. To hear the banter and the arguments, the sorrow, the loss and the happiness that brought a family together and closer." – Nerdy, Dirty, and Flirty

Just The Way You Are

"An alpha cowboy and a smart, sassy princess collide in JUST THE WAY YOU ARE in Erika Kelly's latest, and it was fabulous! I was cheering for Brodie and Rosalina with every page. If you love stories with heart, steam, and plenty of swoon, don't miss this one!" -- USA Today Bestselling Author J.H. Croix

"With the Calamity Falls series, Kelly doesn't shy away from charming. She captivates with delectable characters that wrap themselves around a heart. From the first hello to the final goodbye, Rosalind and Brodie are a match made out of the unpredictable, but the sweetest kind of heaven. JUST THE WAY YOU ARE is the perfect example of why I am hooked on this series. SWOONWORTHY READ!" -- Hopeless Romantic Book Reviews

It Way Always You

"This book was full of every emotion you could ever feel. Gigi and Cassian proved you can conquer anything with true love." – Cat's Guilty Pleasure

"I could not put this book down! Erika Kelly always delivers a great love story and never disappoints! I recommend this book for romance lovers looking to get lost in a great love story." – Reading in Pajamas

This book is dedicated to Kristy deBoer. Because it wouldn't be half as good without you.

Acknowledgments

- To Superman: you're my favorite person in the world.
- To Sharon: I don't know what I'd do without your friendship.
- To Kristy deBoer: you get my books across the finish line.
- To Melissa: I might be green with envy over your design skills but that doesn't take away from the fact that I am so grateful you're doing this with me.
- To Erica: you're so chill about the way I totally rely on you for All the Things.
- To the romance writing community: I am so grateful to all the bloggers and reviewers who take the time to read and celebrate my books and to the supportive friends in writer groups like the Dreamweavers, the DND Authors, Indie AF, and The Plotstormers.

Prologue

CoCo CAVANAUGH HAD NEVER MINDED BEING unexceptional.

It came in handy during times like this, when she was surrounded by her sister's friends in a loud, frenzied club in Las Vegas. She could pretend to be having the time of her life, and none of these bright, shiny people would notice.

If she thought it wouldn't ruin her sister's night, she'd be back in their suite, heels kicked off, stripped of her too-tight dress, and butt-naked. She could almost feel the hot water saturating her scalp, as it washed away the make-up, perspiration, and bad choices.

Except, she was pretty sure she wouldn't make it to the shower. She'd walk in the door, collapse on the bed, heels dangling off her blistered feet, and bawl her eyes out. Wake up in the morning with mascara streaks on the white pillowcase.

Nope, we're not doing that. It's Gigi's night. It had taken her older sister a long time to come back from a devastating high school heartbreak, but two years ago she'd grabbed hold of an opportunity that turned her into an international pop star. She was finally healed and kicking ass. Coco wouldn't do anything to bring her down.

At that exact moment, her sister, fresh from her sold-out concert, hiked herself up on a chair and lifted her lemon drop martini. "To *Colette*,"—Gigi used her real name as if to emphasize how mature Coco had become —"happy graduation and, more importantly, happy birthday. Finally, you're old enough to drink, old enough to—"

"Gamble," one of the women shouted over the insanely loud club music.

"Become a pilot," someone else shouted.

"Play with the big boys," a deep voice called.

All of them whipped around to find a group of men sauntering over. Where everyone else in the club dressed in suits and cocktail dresses, these guys wore T-shirts and jeans. With their overgrown hair, tan skin, and laidback attitudes, they could easily have been surfers.

Her sister's entourage broke out laughing, an invitation for the guys to join them.

Gigi, still on the chair, shouted, "She's already got a boyfriend, so there'll be none of that."

The words splashed cold water on her heart, giving her a shock, but her sister didn't need to know that. She'd catch Gigi up tomorrow. For now, Coco held her drink high and said a cheery, "Thanks, guys!" She sipped her martini, fighting back the roar of anxiety that threatened to pull her under.

I don't have a boyfriend.

I don't have a job.

She didn't have *anything*.

A moment later, Pitbull's "Timber" came on, and the

2

whole group jumped up and dashed onto the dance floor, waving their arms and shaking their booties, leaving Coco blissfully alone. *Thank God.* She could finally relax her straining facial muscles.

When her sister motioned her over, Coco pulled off her stiletto and winced, using her aching feet as an excuse to stay put. Gigi blew her a kiss and lost herself in the wild crowd.

Coco could probably go now. No one would notice if she slipped out. She'd just text her sister, let her know.

A prick of awareness had her looking over to find one of the guys still sitting at the table. Watching her, he cocked his head. *You all right?*

She nodded. *Sure.* With his honey-blond chin-length hair and muscular build, he was undeniably hot, but Coco hadn't even been single twenty-four hours. *Too soon.* It really was time to leave. The flashing lights and pounding bass held her brain in a vise.

She finished off her drink, just for the snap of lemon and rush of sugar in her mouth, and then punched in the code to open her phone. She couldn't stop the leap of hope that she'd find something from her boyfriend—

Ex-boyfriend.

Face it. He ghosted you.

She could stop waiting for him. He wasn't going to magically appear, apologize for blowing off their appointment with the realtor, and tell her he was ready to build the future they'd planned.

Nope, she was on her own.

Fear knocked the air out of her lungs.

What am I going to do now? She'd banked everything on him.

A heavy body dropped onto the couch. Long, athletic

legs spread out, as the surfer dude slouched beside her. "House music sucks."

Not expecting him to say that, she actually smiled. "Then, what're you doing here?"

"Jimmy…" He leaned in so their shoulders touched and pointed to a red-haired guy on the dance floor. "He's never been to Vegas. We promised him a survey tour."

"Gotcha. So…" She ticked off one finger. "Casinos."

"He already lost two grand."

"Yikes. That's not good." She touched the tip of the second finger. "David Copperfield or Celine Dion?"

"Worse. Everything was sold out. The only tickets we could get were for the fuckin' Lollipops, which is proof just how much I love that guy, since I'm willing to lose a piece of my soul for him."

Her grin grew wider. Her sister was the lead singer of that band, but she didn't see a reason to tell him. She didn't want to embarrass him as much as she didn't want to draw out the conversation.

"Now, that's a smile." He leaned forward, drawing his legs in. Elbows on his knees, he cut her a look. "And I'll bet that one doesn't hurt."

Heat rushed up her neck and fanned across her cheeks. "Please tell me it's not that obvious?"

He watched her for a moment—studying her expression, as if he actually cared.

And it just cracked the dam she'd worked so hard to build. All of it—the fear, the hurt, the *humiliation*—started slowly trickling in.

Oh, hell, no. I'm not breaking down in front of this guy.

She needed to go to her room and have a good, long cry. She needed to wallow. Just for a few hours, and then she'd be good as new. She'd make new plans.

A muscle in his jaw ticked. "Anyone gonna miss you if we take off?"

She glanced to the dance floor, so crowded she couldn't even see her sister. "I don't think so. I was about to head back to my room anyhow." With a jolt, she realized how that sounded. "By myself. That wasn't an invitation."

"Yeah, no worries. I'm not looking to get laid." He stood up and reached for her hand. "Come on."

As they chugged to the top of the incline, gravity nailed Coco to her seat and the cool night air washed over her skin. She thrilled in anticipation of the imminent fall.

She'd never been on a roller coaster at night, and certainly not in a city lit up in flashing neon lights. The wheels clacked, and she clutched the padded bar. "Oh, my God. I hate roller coasters. You have no idea."

Becks—that's what his friends had called him when he'd let them know they were taking off—covered her hand and gave it a squeeze. "I got you."

At the pinnacle, they paused, giving her a moment to take in the brilliant lights of Las Vegas, and then…it was on. The car plummeted, the dramatic descent whooshing the hair off her face.

Her stomach lurched, and her body smashed against the restraining bar. She laughed so hard tears streamed down her cheeks.

The moment the ride evened out, it twisted, flinging her sideways and speeding along the track. The passengers behind them shrieked. Between the G-forces and her crazy laughter, Coco had to look like something in a fun house mirror.

When they rotated upside down, the blood rushed to her face.

Finally, the ride slowed, and they passed through a dark tunnel. Easing her grip, she released a breath she hadn't even known she'd been holding. The car jerked to a stop, the safety bar released, and Becks stepped out onto the platform, reaching back for her hand.

She clasped it and got out. "That was insane." She took a step, but her knee buckled.

He tugged her up against his hot, hard body, holding her gaze for a long, intense moment. One arm around her waist, the other lifted so he could smooth a lock of hair behind her ear. "Look at you, all wild and sexy."

"I feel wild." Did she feel sexy? Normally, no. But under his hot gaze, looking at her like he wanted to know what she tasted like…everywhere? *Hell, yeah.* "Thank you. That got me out of my head."

He nodded, releasing her slowly, as if he didn't want to let go. Reaching for her hand, he led her off the platform, his scent lingering—clean cotton and spicy shaving cream. Desire hummed, making her feel more alive than she had in ages.

Once out on the sidewalk, he said, "You want to go back to your hotel or do something else?"

She chanced a look into his icy blue eyes. It wasn't just his startling good looks that affected her; it was his kindness and concern. But what was the point in pursuing this attraction to a stranger? She had a future to figure out.

Then, again, she hadn't thought about her ex in a whole hour. "What else have you got in mind?"

· · ·

As the spacious pod of the High Roller Observation Wheel ascended, Coco gaped at the view. Beyond the cluster of massive hotels and the glitter and sparkle of the Strip sat the vast blackness of the valley floor. "It's crazy to think they built all of this in the middle of a desert."

Though they were alone, Becks stood right beside her. Each time their arms brushed, it sent a flurry of sensation through her. She hadn't felt this butterflies-in-the-stomach, oh-my-God-he's-talking-to-me crush stuff since high school.

And she loved it.

"That's the club." He tipped his chin.

"Where?"

He came around behind her, boxing her in against the window. Extending his arm, he pointed. "That hotel right there." His warm breath at her ear sent a shiver down her spine. "The one with the weirdly shaped O spanning across the windows."

The moment felt dangerous. She could imagine turning in his arms, looping her hands around his neck, and pressing her body up against his. She could picture his hands grabbing her ass and lifting her against the window.

And she really, really wanted to feel his fingers push aside her panties and—

"You okay?" He perched his chin on her shoulder.

"Yes. Fine." But she didn't move—not a single twitch of a muscle or shuffle of a foot—because she wanted him to stay right where he was. She didn't want to lose these delicious sensations flowing through her. "You think they're still there?"

"Oh, yeah. My friends'll close it down."

"So will mine." Licking her bottom lip, she turned to look into his eyes. The connection sent a blast of excitement through her. "Why don't you want to be with them?" Was that her voice? All low and raspy, with the promise of a great blow job?

She should probably knock it off. She didn't want to give him the wrong impression. She wouldn't be going back to his room.

But...he hadn't shaved in several days, so he had a good amount of scruff. It accentuated the sexiest mouth she'd ever seen.

He's gorgeous.

And that hard, muscular body.

"I'm more of an outdoors guy. Clubs, loud music, shouting to have a conversation...it's not my thing." As the ride continued its descent, he stepped away. Reaching into his back pocket, he pulled out a small plastic bag. "Here."

Happiness danced on her heart. "You bought something for me?"

"Happy birthday and congratulations on graduating college." The contrast between his laidback attitude and gruff tone ignited something in her.

Sparked a hunger she'd never felt before. "I can't believe you got me a gift." Opening the bag, she pulled out a plastic Las Vegas sign jutting out of a black base. When she flicked the red switch, it lit up. She laughed. "I love this so much." In an impulsive move, she leaned in and kissed his cheek. His scruff tickled her lips, and she filled her lungs with his clean, masculine scent, as if she could bottle it and keep it forever. "Thank you."

"You're welcome."

Something about the intensity of his gaze had her staying right where she was, a whisper away from him. "This whole night...it's been perfect."

The pod landed. In a moment, the doors would open, and they'd get off.

But neither of them budged.

His big hand grasped the back of her neck, and the thrill of his possessive hold rocketed through her. "Know why I got it for you?"

She barely shook her head.

"Next time you have to fake a smile, I want you to look at this and remember to get out there and do something different. Shake things up."

"You got any other ideas for shaking things up?"

He gave her a devastating grin. "You know I do."

The waiter set a huge stack of buttermilk pancakes in front of her. A melting ball of butter sat on top. "What else can I get you?" he asked.

The table was loaded with syrup, a plate of bacon, a bowl of mixed fruit, two mugs of hot coffee, and two icy water glasses. "This is perfect." Coco smiled. "Thank you."

"You got it. Enjoy." He took off.

With the edge of her fork, Coco cut into a pancake and took a bite. Drenched in butter and maple syrup, it was the most amazing thing she'd ever tasted. She closed her eyes and savored it. "Oh, my God, this is unbelievable." She noticed him watching her instead of eating and grew self-conscious. "What? We can't all be mean, lean, fighting machines." She pointed to his vegetable-stuffed omelet. "No booze, no carbs...that hunky body. Professional surfer?"

He chuckled. "Not professional, no. But we did just fly in from Portugal. Ever hear of Ericeira?"

"No, but from the look in your eyes, I'm going to

guess it was pretty awesome."

"It was insane."

"You travel a lot?"

"Used to, but not the good kind. The grind ended a couple months ago, though. From now on, I'm free as a bird and plan on staying that way the rest of my life." He drank some coffee.

"Good for you. I know all about the grind…and what does it get you? I mean, I've done everything I'm supposed to do. Studied hard, never skipped classes. Since I don't have a…you know, passion for anything in particular, I chose a business major. Can't go wrong with that, right?" Hearing herself get all ramped up, she set her fork down and washed the taste of syrup away with some milky coffee. Just thinking about all this made her stomach squeeze.

"You going to tell me how it all went sideways?"

Why not, right? It's better than bawling my eyes out alone in my hotel room. "I had a plan. A very good one. My boyfriend—" *You have to stop saying that.* "The guy I dated in college…okay, let me go back a little bit. Keith and I decided to take a class together, and we partnered on an assignment where we had to put together a business plan. We chose my hometown, because it has two really big tourist seasons. We did a bunch of research and figured out the one thing it needed was daycare. You know, you're on a family vacation, and Mom and Dad want to go out to dinner without the kids, or maybe they want take a harder hike, go skydiving, whatever."

He nodded like, *Makes sense.*

She drank some more coffee to melt the knot of fear in her throat. "It was such a good idea that our professor asked if she could use it as an example in future classes.

That got us thinking...why not really do this? So, while everyone else was applying for grad school and jobs and freaking out about their futures, we were busy starting a viable business."

His brow furrowed.

"Correct. This story has a bad ending. So, for the past two years, I've been taking jobs to save money, getting licenses and permits, lining up contractors and real estate agents." Now, the smell of food was making her sick. She pushed her plate away. "My boyfriend—" *Dammit.* "My *ex* went home after graduation. The plan was to work and live at home until we saved up enough money to launch our business. That was five months ago. Well, the perfect location became available, so I made an appointment with a realtor, and..." She hunched her shoulders in a gesture of helplessness.

Eyebrows raised, he sat back in his seat. "And?"

"And he didn't show." She still couldn't believe it. "I haven't heard a word from him since. Granted, he's been pulling away for a while, but I figured he was just partying with his friends, celebrating being done with school, whatever. But this? Not a single word of explanation? I mean, what kind of person just blows you off like that?"

"A fuckstick"

"That's exactly right. He's a fucking fuckstick." Anxiety rising, she swiveled around to check out the diner. "Does this place serve booze? I could go for another lemon drop. That was really good."

"They don't. But we can walk out that door and find all the booze we want." He held up his hand, gesturing for the bill. "You have any idea what he's doing? Maybe he got in an accident...?"

She let out a bitter laugh. "Unless he accidentally

caught a flight to Hawaii with his high school girlfriend, then I don't think so. For three days, I've been reaching out to his friends, his parents, everyone I could think of. And then, out of total desperation, I checked out her social media pages. Get this, they're going to teach surfing. And the thing is, I can't even be angry about the fact that he's with her, because I'm too worried about my own future. I counted on opening this business, so I have no backup plan. Why would I? He was seriously in it all the way up until a few weeks ago. I have no idea what I'm going to do."

He reached across the table, turning his hand over. She set her palm on top of his, and his fingers closed around her in a warm, solid grasp. "You're going to shake things up."

The waiter appeared, scanning their full plates. "Everything all right?"

"Yep. Everything's great. We've just got somewhere to be." Becks handed over his credit card, and the waiter took off. He shifted out of the booth and slid in next to her, slinging an arm around her shoulders. "It's not over, you know." He picked up her hand, pressing his thumb over her finger. The simple gesture made her realize she'd been mutilating her cuticle. "You can still open this business. Find another partner, get some investors. You don't want a chickenshit for a business partner anyway."

She could do that. She'd thought about it. It was just...

"You don't want to do it?" he asked.

Warmth spread through her. She loved how easily he read her. "How do you do that? Read me so well?"

He brought the back of her hand to his mouth and kissed it. "It's all right there. You can't hide anything."

"Maybe, but I have a feeling it's your superpower."

He shifted. "I don't know about that."

Hm, she'd obviously tapped into something. "Oh, I do. All night, you've nailed me." She laughed. "Oh, my God, what is coming out of my mouth tonight? I swear I don't normally have such a dirty mind. Is there a portal? A wrinkle in the time-space continuum I could drop into?"

"Even if I knew of one, I wouldn't tell you about it." He made a face that said, *Forget about it.* "You're too much fun."

"And you're awesome at deflecting. You don't think you're good at reading people?" Had past girlfriends said he didn't pay enough attention to them?

He settled back in his seat, tapping his fingers on the table. "I know I'm good at it."

"But you don't want to tell me why?"

He glanced away. "I thought we were getting alcohol?"

"Do you even drink?"

"Not much, no."

"So…" She made a circular motion with her hand. *Go on and tell me.*

"Fine. Well, I lost my sister when I was twelve. She was six."

Oh, God. She rested her hand on his thigh.

He went quiet, emotions flickering across his features, like shadows beneath a frozen lake. "Worst thing that ever happened to me." He stared at the syrup bottle.

"I'm sorry."

"I was there. Saw the whole thing." He plucked a sugar packet out of the plastic caddy. "Anyhow, it wrecked my family. And I guess I learned to watch my parents' expressions, so I could…I don't know…" He shrugged. "Fix things. I could tell when my mom was sinking into a depression, so I'd get upbeat, try to cheer her up. Or she'd be gunning for a fight, and I'd distract her."

"That's a tremendous amount of responsibility for a twelve-year-old to take on."

"People show up the first couple of months after a tragedy. After that, they go back to their lives. Maybe they think bad luck is contagious, or they just don't want to be pulled into the sadness. In any event, it was just me and my parents, and they didn't much like each other." He tapped the sugar packet on the table. "So, yeah, I'm pretty much expert level at reading expressions."

"That must get exhausting."

"Oh, I don't do it with everyone. In fact, I hardly ever do it."

"Really? Why me?"

"Here you go." The waiter dropped off the check. "Have a nice night."

"Thank you." Becks signed it and put his credit card back in his leather wallet. "Let's get out of here." He slid out of the booth and, once again, reached for her hand. Like before, he didn't back up to give her room, so when she stood, she was right up against him. He brushed the bangs off her forehead. "Because there's just something about you." His breath gusted over her, warm and scented with coffee. "I *like* you." He grabbed her hand and led her out of the diner.

Out on the street, the nightlife was electric.

"Want to walk?" he asked. "See what we find along the way?"

She loved the idea, mostly because it prolonged their time together. With each passing minute, she was aware of the clock running out. "Sure."

Even at one in the morning, cars jammed the

boulevard, bass thumping. A limo went by with a woman poking out of the sunroof, her arms waving, the wind in her hair.

"You were trying so damn hard," Becks said quietly. "That's why I paid attention. You did a good job—I'm not sure anyone else noticed—but I did. You're different, Coco. Elegant, quiet, and yet you've got this funky look." He tipped his chin toward her deep purple satin bustier-style dress, the skin-tight skirt covered in a flare of dark lavender tulle. "You think no one notices you, but they do. You stand out. You're confident, strong, kind…"

"And funky?"

"Yeah, funky."

"My mom's a retired model, so I grew up with…let's just say an emphasis on hair, make-up, and fashion. My sisters rebelled in other ways—boys, booze, sneaking out…the usual—but I didn't care about any of that. I don't know why, but I just didn't."

"That's the confidence I was talking about."

She hadn't thought of it that way before. "The thing I did care about was my mom telling me how to dress. When we were little, she used to set our outfits on the bed the night before school, but I didn't like what she wanted me to wear. It wasn't that I was into fashion. I just had a preference. Things that I liked. I don't know about funky, but I knew my own taste." Self-consciously, she touched her hair. "I'm the only one with shorter hair."

"And, again, that's the confidence I'm talking about."

"I hated the ritual of blowing it out, adding product to make it all sleek. Just hated it. And when I looked in the mirror, I felt…I don't know. It just wasn't me. So, I cut if off." She didn't style it, either, so she always looked like she'd just come home after a day at the beach.

"I like it. I like your style. I like everything about you. And I really liked the way you held yourself together for the sake of your friends. No matter the shitty place you're in, you genuinely wanted to be present for them. I like that."

"You're a really nice guy, Becks." Affection...desire... just so much emotion crashed over her, and she tugged on his hand, making him stop. Standing up on her toes, she pressed a kiss on his cheek.

Only, he shifted at just the right moment for their mouths to meet. The brush of lips made him inhale sharply.

He smelled so delicious—a hint of salty ocean air, the remnants of a coconut sunscreen. She wanted her hands all over him. "Becks?"

"Yeah?"

"Do you have a minibar in your hotel room?"

A noise...a hum...no, a vibration. Coco fought to awaken.

My phone.

Too sluggish to move, she willed herself to rise through the levels of consciousness.

Where am I? Her dorm? No, her mattress didn't feel like this one. Her sheets didn't smell like these.

Wait, school's over.

I'm home.

Keith.

Yes. Finally. The dick. She was going to rip him a new one.

When her eyelids popped open, two things happened. One, a shaft of artificial light blinked from the gap between the curtains and, two, someone shanked her skull with a blade.

Her phone was still vibrating, though, so she reached for it. But it wasn't where she usually kept it.

To find it, she'd have to lift her head. *God, no. No, no, no.*

For a moment, she let herself wallow in the absolute torture of the worst hangover she'd ever experienced. Gazing at the ceiling, she blinked the sleep from her eyes.

Hang on a sec. This is a hotel.

Reality seeped in. Keith had ghosted her. She'd flown to Vegas for Gigi's concert.

Something bristled against her bare leg, and she jerked it away. *What the hell?* Slowly, so her brains wouldn't slosh around, she turned to find a man sprawled out beside her.

On top of the sheets.

Buck naked.

Tan skin, broad shoulders tapering to a trim waist, and round ass cheeks with matching, deep indents.

Holy shit!

She'd had sex.

With Becks.

Her eyelids fluttered shut. *Oh, for the love of God. What are you doing with your life?*

She'd never had a hookup in her life. Always the serious one, her dad liked to say.

But then…images started to roll in. Laughing so hard on the roller coaster tears had streamed down her cheeks. Making faces at the sharks in the glass tunnel of the aquarium.

Making out like high school kids in the elevator.

And, then, the dash down the long hallway to his hotel room. Him pushing her up against the wall. She could still feel the caress of his hand on her breast, the lusty squeeze. The way he'd groaned, like he couldn't stand one more minute of being separated by clothing.

Desire streamed through her body, making her hot.

Actually...she'd had the best sex of her life.

Oh, yes. That had literally been the best night ever.

Becks had held *nothing* back. Comfortable in his skin, he'd had zero inhibitions.

Had they done it *three* times?

She grinned. They sure had.

The throbbing in her head only got worse, and she knew she needed to hydrate, like, immediately.

She reached for her phone and saw Gigi's name. *Oh, shit.* When was the last time she'd checked in? Carefully, she peeled back the sheet, shifted her legs off the bed, and eased them onto the floor. In the bathroom, she answered the phone. "Hey," she whispered.

"Hey?" Her sister sounded outraged. "*Hey?* Where *are* you? The only text I have from you said you were leaving the club to go back to our suite. You're not here. It's *five in the morning.*"

"I'm sorry. I'm so sorry."

"Why are you whispering? Are you in the trunk of a car?"

"I'm—*what*? No. I'm totally fine. But I need to find my clothes right now and get out of here before this guy wakes up."

"This *guy*? My head just exploded. There are bits of brain matter all over the floor. Coco, my level-headed, smart sister went to a strange guy's hotel room?"

"Yes. And I loved it."

"I am seriously about one martini away from snatching you bald."

"Sorry not sorry? Let me get dressed so I can get out of here." She disconnected and crept back into the room.

Clothes. Where were they? She crossed the plush carpet to find her dress by the door, her heels kicked against the wall, and her bra on a table.

Where are my panties? She didn't see them. Maybe the bathroom?

Becks shifted, his head turning toward her. She froze. Held her breath.

She had no interest in small talk. Zero. Frankly, she might've had the best time ever, but it was time to get on with her life.

Because one thing had come out of her wild night— she was going to have an adventure. She'd followed the rules for her entire life, and what had it gotten her? It was time to go wild, have some fun.

She'd take some of the money she'd saved for the business and go somewhere amazing.

By myself.

Yes.

When Becks showed no signs of waking, she quickly dressed and grabbed her purse, the light-up Vegas sign sticking out of it.

Do something different. Shake things up.

She smiled. *That's exactly what I'm going to do.* She'd take this baby home, keep it front and center, so that every time she got too mired down in work, routine, the grind, she'd remember to take an adventure.

She took one more look around the room to make sure she hadn't left anything.

A bright spot of red peeked out of his jeans pocket.

My thong.

She smiled. *And that's his souvenir.*

Chapter One

TODAY

"You get back to her yet?" his dad asked.

Phone pressed to his ear, Beckett O'Neill stood on the deck of his overwater bungalow. A flower-scented breeze fluttered across the turquoise water.

At his dad's question, a corresponding ripple passed through his body, only it felt like guilt. "Nah. Been busy."

"Just to put it out there, I don't care either way. You don't want to talk to her, that's your choice. You're a grown man. I'm not going to tell you how to deal with your mom."

They didn't talk all that often, so his dad wouldn't have called unless he had something to say. "But?"

"But I don't see why she'd be reaching out if she hadn't changed."

Rustling palm trees and murmuring voices from nearby cottages made a strange contrast to the clash of emotions the conversation stirred up. "Okay. I hear you."

"Beckett?" his girlfriend called. "I need a towel."

He wandered back inside, smiling when he found her bare-ass naked, dripping wet from a shower.

She sashayed over and pressed herself against him. "Maybe I'll use your body to rub myself dry," she whispered in his ear.

"It can't hurt to hear her out," his dad said.

When she clutched his ass and did a little shimmy, he gently pushed her away. *My dad*, he mouthed.

Pouting, she swiped her see-through cover up off the chair and threw it on, before flouncing on the unmade bed.

"I don't see the point." Beckett stepped back onto the balcony, lowering his voice. "I've thought about it a lot over the years, what I'd do if she came back." In the beginning, after his mom left, he'd imagined all kinds of scenarios.

Like her pacing around his living room, wringing her hands. *I can't believe I walked out on my own son. What the hell was I thinking? I'm so sorry.*

Or—a favorite—he'd show up at her apartment and ream her out. *I lost Ari, too. What kind of mother abandons her own son? I was grieving, and you left.*

After seventeen years and countless possibilities, though, he'd run out of gas. "I just don't care anymore. There's nothing she could say that would matter."

"Sure, sure," his dad said. "I get that."

His dad had never pressured him to talk to his mom before, so he couldn't help wondering why now. "Is there something you're not telling me?"

His dad blew out a breath into the receiver. "She's not dying, if that's what you're thinking. Nothing like that. She's moving again, going through her boxes, and I'd bet it's bringing up the past."

"Wait, you've talked to her?" His parents divorced two

years after Ari died and eighteen months after his mom had walked out the door. As far as Beckett knew, they hadn't spoken since.

"Sure, I have."

"How does Marcia feel about that?"

His dad chuckled. "You're not seriously suggesting I'd kick my wife aside and go back to the woman who abandoned my son, are you?"

It helped. When his dad said things like that, it made him feel less alone. "No, of course not. I just don't think Marcia would like knowing you're talking to your ex."

"Marcia's real clear on where I stand with your mom. But this isn't about your mom. It's about you."

"Trust me. I don't need closure. I have no lingering emotions where she's concerned."

"It's not about that." His dad sounded frustrated. "Don't you want more?"

"More what?"

"More out of life. Ever since you retired, you're just screwing around, hopping on one plane after another. No ties, no commitments. How can that be satisfying?"

"Whoa. What are you talking about? I'm not screwing around. I'm running a business. We only launched it in January, and it's already doing well." For their Xtreme Adventures travel app, Chris handled coding, Dave managed finances and advertising, and Beckett handled the trips.

Yeah, he got to have wild ass adventures for a living, but it was hard work. He not only sourced the activities, but he uploaded every photo and video with a link so their customers could immediately book a trip. He also maintained a heavy social media presence, which was their single best marketing tool. Watching him sky surf or swim with sharks got more engagement than he'd ever imagined.

Not even six months into it—the engagement and retention metrics looked good.

"Babe?" Willow called. "Come here. This is hilarious."

"And I have a girlfriend." He glanced into the bungalow to find Willow on her back, knees raised, as she scrolled through her phone. "It's a pretty damn perfect life."

"I misspoke. I'm sorry." His dad sighed. "I'm proud of you for creating this business, and I'm sure I'll like your girlfriend once I meet her. But I'm talking about something more meaningful. Look, even before Ari died, you had a screwed-up childhood. Your mom wasn't there for you, and even though I saw what was going on, I didn't step in. I was so damn stubborn, insisting she take care of you kids since I was earning the money. Your mom and I both screwed up, and I just don't think you had any kind of good model for what a rewarding life looks like."

"I like my life, Dad."

"I believe you. I'm just suggesting that you don't have anything to compare it to. You're twenty-nine years old, and you don't know what a good family feels like. You don't know what roots feel like. I can't help wondering if talking to your mom might shine some light on the choices you make."

"You know, most people envy my life."

"Do they? I don't know that most people would enjoy sleeping in a hotel bed three hundred nights a year."

He was probably right about that. "Well, I do. And I found a woman who wants to do it with me."

"Oh, my God," Willow called. "*Beckett.* Get over here. You're not going to believe this."

"All right, Dad. I've got to go."

"Sure, okay. But would you do your old man a favor and give it some thought? One conversation with your mom might be worth it if it puts some ghosts to rest."

"Sure, Dad. I'll think about it. I love you."

"Love you, too, Son."

Water lapping against the foundation of his bungalow, Beckett let the briny breeze wash over him. Whenever he talked to his dad, the past crept back in for an unwelcome visit.

And it always delivered a memory of his sister.

This time, it was that moment right before the accident. At the top of the slope, when she'd gazed up at him, cheeks red from the cold, eyes full of adoration.

Fuck. Every muscle in his body squeezed, wringing out a cold fluid that made him shudder in spite of the balmy air.

If she'd lived, she would be twenty-three. Would she have gone to college? Or would she have put off school to compete professionally as he had? He'd never know what path she would have chosen, since she'd died so young, but he did know the world had missed out on someone special.

"What're you doing out there?" Willow sat up. "Come and see this."

He gazed out at the endless, flat blue sea and let himself remember her.

I miss you, Ari.

So fucking much.

He'd do anything to go back to that day and just do one thing differently. Change the timeline by one second. *That's all it would've have taken.* If he'd finished boarding one second later, if they'd lingered with their parents one second longer, if they'd taken one extra second before pushing off the slope…

But he couldn't change anything. And all he had were the bittersweet memories of a sister he'd loved fiercely who'd died before she'd had a chance to live.

Shaking it off, he stepped inside and tossed his phone on a chair. "What's up?" He sat on the edge of the mattress.

"We just got the most unbelievable offer." Her eyes shone with excitement.

"Yeah?" When they'd met, Willow had already been a top Splashagram influencer thanks to her page, *@WillowtheWanderer*, but once they'd gotten together, her engagement had exploded. Now, she not only traveled from one exotic location to another, all expenses paid by the venues looking for exposure, but she also occasionally joined him on his trips.

They made a good team.

She sat up on her knees. "Oh, my God. I'm *shaking*. Look." She thrust the phone at him. "This is the opportunity of a lifetime for both of us."

He scanned the lengthy private message…*love your vibe…massive engagement…*yeah, yeah, he'd heard it all before. She never tired, though, of hearing how much people loved her style and page.

But then his gaze snagged on one word in particular. *Wedding*. "What wedding?"

"*Ours*." She grabbed the phone back, clicked on a link, and handed it back to him. "Look at this place. Owl Hoot Resort and Spa. It's a living museum in Calamity, Wyoming. Some billionaire family turned a ghost town— the original settlement of Calamity—into a tourist attraction. It's like going back in time to the gold rush days. They've got gunslingers and shoot-outs, a jailor, a saloon…all that kind of stuff."

"Sounds cool." He'd heard of Calamity, of course— most extreme athletes knew about it—but not the resort.

She shook her head, like he wasn't getting it. "They're still building the place out. They've added an amphitheater for live shows, a gondola ride up the mountain, and now they've built a gorgeous mountain chapel with stained glass windows and reclaimed wood so they can start a destination wedding business." She paused for dramatic effect. "And they want us to launch it. All expenses paid."

"Launch it how?" He had no idea what any of this had to do with them. "What do they want us to do?"

"Oh, my God. We're getting married in Owl Hoot. All expenses paid. But the craziest part is that you used to know these guys, so instead of a chapel, we're doing it on a glacier."

I'm not getting married. "Who? Which guys?"

"Apparently the billionaires used to snowboard, too. And they think we've got the kind of following that will draw attention to their venue."

"Are you talking about the Bowies?" The four brothers kept mostly to themselves, but since they'd competed at the same events, he'd hung out with them a lot during those years. He hadn't seen them since he'd retired six years ago. "They run a resort?" That didn't sound like them at all.

"You're so missing the point." She grew impatient. "I don't know the details. I literally just got the message from her while you were talking to your dad. The wedding planner introduced herself, I asked some questions…

mentioned you've won the X Games five times and she's like, You're *kidding* me. The guys I work for did, too, and then she went and told them about us, and we all decided to screw the chapel. Let's do it on a *glacier*. Can you even believe this?"

"But we're not engaged."

She hurled herself at him, knocking him down on the bed. Scraping his hair back, she smacked kisses all over his face. "Beckett O'Neill, honey bunny, sugar dumpling, will you marry me?"

He cupped her cheeks, looked her right in the eyes, and said, "No."

She sat up. "I know, I know. You're never getting married, never having kids. And that's exactly why we're so perfect for each other, because I don't want those things, either. We both want the same kind of life." Straddling him, she sat up. "Which is why this wedding makes so much sense. We'll both get more exposure than we've ever had. Your subscribers will go nuts over a wedding on a glacier. Can you just picture me dropping out of a helicopter in a wedding gown?"

"Well, now I can."

"You said it yourself, this is your time to level up. The first year is make-or-break. Well, here you go."

"I'm not going to lie to get followers."

"It's not a lie. It's a real wedding."

"How did this come up if we're not engaged?"

"Well…" She turned a single syllable into three and grinned at him. "Remember the other morning when we got coffee in town? I might've taken one tiny little picture of our reflection in the window kissing."

All his good humor died. Lifting her, he set her aside, rolled off the bed, and got to his feet. "Not cool. You know how I feel about that." She might get off on the attention, the selfies…all that shit. But he didn't. For him, it was about growing his app. He uploaded pictures all day long—but only ones that revealed the place he was promoting.

Since he wouldn't let her post selfies of the two of them, she'd made a joke out of showing images of his feet, his hand, the back of his head, and her followers loved it. They'd even made a page for his ass. As long as she didn't post his face or reveal anything personal about him, he didn't care.

"I swear, you can't see your face. Look, I'll show you." Brow furrowed in concentration, she clicked on the screen and then held up the phone to show him. "See, it's just a reflection. You can't see any details about you at all." Reaching for his hand, she said softly, "You know I'd never betray you like that."

While he couldn't be identified in the shot, the whole thing pissed him off. "I still don't see how a picture led to a wedding."

"I guess, because I showed us *kissing*, they got the idea we were making a statement. Someone goes, *Are you engaged?* And then it just got out of control. It got tons of comments. You can't even believe how many new followers I got just from the speculation."

"I really wish you hadn't done that."

"Well, anyhow, all that led to a private message from the wedding planner. This will be amazing for both of us, babe. I've never seen anything like Owl Hoot. Here, check it out."

She handed him the phone again so he could see the images. He barely glanced at the landing page—the elevated boardwalk, the costumed actors walking the streets, the saloon and jail. The place looked interesting, for sure, but he wasn't getting *married*. "Where did you leave things with her?"

"I told her I was interested and would be in touch, and she wrote right back to say they'd even throw in a custom-made wedding dress by a famous designer who lives in Calamity." She wrapped her arms around his neck. "Come on, babe. We're perfect for each other. Who else are you going to find that doesn't want the whole kids, dog, and picket fence gig? Who wants to legit spend her life on the road the way we do?"

True, she never had a problem with his schedule, the fact that it kept them apart so much. And, when they were able to be together, they were perfect travel companions—they both liked to explore. She'd been a professional volleyball player, so they both favored athletic adventures over spas and beaches.

"I mean, honestly, there's no one else I'd rather be with." She hugged him, the coconut and vanilla scent of her body lotion swirling around him. "We're so good together. Let's do this." She pulled back, arms still around him. "Okay?"

"Because you want a million more followers or because you want to marry me?"

"Don't even try to make me feel bad for wanting both. This is my career, and I love it. Besides, that's a trick question. Neither of us wants to get married. We'd both be doing it for our careers. You need to level up? Here you go. I'm handing it to you on a silver platter. We won't have to do a thing but show up."

He saw her point and was on the verge of agreeing to the ridiculous plan...but his dad's concerns still clung to him like smoke. He couldn't deny the truth of it—he was twenty-nine and had no roots, no ties.

And marrying Willow would only cement that. Which seemed an odd thing to say, since marriage meant spending their lives together. But he knew a certificate wouldn't change their relationship. It wouldn't deepen it. *That's just not what we have.*

On the other hand...*I am who I am.* He couldn't imagine anything better than a life full of travel and good times. Still, there was one sticking point. The one that mattered more than any other. "If we do this, if we get married, we're still not having kids, right?"

She shook her head. "God, no. No kids. I'm not going to change my mind ten years from now and beg you for one, believe me." She pressed a soft kiss on his mouth. "There's no one on this earth I'd rather spend my life with than you, Beckett O'Neill. Are we going to do this?"

What the hell. "Yeah, okay." *Why not?* "Sure."

Coco Cavanaugh stood a few feet back from the picnic table, recording her daughter's birthday party on her phone.

Five years. God. Her heart clutched. It was all going so fast.

Bright balloons clobbered each other in a brisk breeze, and the tablecloth fluttered around the rocks anchoring it. Everyone gathered around her daughter to sing.

"Happy birthday to you, happy birthday to you, happy birthday, dear Posie, happy birthday to you."

Sunlight glinted off the sparkles on her daughter's

headband and dress, as her parents stood like sentries around the cake to protect the candles from the wind.

Her little girl puffed her cheeks out like a blowfish, but instead of exhaling, she closed her eyes to make a wish. Posie took these opportunities very seriously.

Because she wished fervently for one thing: to be a fairy. A real one.

Coco's ex, a graphic artist she'd dated a year ago, had told Posie she could be anything she wanted, if she just wished hard enough. And then, of course, he'd moved away before clarifying that it didn't include things in the magical realm.

Which meant, since Coco wasn't a Santa Claus or Easter Bunny killer, she had to keep deflecting until Posie was old enough to figure things out on her own. Another breeze swooped down from the mountain, ruffling Posie's silky, golden hair. The candles nearly flickered out.

"Okay, sweetheart." Coco motioned for her mom to get Posie's attention. Her classmates were getting antsy. "It's time to blow out the candles."

Stubborn as could be, Posie kept her eyes closed. "I'm wishing, Mommy."

Coco smiled. Her daughter was adorable.

Even with grandma whispering in Posie's ear, the little girl still shook her head vigorously. "Wait."

At that exact moment, Jessie—a little boy from Posie's preschool—lunged forward and blew out all five candles.

People gasped, as the boy's mom grabbed him around the waist and hauled him off. Posie stood on the bench looking like her last hope in the world had just sputtered out.

"It's okay." Coco's mom pulled a matchbook out of her bag and immediately set to lighting the candles again.

"No, Grandma. Stop." Posie couldn't have been more upset if Jessie had shoved her cake onto the ground.

"It's okay. We got this. We'll just do it again." Always the fixer, Coco's mom remained cheerful as she set the flaming match to each of the candles. "See? Look, they're all lit up. Now, go ahead and blow them out."

Expression mulish, Posie's lips clamped shut.

The group gathered more tightly around her, everyone issuing encouraging words.

But Coco knew better. Pocketing her phone, she came to sit beside her daughter. "What's the problem, sweetheart?"

"I already wished."

"That's okay," Grandma said. "You just wish again."

"I can't." Her daughter turned distraught. "I already wished the only wish I want, but stupid Jessie blew out the candles, so *he* gets it."

"Honey, wishes don't work like that." Giving her mom a look that said, *Please handle the guests*, Coco scooped up her little girl and walked closer to the lake. Even this late in June, her mountain town was too chilly for sunbathers, but plenty of people came to walk their dogs or enjoy the bike path.

Sitting on a boulder, she settled her daughter on her lap. "I don't know what Ethan told you about fairies and wishes." *And I sure wish I did.* "But I do know for sure that wishes come from inside here." She patted her daughter's chest. "Which means that nobody can take them from you."

Posie studied her, as if checking to see if she was being humored.

"Do you know why we blow out candles and make a

wish?" Coco tucked a lock of hair behind her daughter's ear.

"Yes. Ethan says the smoke carries wishes to the gods. And now my wish is going to Jessie's god. Not mine." She folded her arms across her chest to show her outrage.

Coco scrambled for a different angle. "Okay. What if I put brand new candles in the cake? Would that work?"

"Yes." Bad mood lifted, Posie twisted around so they were nose to nose. "That would work, Mommy."

Phew, crisis averted. "Perfect. Let's do it." Holding Posie close to her, Coco slid off the boulder. "We'll do this, but you need to know something. Wishes come true when you want them so badly you're willing to work your patootie off to make them happen. So, never mind Jessie or anyone who tries to take your wishes away from you. No one has that power over you."

"That's not what Ethan said."

Well, if Ethan had decided to stay in touch, we could ask him about it. But, since he didn't... we'll take what he says with a grain of salt.

She set her daughter back on the bench and announced, "We need fresh candles." She nodded to her mom. "Can you grab the box from my tote bag over there? Let's try this again."

Within minutes, fresh candles glowed on top of the chocolate cake covered in white frosting and glitter sugar. Her little girl inhaled enough air to conduct a deep dive to the bottom of the lake, and then, finally, blew out the candles.

"Yay!" Everyone broke into applause.

Coco stood up to cut the sheet cake, when her mom took the knife. "I got this, honey. Diane Peterson wants to talk to you."

She scanned the group until her gaze landed on the elegant, older woman. "What about?"

"The Bowies hired her to get the Owl Hoot Resort and Spa's wedding business off the ground. She's looking to partner with businesses in town."

"That would be amazing." Coco had tried a number of marketing angles to get her chocolate shop to the next level, but nothing had taken off quite the way she'd hoped.

"It would be. From what I understand, this first wedding is a high-profile couple."

"Oh, awesome. The timing couldn't be better." She'd gotten a small spike in sales after providing her chocolates for Academy Award swag bags, but now, a little over two months later, they'd fallen away.

"You've had some pretty major successes in your *four years* in business. You're awfully hard on yourself."

"I'm a single mother." And, since Ethan, she'd come to accept she'd always be one. After he'd moved away, she'd made the decision to hold off on dating until Posie was much older. Her daughter had attached so deeply to him that his move had been devastating. How could he do that? Just leave and never talk to Posie again? It was cruel. "I have to think about her college and my own retirement."

"Cake." Posie swiped some frosting with a finger and stuck it in her mouth.

"You're getting cake, silly girl." Her mom sank the knife in and cut one long row. She leaned closer to Coco. "You know we're always here for you, right? You're never alone in this."

"I do." Love bloomed in her chest, spreading sunshiney warmth through her body. She kissed her mom's cheek, getting a whiff of the most familiar scent in the world. Joss Montalbano, a former Eighties supermodel, had worn the same perfume for decades. Created by a designer exclusively for her, it had a spicy, peppery scent with a floral heart and a woody base. "I don't know what I'd have done without you and Dad helping me. But I've still got to build my own career."

"Well, this might be the big break you've been hoping for."

It had taken a couple of marketing efforts to figure out success didn't hinge on one big moment. Her business would grow because she pursued all kinds of ideas. Like establishing Calamity's first Chocolate Festival. Since the Bowies were looking for ways to draw tourists, they'd given her use of the resort's ballroom for the three-day event. She was so excited—the response to her invitations had been phenomenal—she had well over one hundred chocolatiers from around the world. Who knew the idea of the Wild West setting would be such a draw internationally?

Adding a steady stream of business from weddings would be phenomenal. "You've got this?" she asked her mom.

"Of course. Go talk to Diane before she takes off."

Coco headed for the artsy woman with short, silver hair. "Hey, Diane. Thanks for coming to Posie's birthday party."

With a jangle of thin gold bracelets, the woman leaned in for a hug. "I wouldn't miss it." She and Coco's mom worked together on all kinds of philanthropic projects. They'd been good friends for years.

"My mom said you wanted to talk to me?"

She grinned like she was holding backstage passes to a

Rolling Stones concert. "I do. Did she tell you I'm giving the Bowies a hand with their wedding business?"

Coco nodded. "I didn't think you wanted a full-time job."

"Oh, I don't. I'm only getting it started. In fact, I'm already looking for an assistant who'll eventually replace me. Anyhow, after pursuing every angle I could think of— bridal magazines, tourism websites--anything to drive attention to a wedding business in a remote mountain town, I finally got the grand idea to stalk social media influencers. I found the perfect couple and, believe it or not, they happen to know the Bowies. Imagine that? We're going to sponsor their destination wedding here."

"That's a really good idea."

"Thank goodness I spent a little extra on a terrific website designer. I really think it's what sold the bride. Well, that and the fact they're going to have the ceremony on a *glacier*. In return, the bride will talk up our resort and post photographs for the next six months, and the groom will add Calamity as a destination on his travel app."

"I love it. That's such great thinking." Coco had given away a lot of chocolate in her early days, but it had never translated into sales. She'd learned quickly that most influencers just wanted free things. She would love to be included in Diane's plans, but she really didn't want to donate her chocolate. Still, she'd at least hear Diane out. "How can I help?"

"We'd like to put your chocolate in the guest swag bags."

Ugh. That's what I figured. But how could she say no when she wanted Diane to consider her for future— paying—jobs. "How many guests are we talking about?"

"I don't know yet. They're flying in tonight for a meeting at the resort tomorrow. But we're going to pay you for it. I'm not asking you to donate anything. This is on us."

"That's incredibly generous. Are you sure? I mean, if you're doing it for free, it seems only fair I do, too. I'm looking at more than this one wedding. I'd like a partnership with you."

Diane grinned. "You Cavanaugh girls." Her smile faltered, and Coco knew she was thinking about Coco's younger sister. "You've all turned out to be such incredible women."

"We have great parents." She hated that no one knew what Stella was doing. After the scandal, she'd left town and hadn't been heard from since. Which meant no one got to tell her that anything could be repaired. They just needed Stella to come home, so the sisters could work things out.

"I very much appreciate the offer, but the resort will cover the costs. I've already run everything by Brodie. Do you think you could stop by tomorrow to meet the couple and let them taste your chocolates? As part of the sponsorship deal, they'll be sharing photographs of your product, so I'd love for you to bring a couple of your most unique shapes. Let's really grab their attention. Another idea...why not bring some slices of your Chocolate Decadence cake? I'd love it if they chose Coco's Chocolates to make the wedding cake."

"You're wonderful, Diane." She leaned in for a hug. "This is an amazing opportunity. Thank you." She pulled back. "I'm lucky you and my mom are such good friends."

Diane gave her a pointed look. "This is business, honey. I don't do favors for friends when it comes to making money. I'm using your chocolates because they're special. I'm hoping she'll choose your cake because it's the best damn cake I've ever tasted. So, get that favor nonsense out of your head and bring some goodies for the meeting tomorrow at noon."

"You got it. I'll be there."

Diane wagged a finger. "I have a very good feeling this couple's going to change our lives."

Chapter Two

IN THE CONFERENCE ROOM OF THE WEDDING planner's office, Coco set three boxes down on the table. Gesturing to the one with the pink and white polka dot bow, she said, "This is the Doris Day collection. The chocolates are rich, creamy, and mild. They have no additional flavors."

"Oh, I love the packaging." But the bride, a stunning beauty with her bounty of red hair and gorgeous green eyes, grew concerned. "I don't want to give my guests boxes, though. They're pretty, don't get me wrong, but I was picturing chocolates in shapes that tell our story."

"I will absolutely make the chocolates in any shape you'd like. I only brought the different collections so you can choose the flavor palette. For big events, most people choose the Doris Day, because it doesn't contain eggs or peanuts or any of the classic allergens. Your guest list"— Willow had said neither she nor the groom had much family and would prefer to keep it small—"might give you a little leeway, assuming you know everyone well enough to know their health issues."

The bride dug into her hemp tote bag and pulled out a folder. "So, I did a little looking around." She pulled out a photograph of the Eiffel Tower. "I think this could be really, really cool. I saw the chocolate skulls on your website. Can you cover this with the same sparkly silver?"

"Definitely. I can do anything—"

"Because I was thinking we could do a different shape for each guest, and each piece could reflect one place we've traveled." She looked to Diane. "Don't you think that would fit our brand?"

Their *brand*? Was this a wedding or a marketing event?

Diane, the consummate professional, gave the bride a serene smile. "Yes, it would. Another idea that could be fun is if we go with snowboarders and volleyball players."

Coco could learn a lot from this woman. Instead of telling the bride how impractical it would be to create a separate mold for each guest, she'd deflected. *Nicely done.*

"No, that's in our past. And my followers care about my travels, not sports. I wish Beckett was here." Willow glanced at the door. "I really want him in on this."

"You don't have to make any decisions right now," Coco said. "We've got plenty of time." The couple hadn't even set a date yet. "All you need to do while you're in town is taste the chocolates, so you can decide which one you like best." Coco lifted the gold box wrapped with a red satin ribbon. "The Brigitte Bardot collection is more decadent. The chocolates are richer, creamier. Some have alcohol. There are no nuts in this one, either. And this one…" She tugged the glittery silver ribbon on the black box. "The Elizabeth Taylor has all the unusual flavors that've earned Coco's Chocolates its reputation. Do you want to get started sampling them?

Willow waved the box away. "Let's wait for Beckett."

Discreetly, Coco checked her phone. They'd spent nearly an hour talking about Willow's life as an influencer and going over her wedding storyboard. Now, Coco had run out of time. She had to pick up her daughter in twenty minutes, and it was a fifteen-minute drive to her preschool. "I'll leave the chocolates with you, then, and you can take your time deciding."

"Oh, don't go yet, please?" Willow twisted around to the door. "He used to be a snowboarder, so he's probably just yapping away with the Bowies. I'm sure he lost track of time." She cocked her head, as if one of Posie's fairies was whispering in her ear. "Oh, wait, no. That's not it. He had some trouble with work. He's got a travel app, and I guess the wifi's not great in this hotel because he couldn't upload his images. Or something like that." Her eyes lit up. "You know what we could do? Can you make chocolate in the shape of a mountain with us hiking? That's literally how we met. He was there to do the climb for his app, and I'd been invited to the opening of the base camp facility. We spent our first night together in a yurt."

Of course you did. "I've got an artisan here in town who makes the molds for me. So, I can literally make any shape you want." She reached for her purse. "Enjoy the chocolates. Let me know which collection you prefer, and I'll talk to you later."

"Can't you wait just one more minute?" Willow pulled her phone out of her tote. "Let me text him."

"I have to pick up my daughter right now, but my shop's right in the center of town, so feel free to stop by whenever you like."

"We're leaving for Phuket tomorrow, so this is the only time he's going to be able to taste your stuff and make a choice. Please?"

"I'm so sorry. I can't leave my daughter waiting."

"Can't someone else get her?"

While Coco had never been married, she did understand the importance of wedding details. "I'm afraid it's too late to ask someone. I have to be there in fifteen minutes, and it'll take exactly that long to get in my car and drive there, but I can come back, if you like, or you can bring him to the shop. I'll be there the rest of the day." She didn't want to be rude, and she did want the business of making chocolates for an event like this, but her daughter came first. Always.

With an apologetic smile to Diane, Coco started for the door.

"I'm texting him right now," Willow said.

Oh, brother. This woman was not getting it.

"Hang on. Please?"

Coco kept going. Three more steps, and she was out of here. "I'm happy to meet with him later—" She came up short when a tall, broad-shouldered man filled the doorway.

With his messy surfer hair and lazy grin, he exuded charisma and confidence. "Sorry I'm late." But when he laid eyes on Coco, his smile flattened. His eyes went wide.

Time came to a screeching halt.

Shock sent a stinging jolt through her body.

"You...what's going on here?" The groom stood there looking between Willow and Coco with a mix of bewilderment and alarm.

Coco was aware of movement behind her, the breeze of a body flying past. Tall, slender Willow rushed past her, seemingly oblivious to the electricity the air. "Baby, you're here just in time." She slipped her arm through his.

Coco felt the bottom drop out of her world.

It was him.

Becks.

Her one-night stand from six years ago.

And…Posie's father.

Oh, my God.

How is this even possible? Panic swept in like a cold tide. She needed to grab hold of something to get her bearings, but there was nothing around her. Just *him.*

"Baby, this is Coco. She's the one who runs the chocolate shop." Willow gave her fiancé a little shake but couldn't distract him from gaping at Coco. "What's going on?" Willow looked between them. "Do you two know each other?"

"Everything all right?" Diane's calm voice was the hand that reached down and pulled Coco back into the moment.

"Yes. Of course. I…" Coco tried to shake it off, but it was taking a minute for her brain to come back online. "Becks. It's…" *Get a hold of yourself.* "It's nice to see you."

Willow's smile hardened. "How do you know each other?"

"Why don't you come in?" Diane said. "Let's all sit down."

But Coco couldn't do that. "I'm sorry. I have to get Posie." *What do I do? How do I handle this?* "I need you to wait right here for me. Can you do that? I'll be back in half an hour." She'd take Posie to her parent's house. "Okay? Thirty minutes." She looked into Becks' eyes, registering the confusion. "Don't go anywhere." *Oh, God.* Her stomach had contracted into a hard pit. As she breezed past them, she got a whiff of his scent—and it sent her right back to that night six years ago.

His hands gripping her ass, his mouth on her neck, the sheets shushing as they rolled and shifted.

God. She raced down the hallway, catching a snippet of their conversation before the door fell shut.

"What's going on?" Easy, breezy Willow's voice had turned insistent.

"I met her in Vegas a couple years ago," he said.

Her heels clacking across the hotel lobby, Coco dug into her purse for her keys, but she couldn't find them. The valet opened the door, and she stepped out into the cool, late spring air. "Thank you." She rooted around in her purse. Dammit, she was going to be late.

Where are my damn keys?

A drop of sweat rolled down her temple, as she grew increasingly frustrated.

"Ma'am?" A valet came up to her. "Would you like me to get your car?"

Right. She'd been running late and hadn't found parking. "I forgot I left it with you." *Jesus, I'm a mess.* She found the ticket sticking out of an interior pocket and handed it over. "Thank you."

"No problem. Be right back."

Tourists breezed past her, their flip-flops smacking on the boardwalk. Costumed actors strode by, the women carrying parasols, the men in three-piece suits, and a crowd gathered around a staged shoot-out. Life went on as though a bomb hadn't dropped into her world.

She couldn't make sense of it.

How in the world did Posie's father just…appear in her life?

And he's the *groom*?

A chill skittered across her skin, making her realize

she'd left her cardigan in the office. She didn't have time to go back for it.

She didn't have time...for *anything*. She was totally unprepared for this moment. Sure, the first year or two, she'd tried to find him, had rehearsed what she'd say when she did...but she'd stopped imagining the impossible long ago.

Only...the impossible had just happened.

How do I tell him he has a child? Do I tell him in front of his fiancée?

And then, for one wicked moment, she wondered...*do I even have to tell him?*

Anxiety surged through her.

No, of course she did.

It was just...he was getting married. Soon, they'd have a family. If they met Posie, they'd fall in love with her. She was smart and fun and wildly imaginative.

Visits would quickly turn into joint custody. And that meant—God—not reading to Posie every night before bed and laying out her clothes, only to have her choose her own outfit anyway. It meant not spending every holiday with her.

Coco's skin went clammy, and her mind spun.

The idea of sharing her baby girl...it felt like driving too fast on a mountain switchback.

I can't do it.

I can't share her.

She didn't have a choice. No matter the consequence, she had to tell him. It was the right thing to do for him *and* for Posie.

Tires crunched over the dirt road, as her dark green Jeep pulled up in front of the hotel.

"Coco." That voice. Rich, deep...thick with concern.

Slowly, she turned to face him. Becks still had the same chin-length honey-blonde hair and laidback demeanor. And those eyes. A fresh wave of awareness rolled through her.

Those are Posie's icy blue eyes.

When she noticed her cardigan bunched in his fist, he thrust it out to her. "You forgot this."

"Oh." Even though she needed its warmth, she shoved it into her tote. "Thank you."

At the same moment, the valet clambered onto the boardwalk. "You're all set."

And there she stood on the boardwalk, sandwiched between the valet and her one-night stand, and she'd never felt more lost in her life.

She wanted to get it over with, just lay the truth at his feet. To skip ahead five steps to the point where her world righted, and she knew exactly what the new reality looked like.

Sliding a look to the valet, Becks pulled a wallet out of his back pocket and handed the young man a bill.

"Thanks, man." The guy took off.

Coco shook her head. "I'm sorry. I'm just completely in shock."

"Yeah, crazy coincidence, right? Somehow, though, I have a feeling there's more going on here."

"You're right. There is." She gestured to her car. "But I really do have to go right now. You'll wait for me?"

"Of course. I'll be here."

"Thank you." She stepped off the boardwalk and headed around to the driver's side. Gunshots from the shootout ripped through the air, sending her pulse into overdrive. Just as she opened the door, she looked up to see him still standing there, watching her.

"Hey," he called. "Did you ever get your adventure?"

"I did."

And you're about to meet her.

"Did you catch her?" the wedding planner asked.

Beckett nodded, distracted. "Hey, how old's her daughter?"

Because what else could it be?

What else would have a hookup from six years ago so freaked out about seeing him again?

"Oh, Posie just had her fifth birthday yesterday." Diane's tone held warmth. "She's a doll."

Five. He'd met Colette—*shit, her name's Coco*—at the end of September six years ago. He remembered, because it was right after that trip to Portugal. Add nine months… and that made her a June baby.

Something cracked inside him, like stepping on the thin crust of ice on a newly frozen lake. A shiver raced up his spine.

Holy fucking shit.

"Hey, babe, what's going on?" Willow sat on the edge of the conference table, her long legs swinging, her feet bare.

Jesus—how would she handle this? They'd just had the no-kids conversation. They were both very clear on the subject.

Diane gathered her leather sheath. "I'll be in my office if you need me."

The moment she walked out the door, Willow jumped off the desk and approached him. "You okay? You look like you're going to be sick."

Beckett paced to the window overlooking the mountain, but his vision wouldn't focus on anything, the view nothing but a blur of green, brown, and bright spots of moving color.

A kid. The idea darted around his mind, like a firefly dipping and weaving—just out of reach. He couldn't grab hold of it.

Hang on. She'd had a boyfriend. *That's why she was sad that night at the club.* The guy had fucked her over—

That's right. He'd ghosted her.

The kid's not mine.

Oh, Jesus. Relief swept through him.

Of course, it's not my kid. We had one night together.

And we used condoms. He thought back...had they? *Yes, absolutely.* He distinctly remembered grabbing them from his toiletry bag.

He clutched his head, letting out a shaky breath.

Willow put her hand on his back. "You're kind of freaking me out right now. What's going on? You obviously know the chocolate lady, so what's your story with her?"

"I told you. I met her in Vegas six years ago."

"And?"

"And nothing. It was one night."

"Then what's she all freaked out about?"

He turned back around to face the room, folding his arms across his chest. "No idea."

"You didn't know she was from here?"

More information came back. Her ex had ghosted her on a daycare business they were supposed to start in her hometown. A tourist town.

Is this it? Calamity?

49

What were the odds she lived in the same town as the Bowie brothers?

Why did I never ask?

"I mean, if it's nothing, why are you both acting so weird?" Her phone chimed, and she looked at the screen. "Okay, they just got back to me." Her brow furrowed. "When's the Pamplona trip?"

"The first bull run is July sixth."

"Okay, good. I don't want to miss that one. So, then, I'm going to take this one. It's a rock festival in Ireland. Do you want to come with me?"

Ireland didn't have the kind of extreme sports he covered, but he could go just to hang out with her. "When is it? I'd have to check my calendar." *But not right now.*

Now, he could only think about Colette—*Coco, dammit.* Because why, if the kid was her ex's, was she so wild-eyed?

What's going on?

"End of August." Willow's voice sounded like it came from the other end of a tunnel.

Come on, Coco wouldn't be freaked out if the kid was someone else's. Nothing else made sense.

Fear churned through him, the blades hacking away, turning his bones to mush.

He shut down that line of thought. *Hang on. Wait for her to get back.* "I have to be in France September first. Can't miss it." That was the biggest trip he had this year. His followers couldn't wait to see the footage of him with nine other medaled athletes wearing wingsuits and flying off a cliff.

"Oh. I really wanted to go to that. Now, I don't know what to do. We need to synch our calendars, so I can see what you've got going on. With a wedding coming up, we need to do more trips together."

Her words pinged off his brain and clattered to the ground like pellets on aluminum.

He needed answers.

He dreaded them.

Pretty, sexy, sweet, caring Colette—*Coco*—had a kid. She'd gone off on an adventure, only to find out she was pregnant.

Had she *married* the ghost?

A fresh fear sliced through him, though he couldn't say why.

Coco being married was a good thing. *She's a mom.* A business owner. She has a full life.

I'm getting married, too.

Am I, though? Even stringing the words into a sentence felt like wearing shoes on the wrong feet.

"I guess I have to figure out what's more important for my brand," Willow said. "Going to the festival or traveling with my fiancé? At least for the next year, we should probably do a lot more things together. That's what my followers want to see. It gets the most engagement. We'll both just have to compromise. I'll skip some things to go with you, and you'll skip some to show up with me."

"I'm not skipping anything. If it's on my calendar, it's something I committed to." The only thing that distinguished him from every other person with an app and a unique idea was his reputation. He met his obligations and commitments, period.

"Well, that's the thing. It's not just you anymore. It's us. We have to do things together."

"You're welcome to come on any of my trips, and I'm

willing to go with you on days I'm not already booked. That's about all I can offer."

Fuck, he didn't want to talk about work.

He needed answers.

He needed Coco to come back and talk to him.

He needed to know if his life was going to be blown apart.

Chapter Three

Lost in his thoughts, Beckett paced a trail on the carpet.

And then the door opened. Coco breezed in, breathless. "Hey."

She was so fucking pretty. Ridiculous thing to be thinking in that moment, but still. With her dark hair framing her face in loose, gentle waves, the bright red lipstick, and her black and white polka dot dress that showcased her curvy figure, she hit a note in him he couldn't explain.

"Hey." He didn't mean to sound clipped, but...*I'm a fucking mess.*

Willow glanced up from her phone, watching Coco enter.

The two women couldn't have been more opposite. His girlfriend was nearly six feet tall, with long, flowing red hair and a toned, athletic body. She was only twenty-two, but a life spent outdoors had toughened her skin. Not that she wasn't beautiful—she absolutely was.

But Coco...she had a quiet elegance. That's what he'd

first noticed about her, that air of dignity. He'd been drawn to her because, underneath that smile, had been a poignant vulnerability that had grabbed him by the balls.

"Sorry about that." Coco strode to the table and dropped her tote on it. "We have a routine after school, and she doesn't like breaking it."

Willow got up. "So, what's going on? You've got us all twisted up here."

Coco drew in a deep breath. "Right." She looked at him, strong, resolved.

And yet, underneath that determined façade, he could see fear. The look in her eyes said, *Can I trust you?*

Something in him rose, tall and confident. *Yes.*

But then it sat right the fuck back down when he remembered they were talking about a kid.

"There's no easy way to say this," Coco said. "But I've got a five-year-old daughter, Posie, and…she's yours."

Even though he'd prepared himself for those words, the cord tethering him to reality snapped, and he went into freefall.

"That is not only a ridiculous thing to say, but it's dangerous." Willow slapped her phone on the table and pointed a finger at Coco. "I don't want you to say that again—to us or to anyone—until he takes a paternity test."

Oddly, it wasn't his girlfriend's stern defense that brought him back. It was Coco's pride. The tilt of her chin and set of her shoulders reminded him he wasn't alone in this experience. She was struggling, too.

"Beckett *is* her father." Coco said it quietly, calmly. "I'm more than happy to get a test done, but once you see her, you won't question it. That said, let me be very clear." Her whole demeanor changed, went from kind and sweet to stern. "I'm telling you because it's the right thing to do, not because I expect you to be involved in her life in any way."

"You guys had a one-night-stand," Willow said. "Let's be real. It could be anybody's."

"That's enough." He stepped forward, breaking the waves of tension flowing between the two women. "I'm assuming your ex already took a test?"

"Of course." She looked to Willow. "And I hadn't been with anyone other than Keith and Beckett." Turning toward him, she grew more intense. "I want you to know I looked for you, but the only thing I had to go on was your name. Your friends called you Becks, so that's what I looked for. Other than a bar and a couple of women, I didn't find anything."

"That's because I'm Beckett. Only the snowboarding world called me Becks. And I retired six years ago."

Her probing look laid a question out between them. *Did you try to find me?* But she quickly brushed it aside. "I have a picture of her." Coco reached into the tote and pulled out a framed photograph. "I grabbed it from my mom's house when I dropped Posie off." Her hand shook as she handed it over. "I'm sorry. I'm a mess right now."

Part of him didn't want to look at the picture. He didn't want this to be true.

Willow grabbed it before he could. "Wow. She looks just like you."

He glanced over and stared into the blue eyes of a laughing little girl. Her hair was golden blonde, exactly like his. *Fuck.*

Fuck.

"She's got your dimples," Willow murmured. "I can't

believe this is happening." She handed the picture back. "We're still going to need a paternity test."

"I have no problem with that," Coco said. "But, again, I'm not looking for anything from you. I have a very strong support system here, and my business is doing well. I don't need anything." She tucked the frame carefully into her tote, as though it had feelings, and Willow had hurt them.

"I'm not…" He couldn't take his eyes off the photograph peeking out of the bag, too aware that he hadn't touched it, hadn't really looked at the little girl. "I'm not accusing you of anything."

"Neither am I," Willow said. "But it's a reasonable request. We're leaving for Thailand tomorrow, so we need to get it done today. We can deal with the situation when we get back."

Tension crackled around them, and Coco went rock hard. "My daughter is not a situation. She's a beautiful, happy, smart, little girl." She shook her head with a look of disgust. "Okay. I've done what I needed to do, and now I'm going to go. You know where my shop is, so after you pick up a test at the pharmacy, you can drop it off with me. Unless, of course, you'd like to swab her yourself to make sure I'm not pulling a fast one on you." She grabbed the handles of her tote and walked out the door.

"Sensitive much?" Willow reached for her phone. "Like we're just supposed to jump in and start writing child support checks? Come *on*."

She was a flurry of motion, passing by him to grab her purse, reaching inside for sunglasses, but for some reason time had slowed for him. He couldn't get his body parts to move. Glancing out the door, he watched Coco duck into Diane's office.

"Let's go," Willow said. "We need to get this done today."

Coco came out of the office and strode down the hallway, her quick pace causing the silky skirt to flutter around her legs. He felt this terrible tug, like every step she took away from him meant he was going to lose her. "Wait." He bolted out of the room.

She must not have heard him, because she kept on going, pushing through the door that led to the resort lobby.

He chased after her. "Coco. Wait."

Slowly, she turned, taking in a steadying breath. "What?"

"I'm sorry." He didn't have any more words. He just didn't.

But the two he gave, simple as they were, seemed to relax her. "I'm sorry, too. I know this is hard for you, I do. But in all the times I imagined finding you, I was never accused of trying to trap you."

"That…I know you're not doing that. It hadn't even occurred to me."

"This whole thing feels surreal. I can't even believe it's happening."

"I know. I…" He shrugged. "I'm…in shock."

"I'm sure. I probably could have found a better way to tell you."

"I don't think there *is* a better way."

"I should go. I'll be waiting for you at the shop. The lab will post the results online, so you can see it from anywhere in the world."

She'd obviously looked into it. "Okay." He had so much to say to her. Most importantly, *Thank you, for handling this all on your own.* But he'd wait for the test results. Wait until it sank in.

Still, she stood there, their gazes locked, a thousand unspoken words passing between them.

It was like a net of memories had dropped over them, connecting them in a shared experience that suddenly brought it all back to life.

"Right. I'm…" She hitched a thumb over her shoulder. "Going."

His pulse quickened, perspiration beading over his lip. What if she wasn't at the shop when he dropped off the test? He might not see her again. Tomorrow, he'd get on a plane, leaving nothing but his DNA behind. In a few days, he'd read the results from a hotel room across the world. And he didn't want to do that.

Jesus, how the hell could he leave without… "Can I meet her?" The idea sent a shockwave between them.

She looked like he'd issued a threat. When she glanced over his shoulder, he knew she was thinking about Willow's hostility. "I can come alone, if that's what you want."

"She's your future wife. Whatever involvement you might have will include her, so it's fine if she comes. But I'm telling you right now, Posie's *five*. She's sweet and innocent, and I can't have you looking at her with any kind of suspicion or mistrust. It has to be nothing more than me running into some friends, okay?"

"I understand."

"How about this? After dinner, I'll bring her to the resort's indoor pool. Say seven o'clock? If you decide you don't want to meet her, no harm no foul. You can walk away with no consequences."

"That sounds good." Actually, it sounded terrifying.

He'd jumped out of airplanes and snowboarded on uncharted terrain. He'd swum with sharks.

And nothing frightened him more than meeting a five-year-old.

In her shimmery one-piece swimsuit, Posie stood on the side of the pool, fists clenched, her bare little feet stomping in a puddle of water. "Catch me, Mommy."

"You know I will." Coco figured most of the guests had taken advantage of the outdoor pool, because only a couple of families played around them.

The door opened, and a group of teenagers burst in. Loud and reckless, they dropped their skateboards and made a tour around the big room. The sound was deafening.

Since Coco had carved out a safe little corner in the shallow end for her daughter, she was wary but not concerned about them. "I'm right here." She stood in hip-deep water, flicking her fingers. "Come on. Jump."

Posie tugged on the tulle sewn around her waist. Store-bought swimsuits were too plain, so Coco had added frills to get her daughter to wear one. The girl was all fairy clothes, all the time.

Coco's arms grew tired of reaching up. "Jump, sweet pea."

Smiling with glee, Posie chanted, "I can't. I can't. I can't."

"Okay. Well, I guess I'll do some laps then."

"No, Mommy. I'll do it. Stay right there."

"All right. I'll count to three, and on three you'll jump. Ready?"

Posie clutched the tulle. "One second." She looked up to the ceiling and whispered to herself. "Okay, Mommy. I'm ready now."

"One...two...three!" Coco called.

Her daughter stared down into the pool, before lifting both arms in the air and taking that daring leap of faith. Coco caught her, careful not to let her face go under the water. Still, droplets collected on her eyelashes, and she looked stunned, as she adjusted to be being wet and cold.

"You okay?"

Posie nodded, before pushing out of Coco's arms and paddling around like a puppy dog. Coco heard a shriek and turned just in time to see one of the teenagers grabbing his friend fireman-style and hurling him into the water. Hollering, the others cannonballed into the pool, creating a series of waves that crashed over Posie's face, causing the little girl to swallow water and flail.

Coco lunged, but before she could get to her, a man jumped in and lifted Posie into his arms. The sight of big, muscular Beckett holding her little girl—the pink nail polish against his tan skin—hit her hard.

With a threatening look at the teenagers, he said, "Watch it."

For one moment, their smiles froze and fear flashed in their eyes. Then, they swam off to the deep end.

"Mommy." Posie lunged for her, and Coco pulled her close. Those little arms banded around her shoulders, and her daughter tucked her face into Coco's neck. "My eyes sting. It *hurts*."

"Hand me that." Beckett flicked his fingers, and Willow tossed him a hotel towel. Keeping it above the water, he brought it over to them. Gently, he patted Posie's face dry.

Coco caught the moment when father and daughter looked into each other's eyes. Beckett's jaw went slack. It was like he'd seen a ghost.

"Who are you?" Posie asked in her sweet, little girl voice.

The normally easy-going, confident man stood there, awkward, uncomfortable. He swallowed, making a visible effort to get a hold of himself. "I'm Beckett. I'm…a friend of your mom's. Are you okay?"

Posie gave an exaggerated nod, like the little drama queen she was.

"Can you say thank you to Beckett?" Coco said.

Her little girl turned big, mournful eyes to the man who'd saved her. "Thank you." She stabbed a finger towards the deep end. "Those boys are mean."

"I don't think they meant to hurt you," Beckett said. "They were just having fun."

"That wasn't fun." Posie's tone held accusation.

"No, I didn't mean…" Beckett looked helpless and out of his element. "I meant they weren't paying attention."

Coco jumped in to save him. Kissing her daughter's arm, she said, "You want to get out or stay in the water?"

"I'm getting out."

"All right then." As she walked to the stairs, Beckett launched forward, his broad back and shoulders gleaming, his strong arms carving into the water. He hoisted himself out, droplets coursing down his muscular body. His board shorts clung to him like plastic wrap, outlining a hard, round ass.

A memory struck of her hands clutching those hard globes, as he thrust furiously. A tremor rocked through her, and she forced herself to look away.

She'd never forgotten how hot that night had been,

how passionate he was. Their sex had been so desperate, urgent...so deeply satisfying. She went hot and flustered and had to look away.

The moment Posie's feet hit the concrete, she dashed off to the two loungers that held their towels and tote bag. "Mommy, I want to play now." She dug into the blue and white striped bag, pulled out her fairy dolls, and headed for the kiddie pool.

"I'll be right there." Coco reached for a towel, dabbing the moisture off her face. Laughter had her turning to find Willow, so slender and tall in her string bikini, clasping her hands around Beckett's neck. Where she was loose and easy, Beckett stood rigid.

This is really hard for him.

Compassion softened her. She couldn't imagine finding out she had a child in the world she hadn't known about. Willow was either trying to lighten him up or she was just completely clueless, but his body language screamed, *Back off.*

And then the woman glanced her way, and Coco grew instantly self-conscious. Her tummy had a little pooch and her thighs had never been toned—not like that. She reached for her cover-up, but before she could lift it over her head, she grew annoyed with herself.

I had a baby, and my body changed.

Screw it. She cast it aside.

And, really, what did she care what Beckett and his fiancée thought of her body? She strode to the kiddie pool and plopped down, not even bothering to suck in her stomach.

It is what it is.

Though, just to say, I sure wish I'd worn the one-piece.

Her feet covered in tepid water up to her ankles, she

watched Beckett rub a towel over his hair, while engaging in a heated conversation with Willow.

Why had he jumped into the water like that? Posie might've gotten splashed, but it hadn't been that big of a deal. He'd been so angry and protective.

And she'd liked it. Liked seeing her daughter in the shelter of his arms. Every child needed a father.

God, she has one.

Posie actually had a dad. Her eyes stung, and she blinked back unwanted tears.

Hers had done such a great job of making all four of his daughters feel like his special little girl. There hadn't been a single moment in her life when she'd questioned whether he'd be there for her. And it had always killed her that Posie wouldn't have that. Sure, she had her grandpa, but it wasn't the same thing. She'd thought Ethan could be that...and then he'd left.

What would happen with Beckett, though? Would he want to be Posie's dad—or would he get on a plane in the morning and never look back?

He caught her staring, and she thought she saw a plea in his eyes. He looked shaken, like, *What do I do? What the hell do I do?* She couldn't imagine what this experience must be like for him, but she appreciated that he was here, trying. He could've dropped off the test kit and gone back to his hotel.

She gave him a warm smile and patted the ground next to her.

Dropping the towel, he made his way over, Willow following.

"Well, hey." The redhead used a voice meant for cute little purse-dogs. "Can we join you guys?"

Posie barely spared her a glance, but she did do a

ERIKA KELLY

double take on the man who'd defended her against the mean teenagers.

"Sure," Coco said.

The couple settled down beside her, Beckett between the two women. Willow glanced down at her toes—the nails painted yellow with black dots. "I'm sorry if I came off too aggressive this afternoon. This whole thing has really thrown me."

Coco appreciated the apology. "It's pretty big news."

"Understatement of the year." The woman had a big, throaty laugh.

"When did you find out you were pregnant?" Beckett spoke quietly, so Posie couldn't hear.

But he didn't have to worry. That girl was completely lost in her fantasy world. Holding a doll in each hand, she skimmed them over the surface of the water. "Look, Mommy. They're flying."

"They sure are." Smiling as Posie walked around the pool, making her dolls dip and glide, Coco turned back to the adults. "I don't know if you remember, but I—"

"You'd graduated college in May, your boyfriend had ghosted you, and you didn't know whether to start the daycare business on your own or do something different."

More than a little surprised he'd remembered so much, she automatically checked Willow's reaction—and saw the sharp flinch of hurt.

Well, Willow might not appreciate how much he remembered about a one-night stand, but Coco very much did. They'd created a child together, so it mattered that they'd had a memorable connection.

Because one day she'd have to explain it to her daughter.

"Exactly. So, I remembered what you'd said, about

64

shaking things up. And I did just that. I took some of my savings and went off to Europe for my big adventure. I didn't really notice anything at first. It wasn't until the second month that I got worried." She would never forget waiting in the bathroom of the studio apartment she'd rented in Paris. She'd wanted to crawl out of her skin, the anxiety was so intense.

And then to see that blue line?

God. Her world had crashed and burned. She'd had no idea what to do.

"So much for your wild adventure," Willow said.

Why did everything out of this woman's mouth make Coco bristle? "Oh, no, I had it. I'd only planned on staying in Europe for a month, but I wound up taking a chocolate class. I loved it so much I took another in Belgium and a third in Switzerland."

Beckett's eyebrows shot up, impressed.

"So, I not only got to live in Europe for seven months, but I discovered a business I was really excited about."

"Well, you've got a great attitude about everything," Willow said. "I'll give you that."

Coco wanted to snap back, *I don't need anything from you.* But she kept her attention on Beckett. Willow's opinion meant nothing. "I know I already said this, but I really did try to find you. There were a lot of sleepless nights after she was born, and I spent them searching the hell out of Becks." She lowered her voice even more. "I remember you said you'd just come back from Portugal, so I guess I was fixated on surfing. I also remembered your friend Jimmy. Did I remember that right? The guy who'd never been to Vegas before?"

"Yeah, that's right. He was a snowboarder like me."

"Do I know him?" Willow asked.

"Yeah. Jimmy Wolfe."

"Oh, that's the guy who wanted to get in on your business so bad but couldn't afford the buy-in." Willow said.

Coco really wasn't liking this woman very much. "Well, I better get her home. She's got school tomorrow."

"Is it year-round?" Beckett asked.

"It's preschool, but with a daycare schedule, which is why I chose it. It's great for working parents." Watching her daughter, warmth and affection rushed in. These two would go off on their exotic adventure tomorrow, but she got to be Posie's mom. She got to give her a bath and read her stories and whisper, *Sweet dreams.* She got to make her breakfast and listen to her make up wild stories for her dolls in her car seat.

I love my life. She got up, no longer even slightly self-conscious about her body. "I got both your numbers from Diane, so I'll send you the log-in information as soon as the results are in." She grabbed the two dolls sitting on the top steps. "Come on, sweetie. Time to get home."

"I'm not ready, Mommy."

"You can go swimming with Grandpa tomorrow."

"No, Mommy. We're having a tea party, remember? You said."

"I do remember, and I've got all the ingredients to make cookies. But I'm talking about tomorrow night. We can have dinner with Grandma and Grandpa and go for a swim afterwards. But right now, we have to go."

"Not yet."

She heard a chuckle and glanced back to see Willow giving a Beckett a look that said, *Thank God that's not us.* Coco tried to ignore her, but she felt the couple's attention spreading over her like a rash. "Posie, if you want to do fun things like we did tonight, then I need to know I can count on you to listen when I say it's time to go home. Do you understand what I'm telling you? If you make it difficult, then I'm going to be much less inclined to come up with these fun ideas."

In a crouch, Posie stared at her dolls, their hair floating like masses of seaweed under the water. "Okay, Mommy. I'll go home now. Can I play in the bathtub?"

"Of course." Relieved that she'd managed to bypass a scene, she stepped out of the water.

Beckett stood, too, looking a little panicked. "So, I guess—" His jaw snapped shut.

This is it. He'd met his daughter, and he didn't seem to know what to do next.

But it wasn't something he could figure out in one day. Still, she could see he needed something. "If you'd like, I can set up a private Splashagram page, and I can post pictures of her there. You can watch her grow up."

Something flashed in his eyes—fear? It passed too quickly for her to discern. "Yeah. I'd like that."

"Come on, lovely." Coco headed back to the lounger and grabbed the beach towel. Posie walked right into her arms, and Coco folded the soft cotton around her. "Did you have fun?"

"Why did that man jump in the pool?" She twisted around to look at Beckett.

"Because he didn't like the way those kids splashed you like that."

Her daughter watched him slip his feet into black flip-flops. "I like him, Mommy."

"Yes, he's a nice man."

Beckett joined them, leaning over, hands on his knees,

so he was eye level with Posie. "Well, I guess I have to say goodbye."

There was no mistaking the conflict in his eyes. And she got it. She did. Because Posie didn't know it, but she was talking to her father. It seemed so wrong not to tell her. *She needs a dad.*

She deserves one.

"I'm glad I got to meet you." Beckett held out his fist. "Take care of yourself."

Posie bumped it. "Do you want to come to my tea party tomorrow?"

Beckett looked stricken. His mouth opened and then quickly snapped closed. He didn't speak for a moment that went on so long, Coco couldn't bear the tension.

Just when she was about to say something, she remembered.

That look on his face? Like he'd seen a ghost? He had.

He'd lost his sister. *Oh, God.* She'd been young when she died.

Six. And Beckett had been twelve.

Posie must remind him of her.

How awful.

The man was dealing with layer upon layer of complicated emotions.

Willow set a hand on Beckett's shoulder. "Babe, let's go. We've got to get up at four-thirty."

Beckett rose to his full height. She didn't think it was intentional, but it sure looked like he was telling her to back off. "Thanks for inviting me, Posie. I can't go to the tea party tomorrow, but next time I'm in town, I hope you'll invite me again, because I'd really like to go." He reached out a hand, as though he might touch her, but froze before letting his arm fall to his side. "I'm glad I got to meet you." He hesitated a moment longer, and then headed back to the table that held their belongings.

Lingering, Willow said, "You should follow me. At Willow the Wanderer. It's a super fun page, and we have the most amazing adventures." And then she took off, her long hair gleaming, her hips swaying.

Coco watched them go, Beckett striding several steps ahead of his long-legged fiancée.

Would she ever see him again?

She wished she could say she didn't care. But it just wasn't true.

It would break her heart if he chose to ignore his daughter.

Chapter Four

BECKETT HADN'T HAD A SINGLE DROP OF COFFEE, AND yet as he stared at the images on his computer screen, he felt as wired as if he'd downed a whole pot.

True to her word, Coco had set up a private Splashagram page last night, and she'd already uploaded pictures. Lots of them.

In the dark hotel room, Posie's face was the only thing he could see. He was focused on the one taken last night. She was staring into the mirror as she brushed her teeth.

All that honey-blonde hair.

Bright blue eyes, like crystals.

Like mine.

He scrolled to the bottom of the page again to see her as a red-faced newborn, features scrunched up, damp hair plastered to her head. The next one showed her swaddled in a soft, white blanket, held snug against a chest. The muscular, hairy arms most likely belonged to Coco's dad.

Should've been me.

No, he didn't want kids, but he would've been there if

he'd known. Coco should never have had to go through it alone.

In the third photograph, Posie sat in a high chair with a fistful of birthday cake.

In another, she toddled away from whoever took the picture. Those chubby calves, the long, bouncy hair… from behind, she looked so much like Ari.

His heart pinched hard.

Ari.

Fuck.

His sister had been his little mini me, and he'd loved her with everything he had, but the memories had stopped slicing him open a while ago.

It was kind of like the way a constant stream of water smoothed the sharp edges of rock, carving it into a whole new shape. He'd become a whole new shape.

Willow swept out of the bathroom and came to an abrupt stop. "What're you doing? Put your laptop away. We have to go."

They didn't just share the same eye and hair color. Posie had Ari's feisty spirit, her mercurial mood swings.

And, right then, in the bed of the Owl Hoot Resort and Spa at five in the morning, his past surged forward to merge with his present, leaving him disoriented, exhausted, and filled with a longing he couldn't name.

Willow's herbal shampoo scent surrounded him, as she stood looking at the screen. "What're you thinking right now?"

"How alike they are, Posie and my sister."

"Isn't she the same age as Ari when she died?"

"Ari was six, but yeah. Close enough." A million memories burst out of the box, and for the first time, he needed to talk about her. Not keep it all locked inside.

71

"Ari was this crazy ball of energy. She would go, go, go, and then the next thing you know, she'd be crashed out on the couch. She never just walked anywhere, she skipped. Everywhere she went, she made people laugh, because she was just so…extra. About everything."

Willow sat on the edge of the mattress, tipping her chin to the screen. "She wasted no time putting that page up."

And just like that, the memories scuttled back into the box. *Wrong time to share them.* "You act like she's been waiting for me to find her, like she's got a list of demands. That's not what's happening here. You saw her. She was just as blown away as I was. This is tough for all of us." He reached for Willow's hand, understanding she had to feel threatened, too. "We're going to get through this. It's just going to take some time to figure things out."

"You say that, but I'm telling you, it's got to be a big relief for her. I mean, I was raised by a single mom, and mine would've jumped at the chance to have some help."

"Pretty sure she said she doesn't need anything from me. Her dad's Tyler Cavanaugh, one of the greatest quarterbacks to ever play football." His gaze fell to the photo of the retired ball player squeezed onto a slide, Posie on his lap, both of them laughing as they raced down.

Damn, Coco. Who knew that night in Vegas he'd been hanging out with Joss Montalbano and Tyler Cavanaugh's daughter?

"I'm not talking about financial stuff." Willow shifted beside him. "It's hard to raise a kid by yourself. It's lonely, and there's always something in the house that needs fixing or decisions that need to be made. But, honestly, there's no point in thinking about any of this until we get the test results." She nudged him. "Come on. The car's waiting.

We can talk on the way to the airport. It's a two-and-a-half hour ride." She dug into her purse and pulled out her passport. "Oh, shit. Where's yours? I swear I put them both in here." She flicked on the lamp and scanned the room.

"I took mine out."

She whipped around. *Why would you do that?*

"I'm not going."

"What? You have to go. No, no, no. You can't do this. The island's closed in June. They're only opening it for you. This is your *business*, Beckett. You can't bail on this trip."

She couldn't relate, he understood that. Posie might not be her child, but did she really not grasp the enormity of the situation? Did she really think swimming with whale sharks carried more weight than his kid? "I need another day or two to figure things out."

"Which we'll do in Thailand. By the time we get back, we'll have the test results. One week isn't going to matter."

"Wills, I just found out I have a kid. I can't take off."

"Did she say something to you?"

Everything in his body strained to get back to the pictures of Posie. To seal himself in her world. He didn't want to have this conversation, but he knew he owed it to his girlfriend. "Of course not." There wasn't a single chance in hell he could get off this bed, zip up his suitcase, and head to the airport.

"If you were a lawyer, and your hearing started tomorrow, are you telling me you'd bail on your client? You wouldn't. Thailand is your court date. It's your career. God, Beckett, it's been five years. One more week isn't going to matter."

His pulse quickened. Panic stirred inside him like a

dust devil. "That's exactly right. Five years, and I've missed every minute."

"You don't even want kids."

"Willow…stop. I'm not getting on a plane when the only thing on my mind is the fact that I *have* one." She didn't get it, but she was making it worse. Panic hardened into a choking fear.

She drew in a breath, working to tame her frustration, to find the right words to convince him. He knew her. He knew how she worked. He knew what was coming.

And he didn't have any room in him for it.

"Okay, I'm sorry." She held up a hand, palm facing him. "I'm in travel mode. That's just how I get. Between the drive to Idaho Falls, the plane change in New York, there's a lot of moving parts." She drew in a breath and looked to the curtains. "Here's what we'll do. I'll go on ahead and meet the tourism minister. That way, you not showing up won't be considered rude. My followers are going to freak out and want to know why I'm not with my fiancé, but it's not like I can tell them what's going on. At least not until you get the results back."

"I'm not talking about her, period. That's never going to happen."

She reeled back from his aggressive tone. "God, Beckett. Chill out. I'm sorry if I'm not handling this the way you want, but you have to understand this isn't just affecting you. It's my life, too." Slinging the purse strap over her shoulder, she reached for the handle of her carry-on. "I should go. Take a day or two to do what you need. As long as you're there by Friday, we should be okay."

"Sounds good." He scrubbed a hand over mouth.

"I love you, you know that, right?"

They didn't really say romantic things. That wasn't the

nature of their relationship. So, he just gave her a curt nod. That was all he was capable of. She couldn't see, but he was lost in the shadows, the nowhere land between this conversation with Willow and the Splashagram world of Posie.

And the pull toward that world was too powerful to ignore.

When he didn't set the laptop aside and get off the bed to walk her out, she came back to him, smoothing her hand down the back of his head. "It's going to be okay, I promise. We'll get through this. I'll see you in a couple of days." She went in for a mouth kiss—hers soft and open, his closed. She pulled away, studying him.

And then, sighing, she, rolled her suitcase to the door. Once there, she paused and waited for him to look at her.

He knew she needed him to be okay, so he said, "Text me when you land."

She rolled her eyes, her relief clear. "When do I not text you? See you soon."

The moment the door clicked shut, he turned back to the screen to find a picture of

Posie bundled in a red snowsuit, the hood drawn tightly around her face, exposing only her blue eyes, nose, and rosebud mouth.

He skimmed down to see her at the lake, standing in a shallow puddle on wet sand, the sky filled with dark, heavy clouds. She'd lifted the hem of her shorts and dipped a toe daintily into the water. He cracked a smile. *How cute is that?* Lifting her *shorts* like they might get wet.

Another birthday, this time the cake was lit with two candles. Posie stood on a chair, cheeks puffed out.

His blood pumped hard. A sense of urgency getting him moving. He set the laptop aside.

Looking at pictures wasn't enough.

Had he not gone to the pool last night and met her, it might have been different.

But he had.

And now it was too late.

He needed to see her.

Beckett felt like an asshole. After showering, extending his stay at the front desk another night, and driving from the revitalized ghost town into the heart of Calamity, he hadn't once thought to check the time.

Now, he stood on the sidewalk, hands jammed into his pockets, with nowhere to go.

At six in the morning, the small western town was just waking up. A man walked his dog under the antelope-horn arch and onto the dewy green, while two women in cowboy boots and jeans jumped out of the bed of a pickup truck and headed into the only store open at this hour, Calamity Joe's coffee shop.

He should've thought this plan through. Not only didn't he know where Coco lived, but he had no idea what time her store opened. Somehow, he'd had a vague notion chocolate shops worked like bakeries. He'd imagined her up at four, making fresh truffles for the day.

But he didn't see a single light on in the store.

She's got a five-year-old. She's probably home.

He got an image of Posie jumping on her mom's bed, demanding she wake up and make waffles for breakfast. Actually, with that girl's independent streak, she was more likely to be dragging a chair to the counter and pulling a box of Cheerios down from the cupboard. He could picture the scene so clearly, all the way to the spilled milk on a kitchen table.

It killed him, the idea that while he'd been jumping on —and out of— planes and waking up when he felt like it, Coco had spent every single moment of the last five years feeding, bathing, and dressing a child.

My child.

A woman in shorts and hiking boots dashed out of Calamity Joe's, carrying a tray of drinks and a bag of food. She headed for a car idling at the curb. The driver pushed open the door, and she passed the tray to him, before getting in.

The air smelled of coffee and something sweet, like muffins. His stomach grumbled. Maybe he'd grab a bite while he waited.

But his feet were rooted to the sidewalk.

He couldn't do anything, go anywhere. He just needed to see them.

That's right. Them. Not just Posie, but Coco, too.

There was something about her that drew him. Just like that night in Vegas, he felt a weird, magnetic pull.

It wasn't sexual—he had a girlfriend, for Christ's sake. It was just…something.

His phone vibrated, and he knew it was Willow. She'd probably checked in at the airport and wanted to talk. But he just wasn't in that mindset. He hovered in some strange place of anticipation, fear, and anxiety.

His life had irrevocably changed. Either he altered his lifestyle to fit in with Posie's—or he didn't. He could catch a flight tomorrow and go back to life as he knew it.

Posie wouldn't notice.

The way she'd kept sneaking looks at him last night, though…that look in her eyes…

His mind kept snagging on it. She'd liked the way he'd protected her—and that made him feel big, powerful.

Important.

Beckett could remember being at a park—*what was I? Eight? Nine? No, we moved to Lake Placid when I turned eight. So, seven.* His dad had been teaching him how to ride a bike when some cyclists soared by. One of them accidentally knocked him over. His dad had picked him up carefully, dusted off his jeans, and then approached the guy, who'd gotten off his bike to check on him. His dad had cornered him against a tree and yelled at him.

Beckett could remember being mortified, wishing his dad would stop, but also, underneath that, feeling safe... protected. Cared for.

Posie didn't have a dad.

He rubbed his chest, as if he could somehow soothe the ache deep inside.

She needed one. Every kid did.

I just don't think that's me.

Then, what am I doing here? They're not expecting me, so I can just go.

But he couldn't seem to make himself leave town. Tipping his head back, he scraped his hands through his hair. Pretty sure he caught a whiff of chocolate, he swung around, wondering if she'd opened the shop. *Nope, lights still off.*

Inhaling again, he got a hint of sage, exhaust, freshly mown grass, and...yeah, chocolate. Definitely chocolate. Someone was making it. He'd go around back.

Heading down the street, his heart thundered. And not out of fear.

He was excited to see her. *Coco.* His Vegas girl.

That night had been the best sex of his life. They'd

connected in a way he never had with anyone else—not before or since.

As he turned into the alley behind Main Street, sunlight crested the horizon, glinting off the windshield of a green Jeep.

She's here.

His boots crunched on gravel as he headed toward the back door. He knocked, stupidly eager to see her.

A bearded man in an apron answered. "Oh." He seemed startled. "Thought it was early for a delivery. Sorry, we don't open until ten."

"I'm actually here to see Coco."

Interestingly, the guy stepped forward, pulling the door closed behind him.

Protective. That's good.

"Is there something I can help you with?" He had chocolate smeared across his apron.

"I met with her yesterday to talk about chocolates for the guests at my wedding."

"You're the Splashagram influencer?"

"My girlfriend is, but yes."

"You mean fiancée." He flashed a wedding band. "Takes some getting used to. Yeah, she said you had an early flight today. Come in. She's on a call right now, but if you don't mind waiting…" He ushered him inside. "I've got to get back in there. The beans are a-roasting." After shutting and locking the door behind them, he took off.

Metal shelves lined the hallway, all of them stuffed with neatly packed boxes. He passed a bathroom on his right, and further down he came upon an office, the door cracked open, yellow light spilling onto the concrete floor.

"No, no, no," Coco said from inside. "You're coming. I'll find a place for you to stay."

ERIKA KELLY

As he headed toward the kitchen, it occurred to him that he had no idea what to expect. Did they melt chocolate bars and turn them into truffles? Did they dip a ladle into a river of chocolate? He didn't have a clue.

To his surprise, it was nothing more than a large industrial kitchen. Several employees clustered around workstations. Against the walls, more shelving units were stuffed with supplies, and sections of both marble and butcherblock topped the island in the center of the room. He didn't recognize a lot of the small appliances.

The shelf nearest him had various molds—from small plastic trays with shallow wells to larger ones shaped like a rabbit, a race car, and a balloon bouquet.

"Look, at the very worst, you can stay with my parents," he heard Coco say. "They have plenty of room, and they'll pamper you better than any five-star hotel." She paused. "Laurent, I wouldn't be planning this festival if it weren't for you. If you want to come, I'll move heaven and earth to make it happen."

Through the crack of her doorway, he could see a large desk covered in papers and a wall of framed photographs. From the slice he could see, it seemed like her entire life was documented on these walls.

Did he even have any family photos? He thought of his cabin in Boulder, the boxes stacked in his office. Maybe in there? At the very least, he should find one of Ari and get it framed.

"Oh, I'm so glad," Coco said. "All right, let me make some calls. Au revoir."

He reached to knock on the door, but the moment she disconnected, she tapped the screen to make another call. *She's busy. I should go.*

80

I'll grab something to eat from Calamity Joe's. Leave her a note, letting her know I'm in town.

"Hey, Dad. I need a favor. Apparently, the whole town's booked—" Her chair creaked as she sat back in it. "Ha. I *wish* it was all because of my little chocolate festival. I'm pretty sure it has more to do with the Economic Summit but way to support your second born."

Her laughter was rich, a little throaty, and incredibly sexy.

It reminded him of how he'd felt that night in Vegas, when he'd scored a hard-won laugh out of her. She'd been working so hard to keep up a cheerful façade, and he'd wanted to know what a genuine smile looked like. Wanted to be the one to coax it out of her. He'd never forget the first time she'd given it to him. *Such a rush.*

"Anyhow, Laurent's decided to come—" She tipped her head back. "I know, right? Who knew I'd get such a good turnout? I'd only booked the small conference room, but now I've got overflow in the banquet room." She sat forward in a snap. "I just hope I can pull this off. Anyhow, so Laurent needs a place to stay. If we can't find anything, he can stay in my house and Posie and I will move in with you—" Sliding her fingers through her hair, she caught Beckett watching. "Oh." She waved him in. "Dad, I have to go. Someone's here. But, yes, please do that. I'd really appreciate it."

Beckett came in, catching a glimpse of some of the photographs on the wall. Four girls—obviously sisters—dressed in matching red and white snowflake Christmas pajamas—and a framed cover of Sports Illustrated featuring her mom.

"Thank you so, so much, Dad."

He couldn't help thinking back to his own childhood.

He and Ari had never posed for a Christmas card. Scanning the wall, he saw the Cavanaughs at graduations and birthday parties, gathered around the pool, sitting around a restaurant table…

He sure as hell didn't need to worry about Posie. *She's all set.*

"Okay, let me know." She disconnected and set the phone down, quickly standing. "Is everything all right? What're you doing here?" She checked the time on her computer. "You've missed your flight."

"I'm staying. If it's all right with you, I'm here for another day."

"I mean…sure." In her black leggings and ballet flats, she perched on the edge of her desk. "What's going on?"

He started to answer, but the only thing that came out of his mouth was a huff of breath. "I can't do it. I can't get on a plane when I know I've got a kid. I don't know what kind of involvement I should have, but I know I can't make the right decision if I leave."

Her features softened. "I'm actually relieved to hear you say that." And then she went on alert. "Hang on a sec." Leaning out of the office, she called, "Ian?"

"Yeah?" the man called.

"Are you checking the beans? They smell ready."

"Dammit, dammit, dammit."

Coco dashed out the door, waving for Beckett to follow. "Let's talk in the kitchen, so I can stay on top of what they're doing." She hurried down the hallway.

The aproned man that'd let him into the kitchen opened a strange-looking oven, pulled out a tray of beans, and examined them, shifting them around with a finger. "They're fine. Perfect."

"You could tell by the smell?" Beckett asked.

"Well, I had a timer set, but she's right," Ian said. "They're definitely ready." He tipped his head toward Coco. "She's got a nose like nothing you've ever seen."

"It's just experience." Coco sifted through the beans. "After they've been roasting awhile, they kind of smell like fresh hay and warm chocolate brownies. That's the exact moment you take them out."

Ian checked another oven. "The rest of us mortals wait until we hear the beans popping."

"This place is nothing like I expected." One shelving unit had chocolate-shaped flags wrapped in clear cellophane and red, white, and blue ribbons. For the Fourth of July, obviously.

"It's actually a lot of fun." Coco smiled at him, and he felt something big, bright, and alive burst open inside him. "Sometimes bakers or chefs complain because they have to make the same exact thing every day, but with chocolates, we're always experimenting. And not just with the beans but with the flavors and shapes. Actually, your fiancée left without taking the boxes I brought her." She crossed the kitchen. "Come with me." She pushed open a door and headed into the shop.

When she flicked on a light switch, he said, "Holy shit." Since she lived in a western town, he'd expected more cowboy-chic. Instead, her shop had a European feel, with tin ceiling tiles and pale green floor to ceiling bookcases stuffed with packaged chocolates. Three ornately carved dark-stained display cases faced the center of the room, with enough space for the employees to stand behind them and bag the chocolates. In the center stood a glass table covered in antique cake plates.

"You like?" Coco asked.

ERIKA KELLY

"It's you, sophisticated and elegant, with that little bit of funkiness."

"Well, thank you." She gave a shy smile. "I'm really proud of it."

"Posie must love it here."

"She doesn't come to work with me all that often. Not with hot ovens and granite wheels and power tools."

"Who knew chocolate was a dangerous business?" He tried for a humorous tone, but he just wasn't feeling it.

Because, really, what kind of alternate universe had he dropped into? *This is fucking crazy.* "I don't want you to take this the wrong way, but this is weird."

She laughed. "Are you kidding? I still haven't recovered from seeing you in the conference room. I nearly plowed into a pick-up truck on my way to get Posie. Oh, my God, I was shaking so hard. I just can't make sense of this. How can you, of all people in the world, be the one chosen for a destination wedding in Calamity?"

"That's the part that makes sense. I used to snowboard, and I spent a lot of time with the Bowie brothers."

"I know, but Diane chose you guys based on Willow's page—*before* she knew about the connection."

"That's true. Do you know them? The Bowies?"

"Sure. Gray's my age, but we all went to school together."

"It's crazy enough to run into you again." His gaze wandered out the plate glass window that looked across the street to the town green. "But to find out I have a…" He swallowed. *Just say it.* "A daughter." His voice came out strained, tight.

I have a daughter.

Reality slammed him. He stepped back and leaned against the display case.

84

Fuck.

Shit.

I'm a father.

How the fuck had this happened?

She touched his arm. It should have been innocent. It *was* innocent. She was only looking to comfort him, but instead it incited a riot of sensation. "I know it's a lot to take in. Just know that you don't have to make any decisions right now. We can take this one day at a time. For now, let's just stay in touch, and you can check out the Splashagram page to keep up with how she's doing." She stepped closer to him, her sweet scent filling his senses. "I'm not asking anything of you, I promise."

Her words offered a relief valve, and it helped. But he was just so caught up in her. That red mouth—so fucking kissable, the flirty hairstyle, and her scent—a hint of flowers, warm chocolate, and clean clothes.

It was happening all over again, the way, six years ago, he'd raced through the stages of attraction. From the surprise of liking her to the deepening into something darker, richer...something sexual.

She felt it, too. He knew she did. Her eyes went lusty, her mouth soft, lips parted. And then she shook away the desire and stepped back. Straightening the cheerful yellow bow on a cellophane-wrapped chocolate moose, she said, "So, you've got twenty-four hours in town. How would you like to spend them?"

"With you." Shit. That came out wrong. "I'd like some time with you and Posie, if at all possible."

"You're here for one day. I'll make it happen."

"Thank you."

"She spent the night at my parent's house last night.

85

Seeing you really threw me, and I just needed to be freaked out and not pretend that everything was okay."

Exactly how he'd felt around Willow, but he wouldn't say that about his fiancée. She was impacted, too. "When does she get home?"

"My mom's supposed to take her to school, but like I said it's not much more than daycare. She doesn't start kindergarten until the fall. I'll ask her to bring her home instead. In fact, why don't we head over there now? That way you can see her room, look through her baby book… get a feel for her life."

"Yeah. I'd like that." From the moment he'd heard the words-- *I've got a five-year-old daughter, Posie, and…she's yours*—the world had been spinning. But, with every second that passed, it slowed, his perspective growing sharper, clearer.

"Okay, let me talk to my team and grab my phone."

And, right then, the picture became crystal clear.

Because he understood that, even if he walked out the door, called a taxi, and headed to the airport, he would never have his coveted freedom again.

He was now, always and forever, a father. It was inescapable.

Which meant he had to figure out how to fit her into his world.

And that started right now.

Chapter Five

STEPPING INTO THE ALLEY, BECKETT TOOK IN THE peach-infused clouds streaking across a wide, blue sky. A van pulled in outside of Calamity Joe's. The driver hopped out and opened the side door, hauling out a box.

"Morning, Dave," Coco said.

"Going to be a beautiful day," the older man said.

"There's nothing like June in Calamity."

"Isn't that so." The man pulled open the door and headed inside the bustling coffee shop.

The crisp mountain air cleared Beckett's head and gave him a little breathing room. "Friendly town."

"I love it here. My sisters all moved away, but I'd always planned on staying here."

"Never wanted to experience city life?"

She laughed, but it wasn't full of joy. "Something like that. It's a long story."

"I'd like to hear it."

At the end of the alley, they turned onto a quiet residential street, the kind where everyone mowed their lawns, painted their front doors, and maintained their gardens.

So unlike his rustic mountain cabin in Boulder.

"My mom—you'll meet her when she brings Posie home—is a force of nature. Her goal in life was for each of us to find our passion. If we came home from school and said we were thinking about joining the debate team, the next thing we knew we were on a plane heading to D.C. to intern with a lobbyist."

"Ah. So, you did a lot of traveling as a kid?"

"Well, my other sisters did a lot more. My older sister —actually, I didn't want to tell you at the time, but Gigi Cavanaugh? She was the lead singer of the Lollipops—"

"Wait, that's who was standing on the chair, toasting you?"

"Yep."

"Why didn't you tell me?"

She stepped off the curb to cross the street. "Uh, because you'd just told me how you'd lost a piece of your soul by going to the concert?" She flashed a warm, sweet smile.

His blood turned hot and fizzy. "Is that what I said?" Damn, she was gorgeous. "I might've overreacted."

"Oh, believe me, Gigi felt the same way. But she's moved on. She's got a new band now, and she's performing her own songs." They crossed a patch of crisp, green grass before heading down the sidewalk. "So, anyhow, since nothing really struck my fancy, I only had a stint in LA to work with a fashion photographer, and one in Manhattan, to help with Fashion Week." She gestured to a dark-stained Craftsman-style house. It had a low-pitched roof and roomy porch, a paneled door and multi-paned stain glass windows. "This is it. This is home."

"Nice."

"Yeah, I really love it. I like that I can walk to work, and it's just me and Posie, so it's the perfect size. Plus, it was affordable." They headed up the walkway.

"Sounds like you were into fashion."

"I really wasn't. I think I've just always known what I like, and it's never had anything to do with what my friends were wearing. I had—"

"Flair."

She smiled as they climbed the porch steps. "That's a nice way to put it. I'll take it." She dug around her tote for her keys. "To my mom's endless disappointment, I didn't find my passion until I was out of college and on my own. Luckily, she had my other sisters to focus her energies on and left me alone."

"Gigi was obviously into music."

"Yep, and Lulu was into cooking. My youngest sister…" Her gaze flicked up. "Well, if anyone had style, it was her."

He was getting a strange feeling about the youngest. The way Coco referred to her in the past tense…had something happened to her?

"It was a relief when my mom gave up on me, because I just wanted to be home." Keys in her hand, she unlocked the door. It was still early enough that she had to flick on the lights.

Before entering, he took a moment to gaze out on her street. Beyond the two-story homes, the Teton Mountain Range loomed harsh and intimidating, its jagged peaks capped with snow. Then, he turned back and followed her inside.

Dark wood paneling matched the hardwood floors, and sunlight poured patches of color through the stained-glass windows. His gaze was drawn to the intricately carved features on the mantelpiece over the river rock fireplace.

Damn. This place is nice. He turned back to find her kicking off her flats, leaving them on a mat by the door, and he quickly followed suit. Untying his boots, he pulled them off, and set them beside the others. A pair of sparkly silver shoes caught his attention, and he crouched to pick one up. "It's so tiny."

"I know. And the thing of it is, she outgrows everything within a month. I hate it. Sometimes, I just want to stop time and let her be little and adorable forever."

He remembered the initial wallop of attraction he'd felt that night in Vegas—and not just because of her beauty, though he did love that twist of funkiness in her otherwise fresh, girl-next-door look.

But it was the glint of mischief in her eyes that had caught his interest, an underlying sense that she got the joke. She was an old soul, someone who handled life's twists and turns like a pro.

That's it right there.

His mom had fallen apart. She'd handled grief by shutting down and abandoning her family. But Coco had an inner strength that commanded his attention.

That's what I'm drawn to.

Which was a good thing to figure out, since he shouldn't have these feelings for her. Not when he had a girlfriend.

Shit. Fiancée.

He was pretty sure it meant something that he had to keep reminding himself of that fact.

"How about I make some coffee? You're welcome to

have a look around." She gestured to the framed photos lining the mantel and hanging on the walls. "I *might* have chronicled every moment of Posie's life."

"I see that. Noticed it in your office, too."

He couldn't help following her into the kitchen, though. Small, cozy, it had cherry wood cabinets and a row of cheerful flowers on the windowsill. And...was that...he headed over to the sink and picked up the Vegas sign he'd bought her. "You kept it?"

"I did." Grinning, she came over to him. "This is the reason I went to Europe. It's the reason I started my business. When you gave it to me, you said the next time I fake a smile, I should do something different."

"Shake things up." Their gazes locked. "I remember."

He remembered *everything*. The feel of her warm, curvy body pressed up against his, the sexy gust of breath she'd make when he'd touch her right where she needed it, and holy shit did it stir him up.

And in that moment, he knew she remembered, too.

It was in the way she pressed her thighs together and the faraway look in her eyes that made her expression go lusty and hot.

She broke away first, plucking the sign out of his hand. "I keep it right here as my daily reminder."

What the fuck, man? Stop thinking about her like that. He scraped off the memories to focus on what she was saying. "So, you went to Europe for a month and wound up taking chocolate classes. How'd that happen?"

She set the sign back on the windowsill. "Right. I started in Paris, but I still wasn't over Keith ghosting me, so I pretty much ate my way through the city. It seemed like there was a fancy chocolate shop on every corner, and by God, I went into each one."

He liked listening to her, liked the animated way she told a story, the sparkle in her eyes, the gestures of her hands.

"They were just so pretty, but the thing I noticed is that they didn't all taste the same. In fact, some didn't taste much like anything. And that surprised me." She brought the kettle from the stove to the sink and filled it. "There was this one tiny shop on Rue de Faubourg, and I was standing there savoring the most luscious, delicious bite of chocolate I'd ever had in my life, and the owner comes over and says, You like? And I said, What *is* it about this? What makes it so good? He started explaining how the beans have a different flavor depending on where they're grown. I kept asking questions, and he told me about a chocolate class. It lasted twelve weeks, but I had all that savings, so I just went for it."

"Even after you found out you were pregnant, you still stayed."

"I did. I kept it to myself for a while."

"Did you worry how your parents would take it?"

She set the kettle back on the stove and turned up the flame. "I mean, I figured they'd support me no matter what, but yeah, I knew I'd disappoint them. My mom wanted us to do great things with our lives." She gazed out the window with a smile. "It took me a couple years to realize I'd done that—just not the way anyone expected."

I'd done that. She had no idea how deeply her words resonated with him. Having Posie was her great thing, and it made his resolution to never have children seem... shallow. "When did you decide to make chocolate for a living?"

"I guess, from the moment I found out I was pregnant, I felt the pressure to come up with a plan.

Would I go to grad school? Get a job? But, with either of those options, Posie would've been in daycare. And I just didn't want that. I don't know…it just hurt my heart to think about being away from my baby, not nursing and holding her, so at the end of that first class, I thought… why not start my own business? When Keith and I were thinking about our proposal, our main thought was, What does Calamity need? Well, it didn't have a chocolate shop, so….why not? Worst thing that happens is I fail and have to get a full-time job. So, I went back to Laurent and talked to him about it, and he suggested I take this special class in Belgium."

"That took some big-ass lady balls."

She laughed—and fuck, if that didn't light him up—as she reached into a cabinet for a bag of coffee beans. "Believe me, I spent a lot of time taking career tests and looking up graduate school programs while eating croissants and crying my eyes out. But, no matter how close I came to filling out an application, there was something in me…"

"Yeah, I know. And that's the something that drew me to you in Vegas. That quiet strength."

"What do you mean? In Vegas, I was a mess. I was devastated that Keith had ghosted me, terrified of not having a job…"

"And yet you held it together so you wouldn't ruin your sister's night. You could've easily made it about you. Instead of celebrating her sold-out concert, she could've been in the hotel room with you, handing you tissues and promising things would work out. But that didn't happen, because you rallied for her. And, even after you told me what happened, you still didn't fall apart. You're strong and determined…and I like that."

"Well, thank you. That's nice to hear." Scooping out some beans, she poured them into the grinder and twisted the plastic top.

"Not that you keep it inside. I don't mean that. Just that you handle life's curves with grace."

She looked touched, and after holding his gaze a little too long, she turned back to her work. As the motor whirred, he glanced at the art work stuck to the refrigerator with magnets.

Stick figure families, flowers, a mountain...but it was the frame made out of popsicle sticks with the photo of a little girl inside that pried loose a memory. "My sister had one of those." She'd colored the sticks with marker, just slashes of primary colors.

"Pretty much every kid in America has made one." Finished grinding the beans, Coco poured them into the French press. "You want to get the cream out of the fridge?" After letting the hot water steep for a while, she pushed the rod down.

He opened the door to find the shelves packed with vegetables, yogurt, and storage containers filled with chicken, vegetables, pasta. "You cook a lot?"

"I do. I keep it simple, but I really want her to grow up making food, you know? I want her to see it's a way of life, versus ordering in or passing through the drive-through window on the way home from soccer."

He was more impressed than he could say. Because it took effort to shop, cook, and clean up after a long day. Something his mother had never bothered with. He pulled out a small container of heavy cream. "Here."

"Thanks." She took down two mugs. One said, *May Your Coffee Be Stronger than Your Daughter's Attitude*, and the other had a photograph of her daughter wrapped around it.

Our daughter. *I have a child with this woman.* "Coco."

Opening the silverware drawer, she glanced at him over her shoulder.

The sun streaming through the window poured a golden glow over her dark hair and warmed her rosy complexion. Her beauty made his heart stutter. "Of all the women in the world..." Emotion swelled, tightening the muscle in his throat. "I'm glad it's you."

She smiled as she removed a spoon and shut the drawer. "That's the strangest and yet nicest compliment anyone's ever given me."

"This whole experience is strange." He tapped a fist on the counter. "I never thought I'd see you again."

"Did you look for me?"

He hesitated. "I did."

"Really?" Her tone said, *You're not just saying that because we're alone in my house and it would be awkward to say no?*

He chuckled. She was so easy to read, and he liked that. "Really. I liked you. I'm not that into hookups. If I'm going to kiss someone, I have to be attracted to her. And if I'm into her enough to kiss her, I'm probably going to date her. I didn't plan on landing in bed with you that night."

"That's what you said. You said, 'I'm not lookin' to get laid.'"

He smiled at the way she lowered her voice to sound like a surfer dude. "Did I?"

She nodded, pouring coffee into both mugs. Lifting them, she nodded to the cream. *Bring it with us.* "That's why I left with you. For whatever reason, I trusted you." She brought the mugs to the small kitchen table, and he set the cream down. The only seating was a C-shaped, cushioned bench, so they sat down on opposite sides.

She spooned sugar into her mug and stirred. "Hang on one second." Sweeping out of the room, she left him alone in this homey kitchen filled with the presence of his daughter...the plastic cups hanging upside down in a dish rack, the painted rocks lined up on the counter, and a ladybug umbrella hanging off a hook by the back door.

He wrapped his hands around the mug, let the heat sink into him. As surreal as this moment was, there was nowhere he'd rather be.

A sharp pang hit his chest. *Willow.*

Isn't that where I should want to be? With her? To be fair, with their heavy travel schedules, they didn't spend much time together. Still...he pulled out his phone to see several missed texts and calls from her. He needed to check in.

Beckett: Glad you made it to the airport. I'm with Coco and Posie. Call you when I'm done.

She responded immediately. **I'm so glad to hear from you.**

One after another came in, as if she didn't want to lose his attention.

Willow: I was freaking out.

Willow: The way we left things.

Willow: I didn't handle it well, and I'm sorry. It was like everything I said made you mad.

Beckett: Not angry with you. Just thrown by the situation.

Willow: I know! It's so wild. But let's not worry till we have the results.

His temper flared. *This is why I don't want to talk to her.* Because Willow wanted to deny and distance herself, while he needed to accept his new reality.

Because she's mine. He didn't need a test to prove it.

Beckett: I'll call when I'm back at the hotel.

Willow: I've got hours till my next flight, so I can go ahead book your travel plans for tomorrow. Can't wait to see you!

Coco came back in, waving a photo album at him. "You ready for this?"

He'd bet those pages held Posie's entire life.

Beckett: Hold off on booking my flight. I'll call you later.

Lifting a hip, he shoved his phone into his back pocket. "I am."

Dragging her mug across the table, Coco motioned for him to scoot over. She sat close enough that he could feel the heat from her body, breathe in her lovely scent, and while he knew he should give her more room, he needed that connection, as she flipped the book open to the first page.

She skimmed past the first few shots of Coco pregnant, but he rested his hand on top of hers. "Hang on." He leaned in. "I want to see you." *Pregnant with my baby.*

Her face looked fuller, a little splotchy, but there was no denying she *glowed.* "You looked happy."

"That was when my parents picked me up from the airport. I was seven months pregnant and a hormonal mess. I was happy to be home, excited to start my business, scared that my parents would be disappointed in me, and terrified that I wouldn't be able to handle being a mom and running a business."

Without thinking, his finger touched the swell of her belly in the photograph. "What was it like?"

"Pregnancy?" She smiled. "It was pretty easy right up until I hit thirty-eight weeks. Then, it started to get uncomfortable." She turned the page, tapped her finger on a newly born Posie. "She was ten days early, which is so her personality." She sat back and used both arms to show bursting out of a box. "Lemme out of here. I got things to do."

Smiling, he tapped the picture of Coco in a hospital bed, a baby on her chest. "You're laughing?"

"Well, I had an epidural, so the pain was manageable, but I was laughing because Posie came out *pissed*. She had this grumpy expression, and my mom said something like, 'Oh, look out for this one.' And, also, to be honest, I was just relieved. It was so stressful to be pregnant at twenty-one, with no income, no partner, no idea if my baby was healthy. I didn't have a clue what it meant to have an infant—like, how do I bathe her? Feed her? How do I *do* this? But, then, to see her with all ten fingers and toes, perfect ears, nose, mouth…it was such a relief. Now that she was here, I felt like, okay, I got this."

When he turned the page, she touched the back of his hand. "You're shaking."

He'd never felt this kind of intimacy before. It was trust, plain and simple. He knew he could show himself to this woman. "I missed all of it."

"But you're here now."

"Yeah, but you did it by yourself. I want you to know, if I'd known, I would have been here. I wouldn't…"

"I know. I know you would have."

"I'm just so damn sorry you had to do it alone. But she's a great kid because of you. You're amazing, Coco."

"Oh, I don't know about that. You know that big conversation about nurture versus nature? I've only got one child, but from what I can see it's nature. She was born with her personality."

He flipped the page to find more hospital photographs. A nurse helped the baby find Coco's nipple. In it, Coco was laughing, her eyes wide in disbelief. "Did it hurt?"

"Like nothing I've ever experienced."

In another picture, big, male hands held the infant on a thick yellow sponge in a sink. "Were you dating someone?"

"That's my dad. He gave Posie her first bath. Changed her first diaper, too."

In another, Coco sat on the couch, pale, hair tucked behind her ears, the baby nursing under a blanket. "I guess it stopped hurting?"

"Sure, after *three months*. Oh, my God, every time she latched on, I had to grab hold of something. It was like razor blades every single time."

"Then, why'd you keep doing it?"

"Because it felt right to me, to nurse her. It only hurt the first five minutes or so. After that, the pain would subside."

"How long did you do it?"

"A year."

"So, wait, when did you start the chocolate shop?"

"I started setting up the moment I came home. Everyone loves to talk about how they'd see me in the grocery store with a blanket over my shoulder, pushing my cart with one hand and nursing Posie with the other. You can't imagine how many times I nursed while winnowing beans. I had a little playpen in the office, and when she slept, I worked. For the first year I couldn't afford to hire anyone, so I got interns. My friends were like, 'No one's going to work for free,' and I thought, well, I won't know until I ask. There's a group of retired people who meet at the diner every morning, the Cooters. I asked if anyone wanted to learn how to make chocolate, and a bunch of them said yes. I put up a notice on the high school job board and got some help that way, too."

"Resourceful." It was really hitting him, the freedom she'd given up. Her time wasn't her own—at all.

He prided himself on being rootless. He had a small house in Boulder but only stayed there when he had a few days between trips. He lived out of a suitcase and loved every minute of it.

A cold sweat broke out on his forehead.

Coco was a mom, a daughter, a sister, a business owner. She was the exact opposite of him.

How would this work? It struck him, everything that was involved in being someone's father.

Would Coco expect him to move here? She kept saying she didn't need anything from him, but that didn't absolve him of obligation. Instead of going to Boulder, would he visit here between trips? Send her gifts from his exotic travels, postcards from around the world?

That's not a dad.

That's a fun uncle.

Okay, but what would it look like if he moved here? He'd get a nine-to-five job, a condo, a minivan...

His axis tilted, wobbled, and he got walloped with motion sickness.

He couldn't do that. He couldn't be what Coco needed.

That's not who I am.

He needed to tell her. Right now. Before she got ideas in her head, formed some kind of picture of them co-parenting.

He shut the photo album. "I'm leaving tomorrow. I've had this trip on the books for months, so I can't miss it."

"Of course." She sat back, that warmth and open spirit snapping shut like a fist. "I didn't ask you to stay."

He'd fucked up. Come off too aggressive. *Calm down.* "No, I know that. I'm just…trying to get my bearings here." He lowered his head into his hands. *What am I supposed to do? How do I handle this?*

"I'm going to reiterate the first thing I said to you." Her tone turned businesslike. "I don't need anything from you. I don't expect anything. You wanted to stay in town an extra day, well, I'm here, taking off work, giving you what you asked for. If you decide to get on that plane tomorrow and never talk to us again, that's fine with me."

"I'm sorry. I got a little edged out."

"Well…" She lifted her hands and let them drop into her lap. "Talk to me. Tell me what just happened in your head to make you freak out like that."

"After nearly six years of development, I launched an app with two partners in January. We're all working twenty-four-seven, and it's just now starting to pay off. But my end of things…it puts me on the road three hundred days a year."

She watched him carefully.

"Our lifestyles are very different," he said.

"I know that."

"And, so, I'm not sure how to be in Posie's life."

Coco shifted off the bench, grabbing the photo album, and clutching it to her chest. "First of all, I want to be very clear about something. Posie's not going to know anything about her paternity. This is between you and me. As far as she's concerned, you're a friend in town for a few nights." Her expression demanded a response. *Got it?*

He gave a sharp nod. "I hear you, but I'm talking about the situation. I've only been thinking in terms of my schedule, but I'm just realizing it's about so much more. It's about what's best for all of us."

The front door opened, and heels clacked across the wood floor.

"*Mommy.*" Posie ran into the kitchen, cheeks wet with tears.

"Oh, baby, what's wrong?" Coco reached for her, but Posie kept her distance, planting her hands on her hips.

The girl was pissed. "I'm going to school today. I *have* to."

A tall, elegant woman walked into the room and shot Coco a look. "Thanks for that." Her tone held sarcasm.

Coco shot her an apologetic look but turned back to her daughter. "It's okay, sweetheart, you can miss one day."

Posie stomped her foot. "No. I can't miss today. I'm going to school."

It took a moment for it register, but she was wearing a Halloween costume. It had glitter and frou frou stuff all over it. Her shoes were the red version of the sparkly silver ones by the front door. "Is it dress-up day?" he asked.

His daughter sighed with such utter disgust he could hardly believe she was only five. "I'm a *fairy.*"

"Oh. Okay." *It's June…no holidays…maybe they're doing a play in preschool?* He'd keep that thought to himself.

Coco leaned over so she was eye-level with her daughter. "I thought, since my friend's in town, and he's never been here before, that it would be fun to show him around. We could ride the chairlift to Bear Mountain and have lunch up there. He'd get to see the backcountry, and what do you bet we're going to see a moose or a bear?"

"I'm not going." She stomped a foot, both hands curled into fists. Tears welled in her eyes. "I have to go school, Mommy. I have to."

While Coco talked to her daughter, the older woman reached out a hand. "I'm Joss, Coco's mom. The fabulous benefit of being a grandmother is that when they fuss, I can get into my car and drive away."

He couldn't help smiling as they shook hands. "It's nice to meet you, Joss. I'm Beckett O'Neill."

"Well, you enjoy your visit." She leaned in. "And don't be scared. You'll blink, and just like that, she'll become her charming, adorable self." Smoothing the hair off her granddaughter's cheek, she pressed a kiss to it. "Goodbye, my love. I had a very fun sleepover with you. If you want to come back tonight, I can leave our fort just the way it is."

Posie wiped away tears with the back of her hand. "I want Grandpa to sleep there with us."

"Oh, you know what a fuddy duddy your grandpa is. He's a big, old bear who likes to sleep in his own bed. But I *will* make him fly you around the whole house."

"Okay." She flung her arms around her grandma's neck and hugged her fiercely. "Thank you, Grandma."

"You're welcome, my angel. Have fun today."

After her mom left, Coco sat on the edge of the bench seat. "Why don't you tell me what's so important about school today?"

"It's my day for Show and Tell."

She said the last word tell like "tail," and he cracked a grin. She was a handful, but she was cute.

"And what are you bringing again? Remind me."

103

"My glitter tattoos. I promised."

"We can always bring them in next Wednesday."

"No, Mommy. It has to be today. I promised all my friends they could have one."

"Okay, well, if you promised them, then you should definitely go to school. It's important to keep your promises. But, if you want to come with us to Bear Mountain, we might be able to come up with another option."

"Like what?"

Beckett had no idea why, but he found the conversation fascinating. Coco's calm demeanor juxtaposed with Posie's strong personality…it presented quite a show.

"What if we have your friends over on Sunday?" Coco said. "We can make cupcakes and put the tattoos on ourselves."

"If I go to school are you going to Bear Mountain without me?"

He got a kick out of watching this little girl work through the possibilities.

"Yes. My friend is only here for a day, so I want to make sure he gets to do something fun."

"I want to go to Bear Mountain. And I want a milkshake." Posie looked torn, worrying her bottom lip. "But I promised my friends."

"School doesn't start for two more hours, so we have time to send them an email and let them know you're not coming to school, but that you'll give them the tattoos on Sunday. That way, you'll be keeping your promise." Coco got up. "Did you eat breakfast at Grandma's?"

"No. How could I eat? I'm too upset. You made me very mad, Mommy. You should have told me first. You made the whole decision without me, and it's a very important day."

"You're absolutely right. I definitely should've asked you first." Coco brushed her fingers through Posie's long hair. "I thought my friend was leaving yesterday, but he surprised me this morning at the chocolate shop and told me he was staying a little longer." She moved to a cupboard and pulled out a plastic cup. "I'm going to make breakfast. Let me know when you make a decision."

"I want to go with you."

"Oh, good. I'm so glad. So, are we having your friends over on Sunday?"

"Yes. I want to make cupcakes."

"Awesome. I love it. Okay, let me go email everyone right now." She went to the refrigerator and pulled out a jug of milk. "Toadstools or oatmeal?"

"*Mommy*, fairies don't eat toads." Her tone said, *Duh*.

"Oatmeal it is."

"But only if you put fairy sprinkles on it."

"You got it." Coco pulled out a pan and filled it with water. "Beckett, did you eat? Do you want some oatmeal?"

"I mean, are there enough fairy sprinkles for me?" he asked.

Coco threw open a spice cabinet. The top shelf was stocked with sprinkles in all colors—pastels, green and red, pink, red and white, bright orange and black. "I think we're good well into the apocalypse."

"Then, I'd love some. Anything I can do to help?" He started to slide out of the booth, but Posie climbed up next to him.

"My grandma did my nails last night. Look. They're sparkly. Fairies have sparkles everywhere."

"I see. Very pretty."

"She won't let me take the polish home 'cause she says that's special stuff for us to do when I've over there." She twisted around. "Mommy, can I have some milk?"

"Sure, hon." Coco poured some into a plastic cup and set it on the table.

"Thank you." She used both hands to grasp it and bring it to her mouth.

Back at the stove, Coco lowered the flame under her pot. "While this is simmering, I'll send those emails. Be right back." She glanced at him, as though checking to see if he minded being alone with Posie.

He tried to give her a reassuring smile, but he doubted he could hide his discomfort.

Because what the hell did he do with a five-year-old?

Chapter Six

"HOW COME YOU'RE HERE?" POSIE ASKED HIM.

Because I found out you're my daughter. "I'm visiting friends."

As she gazed up at him with icy blue eyes identical to his, he noticed she had a tiny little scar the color of the moon on her cheek. How did she get that? Did she need stitches?

He wanted to know.

I want to know every moment I missed.

"Where's your house?" she asked.

"In Colorado."

"Is it pretty?"

"Not as pretty as yours, but it's in the mountains. That's why I bought it. For the location." *Jesus, she's not an adult who understands the real estate market.*

She finished off her milk and then licked her lips. "Do you have a doggy? I want one, but Mommy says I can't. She says we're not home enough to give a doggy lots of love. Do you have a doggy?"

"I don't have one, but my neighbor does." *That's a weird answer. Who cares if my neighbor has a dog?*

She asked if I have one.

"Where is he? Can I see? I want to play with your doggy."

"He's in Colorado right now. But, like I said, he's not mine. He's my neighbor's."

"You get to play with him?"

"When I'm home, he pretty much lives with me."

"Because you gots good treats?"

Because my elderly neighbor's health is failing, and I suspect there are many days when he doesn't get fed. "I do, yeah. I keep treats for him."

"I want to play with him."

"Maybe one day. But he's in Colorado right now."

"Do we have time to go to Callrado before we get my milkshake?"

"No. Colorado's another state. It's…well, here." He grabbed a napkin from the basket and a crayon from the plastic cup. "So, we're in Wyoming." He drew a line going east then straight down south. "And this is Colorado. It's about an eight-hour drive in the car."

"Eight hours? How long is that?"

"That's how long you sleep at night."

Her eyes went wide. "You live far away. My grandma and grandpa has doggies. You can come see them. They don't like to play with me, because they're old, and I'm too much for them. I'm hungry." She got up on her knees and reached for a banana in the fruit basket. "I want peanut butter."

"Okay."

When she scampered out of the booth and just stood there watching him, he realized she expected him to get it.

"Oh." He slid out and found the peanut butter in the refrigerator. "How do we do this?" At home, he'd stick a knife in the jar and smear it right on top of the banana.

He found a plate in a cabinet and a knife in a drawer and brought them to the table. "Now what?"

"Put it on the banana." Her tone held an eye roll.

"Obviously." He peeled off the skin and then set it on the plate.

She recoiled, waving a hand at the naked banana. "You have to get that stuff off."

"What stuff?"

"That yucky, stringy stuff."

"Oh, that. Want to know something? It's called a phloem bundle." With the tip of the knife, he lifted it, and then used his fingers to strip it off.

"A what?"

"A phloem bundle."

"What's that?"

"It's how the nutrients are distributed throughout the banana. You know how our veins deliver blood throughout our body?"

"No."

"Well, the phloem bundles deliver nutrients to the banana."

"I'm not eating flow bundles."

He chuckled. "Yeah, that does sound unappealing. Okay, let's get 'em off." After removing one more, he stabbed the knife into the peanut butter. Just as he started to smear some onto the banana, she pushed his arm.

"No. I'm not eating that."

What? "You don't want the banana?" What the hell was he missing? "You said you wanted peanut butter on a banana."

"I don't want that." Her voice rose. "I'm not eating it."

"Hang on. Instead of getting upset, just tell me the problem."

"I'm not eating flow bundles."

"I took them off."

She pointed at the banana like there was a spider on it.

Rolling it around, he found a tiny string on it and burst out laughing...until he saw her flushed cheeks and realized she was genuinely upset. It really was like a spider to her. He quickly removed the string. "Okay?"

She examined the banana and pointed at one more string.

This girl was hilarious. He peeled it off. "Now are we good?"

She nodded, looking as though she'd suffered through a trying time.

"So, now what, Your Highness?"

She tapped the handle of the knife. "Put the peanut butter on."

"This is how I do it." He swiped the top of the banana with the peanut butter and bit it off.

"Hey, that's my banana." She reached for it.

"How does your mom do it?"

"She makes it pretty for me. Fairies eat pretty food."

"Ah, gotcha. Okay, let's see what I can do." He sliced the banana into thin chunks. Then, he cut out triangles so that each piece looked like a star. Then, he carefully put a dot of peanut butter in the center of each one. "Hang on. Let me get the sprinkles." He found the container and shook it out over the food.

Clapping her hands over her mouth, her eyes went wide. "That's the prettiest fairy food ever." She pulled the plate in front of her. "Thank you, Beckett."

"You're welcome." He felt ridiculously happy he'd done a good job for her.

"Does your doggie eat peanut butter? Marcy's mommy hides doggy pills in peanut butter. Her doggy eats it like this." With her mouth full of peanut butter and banana, she flicked her tongue out a couple of times.

He laughed. Pointing at the triangles he'd removed, he said, "Can I eat those?"

"Yes, we can share." She shoved the plate, so it sat squarely between them.

In this cozy kitchen, sitting with a five-year-old, and listening to Coco's voice on the phone in the living room, Beckett felt strangely comfortable. The refrigerator hummed, Posie's heels slammed rhythmically against the bench seat, and there he was eating peanut butter and bananas with…his daughter.

It was starting to sink in, and it wasn't half bad.

Coco came back into the room. "Okay, let's get rolling with the oatmeal. Do you want a banana in it? Or blueberries?"

"I'm not hungry." With sticky fingers, Posie dropped off the bench seat. "I'm getting dressed for Bear Mountain." She ran out of the room.

Coco glanced at the plate of food he'd prepared. "You fed her?"

Oh, hell. "It was just a few pieces of banana." He'd messed up. "She said she was hungry and gave me step-by-step instructions. There wasn't a chance in hell I was going to throw down with my kid on day two."

She grinned. "Posie's a grazer. If she eats a few bites of banana, she's done."

"Shit. Sorry."

"Another hot tip. She'll repeat your words. Not right

now, not in the safety of her home, where you can explain why we can say some words and not others, but in the middle of circle time at school."

"Shit." He shook his head. "I mean…I'll do better."

But he caught her expression—it was fleeting, before she turned away and headed to the stove. But he saw it.

Will it matter, though? Will you even be around to do better?

He didn't have an answer for that.

And it felt like he had less than twenty-four hours to figure it out.

On a chairlift meant to accommodate two adults comfortably, Posie straddled both their laps, which meant Coco had to sit right up against Beckett's hard, warm body. A black ball cap shaded his face, the shadows only accentuating the masculine cut of his scruffy jaw, high cheek bones, and ridiculously sensuous mouth.

For a man who'd traveled the world, he seemed awfully impressed by the scenery spread out before them. As they ascended the mountain, the bowl-shape of the valley became clear. The Teton and Gros Ventre Mountain Ranges thrust aggressively from the earth, while patches of green meadow, clusters of houses, and ribbons of silver rivers covered the floor.

"Show me what I'm seeing." He had a lovely way of talking to Posie as an adult, asking questions that empowered her, and Coco really liked that about him.

"That's Jackson." Pointing to the largest sprawl of buildings beneath them, Posie turned toward her. "Right, Mommy?"

"You got it."

With a more confident expression, Posie pointed farther off to the left. "And that's Calamity. That's where I live."

"And that mountain right there?" he asked. "The closest one? What's that called?"

"What's that mountain called, Mommy?"

"Mount Owen. That's where Grandma and Grandpa take you hiking."

"Right. Mount Owen. And all the way back there, the big one with the snow on top? That's the Tetons."

Beckett cut her a look, clearly impressed. "It's beautiful here."

"It really is." Coco had seen a lot of the world, thanks to family vacations and the trips her mom had sent her on over the years, but there was just no place like Calamity. "And we have a very cool history. Because of its location and brutal climate, it was nearly impossible for people to live here. Starting in the Eighteen-sixties, the government gave out free land, but the settlers couldn't make a go of it. It's just too rocky and cold to grow food. And, in the winter, there was only one pass in and out of the valley. Actually, it was called Owl Hoot."

"I wondered where that name came from," he said.

"And the only people who'd brave that pass were outlaws."

"Is Grandpa an outlaw?"

"No, sweetheart. Grandpa played football. Anyhow, they'd lead their stolen horses or cattle in, rebrand them, and then take them out when the weather cleared to sell in Utah. So, this whole area was founded by outlaws."

"And now the Bowies finally make sense," he said.

She smiled. "Right? They're literally descended from

outlaws. But everyone who lives here is wild at heart. Someone once said Calamity's the Western capital of whoop-ass, and I think that nails it. We're outdoorsy, we think outside the box, we're fiercely independent, and we don't like rules."

"I'm confused," Beckett said. "You talk about outlaws, but I only see fairies."

"I'm a fairy outlaw, right, Mommy?"

"That's right." Coco held out her hand for a fist bump. "Outlaw fairies."

The wires creaked, and the chairs rocked. The higher they got up the mountain, the cooler the air, and when she rubbed her arms for warmth, Beckett reached across her shoulders and pulled her in tighter.

The small gesture unearthed a longing—to lean against him, give him some of the weight she carried. It was scary, because she couldn't afford weakness—not as a single mom. But this moment...this precious, perfect moment, with the three of them connected physically...it gave her a burst of true and perfect happiness.

Her heart said, *We're a family.*

How many times had she dreamed of this exact scenario? Well, maybe not this exactly. She hadn't expected to see Beckett again, but she'd wanted so badly to fall in love with a man who would adopt Posie, treat her like his own daughter.

And now—unbelievably—she had Posie's actual father sitting with them, and it made her heart soar.

But it was all a lie. She knew that. She couldn't get carried away with silly fantasies. *We're not a family.* All he'd said was that he couldn't get on a plane knowing he had a daughter. He wasn't here to take on the role of Posie's father. He was here to figure things out.

And just like that, happiness turned to anxiety. Because she didn't know what would happen. Would he leave, go back to his life, and send an annual birthday card with a twenty-dollar bill tucked inside?

Or would he want more? She could see her little girl joining him on his trips, becoming a little daredevil.

Fear wrenched her, and she felt sick. It would kill her if Posie wound up spending half of the year traveling with Beckett and his adventure-seeking fiancée.

Would she have to share *holidays*?

Stop it. Oh, my God, just stop it right now.

"*Mommy.*" Posie sat up and lunged forward, causing the chair to rock wildly. "*Look.*" Her shriek split the peaceful, summer day wide open.

Just as Coco tightened her hold, Beckett wrenched Posie right out of her arms and hugged her tightly to him. "*Jesus Christ.* Don't do that."

Posie's eyes flared with fear, and she looked to her mom to find out if she'd done something wrong. Where Coco's first instinct was to protect her daughter, she couldn't miss the terror in Beckett's eyes.

Even before the chair quit rocking, Beckett seemed to recognize his overreaction, as he loosened his grip and let out a rough exhalation. Posie pulled away from him, pressing her face into Coco's side.

Heart racing, she soothed her daughter with gentle strokes on her back, while rallying a comforting look for Beckett. "That was scary." She tapped Posie's shoulder. "Sweetie, we're thirty feet off the ground. You know you have to sit still."

"But I saw a bear." Her voice sounded muffled. "I was showing you."

Perspiration beaded on Beckett's forehead, and he

scrubbed a hand over his face. "I thought…" He looked away, popping his ball cap off his head and scraping his hands through his hair. Setting the hat back on, he patted Posie's shoulder. "Sorry."

Keeping her forehead pinned to Coco's shoulder, she swiveled to look at him. "Why'd you do that?"

"I got scared. I thought…" He looked down.

"I wasn't going to fall." Posie sounded defensive.

"Yeah, I just…"

"Hey, you scared me, too." Coco gave her daughter a gentle shake. "You know better than to lean out of a chairlift like that." Thankfully, they'd reached the summit. She needed to get off this thing. "Come on. Let's go." With her daughter still shaken, she handed the tote off to Beckett and lifted Posie into her arms. Under the broad roof of the platform, she stepped off, relieved for the shade.

As they stepped off the pavement and onto the pine needle-strewn ground, Beckett remained quiet. She knew how overwhelming all this was for him, so she wanted to put him at ease. "We love it here. We probably come up once a month or so."

Posie squirmed. As soon as Coco set her down, she said, "I want my milkshake now."

Sunlight glinted off the copper drainpipes and windows of the two-story pine lodge. Several yards away sat the bath house, where visitors who'd come only for a soak in the hot springs could change into their swimsuits and then rinse off afterwards.

"But we usually swim first," Coco said. "Which would you rather do? Eat lunch first or go in the hot springs?"

"Swim, Mommy." She tugged on Coco's hand.

"Okay." Shielding her eyes with a hand, she gazed up

at Beckett, only to find him still shaken. "Would you rather have lunch first? We have a favorite spot right over there in the woods for our picnic."

"No, swimming sounds good."

"Okay, well, why don't you grab your swimsuit out of the bag, so I can get Posie changed?" Because, of course, her daughter couldn't wear her suits under her clothing, not with all the added tulle and lace.

"Sure." Kneeling, he set the tote on the ground and dug underneath the stack of towels. His hands shook, and Coco's heart wrenched for him. It was enough to find out he had a child, but at the same time, he had to deal with the memories of losing his sister around the same age.

If she remembered correctly, he'd watched it happen.

The first time Coco had heard it, she'd ached for his loss. This time, though…she had a five-year-old, and it wrecked her. She wanted to drop everything and hold him, let him know she understood what he was going through.

Finding his trunks, he started to get up, when Posie came right up to him. The two stared at each other for a long moment. And then she reached out and patted his shoulder. "I'm sorry I scared you, Beckett."

A tremor went through his body, rocking him hard enough to set him back on his heel. With an expression of awe, he said, "That's okay. I overreacted." He broke into a heart-stoppingly beautiful grin. "You think we can hug it out?"

Posie moved right into his arms, and he closed his eyes, abandoning the tote to wrap her tightly against him. Coco had never seen a man's features express such a complicated mix of emotions, happiness, confusion, and true, raw pain.

Emotion tightened her chest, as she witnessed the bond forging between Posie and her father.

Alarm bells sounded in her mind.

Everything's going to change. She didn't know how, but it would.

Because this man had crossed a line. He might not know it yet, but he wasn't going back to his old life.

And that meant her carefully balanced world was going to come crashing down.

Chapter Seven

BECKETT COULDN'T SHAKE OFF THAT MOMENT ON THE chairlift, so on their way home from Bear Mountain, he'd asked Coco to drop him off at the Bowie training center.

He'd seen accidents like that happen before. Once, a teenage boy had dangled precariously, until a group had gathered beneath the chair to catch him.

This time, though, it was Posie. Jesus, she was so frail, so slight...she'd have shattered like a Christmas ornament if she'd hit the ground.

Fear rippled through him, and he shook the image of her broken body out of his head. *Cut that shit out.*

Posie wouldn't have fallen. They'd both had a grip on her.

So, yeah, he needed a break. Needed to hang out with old friends and feel like himself again. Because that whole thing—the three of them together like that—had started to feel way too much like a family.

Which they weren't. *I'm leaving tomorrow, and I don't know when I can be back.*

He entered the main building and headed straight for the reception desk. "Hey, are the Bowies around?"

But, before the guy could answer, they heard a burst of male laughter. The receptionist smiled and tipped his head toward a hallway.

"Got it. Thanks." He only had to walk a few feet before he found Brodie, the owner of the Owl Hoot Resort and Spa and the guy who'd offered to sponsor his wedding, in the main office.

The new dad offered him a big grin and a side hug. "Hey, man, good to see you."

Side because the mountain of a man had a carrier strapped to his chest. "Look at you with this pretty new accessory."

Brodie grinned at the tuft of wispy hair peeking out. "This is Lou. Well, actually, she's Princess Lucia Grace Mathilda Bowie, but that's what happens when you marry a princess."

"You're *married*?" He hadn't heard anything about a Bowie getting married.

"Not officially, but yeah." His smile was soft, warm. "Heart and soul, man, they're my heart and soul. So, you here to talk wedding plans? Or do you want a tour?"

"I'd like a tour, if you have the time."

"Well, that's a fuck of a lot better than talking wedding shit, so yeah, I'm in. Come on." Brodie led him back out of the building, where a group of athletes were just leaving a state-of-the-art gym with floor-to-ceiling windows. Sweaty and exhausted, they toppled over like dominoes, crashing on the lawn.

The campus spanned across acres, and Brodie pointed out the massive and deep swimming pool for water ramp training, a trampoline gym, a physical therapy wing, and a co-ed dormitory.

Beckett had never seen anything like it. "This place is amazing."

"You trained in Lake Placid, right?" Brodie walked alongside him, his daughter's tiny legs dangling out the bottom of the carrier. In the shade of a white, floppy sunhat, the baby stared wide-eyed at the world, blinking.

"I did. But that was a decade ago, and it didn't look anything like this."

"Yeah, it's cool." Brodie playfully patted his baby's feet with his palms. "Fin's done a good job."

It was hard enough to imagine the fearless, wild Bowie brothers locked down in committed relationships, but Brodie with a *baby*? And looking so damn happy about it? It didn't compute. "You all work here?"

"It's Fin's place, but we stop by when we can. Keeps us out of trouble." Opening the door to the gym, he headed right for the stairs and led them to a second-floor viewing room.

Rows of trampolines bolstered with blue landing pads filled the large rectangular space. Scattered around the room, coaches in red T-shirts worked with small groups of athletes.

One coach stood out. "Is that Will?" The tall, muscular man bounced on a trampoline. A freestyle skier, he'd retired after winning an Olympic gold medal. *Wait... isn't that Gray?* "You're all here."

"Will just dropped Ruby off at camp. I thought Gray was supposed to be running errands." Brodie chuckled. "I guess we're here more than I realized."

"Ruby? Will's got a kid, too?" He had to be living in an alternate universe. One where the men least likely to settle down found themselves with children and committed relationships.

"Ruby's our half-sister. Will's raising her. We're the only two with kids so far, but the others won't be far behind."

"Not Fin." No way would the ultimate rebel and badass settle into a traditional life.

"Couple years back, he worked things out with his high school girlfriend. He's been busy building the training center, and she's been working on her museum, but things are on an even keel, so any time now."

Most of his friends had settled down—no big deal. But the Bowies? "You seem…happy."

"Never been happier."

"Figured you guys had it all—family, the Tetons as your gym…I remember those trips you'd take with your dad, the remote mountains, uncharted terrain."

"Yeah, we had some good times."

"Why would you give it up to be saddled with kids?" The ugly words landed before him like roadkill. "Shit. That didn't come out right." The last two days had left him rattled.

Brodie chuckled. "No, I get it. Before I met Rosie, I felt the same way. Couldn't figure out what my brothers were doing. Fin had never wanted anyone but Callie, so fine, I got that. But Will, man, he's a stay-at-home dad. And Gray's *married*." He shook his head. "Couldn't wrap my head around it. Why give up your freedom and all the good times to be tied to one woman? But then I met Rosie." His expression changed, lightened. "When I weighed the things I thought were so great against what it felt like to be with her? No comparison." He nudged

Beckett. "You know what I mean. You're doing it, so you get it."

"It's not like that for me and Willow."

"What're you saying? The wedding's not real? Is this some kind of social media stunt?"

"No, we're getting married. But only because Diane made the offer. It's not like I proposed."

"I thought you were already engaged. That's *why* we made the offer."

"Nah. Willow posted a picture of us kissing, and her followers took it as an announcement. It wasn't. I've never even thought about proposing." Even while focused on the athletes bouncing and flipping, Beckett could feel Brodie watching him. And it made him feel like shit. Because he hadn't taken the idea of marriage seriously. He'd viewed it as a means to draw attention to his business. "I never wanted to get married." He glanced at the baby. "And I don't want kids."

The moment the words left his mouth, the reality of his situation zapped him with an electric prod.

Because I have one.

A beautiful, spirited, sensitive daughter.

And, after spending the day with her, she'd become a person. She wasn't just a source of guilt for not helping Coco with a problem they'd both created. She wasn't an idea, a concept.

She was a little girl full of sass and compassion, with idiosyncrasies and quirks.

Fuck.

He wanted to talk to Brodie about it, but he couldn't do that until he checked with Coco.

Until I figure out what I'm doing, what role I'm going to play in her life.

Coco had made it clear he could leave tomorrow morning, free and clear. Go back to his life. She didn't need anything from him. It could be as simple as sending child support each month. Or he could set up a college fund. *Both.* He'd do both, of course. She'd shouldered the financial burden on her own for five years. He owed her.

Maybe he'd pay off her mortgage, or he could buy the building, put the deed in her name, so she didn't have to lease space for her chocolate shop. He needed to relieve her burden in some way, and it didn't require his physical presence.

Except…he knew exactly what it felt like to have a mom alive in the world who didn't give a shit about him. And he couldn't do that to his own kid.

"You all right?" Brodie asked.

"Sure." He dug his hands into pockets. "Great."

"You don't have to do this, you know. We haven't announced anything yet. I don't think you've even chosen a date, so if you want to back out now…it's not a problem."

Beckett tugged on the neckline of his shirt. It felt like it had shrunk two sizes in the wash. "I think I need some air."

"Sure, man." But Brodie hesitated. "You love her?"

"Willow?"

Brodie looked at him like he had a screw loose. "Yeah. Willow."

"I like hanging out with her. We have fun." He cringed.

Jesus Christ. How shallow am I?

"Okay, but we're talking about marriage. When you see yourself ten, twenty, thirty years from now, is she with you?"

Beckett let out a humorless laugh. "I haven't looked that far ahead. You know what it's like to be a competitive athlete. I grew up at the academy. Every minute of my time was scheduled. Meals, workouts, training, school from one to six, unless I was on the road for a competition."

Brodie nodded. He knew.

"From the moment I retired, the only thing I've wanted is freedom. I don't want anyone telling me where to be or when."

"I hear that. You know the crazy thing? After I met Rosie, all that freedom I thought was so great? Turned out to be pretty fucking lonely. My life was about me. But with Rosie and Lou, my life's about so much more. Making my woman and daughter feel safe, loved, wanted, protected…that shit runs deep. There's nothing like it."

They headed down the stairs and out the door. Outside in the bright sunshine, clapping and whistling came from the pool. He glanced over, but he couldn't see anything past the memory of Posie paddling around the hot springs in her inflatable arm bands. So fucking cute, it killed him.

And to have Coco there with him? The way, when Posie did something adorable, they'd share a look. That hot, electric connection between them? Seriously, if he had to have a kid…he'd lucked out with Coco as the mom.

Fuck, he wanted to talk to Brodie about his situation. *I'm a hot mess.* "I can't wrap my head around it."

"Around what?"

Shit, he'd said it out loud. "You with a kid. That's… serious stuff."

"It is." When his daughter looked up at him, Brodie grinned like she'd just pulled a one-footed double-backflip.

"I'll tell you something. I'm twenty-eight years old. I've looked around every corner, been to every party. I know what's out there. I don't need to do any of it anymore. I don't need anything but them." He gazed out over the lawn, the tree limbs rocking, leaves shushing in a breeze. "Rosie…she's like an essential piece of me I only realized I was missing once I met her. I don't know how else to describe it, other than to say there's symbolism in getting married. It's like fusing the missing piece to me so I never have to feel that emptiness, that hole…"

"I don't feel empty."

"I didn't either. Until I met Rosie. And, let me tell you, once you have *that*—that kind of passion? How the fuck can you go without it?" He looked down at his daughter. "I've got a few more months to get my language under control. We all do. Can you imagine a Bowie family dinner with all the kids telling each other to fuck off and shove it up each other's asses?" He grinned. "Gonna have to be careful."

As they neared the main building, Brodie said, "Frankly, the only reason we're not married already is because Rosie wanted to wait until she had the baby. A wedding's going to be a big deal, because she's from San Christophe. So, there has to be two ceremonies—one there, and one here. But I wouldn't do it, man. If you're not feeling it, I wouldn't get married. Not for some Splashgram moment."

Once inside the main building, they ran into Fin Bowie. "Oh, hey, man." The rugged-looking man shook his hand. "Beckett. Good to see you." He looked to the doorway he'd come out of. "You know who this is?"

A tall, lanky teenager stepped out of an office. The moment he saw Beckett, his jaw dropped. "Holy shit. Are you kidding me right now?" He cupped his skull like he was trying to keep it from toppling off his neck. "You're Becks O'Neill, five-time X Games gold medal winner."

"Good to meet you," Beckett said. "You training for Slopestyle?"

"Yeah, literally because of you."

"Hey, no sucking up, man. I retired six years ago." Sure, he got recognized when he judged competitions but rarely by anyone this young.

"Are you kidding? I watched you compete every single year when I was a kid. My coach plays tapes of you because he says, to this day, no one's ever been as stylish as you while doing the most creative and technical tricks." His eyes went wide. "Are you a guest coach?" He turned to Fin. "You got Becks as a coach? This is like my dream come true."

"No, no," Beckett said. "I'm only in town for a meeting. I leave tomorrow morning."

"It's a good idea, though," Fin said. "You can coach here any time you want."

"Thanks. I'd like that." He shook the kid's hand. "Good luck, man." He turned to Fin and Brodie. "Good catching up with you guys. I'll be in touch."

As he headed to the parking lot, he tugged the bill of his hat lower to block the sun. Since retiring he'd done a lot of judging—because it was fun, and he got to catch up with old friends—but he hadn't done any coaching.

And it'd be a good way to spend more time in Calamity.

Dammit, just thinking about leaving in the morning, heading off to Thailand…

He felt that same tug of resistance he had this morning, only this time it was stronger. Because now he'd felt Posie's little hand on his shoulder, saw the compassion in her eyes when she'd apologized to him.

She was sweet and fiery and smart and…

Mine.

He'd just have to figure it all out from Thailand.

As soon as Beckett got into his rental car, he checked his messages. In the shade of a willow tree, windows open so he could hear birds singing, the breeze rustling the branches, and the occasional bursts of clapping from the training pool, he caught up with the most pressing business issues.

Then, finished, he opened the thread of texts from Willow.

Willow: Did you book your flight for tomorrow? You need to get here before Friday. They never open the island this late in the season, but they're doing you a huge favor.

Willow: I hate the time difference. You're sleeping when I'm playing. I stayed up till four this morning. This city never sleeps!!!

Willow: You won't believe this, but they're throwing us a traditional Thai engagement party. Well, not the whole thing, obviously. But we'll have the procession and the Buddhist blessing. I'm telling you, our followers are going to go nuts.

Willow: How was your day? They're treating me like royalty here. When I checked into the hotel, I found out they'd upgraded us to the honeymoon suite. I get in there, and there's all these orchids and champagne and chocolate-covered strawberries. I'm sure you've already seen it. It's all over my pages.

Willow: Ugh. This is so frustrating. Call me. I have so much to tell you.

The conversation he needed to have with her couldn't be done over text, so he tossed his phone into the cup holder and started the engine, heading for the highway.

He liked Willow. She was a lot of fun and down for any adventure. But she didn't affect him the way Coco did.

Where Willow was a free spirit—fearless, fun, and uninhibited—Coco was steadfast. Elegant. Smart. Ambitious.

Coco met her challenges head-on. And her inner strength? Such a fucking turn-on.

She also had roots. Deep, meaningful ties to a community.

Something he'd never had. Nor particularly wanted.

All he knew was that he couldn't plan a wedding with Willow, when he had strong feelings for someone else.

Tourists heading back to their hotels after a day in the park traveled southbound on Highway 191. Fortunately, the training center wasn't far from Owl Hoot, so he turned off quickly, heading for his hotel.

Right at dinner time, Owl Hoot was vibrant with activity. Costumed actors strolled the elevated boardwalks, and tourists waited to get into the saloon for dinner.

But the action in town only accentuated the silence inside his car.

He'd never felt more alone. Two days ago, he'd belonged in Thailand with Willow. And now? He wanted to say he didn't belong here in Calamity with Coco and Posie…and yet he felt the connection, the pull.

Nothing made sense.

A shuttle bus stopped in front of him, causing Beckett to hit the brake. Jogging around to the back, the driver gave him an apologetic wave, before swinging open the double doors and unloading backpacks. As soon as he set them down, the occupants snatched them up and headed into the resort.

Beckett drove around to the parking lot behind the hotel and pulled into a spot. But he couldn't cut the engine. Couldn't get out of the car. He couldn't go to his room, order room service, set his alarm...and act like he didn't have a daughter five miles down the road.

Any more than he could go through the motions of a Thai engagement ceremony.

I'm a Dad. I can't go back to my life and pretend that Posie doesn't exist.

I'm not a fun uncle, so sending her postcards from the road isn't cool. That would be a douche move from a guy unwilling to change his life.

She's a precious little girl and popping in and out of her life at random will fuck her up. Make her doubt herself.

And, frankly, it'll fuck me up, too.

He either came up with a way to be in her life with some degree of consistency, or he stayed out of it.

Which meant he shouldn't be around her until he made a decision.

He couldn't get out of his next trip. The island had closed for monsoon season two weeks ago, but since the weather looked good, they'd granted him an opportunity for this private scuba diving experience.

I don't want to get out of it.

Okay, so go to Thailand. Take a few days to figure it out. Then, he could come back to Calamity and talk to Coco. Tell her how he'd decided to handle the situation.

Excellent. Made perfect sense.

He thumbed the recent calls screen and scrolled until he found the airline.

But he stopped when he saw Coco's name.

And texted her instead.

Making his way up the stone walkway to Coco's home, Beckett found himself drawn to the yellow light in the windows.

Home. The concept kicked up a flurry of strange emotions for him. He'd always felt like an outsider, like a kid pressed up to the window looking in.

Standing on the porch, he hesitated.

You better be sure about this.

There's no turning back.

He glanced at the quiet street, moonlight dousing the neighborhood in its milky glow. A block away, music from the live band playing in the town square traveled on a cool breeze, and the sky glittered with a spray of twinkling stars.

Images of Posie filled his mind, like photographs scattered on a table. That sly look she'd given him when asking him to put the peanut butter on her banana. The way she'd pressed a hand over her mouth to cover a giggle, her tiny fingernails painted a shimmering pink.

And that hand on his shoulder.

The memory sent warmth streaking through him.

There's no other decision to make.

He knocked lightly, part of him hoping Coco wouldn't answer. That was the part that didn't want his life to change. The part that wanted to stay unencumbered.

That's scared to death of having kids.

Because that's what it comes down to.

I'm terrified of being responsible for the life of this little girl.

The porch light flicked on, and the curtain hitched up. Coco's hand pressed to the glass. She smiled at him, soft, sweet.

And he knew. He fucking knew he'd made the right choice.

The door opened. Warmth spilled out. That pretty smile, the glow of lamplight surrounding her…an unnamed emotion pulsed through him.

He forced himself to speak. "Hey."

"Everything all right?" She leaned against the frame. "Your text was pretty cryptic."

Can I stop by? Yeah, maybe it was. "Everything's fine."

"Come on in." She stepped aside, closing the door behind him.

They stood in the entryway, neither speaking. Without make-up, she looked younger, more innocent. Very girl-next-door. Fresh, clean…

Fuck, this woman undid him. He'd felt the same pull to her in Vegas as he did right then. "I'm staying."

Her eyebrows shot up.

"In town."

"Oh. That's…." She straightened, wrapping her arms across her chest.

"For the summer." For the first time since finding out he had a child, he felt like himself again. The confusion had evaporated. He didn't know how exactly, but he felt certain he didn't have to choose between two completely different worlds. That he could find a way to be the same man, only with this new dimension added to his life. "I have to be in France on September first for a big event, but I'll find someone to cover the others for me."

"I thought this week's dive was important."

"It is." *And not just to me, but to my partners.* "But Willow's already there, so maybe she'll do it for me."

"Okay. What changed?"

"I need more time with you guys."

"Do you want to…" She made a circling motion with her hand. "My tea's getting cold." She led him to the couch, sat down, and curled her legs under her. "Not to be rude, but I'm not going to offer you anything until I finish this."

He smiled. "I don't need anything, so no worries." It only occurred to him then that he hadn't eaten since the picnic she'd brought to the hot springs.

"It's my nightly ritual. After I get her to bed, you don't know how easy it is to get lost in work. There's always a million things to do. But I realized early on that I needed to put breaks into my day." She lifted her mug, closed her eyes, and breathed in a floral fragrance he could smell from a few feet away.

The sweep of her eyelashes against her pale skin was so…feminine. "That's a good idea."

She sipped. "I actually have a few breaks built into my day. In the morning, before I wake Posie up, I make coffee and, instead of looking at my phone, I sit quietly. If it's nice out, I'll sit on the porch. If it's cold, I'll just sit right here on the couch. Sometimes I'll just listen to music, maybe read if I'm really into a book. In the middle of the day, I always take a lunch break. I like to go out with someone, because if I don't make a point of it, weeks can go by without me interacting with anyone but my daughter."

The way she was looking at him…it finally clicked. She was sending a message. "What're you saying?"

"I'm not like you and your fiancée. I have a job and responsibilities. I took off yesterday to give you the chance to get to know Posie."

Posie. Not "your daughter."

"We didn't really get into it, but in addition to running my business, I've got the chocolate festival coming up. It's my baby—I've organized it, so I can't screw up. I'm saying the foundation of my life is Posie. Then, there's the business, the festival…I keep a lot of balls in motion, and I can't afford to drop a single one."

He shifted to the edge of the couch, a little ashamed of himself. This big decision he'd struggled to make—he'd made it all about him. "Would you rather I not stay?"

She set the mug down. "That's not what I'm saying. Please don't think that. You're welcome to stay in Calamity, and I promise I'll include you in anything I can with Posie. She's your daughter, and I want you to get to know her. But I need you to understand that we're not free spirits. Kids need schedules and routines. Posie needs them or she gets grumpy and throws tantrums. I need them so I can accomplish everything I need to do in the course of the day."

"I understand."

"Do you?"

He grinned. "No. Not really."

She picked up her mug and settled back in the cushions. "Were you imagining more days of picnics and hanging out?"

"Honestly, I wasn't imagining anything. I just knew I couldn't leave. Not yet."

"I like that. I do. Just know that you'll have a lot of time on your own. Posie's at school for three hours a day —and you saw what it was like to get her to skip a day. I don't know you well enough to let you pick her up and spend time alone with her. I hope you understand that."

"Of course." Alone with her? He hadn't even considered it.

"Then, maybe hanging around to read her bedtime stories isn't going to be reason enough to stay."

"It's enough." He would take whatever he could get.

"What will you do with your time?"

A new energy started rolling in. "I'm going to be a guest coach at the Bowie training center. They invited me." *This is going to work.*

"That's great." She drained her mug and got up. "Let me make you some tea."

"No, tea. Thanks. You don't need to do anything. I just came by to tell you I'm staying." He got up. "We can talk tomorrow."

"You obviously haven't had dinner, so let me make you something."

Why would she say that?

She laughed. "Either there's a monster truck jam going on in your stomach or you're hungry."

He grinned. "I haven't had anything since lunch. I could eat."

"Well, come on. I've got leftovers for days."

He followed her into the kitchen, watching the sway of her hips in those pink and white striped pajama shorts and the slope of her shoulders in a worn college T-shirt.

A dangerous attraction stirred to life, and he had to remind himself.

Nothing's going to happen with Coco.
You're here for Posie.

Opening the refrigerator, she scanned the contents.

"There's mac and cheese." She turned to him with a question in her eyes.

With that dark hair framing her face in tousled waves, the long lashes and pouty lips, she made his heart thunder. And there wasn't a damn thing he could do about it.

Her bare, smooth legs, the toenails painted magenta, reminded him how they'd felt in Vegas, when he'd skimmed his hands up her thighs and gripped the back of her knee.

He could feel it.

His cock sliding into that tight, wet heat.

Fuck. His body went white hot with desire.

He couldn't go there, couldn't reignite the attraction.

But that was the problem. It wasn't just physical. Never had been. She was honest and warm and real...and he liked her. Liked being in her home.

Liked every damn thing about her.

She turned back. "How about roasted chicken? Posie loves chicken quesadillas."

Don't just stand here. Say something. "That sounds great. I'll have one of those."

"Perfect." She pulled out a bag of tortillas and another of grated cheese, the storage container of chicken, some salsa and, when she reached in for something else, trying to shift everything in her arms, he darted over.

"Let me grab those." Relieving her of the cheese and chicken, he set them on the counter.

"Where are you going to stay?" She turned on the oven.

"Haven't even thought about it." Brodie had comped the hotel room for two nights, but he knew the resort was booked for the rest of the summer season.

"I'm sure you could stay with the Bowies, but then

you'd need to keep your rental car. That'll add up. Actually, they probably have an extra car for you, too."

"I think I'd rather stay in town. Closer to you two. I'll check rentals."

"Oh, I can tell you right now, you won't find anything. The Economic Summit starts in a few weeks, and every business in the valley comes up with some kind of event or festival to take advantage of it. I'm having trouble finding accommodations, and I started organizing this event over a year ago." She set a tortilla onto a baking sheet and sprinkled it with cheese. "Actually, I have a carriage house. I use it for storage, but it's an actual house." She stepped to the sink to wash her hands. "Here, why don't you finish this while I make a quick call?"

As she reached for her phone, he stepped over to the counter and opened the container of chicken.

"Hey, Dad." She went quiet, as she listened. "Oh, yeah, you settled her right down. Thank you for that. Hey, how's your day looking tomorrow?" She broke out in an affectionate grin. "That's really sweet. I love you, Dad. So, I've got a guest in town, and I'd like to put him up in the carriage house." She cut a look to Beckett. "Not *that* kind of guest." She rolled her eyes. "Very sure. He's got a fiancée. But can you come over in the truck tomorrow and take all my boxes to your house?"

He pulled apart the chicken and set strips on top of the cheese.

"I'd love that, actually. A dresser, too, please. The only things in there are boxes of supplies for the shop." She flicked a glance at Beckett. "He's starting a job, but I'll ask." She lowered the phone away from her mouth. "Do you think you can be here around ten in the morning to help my dad take out the boxes and bring in a bed and dresser?"

"Absolutely." *Holy shit. This is happening.*

I'm staying in Calamity.

Living in Coco's house.

"Great." She brought the phone back. "Yep, he'll be here." She paused, looking uncomfortable. "Actually, I need to talk to you before then. Do you think I can come over right now?" She listened. "Thanks, Dad. See you in fifteen minutes." She disconnected and let out a breath. "I can't have you meet my dad without letting him knowing who you are. That wouldn't be right."

"Makes sense."

"Would you mind staying here for about an hour? Posie's sleeping. She rarely wakes up, so you won't have to do anything—"

"Don't worry. I don't mind, but should I be there when you do it? So they can meet me?"

"No. I can't spring it on them with you there. They need a chance to react. But if it's a problem, I can ask my neighbor. She and I watch each other's kids like this all the time."

"I don't mind. I just didn't want you to have to do it alone."

"You'll meet them soon enough. So, what about Willow? Is she going to be here with you? It's a pretty small house. Maybe you should take a look at it and see if you'll need something other than a bed and a dresser."

"Uh, no. She won't be coming." But he couldn't tell her the reason why before he talked to Willow.

She studied him for a moment. "This is hard enough for both of us....I can't even imagine what it's like for her.

I don't know what I'd do if I found out my fiancé had a child with another woman."

"It'll be fine."

She watched him for a moment with an expression that said she knew he was full of shit, but since he wasn't offering more, she said, "Okay, well. I'm going to get changed." She gestured to the oven. "You're good?"

"Yep. Don't worry about me."

The moment she left the room, he realized the obvious. He should've talked to Willow first. Before sending that text to Coco, before driving over here. Forget that she was sleeping, Willow deserved to know where things stood.

He pulled out his phone.

Beckett: Call me when you get up. We need to talk.

It's going to suck, but it has to be done.

Because, strangely, he hadn't looked this forward to an adventure in a long time.

Chapter Eight

Coco kicked off her flip-flops. "Mom? Dad?"

"In here, hon," her mom called from the kitchen.

Her parents stood at the island, making a salad together. Her dad cut the avocado, and her mom broke apart some feta and crumbled it into the bowl of greens.

"Hey." Reaching them, Coco popped a walnut into her mouth.

"You have a guest, huh?" her mom asked. "This wouldn't be the same handsome friend you went to Bear Mountain with, would it?"

"Yes, but it's not like that. He's engaged." The whole ride over she'd considered how to break the news to her family. Much like the other day with Beckett, she just didn't see an easy way to say it. "Remember that meeting Diane invited me to? About me providing the chocolate for a Splashagram influencer's wedding swag bags?"

"Yes, how did that go?" Her mom turned to the sink to wash the cheese off her fingers.

No matter what, her parents would feel threatened. They loved Posie like she was their own daughter, and the idea that this stranger would come in and take her away for half the year…they'd flip out.

Because Beckett staying in town for the entire summer meant something. He was getting attached. And that meant Coco would have less time with her baby. No way around it. She would obviously never keep Posie's father from her, but Coco couldn't bear the thought of giving up a single minute with her. God, not having her for Thanksgiving, for whole weeks during the summer? It would kill her.

Come on. Tell them. "You won't believe what happened."

Her dad tossed the avocado slices into the bowl and rested his wrists on the edge of the counter. "Tell us."

"Well, the groom, it turns out…he's Posie's father."

"What?" Her mom swung around with wet hands.

"I know. When he walked in the door, I nearly had a heart attack. I still can't believe the guy I hooked up with six years ago is here in Calamity. In my house. Right now."

"Did he know?" Her dad moved around the island to wash his hands at the sink. "Did he see pictures on social media and figure it out?"

"No, believe me. He's just as blown away as I am."

"You're not letting him live in your carriage house." Her dad yanked a dish towel off the counter and hastily dried his hands. "You don't know the guy."

"I know him. Not well, obviously, but I do…I mean, we haven't spent a lot of time together, but the time we've had…we've really talked. And he's friends with the Bowies —he competed with them for years. I wouldn't take any chances with my daughter."

"I know you wouldn't, sweetie," her mom said. "We're just worried."

"How long is he staying?" Her dad turned hard and stern.

"For the summer."

"What does he do that he can take off that much time?"

The interrogation begins. She understood, though. "He and his friends developed an extreme adventure travel app. He goes around the world meeting the tour guides and venue owners, tries out the experiences himself, and then posts links, videos, and reviews. He says he'll get someone to cover his trips this summer, but he has to be somewhere in September. So…Beckett's here the next several weeks."

"Beckett." Her mom let the word roll around her mouth as if tasting wine.

"Beckett O'Neill. He's a snowboarder—or he was—that's how he knows the Bowies, which is how he wound up having a destination wedding here." She reached for another walnut, running her fingers over its smooth, textured surface. "He said if he hadn't met Posie, he might've been able to leave, but he spent time with her at the pool last night and then again today, and now he just can't. I don't think he knows what kind of relationship he wants, but he needs to spend more time with her."

"And how do you feel about that?"

She dropped the nut. "I'm terrified, Mom. I love every minute I spend with Posie. I don't want to share holidays with him. I can't stand the idea…" All the fear she'd been pushing down finally erupted in a release of hot tears. She swiped them away. "I can't stand the idea of waking up Christmas morning alone in my house. I want to see her face when she comes downstairs and finds the presents Santa brought. I want her to stand on the stepstool while I make her waffles. I want to watch her squirt the whipped cream and shake out too many green and red sprinkles." She looked at her parents through blurry eyes. "I don't want to share her."

Her mom drew her in for a hug. "Oh, sweetheart. That won't happen. It won't. We won't let it."

"She's his daughter. He has rights." She pulled away and blew out a shaky breath. "I already looked it up. Wyoming has no prohibition against intrastate relocation."

"Hey, slow down," her dad said. "We're not getting legal advice off the internet."

"No, I know. I'm just…preparing myself. I mean, it's Posie, you know? He's going to fall in love with her. Today, she did something really sweet. She got excited on the chairlift and made it rock. He thought she was going to fall out, so he grabbed her. It was a total overreaction, and he apologized, but then Posie comes up to him later and says, 'I'm sorry I scared you, Beckett.' Oh, my God, you should have seen his face. He's super easy-going, but when she touched him and apologized, everything in him…he just looked into her eyes, and you could see it all happening. I watched it sink in that this special, sweet, adorable, fairy-loving little girl was his."

"Are you sure you want him living so close?" her mom asked. "In your backyard? What do we know about him?"

"From the minute I saw him in the conference room, I've been researching him. There's not a single negative thing out there about him. He's a good guy. The only bad thing, I guess, is that he doesn't have roots. Doesn't even want them. And maybe that scares me the most. That he'll take her with him on his travels. I guess…I guess I have an idea what kind of life I want for her—family dinners and holidays and best friends she's known since preschool. Ties. History. And then Beckett comes along, and he's the total opposite of that. And I'm scared. I'm just so scared."

Her dad shook his head. "No one's taking Posie anywhere. We'll talk to Sam in the morning, arm ourselves with facts. I'll also get Bradley to do a thorough background check on this guy."

Her parents, both former celebrities, not only ran a philanthropic foundation but several businesses. They had a whole team—legal and security—working for them. Having their support meant the world to her. Every time she thought she was alone in something, her family showed up and reminded her she had an army behind her.

"We need a paternity test, too," her dad said.

"I already took care of it. We should get the results in a few days."

"Let's do it the right way." Her dad sounded resolute. "It'll take a little longer, but I want accurate results."

"Okay. You're right." She felt a little better, knowing her parents were in this with her.

"One step at a time." Her dad's hand settled on top of hers. "We got this."

She wanted to believe him, but he hadn't seen the awe in Beckett's eyes when he looked at Posie.

Up until this moment, she'd relied on her own grit and determination to steer out of a spin. But this time, she didn't have control of the wheel.

And it scared her senseless.

Beckett's phone buzzed, yanking him out of a restless sleep. He fumbled for it on the nightstand. "Yeah?"

"Hey." *Willow.* "Is everything all right? The 'we need to talk' text is never a good thing. What's going on?"

I need coffee for this conversation. "I wanted to tell you I've made some changes." Sitting up, he bunched the pillow behind him.

"Okay." She sounded wary.

"It looks like I'll be staying in Calamity for the next couple of weeks."

"What? No, you can't do that. You've got the dive. Besides, you said yourself this is a critical time for your business, that you have to put in the time now if it's going to take off."

"I know that, but I have a daughter. I can't go scuba diving when I know she's here. I just can't do it."

"Oh, for God's sake. She has to understand that your life can't stop because of this. She can't expect you to take off an entire summer."

"Are you talking about Coco? She hasn't asked me to do anything. This is me." He threw off the covers and got out of bed. Revving from unconscious to fighting in point-nine seconds had his stomach churning. "I can't just walk away. I can't."

"You don't have to walk away from anything, but it doesn't have to change your entire life."

"It already has." It wasn't something Willow could understand.

She'll never find out she's got a child in the world she didn't know about.

"No, I know that. But you don't *change* your life, you adapt. Have you talked to Chris and Dave? Their life savings are wrapped up in this business. You can't bail on them."

Shit. He knew that but hearing it out loud gave him a

jolt. He absolutely couldn't put their business at risk. "I'm not bailing. I'm taking a couple weeks off."

"*Six months* into the launch? You can't do that. What about all the trips you've got scheduled? It took you years to build those relationships with tourism ministers. They've made special accommodations for you. That's not cool, Beckett. You blow them off, and you can't come back from this."

Shit. Fuck. Everything she said was right. He and his partners had not only put their savings into it, but their every waking moment.

Still, in spite of that...he couldn't leave town. Just couldn't. "I don't plan on missing any of the trips. I'm going to find someone to replace me."

"Okay, but then what? What happens after September? You've got a calendar full of travel. Are you going to pass it off to somebody else, so you can buy a house in Calamity? Get a job selling insurance? Come home every night to eat meatloaf and mashed potatoes with your kid? You told me that would be your worst nightmare."

It is. Everything she described was the very reason he'd put so much of his savings into this business.

He didn't want to give it—or his lifestyle—up.

I don't have to. "You're blowing this out of proportion. I'm talking about staying in Calamity for a few weeks, so I can figure out how to fit my daughter into my world. Whatever choice I make will impact her." He had to be careful. No one knew that better than he did. *It's important.*

"Does she know?"

"Not yet. No one knows."

"Look, babe, I'll tell you what I think. You're a good

guy, and your conscience is telling you to do the 'right' thing. But what if you were a lobsterman from Maine, and you found out you had a kid living in Wyoming? You wouldn't quit your job and move to the mountains to be near her, would you? You couldn't. You're a fisherman. You'd just find a way to stay in touch. Send her Christmas cards. FaceTime with her on her birthday. You don't have to become something you're not. Once it all sinks in, you'll figure out a way to stay true to yourself and meet your obligation to your kid."

"You're right. I needed to hear that." Deep down, that idea had been lurking—that he'd have to give himself up to be a father. But Willow was right—he didn't.

"Look, I'm already here. I'll handle Thailand. Just send me the login information, and I'll even upload the photos and videos for you. You take the next few days to get yourself together, and then we'll figure it out from there. Okay? Does that work?"

"No. I'm sorry, but it doesn't. I hear everything you're saying, and I don't want to lose myself to be Posie's father. But I *am* staying for the summer." With a finger he lifted the curtain and peered out the window. He couldn't see it in the early dawn, but he knew the resort backed up to a pine forest at the base of the mountain. "I'm not saying I'll move to Calamity, but I know for sure I'm not sending an annual Christmas card, either. I don't know how it's going to work, but she's my daughter. And I'm not going to minimize it."

Willow went quiet, and he gave her time to let it sink in. "Where does that leave us, then? I don't want kids. I want the freedom to go wherever I want, whenever I want. You want that, too, Beckett. I know you."

And here it came. The tough part. "It doesn't matter

what I want. My circumstances have changed. I'm a father, Wills. And that's my priority right now."

"You're scaring me, because you're only talking about Posie right now, and it sounds like there's no room for me. I'm not disposable. You don't get to set me aside while you figure things out in Calamity. I'm here, I'm your girlfriend. I need to still be your priority."

"You're right, but the fact is…I can't make you one right now."

"God, Beckett. Are you breaking up with me?"

He got a flash of Coco's smile last night, while she'd cradled the mug in her hands, her hair pulled up in a high ponytail. And the excitement pulsing through him was his answer. "Yes. I am."

She let out a breath into the receiver. "Beckett."

"I'm sorry."

"I guess there's no other choice." She sighed. "I don't want kids, and if that's the direction you're taking…?"

"That's the direction."

"Then, I don't think I want to go along for that ride."

It was pretty damn pathetic that they could end a relationship so easily and calmly. Had there been no emotional attachment at all?

"I have to hire someone to take over for me this summer. Before I talk to Chris and Dave, is that something you'd like to do?"

"I mean, yeah, but you've got some pretty intense things coming up."

"How about we go over the list, and you can tell me what you're comfortable with?"

"Yeah, we can do that." Her voice came out heavy with sadness.

"I'm sorry it turned out this way."

"It's crazy, isn't it? One minute we're the happiest couple in the world and the next...we're done."

He didn't know if he would've agreed with her before he found Coco again, but he certainly couldn't now. He'd never known happiness like he did when he spent time with her. "I'll let Chris and Dave know, and we can talk later."

"Okay." She sounded resigned. "Well, I guess I'll talk to you later."

After he disconnected, he tossed the phone on the bed and headed into the bathroom. He had some work to do before checking out of the hotel and meeting Coco's dad at the house.

Flicking on the light, he caught his image in the mirror. He threaded his fingers through his hair. *I was going to marry that woman.*

It had taken two days, his Vegas girl, and his daughter to realize he didn't like the man he'd become.

And he had to wonder if this swerve could turn him into someone he might like a little better.

Fresh from a shower, Beckett came out of the bathroom stark naked and instantly covered his junk when he remembered the window.

Yesterday, he'd helped Coco's dad set up the carriage house with furniture. He had everything he needed... except a curtain. Grabbing boxers and a T-shirt from his duffle bag, he quickly dressed, all while taking in his new view. A neat patch of lawn gave way to the green Jeep in the driveway.

An image hit him of Posie flying out the back door, her long honey-blonde hair fanning out, as she headed for the car in that funny way she walked...step, step, skip, step, step, skip.

His heart squeezed. He needed to see her. Sliding his feet into flip-flops, he headed out into the sunshine and breathed in the coffee-scented morning air. He liked the cool of the mountains—even in summer it never got too hot at this elevation.

As he approached the house, he hesitated. *Is it okay to just go inside?* He didn't know how Coco would feel about him showing up unannounced. With her schedule, maybe she'd prefer set times. He'd have to ask.

Truthfully, he hoped she'd let him share all his meals with them. He wanted to be part of this duo. He was drawn to them. *Both* of them.

As he crossed the dew-covered grass, he didn't see a single toy. Shouldn't she have a swing set, a playhouse...a slide. *Something* back here?

The second he knocked on the back door, he heard little feet slapping on the wood floor. "I'll get it, Mommy."

"Tell me who you see before you open the door, pumpkin," Coco called.

"It's Beckett." The door opened, and Posie gazed up at him with an urgent expression. "I need your help. Come on."

Ridiculously energized by the challenge, he breezed through the mud room and right past Coco, who stood at the stove, stirring a pot.

She smiled. "Hey, let the man have his coffee before you put him to work."

"It's fine." He stood near her. "I hope it's all right that I'm here. I don't want to interfere with your morning routine."

"Not at all. It's not like you can cook out there

without pots or silverware, so just come over for your meals, okay?" She smiled sweetly at him, not a hint of reluctance. "Actually, I had a key made for you." She pointed to the counter next to the sink.

He found the key and pocketed it. "Appreciate it. Thank you."

"Beckett, come on." Posie scrambled onto the bench seat of the kitchen table. "Mommy says I have to wait till after breakfast, but I want to do it now." She shoved a bunch of parts toward him. A plastic dog, some paw prints with arrows in the center, a tree, a slide, and a seesaw.

"Yes, so I can read the instructions," Coco said. "And make sure we do it the right way."

"Beckett can do it." Posie dug into the box and pulled out a sheet of paper. "Here." She smacked her hand on it.

Beckett scanned the information. *Okay, so it's some kind of coding game for preschoolers.* "Well, you're in luck. Because I studied coding in college. In fact, I developed an app with my friends."

"What's an app?"

"App is short for software application, and it's basically a computer program that you can download on your phone." He picked up the dog. When he touched its nose, it wagged its tail, so he knew they'd already loaded the batteries. "Mine's for people who want to have a really cool adventure."

"This." She redirected his attention to the dog. "Make it go."

"Let's figure it out together." As they worked quietly, easily programming the dog to go where Posie wanted, Coco served them each bowls of oatmeal.

When Coco sat down, she said, "Good news. I've

heard back from everyone about Sunday. Alyssa can't come, but everyone else can."

"Jessie can't come." She kept her head down, but he could sense the tension in her little shoulders.

"Did he tell you that?" Coco asked. "Because his mom said he could."

"I don't want him to come. He's not my friend."

"Are you still upset because he blew out your candles?"

"Yes." Posie opened her mouth wide enough to slip a basketball in it and clamped her lips around the spoon.

"Well, unfortunately, I didn't know that, and so I invited him. He's coming on Sunday, but I'll know for next time."

Beckett liked Coco's calm voice. It was gentle, yet confident. Strong.

It gave him chill bumps. He wanted to reach across the table and hold her hand. He wanted to tell her she was ~~fucking~~ amazing.

And that he remembered every detail of their night together.

What he wouldn't tell her was how vividly his body remembered ~~fucking~~ her, how it craved contact with her, relived the experience in his dreams, waking him up with the intensity of it.

Yeah, he'd leave that part out.

"Can I have milk?"

"Of course, sweetheart." Coco got out of the booth and headed for the refrigerator.

"Can I play in your house?" Posie asked him.

So much for the coding dog. This kid was a trip. "There's not much to play with in there, but you're welcome any time you like." Actually, he'd get her some toys. "What do you like? I could get a few things and keep them there for you."

"I like doggies. And dolls. And playing dress up. And arts and crafts. Mommy, what do I like?"

"Books, books, books."

"Yes, I like books. And movies. And cookies."

He caught the way Posie cut a sly look to her mom, but Coco just smiled.

"What kind of cookies?" he asked.

"I like chocolate cookies."

"Maybe we can make some together."

"Mommy, can I make cookies with Beckett? Please, Mommy?"

"Of course. That sounds fun. I might want in on that." Coco gave them both a teasing smile.

"I hope you stay here forever." Posie gazed up at him adoringly.

Looking into those crystal blue eyes, so similar to his own, his heart raced. She was this perfect, precious life... and it scared the shit out of him. He didn't want to ~~fuck~~ this up.

~~Fuck~~ *her* up.

An image of Ari flashed in his mind, her lifeless form on the snow.

A shock of pain radiated through his limbs so fast the soles of his feet tingled.

Fortunately, Coco appeared at that moment with the milk. "Okay, let's eat. We have to get ready for school." Sitting down, she picked up Posie's spoon and loaded it with oatmeal.

The little girl opened her mouth, and Coco delivered the mouthful. With her cheeks puffed out, Posie dropped out of the seat and ran off.

"Don't get scared when she talks about forever."

"No, that's not…" He shook off the vision of Ari. "I'm not scared about that." He reached across the table and held her hand. "Thank you."

"For the oatmeal? Oh, that's nothing."

"No, for being so patient. For giving me time to wrap my head around this. For…letting me stay here."

"You're welcome. I want you to know her. I want *her* to know *you*." She stuck her spoon in the oatmeal and stirred it, but he could tell she wasn't interested.

He studied her, remembering how well she'd hidden her distress from her sister in Vegas. And it struck him that he'd been so wrapped up in his own concerns these past few days he hadn't been paying attention to hers.

Fuck. He'd only ever had to worry about himself. But Posie…Coco…if he wanted to be part of this duo, then he needed to take them into consideration. He squeezed her hand. "This is hard for you, too."

She visibly relaxed. "Yeah. It is."

"Are you afraid Posie will get attached this summer, and then I'll take off and not stay in touch? Because that won't happen. I don't know what role I can play in her life, and I'd appreciate some more time to figure that out, but I won't just disappear."

"Actually, it's the opposite. I'm terrified you're going to fall in love with her and take her away from me for half the year."

What? Not a chance. "I would never do that to you. First, with my travel schedule, it's impossible. These are extreme adventures—definitely not suitable for kids. But, also, I see what she's got here. Your parents, this home, the way you are with her…I wouldn't do that to you or her."

"You say that now, but you're going to fall in love with

her—you'll see. I'm telling you, you will. I'm not saying it'll be wrong for you to spend more time with her. I'm saying I'll be incredibly sad to share holidays with you. But it is what it is, and we'll deal with it as it comes."

Her concerns shredded him. He hadn't once considered how this situation impacted her. "I'm glad you told me."

She set the spoon down and slid out of the booth. "I have to go check on her." She cleared both her and Posie's bowls. "Get ready for fireworks."

"What's going on?"

"You might've noticed she only wears fairy clothes."

He brought his empty oatmeal bowl to the sink. Standing close enough to see her smooth complexion and those luscious lips, made him reel. She smelled so good—a hint of maple syrup, soap, and clean cotton.

"We'll just let these soak. Come on." She headed into the living room. "Time for a crash course on parenting."

He followed her.

He'd follow this woman anywhere.

As they climbed the stairs to the second floor, she grinned at him over her shoulder. "She's got a stubborn streak a mile wide."

In a sparkly silver dress with multiple frothy layers, Posie stood on a stepstool at the bathroom sink brushing her teeth.

Breezing by, Coco said, "I'm going to put out your school clothes."

"I'm dressed, Mommy."

Ignoring her, Coco set out a clean pair of jeans, a pair of white socks with flowers dangling off the top, and a blue T-shirt.

When the faucet shut off, Posie came running out of

the bathroom, her usual eager and excited self. As if she'd come upon a crime scene, she came to a dramatic stop at the threshold of her bedroom. "I'm not wearing that."

"You're going to the dude ranch today, remember? You'll be outside with the animals. They might even take you on a trail ride."

"I can't wear this." Posie's voice rose, and she started to look a little wild-eyed. She stomped out of the room, heading for the stairs. "I'm going to school."

"If you wear that, they won't let you go horseback riding."

"Yes. They. Will."

"Posie, stop for one second and look at me. Let me know you understand that because you're wearing a dress, you won't be able to go on the trail ride. Those are the rules of the dude ranch."

"I'm wearing this."

"Okay, then. Let's go."

As they headed out of her room, Beckett had no idea how this would play out. "Isn't the school going to call you and make you come back with the right clothes?"

"Maybe. But I won't bring them. I'm all about natural consequences. If she misses the trail ride, next time she'll wear jeans, you know?" They crossed the living room. "It's funny, because everywhere I go, I get people telling me I shouldn't dress her in pink or in dresses. I shouldn't make her play with dolls. Which is hilarious, because everything you see around here comes from her. It's what she asks for her birthday, or what she's seen at Target with her aunts or her grandma. All the dresses and fairy dolls, it's one-hundred percent her." She grabbed her keys off the hook by the back door. "Ready?"

Posie slid her backpack onto her slim shoulders. "Ready, Mommy."

"Got your lunch?"

"Oh, I forgot." Her red sparkly shoes glittered, as she ran to the refrigerator and pulled out an insulated pink bag. "Got it."

They headed to the car, Posie dashing ahead in her step-step-skip stride, and he couldn't keep from smiling. As foreign as this whole family moment felt to him, it was the sweetest damn thing he'd ever experienced.

And he wished like hell Ari had had a mother like Coco.

Chapter Nine

BECKETT WASN'T USED TO RIDING SHOT GUN. IN HIS world, he made the plans, booked the flights, and navigated his way around new towns and uncharted terrain. So, being a passive observer didn't feel right to him.

After strapping Posie in, Coco climbed into the driver's seat and turned on the engine.

"I need to know how I can help," he said.

"Help?" She twisted around as she backed out of the driveway.

"You've got your hands full, I'm here for the summer...how can I help you?"

Just before hitting the street, she braked. "I appreciate that. I do. But I've got everything under control. I think the best thing you can do is just spend time with her, you know?"

The refrain was becoming too familiar. She didn't need help. She didn't rely on anyone. He'd have to find ways to help without asking. "I want to reiterate, if I'd known about her, nothing would've stopped me from doing my fair share. I'm going to catch up on the expenses I missed out on, and I'd like you to know, going forward, that I'll contribute financially."

She smiled. "Thank you." Backing into the street, she turned towards town. "I appreciate that. We'll get to it eventually, okay?"

"Sure. Whenever you want. Just give it some thought."

"Hey, I'm sorry my dad sprang that whole doctor's visit on you yesterday. I didn't know he was going to do that."

"I didn't mind. I like your dad." He'd appreciated Tyler's directness. "He didn't even have to use words to let me know what he'd do with my body if I wound up hurting either of you."

"Oh, no." She smiled. "Yeah, he's pretty protective of us."

After a quick trip to the doctor, who'd swabbed him for the paternity test, they'd gone out for coffee, and the retired quarterback had finally lightened up. Maybe Beckett had given him the right answers, or maybe he'd realized Beckett was doing the best he could in a difficult situation, but they'd wound up having a good conversation.

The man was well-liked here. Given the way he'd asked everyone they'd run into about their health, an upcoming wedding, or the colleges they were applying to, it'd be fair to say Tyler took the time to really know his neighbors. He was a good man.

"Are you worried about the results?" she asked quietly as they drove through town.

"No." He tuned into the conversation Posie was having with her dolls to make sure she wasn't listening.

Where he'd initially been struck by how much she

looked like Ari, her personality had erased any comparisons. She was her own, unique, sparkly soul.

"She's mine." He hesitated to tell her his concerns but then realized the only way for this to work was with honesty. Besides, she'd given it to him at breakfast. He owed her the same back. "I'm just...not sure what to do about it. I've been on my own a long time." *I'm selfish.*

The exact opposite of you.

"Ooh. Ouch." At the stop sign, she waited for a group of backpackers to cross the street. "Your fiancée might disagree with that."

"She probably wouldn't like to hear it, but it's true. Even after two years with her, we still did our own thing. She took off on her paid press trips, while I built my business. When our schedules aligned, we'd meet up somewhere. It was fun, we had a good time, but I never thought of her first." It embarrassed him to say that to someone who had such rich, deep relationships. But, since he was being honest, he might as well lean into it. "I didn't talk to her first about staying here. As soon as I made the decision, I texted you. That's how selfish I am."

"I wouldn't be so hard on yourself. You've been hit with a lot."

"Also, you should know, Willow and I ended things yesterday."

"Oh, no. I'm so sorry. Are you okay?"

"At the risk of sounding like a cold-blooded reptile, I'm fine. But maybe it's because I have much bigger things to worry about."

She drove across town, not saying anything more. And then, right before turning onto 191, she braked at the stoplight and said, "I remember what happened to your sister." She cut him a glance. *Is it okay if I bring her up?*

He nodded.

"So, I can't help but wonder if that's compounding an already difficult situation. She was young, too, right?"

"She was six." He didn't miss the way Coco lifted her gaze to the rearview mirror to glance at her daughter.

He noticed the flinch of pain, as she likely imagined losing Posie the way he'd lost Ari. How could she not?

"It was a fluke." He said it to reassure her but given the kick to his gut he always got when thinking about the accident, he knew he needed to hear it for himself. "That's the thing you learn about life. Some things are nothing more than timing. If we'd waited a second longer to head down the slope, if the guy who'd crashed into her had started his run one second earlier or later…"

"It's awful. It's just so awful." She reached for his arm and gave it a squeeze. "I'm so sorry." When the light turned green, she drove across the intersection. "I've noticed your expression sometimes when you're looking at her, and I can't help wondering if you see your sister in Posie."

"That first night, when I saw her treading water? It was like slamming into my past. Ari used to do that. Used to crack us up. She'd have her head as far out of the water as possible, her arms and legs splashing so much it looked like a school of piranhas at feeding time. Why does water on their faces freak them out so much?" He smiled at the memory. "But the more I get to know Posie, the less I see Ari. I mean…" He shook his head. "She's her own person all the way."

"I know. She's a riot. You were twelve, though, right? With six years between you, you were still close?"

"My sister was my mini me. Whatever I was doing, she wanted to do it with me."

"Did that bug you?"

"It probably should have, but it didn't. You know how Posie apologized to me at the hot springs?"

"Oh, man. I told my parents about that. She can be so sensitive and sweet."

"Yeah, I was feeling pretty bad for the way I scared her, and then she looks at me with those big eyes and apologizes to *me*. And it reminded me so much of Ari. My friends and I would be skateboarding or something she was too young to do, and I'd tell her to go inside and leave us alone. And then, like a half an hour later, she'd bring us snacks. Can you imagine this little kid who can't even reach the counter, pulling out a chair to get glasses and lemonade and boxes of cookies and bags of chips? How can you be mad at a kid like that? My friends loved her. Everyone loved her."

Fuck, it hurt. He'd thought time had worn the edges of his grief but talking about her sliced him wide open all over again.

They pulled in front of the school, joining a long line of cars. Coco twisted around and pressed a button on Posie's car seat. "Okay, sweetie pie. Here we are."

"I don't want to go, Mommy. I'm playing."

"The dolls will stay right where you leave them, so you can play as soon as you get back in the car. But, don't forget, today's the field trip, and I know you don't want to miss it."

"What field trip?"

"To the dude ranch. We talked about it this morning."

"What's a dude ranch? Is that the thing with horses?"

"Yes. Remember I said to wear jeans in case you go on a trail ride?"

"I want to ride a horse."

Beckett shot Coco a look. *How are you going to handle this one?*

But Coco just got out of the car, opened the trunk, pulled out a bag, and then swung around to get Posie out of the car. "Here are some clothes for you to change into."

"Bye, Mommy. Bye, Beckett." With her lunch in one hand and the bag in the other, Posie dashed off to a group of kids clustered around a teacher.

Coco got back in the car and inched forward in the drop-off line.

Beckett chuckled. "What happened to natural consequences?"

"I keep an extra set of clothes in the car. It started when she was a baby, when she'd have explosive...never mind. You don't need to hear those kinds of stories. Just... yes, I keep extra clothes for her, so it's easy to give them to her now. If I'd gotten a call from school, I wouldn't have shown up with clothes. It probably only makes sense in my mind, but I'm okay with that." At the end of the driveway, she looked in both directions before turning onto the road. "So, what's the plan? Are you going to keep renting your car all summer? See if you can borrow from the Bowies?"

"I'm going home, to Colorado. I've got to pack up some things, check my mail. And then I'll drive my truck back here. It's only an eight-hour drive."

"Oh. How long will you be gone?"

"If I can get a flight out today, I should be back on Monday."

"And miss out on our tattoo party?" Her eyes went wide in feigned surprise.

"Yeah, good point. But I've got some things to handle with work. Willow's only going to cover some of the trips

I've booked this summer, so I've got to find someone to do the rest." Jimmy came to mind. He really wanted to work with them. "I also have to let my partners know about the switch, and I'd like to do that in person." They both lived in Denver.

"It's nice that you and Willow will stay friends. I haven't stayed in touch with any of my exes. Well, of course, one of them ghosted me, and the other never looked back." She gave him a sheepish grin. "I think I just told you more about me than I'd like you to know."

"I don't think there's anything I could know that would make me like you less."

His words hung in the air between them, a neon sign pulsating light and energy. She looked touched and surprised. "That's an incredibly sweet thing to say."

He felt lighter, happier than he had in a long time. "There's a reason that night in Vegas happened." He knew it then, and he knew it for certain now. It was more than chemistry. Something deep inside him recognized her... and that recognition rang like a bell, waking him up, body and soul. "And, honestly, the fact that Willow and I slid so easily into friendship says more about the depth of that relationship than our maturity."

Looking distracted, she hit the highway and turned right toward town. "Is it okay if I ask how Ari died? I didn't want to ask with Posie in the car."

He shifted back in the seat, stretching his legs out, and groaned.

"Ugh, forget it. I'm sorry." She rubbed her forehead. "Are you desperate to get away from me now? One question away from opening the door and rolling out onto the highway?"

"No, I don't mind. I just…don't talk about it much. She died snowboarding."

"Oh, no. Is that something you guys did together?"

"First time for her." That familiar sadness crept up, circling him, but he wouldn't let it in. Wouldn't let it consume him.

"Weren't you from San Antonio? Do I remember that correctly?"

"I grew up there, but we moved to Lake Placid when I was eight."

"For snowboarding, right?"

He was making her pull the story out of him. If they were going to be up in each other's business all summer, he might as well be as real with her as he could. "The first time I hit the slopes, I showed promise—whatever that means—so my dad made sure I got a lot of attention. But the truth was, he was trying to keep me busy."

His childhood was so damn ugly. Nothing like hers.

But he'd tell her. "It's a long story, but basically my mom wasn't all that into being a parent. Instead of buying groceries, she'd buy new running shoes. Instead of fixing the washing machine, she'd book a climbing trip. She was all about traveling the world and having big adventures. So, I think my dad gave me snowboarding as a way of making sure the money was spent on me and so I had something to do." He glanced out the window. "I was alone a lot."

"That's so hard to imagine."

"Yeah. So, at first, my dad sent me to a lot of camps in Colorado and Utah. But then, when I was eight, we moved to New York so I could live at the National Sports Academy."

"You would've fit in well with my family. Our lives

were so structured, and everyone's an overachiever. Well, except me."

"At least your parents loved you."

He saw her reaction—sorrow chased quickly by a flash of anger. But she kept her words to herself, and he appreciated that.

"They did." She gave him a soft smile. "I never questioned that."

"My parents fought all the time. My dad would come home from work to see no food in the house, me alone, wearing clothes I'd outgrown, and I think the first thing he saw I was good at, he just threw me into it. Like, here's something to do other than watch TV and wait for food to appear in the house."

"Was your mom really that bad?"

"Yep. So, anyway, when I was twelve, we took a long weekend to go skiing in Vermont. Ari was on the bunny slope, while the three of us hit the black diamonds. At the end of the day, we were heading back to the lodge, when Ari said she wanted to go on one run with me."

As he got to the heart of the story, it felt like touching the skin around a wound, the closer you got, the hotter the skin, the more pain. Until you hit the center, and then it stung so badly you had to hiss in a breath and close your eyes.

"I stayed right behind her so I could watch, make sure she was okay. I mean, it was a green slope, meant for beginners, so I wasn't worried. She was coordinated, a good athlete." He cracked the window, let the cool air wash over him. "Out of nowhere some asshole crashed into her. Lost control of his board. Total wipe out."

Coco cringed. "I remember you said you saw it happen. I can't even imagine what that did to you."

He nodded. The sadness rose, swirling around him. He'd never get that image out of his head. "I wish I'd told her no. That I was done boarding for the day. At least, I could have been on her other side, so the asshole would've knocked into me. I'd give anything to go back to that day and tell myself, 'Look over there, man. See that guy? He's coming in fast.'" The deeper he got into the memory, the harder it was to breathe.

She reached for his hand and covered it with hers. It was warm, feminine, and it kept the sadness from sweeping him into that familiar space of panic and regret.

"She was just lying there, eyes closed. I knew not to touch her, but I needed to, you know? That's my sister. People came running over. They wound up Life Flighting her to a hospital in Boston." He would never forget the drive into the city. They'd left everything in the hotel, jumped in their car. His mom had turned into a boulder, silent and stiff. Wouldn't say a word. His dad...his fingers kept flexing on the wheel, his focus intense on the snowy highway, the muscle in his jaw ticking.

Coco kept a firm grip on him, her thumb idly caressing his skin.

"She never woke up. She was in the hospital for a week, tubes everywhere." He glanced at her. Did she even want to hear this?

She squeezed his hand. *Go on.*

He'd never told this story to anyone. Ever. In seventeen years. And, now, he couldn't stop the words if he'd tried. "It was torture, watching her in that bed. I don't know if you've ever experienced anything like it, but you're kept on the razor's edge of hope and utter fucking despair. You hear a sound, and you think, *She's back.* You spend every waking moment bargaining with God, believing you can will her back to consciousness. *If she lives, I'll drop out of the academy. I'll be a better brother.* I mean, I knew what her life had to be like with my mother, right? So, what the hell was I doing living away from home? I would have done anything for her to live. But she didn't."

"I'm so sorry."

"I was there when it happened. We were staying in a hotel near the hospital. The sixth night, I could hardly sleep, because I had an idea. Something to say to her that I knew would get her to smile, get her hand to twitch. She wanted a dog, but if my mom couldn't handle two kids, you know what she'd do with an animal. So, as soon as I got up, I went over there alone. I held her hand, and I told her, if she woke up, I'd quit the academy and come home to live with her, and we'd go to the shelter together, and I'd let her pick out whatever dog she wanted. She had a stuffed animal—it was a big-eared dog. She called him Boscoe. So, I said, Come on, Ari, wake up so we can go get you a real Boscoe."

"You're killing me here," she said softly.

"She coded." He heard the sound like it was happening right there in the Jeep. "Not right then. but a little later. The nurses came running in. Doctors. Someone herded me out of the room." He grew sick, clammy. Smacked the button to open the window all the way.

Only when Coco reached for him, her hand cupping his shoulder, her head tilted against his, did he realize she'd pulled over to the side of the road. She must've done it a while ago.

He stayed perfectly still, letting her warmth seep into him, her kindness pull him from the depths of the memory.

A truck roared past, rocking the Jeep. She didn't say a

word, and he would remember this moment forever, because while he rarely talked about it, when the death of his sister did come up, the way people responded made him feel worse. Nobody knew what to say. They got this desperate look in their eyes, like they wanted to be anywhere but in that moment with him.

And it just made him not want to talk about it, ever.

But Coco...made it all right.

Her head lifted, a sheen of tears in her eyes, and she kissed his cheek.

But he was so desperate for her that he turned and caught the corner of her mouth—and it fucking electrified him. All at once, he was caught up in the floral scent of her shampoo, the warm grip of her hand on him, and he wanted more.

Forget Vegas, forget memories, forget anything other than this moment, this closeness with her.

She roused a hunger he'd never felt before.

And right then he knew why he'd chosen her to share the story with. Because his system was programmed for her.

Fuck.

Her expression turned from compassion to awareness, and she sat up, putting both hands back on the wheel.

She'd seen it, the desire burning in him. And she'd shut it down instantly.

Message received.

We're not going there.

"It must've been hard to go back to snowboarding."

Pulse pounding, he had to look away from her. This woman...she just did it for him. In every way.

Snowboarding. Right. "I didn't...uh..." He swallowed, his skin cooling, desire banking. "I took some time off, but it was terrible at home. My parents were destroyed."

"I can't even imagine. I don't know how I'd function."

"My dad got his shit together. Said he didn't have a choice. Bills to pay, mouths to feed. He enrolled me in public school, stocked the fridge and pantry, and went back to work. But my mom…she disappeared. We don't know where she went, but it was anywhere but home."

"What made you go back?"

"I'll tell you exactly what did it. Ari was only on that slope because she wanted to be like me. And there I was failing my classes, no friends, the saddest fucking home life you've ever seen—I mean, silence at the dinner table so bad that my dad and I just stopped trying. He'd hit the drive-through on the way home, toss the bags on the dining room table, and then just sit in front of the tube. I'd take my bag to my room."

"And you have no idea what your mom was doing?"

"None. In my memories of that time, it was just me and my dad in a house that smelled like French fries. So, one night, I was on my bed, texting a friend from the academy, and I got a notification. My aunt posted a picture on social media. It was of me and Ari. She was wearing a snowsuit and looking up at me like I was her hero. My aunt wrote something like, *Remembering my niece tonight, how she loved her big brother*, and it all clicked into place for me. I needed to be the man Ari knew, not the sad sack eating fast food burgers alone in his room."

She gave him a soft smile. "So, even though she hasn't been physically present, she's been with you every step of the way."

Floored, he could only let the idea wash over him. "I like that idea a lot." He couldn't think of another time in his life when he felt more locked in the moment. When he wasn't thinking about his next step, planning his next move. Coco and he…they just connected. In a very real, very intimate way.

"I've never told anyone the whole story." He gazed out the window, realized they were parked alongside the Bison Preserve. "There's just something about you. I felt it in Vegas, and I feel it now. This…connection."

"I know. Believe me, I feel it, too." She reached for the gearshift. "I should get you home. Have you booked a flight yet?"

"No, I'll do it now." He touched a lock of her silky hair. "I'm sorry if I made you uncomfortable."

"You didn't. Well, I mean, it's not what you said. It's us. This attraction. I just think things are complicated enough, you know? We need to keep things focused on Posie. She's the most important thing in the world for both of us right now."

"You're right." He lowered his arm, rubbed both hands on his thighs. "I left my phone at home, but I'll book the flight as soon as we get back."

"You're not going to forget about us, are you?" Her tone was teasing, but he didn't miss the strain around her eyes.

"Impossible." She didn't trust him to stick around. He got that. But there was one thing she didn't understand.

For him, Coco Cavanaugh was unforgettable.

Chapter Ten

IN THE HOURS SINCE HE'D RETURNED HIS RENTAL CAR to the airport agency, flown to Denver, and finished out the journey to Boulder, he'd discovered something important.

He missed Posie. Throughout the day, something would catch his eye, and he'd wonder if she'd like it. And Coco? She was all he could think about. When he'd nodded off on the plane, he'd dreamt of her. Had his hands all over her warm, soft skin, his tongue tracing every curve...the jolt of excitement had shaken him wide awake.

He missed them. It didn't make sense, considering he'd only known them a short time.

The craziest thing was that he should be in Thailand right now, diving to see whale sharks. That had always been on his bucket list. But he didn't give a damn. He could travel there anytime.

Posie would never be five again. And he'd already missed so much. Right now, it was her bedtime. She'd either be flying around like a fairy or pitching a fit because they'd run out of the sparkly toothpaste, and fairies didn't use the plain stuff. Whichever it was, he hated missing it.

He willed the taxi driver to floor it up the mountain to his cabin, so he could hurry up and get back to Calamity.

Headlights hit the reflective tape on his mailbox. "This it?" the driver asked.

"Yep." He grabbed his duffle bag and handed the older woman a couple of bills. "Thank you."

"Have a good night," she said, before pulling back out.

Beckett's boots crunched on the bed of pine needles and dried leaves that covered his yard. The cab's taillights cast a red glow on his property, revealing a lump on his welcome mat.

His heart jumped into his throat.

"Ollie?" Beckett dashed toward the house. Bushy tail thumping, the dog didn't get up the way he normally would. Looked like he'd lost a lot of weight. "Hey, buddy, how you doing?" He crouched, stroking the dog's fur and combing through burs and clumps of dirt. "Jesus, you're skin and bones."

He glanced toward Mrs. Lionetti's house but didn't see any lights on. "Come on." He stood up, jammed his key into the lock, and swung the door open. "Let's get you something to eat."

As always, his house sat still, empty. A couch, a coffee table. Nothing hung on the walls. He didn't even have a dining room table. He'd either eat standing up at the sink or while watching television. Heading straight for the cabinet, he pulled down two bowls. He let the tap run for a few minutes before filling one of them with water.

In the past year, as Mrs. Lionetti's health deteriorated, her adult kids had wanted to find the dog a new home, but Ollie was the only companionship the old woman had, so she wouldn't let them. Whenever Beckett was in town, the dog wound up on his doorstep. He fed him, bathed him, and took him on walks.

Normally, he could see a single light glowing in Mrs. Lionetti's bedroom window. With the difficulty she faced getting around, she slept with it on. Sadness settled over him. He suspected she'd finally passed. "How long have you been waiting for me?"

He brought the other bowl into the pantry, where he kept a big bag of kibble, and scooped some out. Ollie immediately started wolfing it down.

Beckett sat beside him, stroking his matted fur, too aware of the bones he didn't normally feel on the mixed breed dog. "Dude, go easy or it's all going to come back up." Not wanting him to eat too much, Beckett got up and headed into his bathroom to start the bath.

"Come on, buddy," he called. "Let's clean you up." When Ollie didn't come, Beckett went into the kitchen and gently nudged him aside so he could set the two bowls on the counter. "I know you're hungry, but I want you to keep it all down." The dog's nails clacked on the wood floor as they headed to the bathroom. Lifting him, Beckett set him into the warm water and found the dog shampoo in the cabinet under the sink.

Beckett scooped up water with cupped hands and poured it over him. With the fur plastered to his body, it accentuated the bony frame. Lathering up his hands with some flea and tick shampoo, he gave Ollie a thorough scrub. He couldn't bring a flea-ridden animal into Coco's home.

His heart pinched at the thought that Ollie was now his. One, because his lifestyle didn't work for a dog, but also because tomorrow he'd find out what happened to

Mrs. Lionetti. He suspected it wasn't good. But, if her kids didn't mind, he'd be taking the dog with him. It wasn't like he'd let Ollie go to the Humane Society.

Would Coco even let him bring a dog into the carriage house? Maybe Posie had allergies. He'd text her to find out. Otherwise, his dad would have to watch him until Beckett came back.

And then what? Who'd take care of Ollie after he left for France and resumed his travels?

A week ago, his future had been clear—his calendar was booked well into next year. But right now? He couldn't see anything past the next few days, taking care of Ollie and driving back to Calamity. Getting back to his girls.

After that?

He just didn't know.

Later, after polishing off a can of soup and a sleeve of crackers, Beckett sat on the couch, Ollie crashed out over his thighs. He grabbed his phone from the coffee table.

Beckett: So…I have this friend…and he might want to hang out with me for a while.

Coco: Keggers in the carriage house are a hard no.

Beckett: My friend doesn't drink beer.

Coco: Does he drink champagne?

Beckett: Tap water's fine. Though he does have a clear preference for toilet water.

Coco: Clue #1. Your friend doesn't understand the purpose of a toilet.

Beckett: No, he prefers the woods.

Coco: And fire hydrants?

Beckett: I mean, I can ask…?

Coco: Did you get Posie a dog????

Beckett: No! I wouldn't do that to you. When I got home, I found my neighbor's dog on my porch. He's lost a lot of weight. I'm thinking...the house next door might be vacant now.

Coco: They abandoned their dog? Who does that?

Beckett: That came out wrong. She's elderly. Health declining. Ollie's always spent time with me when I'm in town, so I think if she passed away, it would make sense for him to come to me.

Coco: Damn you, Beckett O'Neill. You know I can't say no to that.

Beckett: I can bring him to my Dad's if it's a problem.

He stroked the dog's fur, and Ollie gave a relieved and contented sigh. He would have a hard time giving this sweet orphan away.

Coco: I think you know Posie wants a dog. My worry is what happens when you leave. She gets very attached.

He absolutely understood. More than anything, he'd wanted a pet as a kid. But they couldn't have one. Not with a mother who neglected everyone's needs so she could travel the world.

But...Ollie.

Beckett: Is that a no? I understand if it is.

His phone rang, and he smiled when he saw her name. "Hey."

"We agreed to be honest with each other, right?"

"Absolutely."

"I'm feeling really uncomfortable about you staying for the summer."

He hadn't expected to hear that. Worse, he hadn't expected the hit of anxiety.

She doesn't want me to come back? "Okay."

Not seeing Posie again? He was back in that kitchen, watching Posie fly her dolls around, while Coco talked on the phone with one of her suppliers. He could smell the clean mountain air breezing in through an open window, feel it wash over his skin.

Contentment. Yeah, that's what it felt like.

"You've only been gone one day, and she's already talking about you, worrying that you left without saying goodbye. Wondering if you're coming back."

"I'm coming back."

"Right. But you *are* going to leave. She got attached to you in a couple of days, imagine what will happen after a few weeks. And then what happens after the summer? Are you going to send her birthday cards every year, show up with presents once in a while, maybe spend a holiday or two with her? And then, as more time passes, will that eventually stop?"

"I don't have answers to that."

"I know. And that's why I'm sitting here freaking out that we're making a terrible mistake. That she'll get attached to you, and then you'll move on."

He didn't think that would happen. Couldn't imagine it. But, at the same time, he couldn't make promises. Not yet. "I can't see that far ahead. I need more time. My life... I'm building a business. But..." He tipped his head back, staring up at the beamed ceiling. "I understand if you don't want me to come back, but...Jesus, she's my daughter. I can't not see her." *I just found her.*

"No, I know." She went quiet for a moment. "This is really hard."

"It is. For both of us. But I can't go back. You understand that, right? I can't pretend she's not my child."

"I know that."

"What's really worrying you?"

"That, for you, this is a lark. You're getting to know her, and it's interesting and it feels important, but then you're going to go back to your life, and you're going to forget about her."

"That's not going to happen."

"I know, I know. I'm jumping ahead. I'm just so afraid she's going to get hurt. It's happened before. The guy I dated last year never even said goodbye. He got a job in Seattle, and he broke up with me. And that was fine, but he never said goodbye to Posie. One day, he was a big part of her life, and the next he was gone."

"That guy's an asshole. I'm not that guy."

"I know. I'm sorry. I'm a little emotional right now." She blew out a breath. "We got the results. You're her father. I mean, we already knew that, but seeing it on a piece of paper…"

"Means I have custodial rights."

"Yes. Exactly. Thank you for understanding how scary that is for me. It means you could give this piece of paper to a judge and take my daughter away from me for half the year. I mean, it's good. I'm glad she has a dad. Especially a good man like you."

She's glad I'm Posie's dad? Warmth spread through him, giving him a sense of something that felt a lot like pride. "Look, I'm not going to make promises about a future I can't see. This is all brand new for me. But you're a phenomenal Mom, and I'd never take her from you."

"Thank you, and I appreciate you saying that. Look,

this isn't your fault. It's the situation. And I shouldn't be unloading all my anxiety on you. It isn't fair."

"I want you to. I want to know what you're thinking, what you're worried about. I need to know—the more we talk about it, the more we can help each other through this."

"You're right. I know you can't see the future, and that's what scares me. I won't know what you want until you spend more time with her. And, so, until that happens, I'll be wondering and worrying every single day."

"I wish I could make this easier for you, and if you don't want me staying in your backyard—if that'll help—I'll find somewhere else to stay. But I can tell you that I care about *both* of you. There's only one thing I want right now, and that's to spend more time with her."

"No, you can stay. It's not going to matter where you sleep at night. If you're going to spend time with her, she's going to get attached. You're good with her."

"I don't know about that."

"Trust me, you are. You don't talk to her in that high-pitched voice people use for babies and dogs."

Like Willow. He'd noticed that, too.

"She's too smart for that. You're also easy-going, and she's pretty high strung, so it keeps her calmer."

He really liked this woman. A lot. "I'm glad to hear you say that."

"I just...can I just ask you to be very careful with her heart?"

"You can. And I will. I promise."

"Okay, one more thing. Since you don't know what kind of relationship you'll want after you leave town, let's not tell her you're her father. I think it's worse to have a dad who sends the occasional birthday and Christmas card than to not have one at all. You know?"

"I understand." *Believe me.*

"Right now, only my family knows. So, let's just leave it at that. I know you're going to be working at the training center, but don't tell the Bowies, okay?"

"I can trust them."

"I'm sure you can, but they have girlfriends and friends and…it's just a really small town. I'd appreciate if you'd keep it between us for now. For Posie's sake."

"Yeah, okay, sure." In his lap, Ollie let out a crazy yawn that made his whole body shudder.

"What was that?"

"That's my friend, Ollie."

"Your friend sounds like he just jumped off the balcony into a pool after having way too much to drink."

Beckett grinned. "He's too cool for that. Ollie wasn't in a frat."

"You think he misses his owner?"

He stroked his fur. "He seems pretty damn comfortable right now."

"I wonder how long he's been waiting for you."

"It's got to be more than a couple weeks. He dropped a lot of weight."

"That's heartbreaking. You're not just saying this so I'll let you bring him home, are you?"

"No. But is it working?"

"Of course it is. I'm not a monster."

"I'll go over to her house tomorrow and find out what's going on. But it's likely—"

"I'm going to have piles of shit in my backyard."

Beckett grinned. "All right. I'll let you get some sleep.

See you soon." He disconnected, still staring at the phone, still feeling her all around him.

And all he wanted was to get back to Calamity.

In the pause between Cheap Trick's "I'll Be With You Tonight" and "Voices," Coco heard the knock at the back door and nearly jumped out of her skin.

Her staff had all gone home, and no one delivered this late at night, so who could it be? Setting the spreader down, she hurried over and called, "Who is it?"

"Beckett."

His deep voice, the lazy drawl of it, sent a thrill through her. *He's back?*

Excitement making her jittery, she opened it to find him wearing worn jeans and a long sleeve T-shirt, looking unbelievably hot. The thin cotton clung to his bulging biceps and accentuated the breadth of his powerful shoulders. He looked so much like the man she'd fallen for in Vegas.

Only this time, she didn't have a broken heart, and she wasn't afraid of her future.

And, worse, she knew exactly what he was like in bed.

Sexy.

Passionate.

Hot.

She'd never felt that kind of intense intimacy with anyone else. At the time, she'd wondered if it had been the thrill of the moment—her first and only one-night stand. But that hadn't been it at all. It was *them*. Their chemistry, their connection.

"I thought you weren't leaving Colorado until

tomorrow morning? Come in." Flustered by her reaction to him, she headed over to the sink to wash her hands. *Don't you fall for him.* "Hope you don't mind, but I have to keep working."

It's complicated enough without developing feelings.

"Not at all." She could hear his boots following her on the concrete floor. He stopped at the melanger, watching the churn of creamy chocolate. "It's so shiny. I hate to sound stupid, but…do you just melt bars and then mold them into different shapes?"

"No, that's not how it works." She hit the faucet with her elbow and then dried her hands on a clean towel. "It all starts with beans. I can give you a tour as soon as I finish this."

"Cool."

She returned to the table and poured the chocolate over the mold. Once she'd flooded each cavity, she reached for the scraper. "How was the drive?"

"Really nice. I saw a mountain goat and a herd of elk."

She shot him a look, unable to hold back her grin, and waited for him to realize what he'd just said.

When he did, he chuckled, tipping his chin down and swiping that sexy mouth with a thumb. "Yeah, well, there it is. I see the world through Posie's eyes now, okay? Been like that the whole weekend. I actually pulled over to record a field of prairie dogs popping their heads out of the ground, thinking she'd love it."

"I do the same thing." She smiled. "And she'll love seeing it." Half of her felt all warm and tingly that he cared so much about her little girl. The other half?

Was sparking like a live wire. This energy between them made her restless…

It made her crave more from him. Their naked bodies

under the sheets, legs tangled, hands roaming, caressing, squeezing.

No one had ever touched her the way he had—like he couldn't get enough.

And, God, she wanted that. She *needed* it.

Finished scraping the excess chocolate off the mold, she set it down and gave it a shake to get the bubbles out. "How's Ollie?"

He winced. "He's okay."

"You look worried."

"Mrs. Lionetti passed away two weeks ago. Her kids said they haven't seen Ollie since."

"He's been wandering the woods all this time?"

He looked like the idea made him sick.

"Thank God you went home and found him. So, is he yours now? You said you needed to talk to her family." Setting out another mold, she dropped a whole macadamia nut in each one.

"He's mine."

Lifting the melanger, she poured the chocolate, watching it glide, like a thick, shiny river. "I went ahead and made a vet appointment for tomorrow afternoon."

"You did?"

"Yeah, is that okay?" She scraped the excess off. "You said you'd hit the road at six, so I made it for three. I thought you needed a day in Boulder? Don't you have stuff to do?"

"I wanted to get back." With a thoughtful expression, he tapped his knuckles on the marble countertop. Then, his gaze swung up to her. "That was nice of you...to set that up." He seemed surprised...almost moved.

"Sure." It made her wonder about his family, his girlfriend. Didn't his people look out for him like that?

He swallowed. "Thank you." Obviously uncomfortable, he looked around the room. "So, this is where the magic happens, huh?"

"It is." She continued clearing away every drop of the excess chocolate. "This is my last one."

"You don't usually work this late, do you?"

"No, definitely not. I've got a great team, and I do my admin work at home in the evenings. But the chocolate festival's in a few weeks, and with Laurent and everyone coming, I really want to create something amazing."

"He's the one who gave you your start?"

"Yes. He's also one of the most revered chocolatiers in the world. So, the pressure's on to do something that'll impress him."

"He's tried your chocolates before, though, right?"

"Of course. I sent him my very first box. You know the sweetest thing ever? I went to visit him in Paris, and I found the box in his office."

"That's nice. Sounds like you've already made an impression."

"He was very kind to me. I was lost and hurt—"

"He didn't help you because you were lost and hurt."

He got her attention with that comment. She set the scraper down.

"He helped you because you were curious and determined. And because he saw that, in spite of the sadness and hurt, you were still fierce and determined. That's what I saw, that night in Vegas. Like I told you before, that's what drew me to you." He moved closer. "Up until now I've had a girlfriend so I couldn't say this, but I find that sexy as fuck."

She wanted to change the subject as much as she

wanted to hear more. She liked the fire in his eyes, the heat in his tone.

Oh, yes, she did.

"I'm making you uncomfortable. I'll stop."

"Are you kidding? I'm a single mother. I want to hear you say things like that all day long. If I'm uncomfortable, it's because it feels dangerous to hear you say that, and it's been a very long time since I've done anything dangerous. And, by that, I mean Las Vegas six years ago."

His eyes flared.

He'd looked at her like this once before, and she knew where it led. Knew what his hands felt like when they'd finally given in to an attraction that had burned out of control.

She'd relived it a thousand times over the years. That first grip of his big hand on her ass, the way he'd hauled her up hard against him. The way he'd cupped her breast and squeezed so lustily.

God, that had been hot.

"But it's different this time. The stakes are a thousand times higher. You're Posie's dad, and you're trying to figure out how to fit into her world. We can't do anything to take the focus off that."

She could actually see him shut off the part of himself that burned.

"How about that tour?" She set the trays in the cooling cabinet.

He nodded, taking a step back. She gathered her tools and set them in a bowl of soapy water in the sink.

"So, this festival…is it an annual thing?" he asked.

"I'd like it to be." She was glad for the change in conversation, but her body hadn't cooled down, and she didn't want to go back to friendly, distant chatter.

She needed his touch like she needed her next breath.

She needed to sink into all those delicious sensations only he awakened.

That night in Vegas, she'd been wild, uninhibited, and it had been outrageous.

A memory flashed in her mind. Riding him, back arched, as she'd gripped his hard thighs, his big hands palming her breasts. A tremor ran through her body.

Oh, God.

"You've come up with some good ideas. I saw on your website that you've supplied chocolates for Oscar swag bags the last two years. That's pretty impressive."

"It's very cool, but it hasn't turned me into an overnight success."

"How does the festival work?"

"It's a ticketed three-day event with chocolatiers from around the world. Each one will have a booth in the ballroom of the resort. We'll have demonstrations and contests…it'll be fun."

"Good response?"

"Better than I could have imagined. We've hit capacity for booths, and the ticket sales are fantastic."

"I don't have much of a sweet tooth, but I'd definitely go to a chocolate festival."

"Oh, for sure. But it's pretty expensive to get in the door, so that's why I'm so pleased with the sales." She rinsed her hands and dried them on a dish towel. "Okay, let's do this. She pointed to a floor-to-ceiling shelf stuffed with jute bags. "It all starts with the beans. It took me a long time to create my signature flavor. I had to experiment with cacao beans from around the world to find the blend I think makes Coco's Chocolates stand out."

"I don't know where I got the idea that a chocolate maker just bought stacks of chocolate bars and melted them."

"That's exactly what launched this whole, crazy trip I've been on. I assumed everyone bought the same high-quality chocolate from a vendor and then made it their own with liquor and nuts or whatever they added. But, nope, it's all about the bean blends, the roasting..." She led him to counter. "Which is done right here in these coffee bean roasting ovens. As you learned the other day, I can smell when they're ready, but for the less experienced nose, we set the timer for fifteen minutes. And then we listen for them to start cracking."

"This is way less Willy Wonka than I was expecting."

"Right? It's science. It's all about weights and calculations." She pointed across the room to a chart. "I base each type of chocolate I make on percentages. That's what gives each piece its distinctive flavor. Fortunately, I'm good at math. Anyhow..." She patted a machine made of aluminum and food-grade PVC that sat on a counter by the wall. "After they're roasted, we separate the husk from the nib with these winnowers." She moved over to a stainless-steel barrel fitted with two granite roller stones. "This baby's the melanger. This is where we get some of that chocolate factory action. It refines the nibs down to about twenty microns." She smiled at him. "Those pesky numbers. Basically, after about twenty-four hours, we have that glassy, creamy chocolate river effect."

"This is pretty fucking cool."

"I think so. So, once the chocolate's shiny and smooth, it has to be tempered. And then..." She gestured to the shelves filled with molds. "The fun begins. I get to experiment with all kinds of different flavors and shapes. Do you want to try some?"

His gaze went hot, and his tongue licked his bottom lip. Desire crested across his cheeks in pink arches. "You're beautiful."

Oh, God. Carnal hunger streaked through her hot and fast. She hadn't heard anything like that in so long. She hadn't felt like a *woman* in so long. "Thanks." Her voice came out breathy and thin.

His gaze drifted to her mouth. "I don't just mean your looks. Well, I *do*, but it's so much more. There's just something about you…that appeals to me."

"Appeals to you?" She said it with a laugh, mostly to break the tension.

Pink flamed to red, and he glanced down.

She wanted to kick her own ass for embarrassing him.

"If I sound like an asshole, it's because this is new to me, and I'm just trying to figure it out. I've never felt anything like this with anyone but you. I know what it feels like to enjoy other people, I know what attraction feels like, but with you…it's the wildest damn thing."

"I know." It came out a whisper. The charge between them got her blood pumping. "I feel it, too. Whatever chemistry we had in Vegas, it's still here."

He shook his head. "No. I know you now, and that makes it so much bigger. Powerful."

God. This man. She wanted him so much.

"I want—"

She pressed her fingers to his lips and stopped him. "One more sexy thing out of your mouth, and I'm done for. Let me finish up, so I can get home for the babysitter. Because let me tell you something Beckett O'Neill, you've got heartbreaker written all over you."

Chapter Eleven

"*Mommy.*"

The blood curdling scream sent Coco tearing out of the bathroom and trampling down the stairs, clinging to the banister so her damp feet didn't fly out from under her. Hair dripping down her back, she called, "I'm right here, baby. Hold on. Almost there." Racing across the living room, she burst into the kitchen to find her daughter standing on the back porch, the door swung wide open.

Her nightgown billowing around her from an early morning breeze, Posie whirled around, pointing out the door. "Beckett has a doggy. A doggy, Mommy. Beckett has a *dog*."

Holy mother of God. Heart pounding in her ears, Coco nearly collapsed against the counter. "Peanut, you scared the living daylights out of me."

"Can I go see him, Mommy? I want to go outside."

Coco glanced out the door to find Beckett waving, while the dog did his business on her lawn. "You better—"

But before she could finish her sentence, he dangled a

plastic bag from his fingers. One second later, the dog made a beeline toward the house, while Beckett headed to the garbage bins lined up against the fence.

Bounding onto the porch, the dog knocked Posie flat on her bottom. Coco waited for the tears...but they didn't come. Instead, Posie's arms went around the dog's neck. Ollie nose-butted her, his tail whacking into the side of the house with a rhythmic drumbeat. Giggling, Posie tried to get up, but the dog straddled her, licking her like a melting ice cream cone.

"*Ollie*. Get off." After Beckett gave the dog a gentle shove, he galloped into the kitchen, heading straight for Coco.

She crouched. "Hey, handsome." She ran her hands through his fur, too aware of his ribs and hip bones. "I don't have any food for you, but I can get you some water."

"He ate." Beckett closed the door and came up beside her. Together, they watched Posie pat the dog's back frantically. "I think she likes him."

"That's what I'm worried about." But she said it with a smile.

It's totally unrealistic to think Beckett's DNA will change, right? He won't suddenly become a homebody?

Uh, no. That's never going to happen. But maybe...just maybe Beckett would fall enough in love with his daughter to find a way to stay in her life in a meaningful way.

That doesn't take her away from me. The clutch of fear gripped her so hard, it spurred her into action. "Sweetheart, go get dressed." Turning away from him, she went to clear the breakfast dishes. "We've got scrambled eggs, if you're hungry." When he didn't answer, she turned to find Beckett sitting on the floor, rubbing Ollie all over, and it about broke her heart to see the dog softly lapping at any area of the big man's exposed skin. If it was possible for a dog to look overwhelmingly grateful, this one nailed it.

"You said you didn't have a doggy, Beckett." Posie stood beside him, leaning over and cupping his cheeks, so he'd pay attention to her. "Did you get one for me? Is this doggy for me?"

"No, sweetheart, that's not our dog." God, she hoped Posie understood that Ollie would be leaving at the end of summer. "He's Beckett's."

Posie knelt, trying to hug the dog, but he was too busy squirming and vigorously wagging his tail.

"Remember I told you about my neighbor's dog?" Beckett asked.

Posie nodded.

"Well, this is him. My neighbor can't take care of him anymore, so she's asked me to do it."

"Why can't she take care of him?"

Coco wanted to step in and answer for him. He might think he needed to be completely honest with her, but Posie didn't need in-depth answers. She just needed something she could understand.

"Because she moved to a place where they don't take dogs." Beckett flicked his gaze over to her. *Wrong answer?*

Coco smiled. *Really good, actually.*

"I love him. I love him so much. Mommy, I'm not going to school today. I'm going to stay with the doggy."

"Ollie will be here when you get back. He's here with Beckett. Can you please go get ready?"

When Posie hesitated, Beckett said, "I'm taking him to the vet this afternoon, and doctor visits scare him. Do you think you could come with me? I think just having you there and loving him will make it easier for him. Will you come?"

Posie nodded solemnly. "I'll help."

"Cool. Thanks."

"Now, go upstairs and get dressed," Coco said.

Posie, for once, did as asked and tore out of the room. "Come on, Ollie. Let's go."

The dog took off after her, nearly wiping out as he made the hard corner out of the kitchen.

"I'll get him groomed when I'm there." Beckett got up and washed his hands at the sink. Pulling a fork out of the drawer, he dug right into the skillet. "I probably should've asked you first if she could come with me. I know you've got a schedule to keep."

"We do, but I like that you made Posie feel important. That was really sweet. You sure you don't have any other kids tucked away at random homes across the globe? Because you're pretty good at this parenting thing." Of course, he'd been six years older than his sister, so he'd probably had some practice.

"Ha. Nope." He brought the skillet to the sink and filled it with water, leaning close to her. "I hope I didn't make you uncomfortable last night. I want to stay here. I want to spend as much time with Posie as possible. I don't want you worrying about me trying to hook up with you. I know why I'm here."

"I don't know whether to be disappointed or relieved." She gazed up at him, her grin fading when the attraction burned between them. She loved the way he looked at her —that stark yearning and need. The answering cry clenched every muscle in her body. It would be so easy to lean in, to wrap her arms around his neck and tip her chin so their mouths could meet. Desire flowed sweet and hot through her. She wanted him. Oh, God, did she want him.

The trampling of dog and little girl feet upstairs broke the tension. She reached across him to dump Posie's uneaten eggs into the disposal, and he stepped aside. "Who am I kidding? I'm definitely more disappointed than relieved. You get me all riled up, Beckett O'Neill. And now I'm going to stop talking. You don't need to hear my ramblings."

His big hands came down on her shoulders. God, the way he looked at her made her heart pound, her blood race.

"I want to hear everything you have to say. So, just keep talking to me, okay?"

She turned to face him. "I really like you, you know that, right?"

"I really like you, too." Even though he kept his hands at his sides, she could feel his gaze caress her cheeks, his thumb stroke her chin. He didn't move an inch closer, yet she could've sworn she felt the warm waft of his breath over her lips.

Yearning rose her from deep within, and those icy blue eyes went flame hot. "I never thought I'd see you again," she said. "I'd resigned myself to the fact that Posie would never have a father." She gave an embarrassed grin. "I've got a whole speech prepared for when she asks, and I have to explain that her mom's a 'ho who got knocked up one night in Vegas."

Finally, he touched her. The moment his fingertips brushed across her cheek, she sagged with relief. "Instead, maybe we could tell her that we got lost, but then we found each other again. That I'm so damn sorry I missed her first steps but can't wait to watch all the ones she takes for the rest of our lives together."

Her whole body tingled, and her breasts felt heavy. "That's a much better story."

His thumb drifted across her mouth, making her tremble from deep within.

"I've never felt anything like this." He sounded awed. "It scares the shit out of me, because it's more than I ever wanted, and I know if I stay here much longer it's going to become something I can't live without."

Her brain ordered her feet to move, to finish cleaning the kitchen and get away from this man who was more dangerous to her than anyone she'd ever known. But the magnetic attraction bound them together. "What exactly is 'this?'" Her voice came out a whisper.

"I don't fucking know."

Water ran through the pipes, so Coco didn't worry about his language. Posie was brushing her teeth.

"That night in Vegas, I remember skimming over all those nameless faces. It was no different from any other club I'd been in. It felt flat. *I* felt flat." He shrugged. "And then I saw you, and it was…"

"Electric."

"Yes. Ripped right down my spine." His thumb stroked gently, languidly.

Her body trembled at the sensation, recalling the same rhythm his tongue had used on her clit, taking his time to bring her to a climax. It had been maddening, but she'd never come that hard in her life. She fantasized about it to this day—the way he didn't rush her to get his own needs met.

"I don't know how to explain it, except to say that, on some level I couldn't understand, I recognized you. And when we talked…it wasn't like the typical getting to know you shit. We dove right in, like we *did* already know each other."

She nodded. It'd been exactly like that.

"It's still there, that crazy connection. Only…"

Deeper…richer.

"…so much more intense." His fingers sifted through the hair at her temple, gliding until he cupped the back of her neck.

Every cell in her body blossomed, opened, as if she were a flower and he were the sun. It was as thrilling as it was terrifying.

I want him more than I've ever wanted anything…but the moment he dumps his dog and his duffle bag in his truck and drives away, he's going to leave a gigantic hole in me.

She could tell from his expression that he saw her fear, because he dialed it down. "It's okay. I get it. Everything's changed, and we have something really fucking important to focus on here. But I like you, Coco Cavanaugh, and every minute I spend with you, I like you more." He leaned in close, giving her a scorching look. "Just so it's clear, *I* want what we had in Vegas. So, if you decide you want it, too…" His nose brushed across her cheek, and he whispered in her ear, "It's your move."

And that was it. Clasping his neck, she brought his mouth to hers and kissed him. That first touch of their tongues hit like a bolt of lightning, practically lifting her off the ground. Her other hand slid into all that silky dark blond hair, and when he wrapped an arm around her back and hauled her to him, her fingers fisted in it.

The kiss turned hot, hungry…carnal. Her toes curled, as she toppled into the rush of desire and lust coursing through her. The desperate, yearning sounds she made in the back of her throat must've done something to him because he turned the kiss even hotter. His palms opened, sliding down her back to grab her ass. When he squeezed, her knees buckled.

Nails clacked down the stairs, and Posie shrieked, "Wait for me, Ollie. *Wait*."

Tearing out of his hold, she dragged the back of her hand across her mouth, her body vibrating with need.

The dog came bounding into the kitchen wearing a hot pink boa around his neck and scrunchies around each leg. "Posie." Her burst of laughter snapped the sexual tension.

Beckett, though…seemed to be having a hard time getting himself under control.

And it was, frankly, one of the most exhilarating moments of her life.

Posie came in with her glittery silver shoes and fairy dress. "Ready, Mommy."

"Are you sure?" Beckett tore his gaze away and looked Posie over carefully. "I feel like something's missing. Oh, I know." He reached into his back pocket and pulled out a slim package.

Posie took it, flipping it over. "What is this?" Ripping it open, she pulled out two pink and purple sparkly bracelets with long tails of ribbons. Her eyes went wide. "You got this for me?"

"I did."

"I love them. I love them so much." She pinched her fingers together to get her hand through one of the elastic bands. "Look, Mommy. Look what I got."

Coco moved closer to help put the bracelets on, but Posie pulled away. "No, Beckett." She handed both bands over to him and held out her wrists.

There was no hiding how touched he was that she wanted him to do it. Stretching one, he slid it on. She immediately went spinning and running around the kitchen, the ribbons fluttering. Ollie barked, his jaw snapping as he tried to nip them.

Posie came back, her eyes shining with joy. "Now, the other one."

He slid on that one, and then stood back, grinning as she danced around the kitchen.

"These are so pretty. Mommy, aren't they pretty?"

"They are."

"I love them." She threw herself at him, wrapping her arms around his legs and hugging him. "Thank you, Beckett."

The unexpected contact made him freeze.

He just stood there, while Posie grinned, holding onto him like a life raft.

Hug her.

So help me God, if you hurt my little girl…

But then, he dropped to a crouch and placed his hands on her shoulders. "You like them?"

She'd never seen him so vulnerable as that moment, eye-to-eye with a five-year-old.

"I love them." She spun in a circle, before gazing up at him. "You're nice."

"Well, thanks." He stood. "You're nice, too."

She whisked away from him, dancing around the room and watching her ribbons flutter. "Can Ollie take me to school?"

"Well, that depends on Beckett's schedule." Coco looked to him. "When do you start coaching?"

"I'll start tomorrow, but it won't matter, because I'll be going to school with you every day while I'm in town."

And with one simple sentence, he snuffed out all her warm, lovely feelings.

While I'm in town.

She needed to type up a banner and print it out.

Enjoy your time with him...*while he's in town.*

Coco reached back to unbuckle Posie's seatbelt. "Have a good day, my lovely. Remember that Grandma's picking you up today."

"Okay, Mommy." Posie dropped down and climbed onto the console. Hanging onto the armrests, she leaned over and kissed Beckett's cheek. "Thank you. I love my fairy bracelets."

He looked dazzled. "You're welcome."

Even after she dashed out of the car and skipped up the walkway, Beckett remained unmoving, as though afraid the kiss would drift away. As she neared her group of friends, Posie turned back to them with a big grin and waved.

"You made her day." Coco checked her mirrors before easing away from the curb.

"Pretty sure she made mine." He lifted his hand to his cheek, in what seemed like an unconscious move. "What's with the whole fairy thing?"

"Ethan, my ex, bought her a costume for Halloween. It came with a book about a little girl who believed she was a fairy. Everyone told her she was wrong. She couldn't be one, because fairies aren't real, but the girl never stopped believing. And then, one day, she sprouted wings. Posie's been waiting to sprout wings ever since."

"That's a terrible book."

"I know, right? But, for some reason, that's the one

that captured her imagination. She asked me to read it to her every night for months."

"I'm all about working hard to turn your dreams into reality, but they have to be humanly possible. What kind of message is that?"

"I'm actually more concerned with the other message he sent. You know, when he left us and never looked back."

"She doesn't mention him."

"You're right. She doesn't." But that didn't mean she'd come out unscathed. "I'm afraid of what she's internalized, and I won't know how she's interpreted him leaving until one day, out of the blue, in some random conversation, she'll say something. And, believe me, it's scary, the stories kids invent to make sense of their worlds."

"Did he live with you?"

"Oh, no. Nothing like that. But since I spend so much time with Posie, he was around her a lot." At the stop sign, she turned to him. "Don't get me wrong. I don't fault him for leaving. He got a great job. He was only twenty-five, and he wasn't ready for marriage and kids. And I wasn't about to uproot our lives for some guy I was casually dating, so I'm not angry with him. I'm angry at myself for not protecting Posie better."

"I'm not sure how much you can protect her from relationships, though. I had this coach once who said his job wasn't to change the world so that I could fit into it better, but for him to give me the skills to live in it. That stuck with me."

That was actually a really good way to look at parenting. "I like that."

"Of course, I'm talking out my ass right now. What do I know about kids?"

"You're doing a good job with yours."

When she looked over at him, she found her words had landed on a bruise. "I'm glad. I need to hear that."

"I know. That's why I keep telling you."

His features tightened. "I don't want to fuck this up."

"Hey, we're doing this together, remember?"

Holding her gaze with affection and warmth, he looked relieved. But then his phone buzzed, and he read the screen. "Excellent." He glanced over at her. "You think you could drop me off at Good Times Outfitters?"

"Sure. What's up?"

"I left a message with them this morning, see if I could rent a mountain bike. It's a perfect day, and I want to check out the area." He wagged his phone. "They just got back to me."

"That sounds like so much fun." When Posie got a little older, she'd do things like that with her. Calamity was a town for outdoor activities—they had a bike path connecting it to Jackson and circling the lake.

"What's that expression for?" he asked.

"What expression?"

"The one like…" With a mournful look, he let out a long-suffering sigh. "That one."

"That's not what I was doing." She grinned because, okay, maybe she had been. "I was just thinking about how long it's been since I've done stuff like that. Probably not since high school. When Posie's older, I'll get her a good bike. There's a lot to do here in the summer."

"Why wait? Come with me now."

"Oh, God, no. I've got too much to do."

"Yeah? Well, I'm here for the summer. Use me. I'm a jack of all trades."

"You're coaching, remember?" Could she make time to

do something fun? Just this once? She thought about her to-do list. She was a delayed gratification kind of person. She saved the best food on her plate for last, and she didn't sit down with her tea until the dishwasher was running, the toys picked up, and the bathroom sink wiped clean of toothpaste.

Thinking about it, she was absolutely on top of her business and the festival. They'd had a little snafu with the license, but she'd handled that yesterday. She'd okayed the banners last night. The extra staff she'd hired to get her through the summer was handling production and packaging. "Actually, I think I've got everything under control at the moment."

"So you're coming with me?"

Could she really do that? Play hooky when the festival was just weeks away? "I'd better not. But why don't we plan something for this weekend? With Posie." She turned onto Crescent Street and pulled in front of the huge sporting goods store. "You need me to do anything with Ollie while you're gone?"

"I'm going to ride home first, knock out a few emails, before I hit the trails."

"Sounds good. Have fun."

"Oh, before I go..." He pulled something out of his back pocket, and then held his fist out to her.

When she opened her hand, a ring dropped into it. The gorgeous blue-green stone practically glowed in the soft morning light. "What is this?"

"I noticed you don't wear jewelry. I'm sure it's because you work in a kitchen, and I probably shouldn't have gotten it, but as I was leaving town, they were setting up an arts and craft festival. I saw the sign for Colorado gemstones, and I pulled over. Just to see what they had. I

201

saw the aquamarine and thought…" His cheeks turned pink. "Well, it's your birthstone."

How did he even know that? "This is stunning." She was so completely touched she didn't even know what to say. "They're usually a light blue—I've never seen one this…rich with color."

"Yeah, that's what drew me to it."

It fit perfectly on her ring finger. Raising her hand, she held it in the sunlight. "Thank you, Beckett. I absolutely love it."

"You're welcome." He tipped his head toward the window. "Okay, so, I'm going to grab my bike." And then he was gone.

Don't go. She watched his easy stride, that sexy as hell bubble butt. She remembered how those hard globes had felt in her hands, how his cheeks had tightened with each powerful thrust.

Longing ripped through her.

He tossed a grin at her over his shoulder. He'd caught her gawking, and she laughed.

"You know you want to," he called.

She really did. Another glance at her ring—*how sweet and thoughtful*—had her buzzing with joy.

She wanted to be with him…*so do it.*

When did she ever take time for herself? And she couldn't think of a better reason than spending time with him.

It took a couple hours to cruise the bike path that zig zagged across a sage meadow and wound its way up the mountain. Coco hadn't ridden in so long, she'd forgotten the thrill of dips on the trail, the stretches of flat road rounding a cliff's edge, and the air…the incredible pine-scented, snow-chilled air.

At noon, they'd stopped for lunch. Now, stretched out on a picnic blanket, hidden in the forest a good half mile off the trail, Coco enjoyed the dappled sunshine filtering through towering trees. "My thighs are going to ache tomorrow, aren't they?" She popped a grape into her mouth.

"Probably. But was it worth it?"

"Totally. I have to make more time for exercise in my schedule. After the festival, I'll do that."

"When I met you, you were going to run a daycare center in town." One arm bent, his hand supporting his head, he gazed up at the trees. "And I remember thinking, *That's not her. You've got too much…flair for that.*"

"Flair, huh?"

"Ever since I found out about Posie, all I can think about is what happened to you. How your life swerved so abruptly." He reached for her hand, lazily entwining their fingers. "While I was out having a good time, you were rocking a baby to sleep. I hate that you did it alone." He brought their joined hands to his mouth and kissed the back of hers.

"I mean, of course I would've liked having someone to go through it with me, but it's made me and Posie really close." She reached for another grape. "I thought about you a lot over the years."

"Where the hell is the bastard who did this to me?"

She laughed. "Not at all. I just hated that you were missing out on something so important. With every milestone, I'd go back to searching for you, but I had nothing to go on. I had all these fantasies about how I'd finally find you."

"Like what?"

"Like I'd be on the cover of the *New York Times* for selling my amazing, fanciful chocolates, and you'd be in your Brooklyn brownstone eating breakfast. You'd be reading the paper, drinking your cappuccino, and your wife would be like, 'Oh, chocolate. Let me see that.' And she'd snatch the paper out of your hand, and you'd get up and chase her around the kitchen, the two of you beautiful people laughing—"

"That's pretty detailed."

"Hey, don't judge. There are a lot of sleepless nights with babies."

"So, while you smell like spit-up and have dark circles under your eyes, I'm living the glamorous life in New York City?"

Coco laughed out loud. "Yep. But I loved the idea of being a world-famous chocolatier by the time you came to find me."

Letting go of her hand, he hiked up on an elbow and raised his eyebrow. "I'll bet my wife wasn't nearly as pretty as you. Bet she wasn't as accomplished either. And I'll bet she didn't put sprinkles in oatmeal."

The breeze rustled the branches, scenting the air with pine and dusty earth. Her body went warm with a rush of sensation. "I love the way you see me."

"I think you're fucking amazing. But finish. So, I'm chasing my wife around the kitchen…"

"And then you catch her and kiss her—"

"Hang on. Do I kiss her like this…" He leaned over, blocking the sunlight, and pressed a chaste kiss on her mouth. "Or this…" He moved closer, so he could kiss her softly, sweetly, and then he swept his tongue along the seam of her lips. When he pulled back, he brushed the hair off her forehead. "If she's anything like you, I'm thinking it was more like this…" Licking into her mouth, he coaxed her tongue into play.

Sensation burst inside her body. He smelled so good—so clean and masculine—and he tasted sweet, like grapes. She loved the way he kissed—soft, slow, like he was taking his time to explore her, *savor* her. He just felt so good.

Wrapping her arms around his neck, she drew him closer, needing more. She scraped her fingernails along his scalp, growing restless for the press of his body. When she couldn't take another second, she tugged him, making him fall on top of her.

He wasted no time situating himself between her legs, reaching under her ass and lifting her so his hard erection pressed against her belly. *God.* He groaned deep in his throat, rocking his hips, like he needed to fuck her but was restraining himself. For her.

Because he'd told her it was her move.

Respect. She liked that.

Everything about this man drove her wild. A simple kiss turned into a flash fire of raw, burning lust.

As his tongue stroked into her mouth and his cock rocked over her clit, he awakened the sexual woman who'd suppressed her desires in order to be the best mother she could be. Her back arched, her hips lifted. *Touch me.*

He must've heard her silent plea, because he skimmed his hand down her chest, shoved up her shirt and peeled back the cup of her lacy bra, exposing her breast to the cool June air. "Did you imagine me sucking my beautiful wife's tits?"

She yanked her shirt up and over her head, pulling it off. "Mm hm." She could barely wrest the words from her throat. "She liked it, too."

"Funny because, I remember how much *you* liked it when I did this…" His mouth covered her nipple, and his tongue swirled around it, teasing it into a hard, tight bead.

Erotic desire flowed through her, hot and electric. "God, Beckett."

He growled deep in his throat, as he plumped her breast and sucked hard enough to make her cry out.

It felt delicious, the press of his hard body, the lavish attention he gave her nipple. Reaching underneath, she unclasped her bra and tugged down the straps.

He pulled it off and tossed it aside. Pressing kisses down her stomach, he licked a circle around her navel. "What about her pussy? Did you imagine me licking it?"

"So many times." She grabbed a fistful of his hair to make him look her in the eyes. "Except it was mine."

"Fuck, yeah, Coco." Unbuttoning her shorts, he tapped her hip, signaling her to lift up, so he could pull them off along with her panties. Sitting back on his heels, he spread her legs, eyeing her with pure hunger. "You're so hot." He lunged forward, hands cupping her breasts, pushing them together. "You've got the prettiest tits I've ever seen." He gave each nipple a lick, before kissing her with lust and hunger. "One day, I'm gonna fuck them."

"Yes." She shifted restlessly beneath him, the pulse between her legs making her crazy with need.

And then he stretched out on his belly, hands sliding under her ass and lifting her, like he was about to indulge in a feast. And he licked the whole hidden length of her.

She cried out, tipping her head back and closing her eyes to seal in the tumult of sensations.

As with everything he did, he took his time, like he was just tongue-kissing her in the kitchen on a lazy Sunday morning. Her body turned molten, her fingertips tingling. And just when she was starting to grow restless, when need turned into desperation, he swiped his tongue over her clit. Hitching up her knees, she clutched handfuls of his hair, holding him right up against her.

"Beckett...oh, God, Beckett." Desire streamed through her, all creamy and hot.

Reaching up, he palmed her breast, squeezing it and plucking her nipple, igniting the path between her two pleasure centers until she burst into flames. The tightening, the quickening came way too soon, but he sensed it, and he licked faster, harder, one big hand caressing her breast, the other gripping her ass, and her orgasm just roared through her, incinerating any shred of rational thought. "*Beckett*." She sailed through a weightless space of pure euphoria.

He read her so beautifully, easing off, slowing down his licks until they turned languorous...and she let out a final sigh of pure relief.

Rolling onto his back, he rested a hand under his head, the other on his chest. "My wife's fucking hot."

"You sure know how to keep her happy. She's a lucky woman." A breeze stirred the branches above, fluttering across her skin like a silk scarf. "I might fall asleep right now."

"Might want to put on your clothes first. Would suck if those trail riders saw you naked like that."

"What?" She jackknifed up, looking around the forest. "Are you serious?"

He chuckled. "Of course not. You think I'd expose you like that if I thought anyone would be riding through?"

She smacked him. "You scared the crap out of me."

All the humor faded, as his gaze locked onto her breasts. Hungry, hot.

God, she loved the way he wanted her. "So, no one's around?"

He grasped his erection, gave it a squeeze. "Hell, no. We're nowhere near the trail."

"Then why are you still wearing pants?"

Chapter Twelve

After coaching the afternoon trampoline session, Beckett popped into the office, where Fin, Brodie, and Will were hanging out. "Got a second?"

"You bet." Brodie waved him in.

"Got a lot of guys wanting private sessions with you," Fin said from behind a desk.

"I'm happy to do it." There was an empty chair, but he leaned against the wall. "Wasn't sure how it would go since I've never coached before." He liked it a lot more than he'd expected. When he'd retired, he'd been done. Sure, he still boarded for pleasure, but getting near a gym, talking about tricks? He hadn't been able to stand the thought of it.

But now, he kind of liked it. He'd had this one kid who didn't get it. Kept landing heavy on his tail and just sliding out on his ass. And Beckett had pulled him aside and talked to him about rotating from his core, not his arms and shoulders. He'd worked with him privately until the kid had a lightbulb moment, and it had felt damn good seeing him finally stomp his landing.

"I watched. You do something not enough coaches do." Sitting on the floor, Will handed his four-year-old half-sister a big, red Lego block. "You break it down, so they understand the mechanics of a trick."

"That's what worked for me," Brodie said. "Our dad hired a coach for us. These guys got it right away." He tipped a chin at his brothers. "They were tearing up the slope, doing crazy-ass tricks, but I wasn't getting it at all. I was pissed and—"

"Temperamental," Will said.

"He was a total diva," Fin said.

"Not even close." Brodie looked offended. "I handled it in a very manly way." His brothers cracked up. "Anyhow, Coach pulled me aside and gave me the physics behind boarding. He explained velocity and centripetal acceleration, and once I understood about my speed, the height of the walls, the weight on my body as I accelerated, it all clicked in my head. That's when I became way better than any of these assholes could ever hope to be."

"You do realize there's a little kid in the room, right?" Will said.

Ruby's head popped up. "I'm not little. I'm a big girl."

"You're *my* big girl," Will said.

For all the years he'd known Will, he'd never seen even a hint of softness. Tall, solid muscle, he took his sport seriously—which explained his Olympic gold medal. So, to see him on the floor, his voice saturated with affection for his sister? Didn't compute. "How old are you, Ruby?" Beckett asked.

The dark-haired little girl glanced up at him. "I'm this many." She held up four fingers, before turning back to her blocks.

He wanted to say, *I have a five-year-old.* But he couldn't do that. Not yet.

Not until he figured out how to fit her into his life. And he just wasn't there yet. He'd talked to his partners, and they didn't like the idea of him hiring someone for the summer—not during this critical first year.

But he wasn't walking away from Posie, so he had to figure out something they could all agree on. And it just felt like he couldn't make anyone happy. His partners wouldn't budge off the original business plan, and Coco wouldn't accept him into their lives unless he found a way to be physically present more than a couple times a year.

The thing is…this is my life.

It might not be a conventional one, but that's just the way it is. Coco might have to change her thinking a little.

He could be a father from the road. He could FaceTime, text…

Text a five-year-old? That was exactly how he'd kept in touch with Ari.

Had it messed her up? Was that why she'd come to idolize him? Because he was elusive and only gave her tiny pieces of himself here and there?

He could see that. Being six years older and in such a different phase of life, he'd been more of a rock star to her than a brother.

That'll mess Posie up, and that's exactly what Coco's talking about. That's why she doesn't want to tell her I'm her father.

I get it, but then…what the hell do I do?

"How long do you think you'll be in town?" Fin asked, pulling him from his thoughts.

"I've got a friend covering some of my trips this

summer, so I'm good until the end of August. I can coach until then."

"Excellent." Fin grinned "Anytime you get the itch to coach, come on back. You're welcome anytime."

"Thanks." He gave Brodie a chin nod. "Anyhow, I just wanted to let you know there's not going to be a wedding."

"Yeah, I figured. I'll let Diane know. She's got some other possibilities, so we're good."

"Does this have anything to do with Coco Cavanaugh?" Will asked.

Surprise had him pushing off the wall. "Where did *that* come from?"

"I saw you biking with her yesterday." Will handed another block to Ruby. "Ruby and I were out riding. You guys flew right past us. Looked pretty happy."

"Nah. I'm just staying in her guest house."

"How do you know her?" Fin asked.

"She was supposed to make the chocolates for the wedding." Even saying the word *wedding* out loud now sounded wrong. He never should've gone along with that plan.

"You just met her, and she let you live in her backyard?" Fin looked to his brothers for confirmation. "She's got a kid."

Well, hell. He'd stepped into that one.

"You and Willow good?" Brodie asked.

Fuck. He grew hot and itchy. "We ended things."

All three stared at him.

They weren't stupid. It had taken them point-three seconds to piece things together. "I lie for shit."

"You really do, man," Brodie said.

Fin smiled. "Don't worry. That's a good quality."

"You don't have to tell us anything," Will said. "It's none of our business."

Brodie gave him a concerned look. "On the other hand, between the three of us, we've probably been there."

Beckett let out a bitter laugh. "Not this."

"Look." Ruby jumped to her feet. "I finished, Wheel." She grinned wide, exposing her missing front tooth, and flung herself into his arms.

"You sure did." Will hugged her, his eyelids flickering closed, and for just a moment, he had an expression of bliss.

Ruby pulled away and tapped Brodie's knee. "Can I have some paper, Uncle Bwodie? I'm going to make baby Lou a picture."

"Yeah, of course. Hang on." Brodie got up and headed over to the printer. Pulling out some clean white sheets, he passed them over.

"Thank you."

"You're welcome, doll."

"Here." Digging into his top drawer, Fin pulled out some pens and highlighters.

"I'm going to dwaw on Maisy's desk." As soon as she left the room, Beckett could hear her talking to the coach in the next office.

"She's cute." It was hard to believe she was only a year younger than Posie. *A lot happens in that year.* "I still can't imagine you as a dad." Of all the brothers, Beckett had spent the most time with Will, thanks to their competition schedules.

"She's our dad's, actually," Will said.

"Yeah, I'd heard she was a half-sister. But you're pretty much raising her?"

"I am." Will got up and sat in the chair. "Our dad

passed away about two months after she was born. He didn't even know about her."

"She showed up on our doorstep when she was two," Brodie said. "We didn't know what to do with her."

"It was a whole different world back then," Fin said. "None of us had kids, I was still trying to get back together with Callie. Marriage, family, wasn't on anyone's radars."

"So, we were going to take turns raising her, but—" Will started.

Brodie interrupted him. "Not our smartest plan. But what did we know?"

"Turns out, we didn't have to make any decisions." Fin smiled at Will. "She chose him."

"What does that mean?" Beckett asked. "Chose him?"

"For some reason we still can't figure out, she latched onto this guy like a spider monkey." Brodie smacked his older brother on the back of the head.

"She took one look at the Three Stooges over here and clung to me like I was her last hope." Will grinned. "Can you blame her?"

The brothers laughed.

"The rotation plan was my idiot idea." Color rushed into Will's cheeks, clearly not proud of it. "It took me awhile to figure out she needed more than a roof over her head, three squares, and an education. She needed—"

"*Deserved*," Brodie said.

Will looked chastised. "She deserves a dad. A family. And, since I was first in the rotation, I lucked out."

"Lucked out?" Even though he stopped himself from saying, *But you gave up your life for her,* he could tell from the way Will's gaze sharpened, that he'd heard it. Which meant he had to clarify. "You guys were the rebels, you

214

didn't follow rules. Now, you're stuck..." He cringed. "I mean—"

"I know what you mean." Will nodded. "I used to see commitment as a burden, too. I get it. But think about it. The only purpose I had before I met my girls was winning the next competition, snagging a gold medal. My life had spikes of happiness, but the in-between times? I spent a lot of time alone." He looked away. "I remember going out for a run late one night, stopping at the Ridge, and looking out over the valley. And I thought, Is this it? Is this all there is?"

Beckett went rigid. He'd had that thought countless times himself, but he'd always chased it away with another adventure. Over the years, though, his friends had married, had kids, leaving it harder and harder for him to find people to join him.

A chill skittered across his skin.

Was that what Willow was? Someone to join him on his travels so he wasn't so alone?

Yes.

Hardcore yes.

"Ruby and Delilah...they're my purpose. Winning a gold medal doesn't compare to reading a book to Ruby before bed, to sleeping beside Delilah every night. It doesn't come close to how it feels when Ruby's crying about something, and I get to help her work it out. Or when Delilah and I are arguing, and it feels like there's no way to resolve whatever the issue is, but we love each other enough to fight through to the end, to a solution that works for both of us."

This conversation was a hundred times deeper than anything he and Will had ever had before, and it made him aware of how he'd skimmed over life, never wanting to dig in.

"When you compare living to win a medal versus living to make the world a safe and beautiful place for my family?" Will shook his head. *No comparison.* "I am one hundred percent responsible for guiding Ruby into becoming a competent, stable adult, and there's no purpose on this earth I'm more honored to have."

The room went dead quiet, the only sound the quiet murmuring of female voices from next door.

"Well, shit, man." Fin got up and swung around his desk. "That was beautiful, big brother."

Will stood up and the brothers hugged.

An outsider, Beckett watched them, his heart pounding, his blood thrashing in his ears. "Posie's mine." He blurted it out so awkwardly, all three guys went rigid. "I'm not supposed to say anything." But he had to talk to somebody, and he knew he could trust these guys.

They stood there, watching him, waiting for him to say more.

"I just found out." He looked to Brodie. "I walked in the door to meet with Diane and the chocolate lady, and there she was. The woman I'd met in Vegas six years ago. We had...one night." One incredible, unforgettable night. "I never thought I'd see her again."

Fin blew out a breath. "Damn."

Going weak, Beckett sat on the edge of the desk. "I was supposed to be in Thailand the next day, but I couldn't go." He looked at them helplessly. "There was no way I could get on that plane. So, I'm here, trying to figure out what to do. How can I fit her into my life?" The guys all gave him identical frowns. The one thing about the Bowies, they were a loyal family. Which meant they didn't understand how he wouldn't drop everything and become a dad. "I never wanted kids. Never wanted to be married. It's…it's not for me."

"Our dad liked to say it's easy to be a good man in a good situation. But the real test of character comes when we're in a tough one." Will faced him squarely. "What kind of man do you want to be?"

"The kind that has no kids." He said it with a laugh, but he winced because not only did it sound awful, but he didn't mean it.

"If that's how you feel, then you should leave now," Brodie said. "Go to Thailand, or whatever's next on your itinerary, and let Coco and Posie get on with it."

"It's gonna suck," Fin said, "If they get used to you being around, and then you take off."

"But my job has me on the road—"

"You travel a lot. We're real clear on that." Will eyed him with his formidable, hard-jawed expression.

He resorted to humor by pointing at Will's face. "I'll bet that's how your dad got you to clean your rooms and stop wrestling in the living room."

"It is," Fin said. "That's exactly how he looked at us."

"Made us shit our pants," Brodie said.

"I'm sure." But he needed to talk this through. "Look, I've thought about leaving. I probably should. I know I can't just send postcards from the road, but I can't do it. I don't want to hurt them, but I can't leave."

"You said you've got a friend covering for you this summer?" Brodie said.

"Right now, it's Willow."

"Can she buy out your share in the business?" Fin asked.

"I'm not giving it up. That's not going to happen. It's

taken me six years to get this app launched, and it's finally starting to take off. I'm not walking away. I shouldn't have to give up my career. There has to be some kind of compromise. I'm just not seeing it right now."

All three stared at him, and he grew too warm, uncomfortable, like someone had starched his clothes. "You think I'm an asshole. Maybe I am. But what am I supposed to do? Move to Calamity, buy a house...wear a suit and go to my job at the bank?"

Will shook his head. "Look, I'm not going to tell you what to do—"

"Yes, he is." Brodie and Fin spoke in unison, cracking themselves up.

"Because..." Cutting them off, Will gave them withering looks. "You already know what to do. It's why you're still here. You're a father. And if you leave now, you'll become the kind of dad that shows up once a year on her birthday, *if* she's lucky and it doesn't interfere with your plans. Distance is going to kill the connection you're building."

"You're telling me I have to give up my livelihood. That's what you're saying. But I worked my ass off for this. I'm not walking away."

"Let me ask you something." Will tipped his chin. "You go back on the road, and then a year from now—or two...five—how're you going to feel knowing you've got a daughter out here, living her life, growing up without you?"

"Like shit. But I'm not exactly father material."

"Like I was?" Will said. "Because trust me when I tell you, I was awful. I treated Ruby like I was her coach."

"Hang on," Fin said. "What's that mean, you're not 'father material'?"

"My family's a mess. I haven't talked to my mom in seventeen years, my dad was barely around...I basically grew up in boarding school. What the fuck do I know about family? About kids?" He was getting all worked up, because the more he thought about it, the clearer it was he had no business being Posie's father.

"Does it matter whether you know how to be a dad?" Brodie asked. "When you already are one?"

The room went silent.

There was only one answer to that question. "No."

This is why everyone likes the Bowie brothers. They might keep to themselves, but people admired their loyalty, their closeness. They were smart, honest, and real. They cared.

And no one was judging him or calling him an asshole.

They were letting him get where he needed to be on his own, and he appreciated that more than he could say. "I'm not going to bail on her. I'm here to figure it all out. But I can't give up my business."

"Wheel?" Ruby called. A moment later, she appeared in the doorway, a streak of yellow highlighter across her cheek. "Maisy has cookies, and I want one. She says I have to ask you, but I told her I don't have to ask you 'cause I'm hungry. So, I'm going to have a cookie. She says I have to tell you."

"Thanks for letting me know, sweet pea. Enjoy that *one* cookie."

The woman in the office next door chuckled. "Loud and clear, Will. Loud and clear."

Will got up. "Okay, I've got to get my girl home. It's time for lunch." He shook Beckett's hand. "I've been there. I had the same doubts and worries." He broke into a big grin that transformed his rugged features. "And look at me now. It all works out. You don't have to make all the big decisions today. You've got time."

When he reached the door, Will turned back around. "Also, don't be a dick. She's your daughter. Make the right choices."

Willow fucked up.

No, I did. I passed my job off to her.

Not cool.

She'd crapped out on the experience. She'd walked across the fourteen-hundred-foot SkyBridge in Sochi, Russia, but she hadn't done the six-hundred-eighty-foot bungee jump or the swing.

And that's the content my followers expected. Not to mention, the experience he'd arranged with his contact at the Federal Agency for Tourism. His partners had reamed him out for letting "Willow the fuckin' wanderer represent our brand."

Fuck. She'd jumped with him before…just never from that height.

But he got it. Walking across a bridge didn't excite their demographic—thrill seekers.

He couldn't argue with his partners. He could only find a solution. And he had.

It's a good one. Now, he just had to hope they signed off on it.

Here goes. At the scheduled time, he hit the call button.

"Chris here."

"Dave."

"Hey, guys. Okay, so I've talked to Willow."

"How'd she take it?" Chris said.

He sighed. "Not well. She didn't appreciate being 'fired' from a job she'd only done as a favor to me."

"Then, she shouldn't have taken it," Chris said.

"The problem is bigger than her not jumping," Dave said. "It's the fact that we lost everyone who checked us out at that moment. They're not coming back. They've dismissed us. We're too lightweight for them."

"I'm not going to argue with you." She *had* done damage, posting the kind of content she'd put on her own page. "But it's only one screw-up, and I've got—"

"It's not just 'one screw-up,'" Chris said. "We've been promoting SkyBridge for a while. That's a once-in-a-lifetime trip for some people. And *our* subscribers have their wallets out, they're ready to book a flight to Russia. When we show a pretty woman taking selfies on it instead, it kills our brand. They take their credit cards to another app and don't come back."

He knew that. *Fuck. Get to the point.* "You're right. And that's why this experience with Willow crystallized everything for me. Look, my situation's changed. I can't travel three hundred days a year."

His partners went quiet—not a good sign. He needed to get his plan out, reassure them. "I'm still going to travel, but I'm hiring someone to be my pinch hitter. You guys know Jimmy, right?"

"Of course," Chris said. "Good guy."

"Jimmy Wolfe, the snowboarder?" Dave asked. "Isn't he still competing?"

"Yeah, he is. Which is why it works out well for me because he's not looking to do this full-time." *Especially good since he doesn't compete in the summer.* "He can cover me all the way up to September. And he's a mad man.

He'll do anything." *Unlike Willow.* Not that he blamed her. "I'll still handle the relationships and source the activities, of course, so it should be smooth sailing from here on in."

"Look, we get that you're in a bind," Dave said. "But, man, this is...it's all I have. I put everything in it. I sold my mom's house, you know?"

He did know, and he'd warned him against it. Beckett had used some of his savings from endorsements and wins. He would never have moved his parent out of the family home to a condo.

Shit. If they didn't agree to his plan, they had the right to buy him out of his share. "Guys, I'm not going to fail. You know what this business means to me."

"Yeah, we do," Chris said. "Just don't make us do something none of us wants to see happen."

He didn't need the reminder that, through nonperformance, he could forfeit the rights to his own company. "Not going to happen."

"Okay, we'll give Jimmy a shot," Dave said. "But you've got to stay on top of him."

"I absolutely will." Relief slammed him. He'd found a way to balance the two things that meant the most to him.

Everything will work out.

Beckett paced to the window, holding the phone to his chest, waiting for his dad to answer. He lifted the curtain, looking out at the neatly mown lawn. How did Coco do it? Not only did she keep the house from being a total disaster, as Posie tore from one activity to another, acting like each thing she did was more exciting than the next, but she ran a successful business, and she always gave Posie her full attention.

Made him feel like an asshole for making such a big deal about his career, as if he couldn't handle more than one thing at a time. Coco multitasked like a boss.

"Beckett?" His dad sounded rushed.

"Hey, Dad. You all right?"

"Storm knocked down my Copper Beech. Just planted the damn thing two years ago. Anyhow, Marcia saw your name on the screen and ran out to get me. She knows I don't want to miss your rare calls."

"Ha. I call." It was the first time it bothered him that Marcia didn't feel comfortable enough to answer when she saw Beckett's name on the screen.

That's not on Marcia. That's on me.

Because, in all honesty, what've I done to get to know her?

"Well, this is the second call in two weeks, so we figured it must be important."

He let the curtain fall. "Yeah. It is." But first… "How's Marcia?"

"She's good." His dad sounded hesitant. Like, *why are you asking?*

Which was fair. He'd never asked about her before. Pacing across the small living area, he glanced at the rocks lined up on his dresser. Posie had painted them for him. Picking one up, he held the light weight in his palm, rubbed a thumb over the smooth surface. "I've got a situation." He cringed, remembering Coco's reaction when Willow had referred to Posie that way. "First, Willow and I broke up."

"Okay. You don't sound too choked up about it."

"Well, that's because I led with the smaller situation."

After a beat, his dad asked, "What's going on?"

"I've got a kid." Jesus, that sounded so cold. "I mean a child. I'm a father."

"I'm at a loss here. You're going to have to give me some more details. We're not talking about Willow right now, are we?"

"No, Dad." And then it hit him. "Wait, you think I'd dump Willow if she was pregnant?"

"Well, it's no secret you don't want kids."

"I would never…" *This isn't the point.* "This has nothing to do with Willow. I met a woman in Vegas six years ago…we spent a night together. I haven't seen her since, until last week, when I came to Calamity to meet the wedding planner. She makes chocolate, Dad. And… she's got a daughter." Everything in him softened when he said the word. "My daughter."

"I'm having a hard time wrapping my head around this."

"Well, it's real. We did a paternity test. Not that I doubted it." *She looks so much like Ari.* But he didn't want to say that. Didn't want to hurt his dad. "Coco's been raising her alone for five years."

"That's a lot to deal with. How're you handling it?" his dad asked.

"She's incredible. She thinks she's a fairy, so she's always wearing sparkly shoes and dresses and hairbands. She's stubborn and funny, and you can't believe how sweet she is. She tells me she's hungry, and then she eats one bite before racing off to do something else."

His dad went quiet.

"Dad? You there?"

"Yeah, yeah. I'm here. I'm just…surprised. You've really gotten to know her."

"I'm staying in Calamity this summer."

"What about your business?"

"I've hired someone to handle the trips I've got scheduled for the next several weeks."

His dad exhaled into the receiver. "Who-ee."

"Yep." He'd been listening carefully to make sure this conversation didn't bring up ghosts for his dad. Did his quietness mean something? Or was he just taking it all in?

Beckett collapsed onto the bed, bunching the pillows behind him. Seeing him settled, Ollie got up from his sprawl and curled up beside him, his rump pressing against Beckett's thighs. He ran his fingers through the dog's soft fur, the sharp bones reminding him how damn glad he was he'd gone back to Boulder.

"You got a picture?"

"Yeah, sure. Hang on." Beckett brought up the photo app and scrolled through the shots he'd taken, before choosing two of the best. *Wait, maybe that one, too.* "Okay, sent you three."

His dad sucked in a breath. "She looks so much like Ari."

Relief flooded him. His dad sounded okay. Not devastated. "Yeah, she does." They never talked about her. He understood why, of course, but he was so damn glad his dad had opened that door. "She's so much like Ari, you wouldn't believe it. She's got the same hair, same blue eyes…and that big personality."

"Is it hard for you?"

"Not at all. Posie's so much her own person, I don't really see Ari when I'm with her."

"So, I'm a granddad." He sounded a little in awe. "Wasn't expecting that."

In the background, he heard Marcia shout, "We're

grandparents? *What?* I'm a grandma? When can we meet her?"

"Marcia wants to know if we can come visit. Let me know if it's too soon."

"Is that going to be tough for you?"

"Ah, you know. It's always going to hurt. It's still a sock in the gut every time I think of her, even after all these years. The loss doesn't ever go away. But Marcia makes me talk about her, and it does me some good. Used to be, I'd feel the punch and then shut it down. But Marcia makes me tell her stories, and it helps a lot. Now, when I think about my little girl, I smile. She was beautiful, happy. It helps to remember." His dad went quiet, as his wife spoke to him. "Marcia wants to know her name."

"Posie. Posie Cavanaugh."

His dad repeated it, and Marcia said, "Posie? What a cute name."

A muffled sound came, and Beckett knew his dad and Marcia were talking. And then he came back on the line. "We'd like to meet her. When you're ready."

"Yeah, sure. I'd like that." A soft knock on the door had him getting up. Ollie grumbled but readjusted himself. "Hey, Dad, I've got to go. There's someone at the door."

"Oh, sure. Drop that kind of news and then take off."

He smiled. "I'll call you later." Tossing the phone on the bed, he hurried to the door. That dark, tousled hair, the jean shorts and cherry-covered tank top turned him the fuck on. He opened it, trying to get a hold of himself. "Hey. Everything all right?"

"Yeah, sure." She glanced to the house, where she'd left the back door wide open. "We're going to my parent's house for dinner tonight."

"Okay." Oh, she meant she wasn't cooking. "No problem. I can walk into town and grab something."

"No, it's…actually, my parents invited you. I know it might be awkward, so you don't have to come if you don't want to."

"Why wouldn't I want to?"

"Because…what could be more *family* than the three of us piling into a car and going to my parent's house for dinner? I don't want you to feel pressure, but they want to get to know you better."

"I'm living in your backyard and spending time with their granddaughter. I get it, and I don't mind."

Relief relaxed her features. "Oh, good. Okay, well, I have to get back, but if you can be ready in twenty minutes, that would be great."

"Sure…I just have to tell you something."

At his tone, concern tightened her features.

"I told the Bowies. I know you don't want me to tell anyone yet, but it just came out. And…I don't know if you know this, but Will's raising his half-sister. Finding out about her blindsided him, too, so—"

"Beckett. I didn't want you to do that. What if, at the end of summer, you decide it's just not for you? You'll go back to your life like nothing happened, but guess what? This is a small town, and one day she's going to find out that her biological dad is friends with the Bowies, that he lived here one summer and then left. That is not all right."

"It *is* for me. I'm not Keith, I'm not Ethan, and I'm not going to leave town and forget about her."

"It's too soon. I'm not ready for this. Not yet. God, I told my parents, you told the Bowies…it's already spreading. Once it's out, it can't be controlled."

"Coco…stop. Listen to me." He reached for her,

cupping her elbows and looking into her eyes. "I'm her father, and I'm in her life to stay. I want her to know who I am. I'm ready for that." Her eyes reflected his own surprise. He hadn't known it until he said it, but he was ready.

And he understood the consequence. Once Posie knew, it was done.

He was committed. There was no turning back.

And while he waited for the flare of fear…it didn't come.

But he saw her doubt, and while he understood it, it stung. *She doesn't trust me.* "We don't have to tell her tonight or tomorrow. We'll do it when you feel comfortable, but you need to know that I'm ready. I'm her father—"

"But do you want to be her *dad*? Do you know what I'm saying? A dad reads to her at night, helps her with her homework, goes to her recitals."

The picture she painted made him tighten up, like a neckline that pulled around his windpipe, cutting off his ability to breathe. "You have great parents, I get that, but not every family's as conventional as yours. I'm never going to be like your dad. He retired and got to stay home with you guys. My job is never going to be nine-to-five." And just like that he shed the image of himself in a suit, heading off to his job at the bank every day. *Thank Christ.* "That's just not who I am." And it gave him breathing room. "But it doesn't mean I won't be here for Posie. And you."

"You're right. You're absolutely right. I've got some idea in my head, and you don't have to fit it. I'm sorry. I'm just so scared of hurting her."

"And that's what makes you such a great mom. But I

have to find my own way to be her dad. Can you let me do that? Because I very much want to." He'd thought he had to do it on her terms, but now the anxiety dropped away when he understood he could do it on his.

"Let me think about it, okay? I have to get back inside, but be ready to leave in fifteen minutes."

"Mommy?" Posie stood in the doorway with a guilty expression.

Coco's eyes narrowed. "What happened?"

Chapter Thirteen

"It spilled." Posie's lower lip wobbled.

"What spilled?" Coco was already on the move.

"The paint." The little girl looked so fragile and frightened.

He wanted to scoop her up and tell her he'd fix whatever was wrong, but this was none of his business.

"On what?"

"On *everything*." Posie collapsed to the floor of the mudroom in a ruckus of tears.

Ollie tried to bolt out the door, but Beckett blocked him. "Hang on, buddy. Let me see what's going on over there."

Where Coco dashed across the lawn and picked up her daughter, Beckett went straight for the mess. He found red paint splattered and smeared across the kitchen.

Jesus, where did he start?

Anything in the kitchen could be mopped up, but the living room—the upholstery and rugs—could stain. Following the trail, he found the coffee table draped in a plastic tablecloth and covered in small plastic jars of paint in primary colors.

Each tub couldn't have held more than an ounce, so he had no idea where all the paint came from. Gathering the corners of the cloth, he bagged the whole mess and dropped it into the kitchen sink.

Then, he followed the other trail to the laundry room. Thick red paint dripped off the step stool. A big jug lay on its side on the dryer, paint glugging out. As he righted it, he looked above to a shelf lined with art supplies, including a row of gallon size paint containers.

Okay, now, it made sense. Digging into the hamper, he pulled out towels, using one to mop up the paint on the dryer and stool. Tossing it aside, he grabbed another and wiped up the floor. Once he'd gotten the worst of it picked up, he dampened a third towel and started cleaning up the smears and residue.

By the time he'd finished, he had no idea where Coco and Posie had gone...until he heard the water in the pipes and realized they were in the upstairs bathroom.

He figured he should leave them be, so he rinsed the towels in the kitchen sink before getting a load of laundry going. Finished, he swiped the perspiration off his forehead and listened to their voices.

They were so comfortable with each other, in a way he'd never been with his parents, and it was just so damn sweet. Something stirred inside him, an emotion he didn't recognize. Maybe it was just the bittersweet recollection of those times he'd sit on the floor while Ari took a bath...

No, that wasn't it.

"Stop it, Mommy," Posie said. "I'm playing."

"Honey, you've got it on the tip of your nose." Coco had a smile in her voice. "Here, let me just..."

It was such a simple moment. It shouldn't mean anything, but this emotion rising in him, bearing down on him—

Only after it crashed over him could he finally name it.

Gratitude.

He was so damn grateful for this family. He knew he wasn't part of it. Not yet. Coco had done this all on her own.

But he wanted to be. Fiercely.

Then, what're you doing down here?

Without another thought, he was crossing the living room, bounding up the stairs, and hurrying down the hallway. Their voices grew louder, water splashing, Posie making her funny flying noises, until he reached the doorway of the bathroom. They quieted when they saw him, Coco stilling as she washed her little girl's hair. Other than the distinctively pink bubbles, you'd never know the mess she'd made.

"Oh, good." Tilting Posie's chin, Coco poured a plastic cup of water onto her head, one hand at her forehead to keep it from spilling into her eyes. Then, she got up and reached for a hand towel. "Can you watch her for a sec? I have to call my parents and let them know we're running late."

"Uh, sure?"

She smiled. "Just put the conditioner on, rinse it out, and let her play with her dolls. I won't be gone long." She started for the door, pausing. "Okay?"

"Yep. Got it."

She touched his arm—it was innocent, just a quick, gentle squeeze—but that woman had the power to make him sizzle. And then she was gone.

He knelt at the side of the tub, his daughter barely aware of his existence, as she seated her dolls in a corner. Her long hair was a slick trail down her back, her delicate shoulders hunched as she worked to bend the knees of one of them.

"Ready for the conditioner?"

Those beautiful, cagey blue eyes looked up at him. "I can do it."

She reached for the big jug, and he quickly swiped it. "Looks like you got your hands full. How about I do it this time?" Pouring a small drop into his palm, he set the bottle back down, rubbed his hands together, and stroked them through her hair. "How does your mom do it?"

She dropped her doll, giving him her full attention. "Mommy does it like this." Those little fingertips massaged the sides of her head, and he couldn't help grinning at her earnest expression.

"Like this?" He took over, giving her the kind of massage he'd get at a salon.

She nodded, causing a glop to slide down her forehead, dangerously near her eyes. He flicked it away.

"That feels good." She closed her eyes, that perfect bud of a mouth opening, exposing her white chiclet teeth. When her eyelids popped open, she said, "Do you have a daughter?"

The question struck his chest like buckshot, the report tearing through tissue and muscle.

Yes.

You.

His heart swelled painfully. *You're my daughter.*

He had no idea what to say. He couldn't lie to her right now and then tell her the truth tomorrow or the next day. Thinking on his feet, he said, "You think I need to be a dad to wash your hair?"

"Yes."

"But I have Ollie, and I wash his hair all the time."

"You do? Can you wash it now? Go get him, and he can take a bath with me."

Crisis averted. "He wouldn't fit. But you can help me wash him next time, okay?"

"Okay."

Coco rushed into the bathroom. "We are so late. Grandpa's already put the salmon on the grill. Come on, bunny, let's get you dressed." She pulled the plug and reached for a towel.

The little girl stood up, arms raised, and her mom wrapped her up like a mummy and carried her over to the sink.

"Beckett says I can take a bath with Ollie next time. I want to wash his hair."

Coco cast him a glance over her shoulder. *You said what?* "I'm not sure the two of you can fit in the bathtub together. He's a big dog."

"Actually, I said she could help me wash Ollie."

"In the bathtub. That's what you said." Posie's exasperated look made him feel traitorous and immature all at once.

He wouldn't last a minute in a verbal cage fight with a five-year-old. "Okay, well, I meant we'd do it outside. With a hose."

Coco set her daughter down and started combing her hair. "We're late for dinner, so we're lucky Beckett was kind enough to clean up the mess you made. If he hadn't been here, we wouldn't have been able to go, because we'd be mopping up red paint."

Uh oh. He thought he'd been helping.

"So, we get to go to grandma and grandpa's tonight, but you're not going to be able to paint again until you can show me that you'll respect the rules."

"I'm sorry, Mommy." With a remorseful expression like that, Beckett had no idea how Coco didn't cave right then and offer her a bucket of paint and a brush.

"I know you are, sweetheart, and I'm not angry about the mess. Art can be messy. I'm frustrated, because we have a rule. If you need more supplies, you ask me, and I'll get them. You knew I went outside to talk to Beckett. You could've waited for me to come back, but you did what you wanted right when you wanted it." She set the comb down and unwound the towel. Pumping lotion onto the palm of her hand, she slathered it all over Posie's body. "Now, since Beckett cleaned up your mess, tomorrow you're going to clean up his."

Her eyes went wide. "What mess?"

"You're going to clean his house."

Say what? He thought of the pile of dirty clothes on the floor, the half-finished glass of water on his nightstand...his toilet.

Tears welled in her eyes. "I don't know how to clean a house, Mommy."

"After tomorrow, you'll know."

"But I don't want to clean his house."

Trust me, I don't want you to.

"I can promise you he didn't want to clean up all that red paint you got everywhere. Now, instead of telling me what you don't want to do, you need to thank him for what he did to help you."

Those soulful eyes found him in the mirror. "Thank you, Beckett."

"You're welcome." But he couldn't help feeling like an asshole.

"Now, let's get dressed." Coco brushed past him.

He reached for her. "Hey. I'm sorry about that."

She smiled. "Don't be. I'm ridiculously happy you did it. You know those pesky natural consequences I'm into? Well, I would've given her one small thing to do, and the rest I'd have done myself."

He nodded, feeling very much out of his element, like he was straddling a divide.

On one side, he had his freedom, the world he knew and understood and could navigate with ease. On the other, he saw two females who'd already formed a tight knit bond.

He didn't know if there'd ever be room for him.

But he knew he wanted in.

He'd just have to keep doing the work to get there.

———

Coco dashed into the kitchen to turn off the stove before the screaming kettle woke Posie. Although, she suspected, after the busy day they'd had, her daughter wouldn't know if they threw a rave.

Pouring the hot water into the mug, she breathed in the heavenly scent of passionflower and lavender tea. She couldn't stop herself from glancing out the window of the back door.

Awareness flashed through her body when she saw Beckett's lights on.

Tonight had been good. Really good. He'd handled her parents well. Though well-intentioned, they'd grilled him all through dinner, really dug into his past, into the choices he'd made.

Why had he retired from snowboarding?

Why did he choose a lifestyle that had him living out of a suitcase?

What would he do after he sold his app?

In other words, would he ever settle down in one place?

She knew what they were doing. They wanted to figure out whether Beckett would one day seek joint custody. Every day, he grew closer to Posie—*closer to me*—and since he was rootless—preferred it that way—what would that mean for her baby? Would he take her away—for the summer? For Christmas vacation?

Fear flowed through her like a raging river, her anxiety constantly on the verge of breaching the banks. Because it didn't matter if he was a good guy, didn't matter that he knew it would kill her to share her daughter. The only way for him to be a father was to take Posie on the road with him. There was no other way for them to spend quality time together.

He's never going to live in Calamity.

Other than me and Posie, there's nothing for him here.

Coco stared at her reflection in the window over the sink, the curl of steam rising out of the mug. Fear pulsed in rhythm with her heart.

Her perfect little girl would change. With an elusive dad, she could very well look for love in every boy that told her she was pretty. Coco couldn't bear the thought of her little girl going through life never feeling good enough, always questioning her worth, just because Beckett didn't want to be tied down.

He's going to break my heart.

Oh. She turned away from the window.

Oh, no.

She felt sick, queasy, as the truth slithered across her skin, cool as a snake.

Because it wasn't *Posie* she was worried about.

It's me.

All this time she'd been so righteous about protecting her daughter. But Beckett was right—Posie never mentioned Ethan.

I'm the one who was hurt that he could move on so easily.

Posie hadn't really noticed.

Am I really that selfish? That self-involved? She hated to see herself that way, but…wasn't it true?

No, she didn't want Posie to know she had a dad who didn't love her enough to spend time with her, but Coco had to face another, deeper, uglier truth.

I'm afraid of falling in love with him and having him leave me.

When Keith had ghosted her after college, she'd been hurt. They'd been together three years, and she'd built her future based on their plans. But she hadn't been destroyed. Frankly, she hadn't even really missed him.

She'd been scared, because she'd had to reinvent herself.

With Ethan? She'd gotten to play happy family. It had been fun. But no way had she fallen in love with him.

But with Beckett, it was so much more. She could fall so hard for this man.

Could? Come on. At least admit it.

I'm crazy about him.

But, seriously, what kind of person keeps her daughter from her own father just because she's afraid of getting hurt?

I won't do that. Posie needs him—in any role he wants to take.

It sucked, but for the first time she had clarity. She had to let the two of them work it out. She'd be there, of course. Her primal instinct was—and always would be—to protect her daughter. But she had to let Beckett bond with her on his own terms.

I fell for a wanderer. That's just the way things worked out.

She wanted to tell him, let him know she didn't need him to fit into their lives. She headed to the back door—

And found him standing at his window. When their gazes connected, she felt the thrill of it pop inside her chest.

It was too late to protect herself. *I'm already here. I want him.*

She opened the door and stepped onto her porch.

Beckett came outside, standing in a puddle of yellow light. His worn T-shirt clung to his muscular frame, the sleeves hugging his bulging biceps, and his intense, hungry expression made her pulse flutter in her throat.

She had to clutch the mug so she didn't drop it. "Surprised you're still here. Thought my parents might've run you off."

He chuckled. "Figured I'd wait to hear if I got the job, though I can't recall which one I was interviewing for. The only thing they didn't ask about is my credit score."

"They were pretty thorough. You handled it like a champ."

"They're good people. I don't blame them for looking out for you guys." He watched her carefully, and she could be wrong, but she got the feeling he wanted to close the distance between them as badly as she did.

She sipped her tea. "How's the wifi in there?"

"It's great. No problem."

"You can come in, you know." With her free hand, she gestured behind her, to her house. "Mi casa es tu casa."

"This is your evening time. I'm not going to intrude."

She loved that he respected her schedule. "I don't mind. Want some passionflower lavender tea?"

"Tempting, but I'll pass."

"How about my company? Want that?"

"Yes."

She tipped her head to her house. "Grab your laptop and come on over. We can work together." Which was pretty clever of her because she knew she wouldn't have sex with him in her small house with Posie right there. Besides, they both had work to do. The countdown was on for the festival. She had a ton of emails to return.

Nodding, he ducked into his house. She shut the door and headed back to the couch. Normally, she didn't work while she drank her evening tea, but she was so anxious, so fidgety, she turned on her laptop. Just to see something other than her hands lifting his T-shirt and exposing all that tan, smooth skin, the hard planes and grooves of his cut chest.

She waited for his big, masculine presence to fill her cozy little home, this world she'd created for her and her daughter. It felt different when he was in it. Fuller, more...complete.

The familiar creak of the door opening sent a thrill through her. In the quiet pause, she imagined him toeing off his sneakers. A moment later, his bare feet padded across the kitchen and then...

He was there, standing in the doorway, laptop cupped in a big hand, watching her. Her world tipped and spun, like a lazy top. She loved the way he looked at her—full of wonder, like she was a revelation, when she was nothing more than a single mother and chocolatier.

Before she melted into a puddle and made a fool of herself, she said, "You don't have to stay out there, you know. I gave you a key. You're welcome to come in here whenever you want."

"My dad likes to say guests are like fish. They stink after three days."

"You're not a guest."

He held her gaze, as he made his way over and dropped down in the middle of the couch. "Still, you have your routine, and I don't want to mess it up. This is your time."

"I don't mind." She pretended to scroll through her chocolate shop's Splashagram feed.

As his laptop booted up, he glanced over. "That's your page?"

She nodded, turning the screen toward him.

"It's really nice. Did you hire a photographer?"

"My mom does it, actually. She stops by every now and then, takes a bunch of pictures, and then uploads one or two a day."

He moved closer, kicking up his scent—mint, soap... Beckett. "I like this one."

In it, she had a look of deep concentration as she constructed one of her enormous chocolate Easter eggs.

He leaned in close enough for her to see the crescent-shaped scar on the edge of his jaw. "You've got this Audrey Hepburn vibe—playful, a little funky—but you're a scientist and a businesswoman, and it's all just a really hot combination."

"You're very good for my self-esteem."

"I mean it, though." He held her gaze, and she felt like a Popsicle on a hot August day. "You're exceptional."

Turning the laptop back toward her, she made a sound of dismissal with her tongue.

"Don't do that."

She'd gone warm, embarrassed. "Do what?"

"Diminish what I said."

"You used the wrong word."

"You don't think you're exceptional?"

She sighed. "Beckett, my dad was one of the greatest quarterbacks of all time. My mom was one of the original supermodels. Gigi's—"

"A successful musician. I know, but those are jobs. Talents. Nothing you just said about them describes their characters or personalities. I don't care what someone does for a living. It's interesting, it gives us something to talk about, but I'm not drawn to someone because he played football. I'm not attracted to a woman because she fronts a band. Are you?"

"I...no. I guess not."

"I was listening to your family tonight, and I got updates on your sisters' careers. I heard all about how your mom took Gigi to recitals and auditions and spent a month in Paris with Lulu for some special cooking class. She took Stella to LA for one thing, Seattle for another. I don't remember which one of your sisters spent the summer in Wood's Hole."

He looked at her like he was expecting a response... but she didn't have one to give. He was describing the good things her mom had done for them.

"But I didn't hear anything about you. She didn't mention you once."

"That's because I didn't have a passion. I told you that.

242

Believe me, if I'd shown the slightest interest in something, my mom would've been all over it."

"Okay, so, while your mom was taking your sisters on all those great trips, what were you doing?"

He didn't know he'd pressed his thumb into a wound that never seemed to heal. "Being normal. I hung out with friends, had a boyfriend." She shrugged. "My mom's great. It's not like she neglected me. My parents are very loving."

Every word was true…and yet, she *had* felt…well, not neglected. That wasn't the right word. "I always knew my mom loved me. But I didn't feel special, you know? Gigi had this gift—not just her voice, but her songs, her lyrics. When she played, the whole room would go silent. You just knew she was destined to be huge. And Lulu was in the kitchen from the time she was little. Always baking, cooking. And Stella…" Her heart twisted for the sister she hadn't seen or talked to in five years. "Stella was larger than life. Everything that caught her interest became the biggest, most important thing in the world."

"Can I ask what happened to her? No one said anything, but I couldn't miss the way everyone talks about her in the past tense. She didn't…"

"Die? No, no. She and Lulu…" She shook her head. *Never mind.* It wasn't her story to tell. "They had a falling out. Right after, Lulu dropped out of college and moved to Paris. The second Stella graduated high school, she left, and we haven't heard from her since." She hoped one day Stella would come back and make things right, but tonight wasn't the night to dig into that hot mess. "But, yeah, I know if I'd asked my mom to spend time with me or take me on a trip just for fun, she'd have done it."

"But you didn't ask."

"No." What was he getting at?

"So, you're used to people not being there for you. I knew there was a reason you're so self-sufficient."

"You say that like it's a bad thing. But, keep in mind, I got pregnant at twenty-one. It was my choice to have a baby, and I promised myself I wouldn't make it my family's problem. It's okay to disrupt my life, but it wasn't fair to impose on everyone else's."

He had this expression—it wasn't pitying, but it was close enough to make her uncomfortable. "I guess it's only a bad thing if you use your self-reliance to keep people from hurting you."

"My family would never hurt me."

"Okay." He looked away, booting up his laptop.

"What?" She nudged him. "Say what you're thinking."

"Why didn't you ask your mom to take you anywhere?" The softness in his voice, the compassion in his eyes…melted the irritation away.

"Because she was busy."

"With your exceptional sisters."

"You don't understand. Everyone could see Gigi was going to be famous one day. And Lulu had pop up restaurants in town when she was *thirteen*. So, of course my mom would take her to Paris for that class."

"You weren't important enough for her to take anywhere."

"I'm her *daughter*. I'm important to her. I'm just not exceptional. There's a difference."

"That's how your family made you *feel*, but it's not true. And I'll bet it's the reason you didn't ask for anything. You didn't think what you wanted was important enough, so you learned to rely on yourself. It was better than putting yourself out there and being disappointed."

Rejected. But, yes, she couldn't deny the truth in what he said.

She would never forget the time she'd spent hours agonizing over the decision to go to Miami University to study marine biology or UCLA for screenwriting. Her mom had been getting ready to go out—dashing in and out of her closet, trying on different earrings, spritzing her perfume—but Coco had assumed she'd been listening. It had been important. But, at the end of her discussion, her mom had remained silent.

"Mom? What do you think?"

"Think about what?" she snapped.

"Between Miami and UCLA?" She'd been accepted by both programs.

Now what did she do?

"I don't know why you'd go to schools for majors you don't even know you'll like. You'll get there and change your mind within the first semester. Just start here at Western and if something catches your fancy you can transfer. Now, let me finish getting ready. I'm late."

"I was the one who'd wanted to go to Wood's Hole. The reason my mom didn't mention my name is because I didn't wind up going."

"She made you feel you're not as special as your sisters because you didn't have one particular talent."

"You know, when I said you could come in, I didn't mean so you could psychoanalyze me." She said it on a laugh, but he'd nailed it.

"How do you think I pay for my trips?"

"With armchair therapy? Now, I get why you're here for the summer. You can't afford an airplane ticket."

"Oh, because I'm wrong?"

The laughter faded, and she saw the truth of herself in those crystal blue eyes. "No, you're not wrong."

"Well, fuck that. You're exceptional. And I don't like that your family made you feel less than your sisters." Shutting his laptop, he set it down on the table. "I have this image of you, my beautiful, sexy Coco, full of energy and intelligence and kindness, and everyone just racing past you on their way to do Great Fucking Things. I hate that they made you feel smaller, and I wish I'd been around to tell you that you don't have to do anything other than be yourself to be worthy of their time. That I've never met anyone I wanted to be with more than you."

Setting her laptop aside, she straddled his lap and cupped his cheeks. "Keep talking like that, and things are going to get very messy here, Beckett O'Neill." She kissed his mouth. "And we can't have that." She shifted restlessly on his thighs—not close enough to feel his cock but conscious of how one punch of her hips would have him lined up right where she wanted him. The zing of it rocketed through her. "I like you." She kissed him again, this time lingering. "I like your face." She licked his bottom lip, and he growled, tipping her onto her back on the couch.

Settling over her, he kneed her thighs apart and rocked his hard length between them. She arched her back, cupping the back of his head, and gave into all the need she'd tried so hard to suppress.

He kissed her with a hunger that swept her away. His hand roamed from her shoulder to her breast, tracing the curve of her waist, and settling on her hip with a squeeze.

Nothing had ever felt as good as the way this man wanted her. He gripped the back of her knee, lifting her leg over him, and surged into her. When she gasped, he tore his mouth off hers and lowered his face into her neck.

"Fuck." It came out a harsh whisper. "I'm sorry." Abruptly, he stood, glancing up the stairs towards Posie's bedroom. "I would've fucked you right here." His gaze swung back to her, landing on her mouth, then sliding down to her breasts, her hips, her legs...all the way to her bare toes.

And she felt it like a caress, her skin tingling. *More.*

"You make me crazy." He started for her, then came to a hard stop. "I've got to get out of here."

Heart pounding, she listened to his footsteps move across the kitchen. Heard the door creak open and closed.

And then she was alone, her body aching for his touch.

She had a choice. She could shut down all this want and need and pick up her laptop, take care of those emails. Stay in her safe little world.

Her gaze snagged on the Las Vegas sign on her windowsill, and she smiled.

Or she could shake things up.

Chapter Fourteen

In her pajama shorts and college T-shirt, Coco padded across the lawn, her bare feet tickled by the coarse grass. Her whole body vibrated with need. She just had to have him. Had to be with him.

The minute she knocked, he opened. Like he'd been waiting for her. He was strung so tight, the muscle in his jaw ticked. He reached for her, hands on her waist, pulling her roughly to him. "I want you. You know I fucking want you so bad, but nothing's changed. I can't make any promises, and I don't want to hurt you."

She wanted him, too. She wanted him more than she didn't want to be hurt. "Make me feel the way I did in Vegas. *Nobody* makes me feel the way you do."

"Get in here." Reaching for her ass, he lifted her, and she wrapped her legs around him.

God, her body thrilled at his touch. He held her so tightly, she could feel the tremble in his arms.

He kicked the door shut, and then tipped his head toward the house. "Posie?"

She waved the baby monitor at him. "I work in here a lot, so I know the signal reaches."

"Good. Now give me that mouth." He kissed her, his tongue licking inside her mouth.

Electric heat sizzled along her nerves, and she sighed. So happy, so…complete.

There was nowhere else she'd rather be than right here, in his arms, kissing kissing kissing him, slow and deep. She'd never known a softer, warmer, more velvety mouth.

The next thing she knew, she was sailing…landing on a soft mattress with a bounce. She'd barely set the monitor on the nightstand before he was on her. His big hand came around the back of her head, fingers threading through her hair, and she loved the possession, the *hunger* in his grip.

Too soon, he pulled away. But it was only to get on his knees and drag her up the bed, until her head hit the pillow. And then he pushed her knees apart and settled between her legs. His hand slid under her T-shirt, skimmed up her stomach, and cupped her breast.

He dipped his nose into her neck. "You smell good. You taste good. You *are* good. So, so good, my Vegas girl."

Palms flat on his back, she glided up his warm, smooth skin until she reached his shoulders. He pulled away long enough to fist the T-shirt behind his neck and yank it off.

A grumble came from the baby monitor, and they both stilled, listening to Ollie snuffling in his sleep. They broke into grins.

The dog had taken to following Posie everywhere and sleeping in her bed.

"He's not going to wake her?" Beckett asked in that deep, sexy voice.

"She goes so hard all day, nothing wakes her." As he

hovered over her, his hair spilled forward, and the concern in his eyes warmed her. She scraped it back so she could see his strong jaw and high cheekbones, those startlingly beautiful crystal eyes. Affection for him swelled to bursting. "I've been so frustrated with myself for falling for a guy who's never going to settle down. Like, what's *wrong* with me? But tonight I realized I'm not falling for a wanderer. I'm falling for Beckett O'Neill. I'm falling for your kindness and intelligence, your honesty and humor. I'm falling for the way you're handling the most life-altering news a man could ever get. I'm falling for *you*."

He kissed her, one hand sliding under her ass and pressing their bodies tightly together. Their tongues tangled and danced, as her fingers mapped every hard ridge of bone and flex of muscle on his powerful chest.

When he pulled his mouth off hers, she cried out at the loss. But his lips skimmed down her jaw to her neck, and he licked a path to her collarbone. "Get this shirt off." As she lifted up, he sat back on his heels. "Slowly. I wanna watch."

She pulled it over her head and dropped it off the side of the bed. Reaching behind her, he unclasped the bra, lowered the straps, and tossed it aside. She loved the way his nostrils flared as he took in her breasts. He immediately filled his hands with them, pressing the mounds together, his thumbs brushing across her nipples.

Desire burst in a shower of fiery sparks. She sucked in a breath, and his gaze flicked up to hers. "We're a good match. I love your tits, and your tits love to be touched." He leaned in. "Do they like to be sucked, too?"

She lay back down and gave a little jiggle just to tease him. "You know they do."

He growled, lunging for her. "Fuck, yeah, I do." As he

lowered his head, his silky hair brushed over her skin. Watching her, he licked the tip of one, the side of his mouth curling when she arched off the mattress.

Lazily, his tongue circled and flicked, working her into a frenzy. "Beckett."

He sucked in her nipple, licking it with the flat of his tongue. Then, lavished the other with equal attention, driving her right out of her mind.

Awash in sensuality, she closed her eyes and let herself sink into everything Beckett, his scent, the way he clutched her, the hungry sounds he made. She felt free, sexy...purely feminine, and she loved it. Loved it so damn much.

Unexpectedly, he released her with a pop. "In Vegas, it was like this little cocoon, you and me in that bed. I wasn't thinking about my retirement, my friends, my family...it didn't even register that I was in a hotel room." Shifting back, he reached for the waistband of her shorts. "You remember that?"

"Yes, but what I remember most was how comfortable I felt with you." She hiked up her bottom, and he pulled them down. "You didn't feel like a stranger."

He took in her body. "Look at you. I don't even know where to begin. I want it all."

She knew he didn't see himself as romantic, as a relationship kind of guy. He seemed to view it as some foreign thing, something he'd irretrievably missed out on because of his family, but he was so wrong. It came naturally to him. She wished he could see that he gave her everything she could ever need. His hunger for her...the way he saw right into the very heart of her *and still likes me*...pure romance. Sitting up, she reached for the button on his shorts. "Let's start here."

He shot off the bed, yanked them down, and started to climb back on when she stopped him with a hand to his thigh.

"Whoa. Not so fast." His hard cock stood straight up, bouncing against his flat, tight stomach. Wrapping her hand around him, she licked the crown. "Mm, you're gorgeous everywhere."

Fingers sifting into her hair, he slid his hand around to the back of her neck. As her tongue swirled around his length, gliding up, then down, she took her own pleasure in learning his sounds and reactions. Grabbing his muscular ass, she sucked him into her mouth, loving the way his hips flexed and his breathing turned harsh.

"Jesus." Both hands cupping the back of her head, he pumped into her mouth.

She loved the way his fingers gripped her scalp, the desperation in his thrusts. Watching, she withdrew him almost all the way out of her mouth, before sucking him back in. His eyelids fluttered closed, and his lips parted in pure sensual pleasure.

She loved the strain in his muscles, the bulge in his biceps. She pulled his glistening length out of her mouth. "Want to see a party trick?" Laying down on her back, the top of her head brushing his thighs, she let her neck dangle off the edge of the mattress. "Fuck my mouth."

"Are you serious right now?"

She grinned, reaching for him and angling him toward her.

"I've been going to the wrong parties." He tried for joviality, but his voice came out strained. Hands on her shoulders, he guided his erection into her open mouth, watching with avid interest as she swallowed his whole length. "Fuck." One syllable came out on a long, drawn-out hiss. When he hit the back of her throat, he rocked in careful, tight thrusts. He looked like he was on the edge of his restraint, trying hard not to hurt her but needing to unleash.

She pulled him out and sat up. "This is a private party, between you and me. So, we can do whatever we want." She lay back down. "I won't be shy in letting you know if I don't like something."

He stuttered out a breath, gripping his cock and easing it back into her mouth. And then he pumped—easily at first, testing her—but she just tipped her head back even more and let him in deeper.

"Fuck, Coco. You feel so good."

She couldn't flick her tongue with her mouth stuffed like that, but she pressed it against him and sucked hard, making him gasp. "Jesus."

He watched her swallow his cock, and his eyes went wild, desperate. And it just made her so crazy she had to reach between her legs to get some relief.

But before she could touch herself, he pulled out. "Oh, no, you don't. I want to feel you come around me." He climbed onto the bed. "Get over here."

She scrambled back onto the mattress, until her head hit the pillow. With her laid out before him, he kissed a path down her stomach to her throbbing center. When he licked inside, she arched off the bed. "*Oh.*" Her body ignited, desire flashing across her skin.

"You're so fucking wet." He licked her into a fever, until her hips twisted back and forth, and the tension grew unbearable. And then he slid his fingers inside her, stroking her into a climax that sent her soaring.

Clutching his head so he wouldn't stop, she rode one

luscious wave after another, the pleasure so intense it made her blood sing.

When she lowered her hips, he reached for the nightstand, grabbed a foil packet from the drawer, and pulled out the condom.

"I can't feel my fingers right now." She watched him unrolling it on his cock. "But next time I want to put it on."

He didn't even smile. "You can do whatever you want. I'm all yours" Once sheathed, he leaned over her, pressing at her entrance. "You ready for me?"

"Mm." She smoothed his hair behind his ear. "So ready."

With a punch of his hips, he thrust inside, and every single cell went white hot. Lifting up on his arms, he took in her body, his gaze fixed on her bouncing breasts. "Jesus, what you do to me."

His ridged abs tightened, and his biceps bunched and bulged. The tendons in his neck strained, and he pounded into her so hard she had to band her legs and arms around him to keep from banging into the headboard.

"Not gonna last. I'm…fuck." He lowered his body so it scraped over hers, his pelvis striking her clit with every thrust. His back grew slick with perspiration, the muscles going rock hard.

Slamming home, he held himself tightly against her, as he threw his head back and came with a roar. One hand under her ass, his hips snapped in short, tight punches.

Collapsing to her side, he wrapped his arm around her, snugging her to him. "Swear to God, the more I know you, the better it is." He sounded like he couldn't believe it was true.

But it *was* true. It just kept getting better with him.

And that filled her with an incandescent joy—matched only in strength by a fear so palpable she wanted to roll out of bed and race out the door. Hide in the safety of her bedroom.

In the heat of the moment, she'd told herself she could handle falling for a man who would leave her. But now she knew she'd told herself lies just to get another hit of his attention, of the way he made her feel about herself.

Because, right then, wrapped in his strong arms, she couldn't help but think ahead to August, when he'd leave, and she knew it would be worse than anything she'd imagined.

She knew herself. She would scour his social media for signs of other women. She'd check her phone, looking for a call or text.

Tonight had been so good—no regrets. But did she really want have a summer fling? Or should she just end it now?

It was time to get her sisters in on it.

She needed their perspective.

With their drinks in hand, Coco and her older sister found a table in the corner of Calamity Joe's. Tourists coming back from a day of hiking and rafting, as well as locals on coffee breaks, made up the late afternoon crowd.

She pushed her chair closer to Gigi's before dropping into it. On impulse, she leaned over and gave her sister a big hug. "I'm so glad you're here. I've missed you so much." Her sister used to live in Los Angeles, making it a quick hour and forty-five-minute flight to Calamity. But since she'd found love with a quarterback from Boston, she came home far less often.

ERIKA KELLY

"I've missed you, too." Gigi sat back, tucking her legs under her and setting an elbow on the armrest. "But you can't drop news like that in a group text message. I had to come and see if you're okay. This is big."

"You're getting ready for a tour." Normally, Gigi would be in Calamity for the summer, since her fiancé ran a football camp for kids here. But her band was opening for Blue Fire, one of the biggest Alt/rock bands in the world, and they were doing choreography in New York.

"Forget about the tour." Gigi whispered aggressively. "Posie has a *dad*. This is huge. It's—"

"Shh. I know exactly what it is."

"Why are we whispering? I thought you said he told her."

"I said he's ready to tell her. We haven't done it yet." She reached for her sister's hand and squeezed it. "But, you're right, it is a big deal. You didn't have to come home for this, but I'm so glad you did."

"So, talk to me." Gigi nudged her. "What was it like to see your hookup after six years?"

"Honestly? It's all still there, the attraction, the chemistry." The other night came roaring back, his urgency, his need…God, the *passion*. It was so good between them. "And the more I get to know him, the better I like him." The visceral sensation of their bodies grinding together, straining to bust through physical boundaries, had her skin on fire. She glanced away, not wanting her sister to see her reaction to him.

"Oh, my God. You didn't."

She shot her sister a look. "I did." And broke into a grin.

Gigi fanned herself. "It was that good?"

She rolled her eyes. "Unbelievable."

256

"Oh, my God, you can't *sleep* with him. Are you out of your mind?"

"When he puts that wicked tongue into action, yep. He drives me right out of my mind."

Gigi burst out laughing. "My quiet little sister's a wildcat in the sheets. Who knew?"

"Quiet?" *This is how my family sees me.* Coco had never been *quiet*. She just hadn't been passionate about anything. Get all four sisters together in a room, and everyone would notice Gigi's voice, Lulu's cooking, and whatever hobby Stella happened to be focused on at that moment.

Coco didn't stand out in any way.

Beckett was right. Her family placed importance on a person's talents, their accomplishments. Not on their personalities, their character.

Gigi leaned forward and grabbed her hand. "What's this? You never wear jewelry."

"I know. It's from him. Beckett."

"Are you serious? He bought you a ring?"

"No, it's not like that. He was just… he saw it at an arts and crafts festival, knew aquamarine was my birthstone…"

"You're making light of it, and I don't know why. He's walking around, sees a ring, and associates it immediately with your birthstone? Sweetie, this man's into you big-time."

"Yeah, I mean, it's really good between us. But I just know I'm setting myself up for a big fall."

"Why do you say that?" Gigi tucked a lock of her dark hair behind her ear. Her sister had an edgy, rocker look, and everywhere she went people did a double take because she looked like someone famous.

"I think I fall for guys who ghost me." *What does that say about me?*

Her sister looked thoughtful. "Well…" Her fingers strummed the ribbed coffee sleeve. "Thinking back on Keith and Ethan, I'd say you choose safe guys."

"There was nothing safe about Keith. He was wild and fun, and Ethan was—"

"Never going to stay in Calamity. By safe, I don't mean boring. I mean the kind you'd never fall in love with, so the lack of an emotional attachment makes it easier for them to cut and run."

Ouch. Is that what I do? She supposed she could see that. "Well, there's nothing safe about Beckett, that's for sure." *Because I have big feelings. Huge.*

"Is this a good idea, though? I mean, he's trying to build a relationship with Posie."

"Believe me, I know." She thought of the way he'd held her that night. She'd known she had to get back to her own bed, but that possessive hold…like he never wanted to let her go? *I want that every night.* "It's not like we can stop it. It's big, Gigi. We really like each other, and the chemistry is so, so powerful. I feel like he's my person, you know?" It felt like a ridiculous thing to say. They hardly knew each other.

One night in Vegas, a week in Calamity…and yet hours, minutes, seconds didn't forge the bond between them. It came from something deeper…a recognition… the missing piece of her soul finally clicking into place.

"I hear you. It's just…your person is a guy who travels most of the year. I can't imagine you being happy with that. And it sounds like it would be awful for Posie."

"No, he knows that's not sustainable, not with a daughter. I mean, it's only been a week, and he's already hired someone to take his trips this summer. He's honestly doing the best he can."

"Well, that's good. Then, why do you think he's going to ghost you?"

"I don't mean ghost, necessarily. But he doesn't want a family. He doesn't want ties or commitments, so I know he's not going to stick around."

"He *didn't,* but it sounds like that's all changing. You just told me he's really into you, and I know he's got to be falling for Posie."

"Don't repeat this okay? But I really need to talk to someone."

"Everything you say goes in the vault."

She believed her. Gigi was awesome that way. "He comes from a really broken family. His mom walked out on him after his sister died. I mean, he grew up in *boarding school.* To be honest, I think he shut down his emotions when he lost his sister, and I can't see him suddenly getting over that to become a family man with a wife, kids, and a dog."

"Does he have to fit into that mold, though? Can you make up your own kind of relationship, something that works for both of your quirks?"

She sat back in her chair, making a face like she was shocked. "What quirks?" But she really did want to know.

"Well, you're pretty closed off yourself."

"I'm not closed off."

"You literally waited an entire week to tell us about Posie's dad."

"That's because I've been trying to get a handle on it. It's a pretty big deal."

"Oh, I know. Which is why you should've told us right away. So you didn't *have* to handle it alone."

"I'm sitting here with you right now."

"Because I flew in from New York. But let's not pretend this is the one and only time you've kept things to yourself. How about the fact that you didn't tell us you were pregnant for five months. *Five.* I couldn't have kept a secret like that for five minutes let alone months. Or the fact that you didn't let us help you with anything for the first year of Posie's life."

"You guys helped plenty. I couldn't have gotten through it by myself."

"I offered to give you a loan for the shop, and you said no."

Okay, now she wasn't being fair. "I was trying not to be a burden on you."

"Hon, I'm your damn sister. If I had one thin dime left to my name, I'd give you five cents."

Fighting back tears, she looked down at her lap.

"Wouldn't you do the same for any of us?"

Her head snapped up. "Yes." She said it so fiercely, the couple at the table next to them looked over.

"Then, why won't you let us be there for you?"

"Because you're busy…you've got more important things to worry about than me."

"Remember that night in Vegas? I didn't even know you and Keith had broken up."

"It was your special night."

"What was so special about it? It was, like, the hundredth night in a row I'd performed with the Lollipops on our American tour. The only thing that made it special was that my sister and friends came to party with me. You think I'd rather *dance* than comfort my sister?"

"You were the lead singer of the Lollipops. How selfish

would I have been to go on and on about my stupid boyfriend problems?"

"Oh, my *God.*" She tipped her head back, blowing out a breath. "Okay, I think I'm starting to understand something. If you'd talked to me that night, I could've given my sister support and love and maybe even some advice. I could've helped you through a really crappy time. But I didn't get to do that."

"I never thought about it like that."

"So, maybe it's not so much that you choose safe men, but that you don't let them help you. You're so self-contained, they don't feel necessary."

Was that true? Did she do that?

Yeah. She totally did. And it made so much sense. "After we graduated, Keith went home. We divided up a list of things that needed to get done to launch our business, but I kept sending him links—for toys, furniture, insurance, licenses. I did everything myself. With Ethan, it didn't seem fair to burden him with parenting, so I didn't let him help." How many times had he offered to take Posie to school, when she had a morning meeting? She'd always said she was fine.

She'd thought self-reliance was a good thing—but she could see she'd used it to keep people out.

Why, though?

"I think that's part of it," Gigi said. "But I'm not really talking about financial or physical things. I'm talking about letting them give you emotional support. People need to be needed. It makes them feel important, like they matter to you. And, even more, it makes you closer. If you handle everything yourself…it's probably pretty easy to ghost you."

Her sister was right, and it made her feel lost…untethered.

"Does any of that ring true?" Gigi asked.

"All of it does. And it scares me."

"Because?"

"Because I'm going to wind up alone."

"Oh, honey, no, you're not. This is the first time you've let me in like this. You really talked to me…and look. You had a breakthrough. And now you have to let Beckett in. If he's your person, you have to open up. Let him be there for you." Gigi leaned in. "If he's The One, then you've got to give it everything you have. You just have to."

Coco had gone off to meet her sister for coffee, leaving him alone with Posie.

Which was great. He wanted that. It was just…he didn't have the ease with her yet that Tyler Cavanaugh had. He didn't talk to her the way Will talked to Ruby, like she was his heart. For Beckett, it still felt awkward, uncomfortable.

Very much how it felt his first few months at the academy. He'd been an outsider—and not just because they'd already formed their cliques, but because they had social and life skills he'd never learned. When he'd first gotten there, he could remember standing in the bathroom, watching the guys get ready for bed. He'd felt like an alien dropped into a strange world, as they showered, brushed their teeth, *flossed*—all habits his parents hadn't taken the time to teach him.

He couldn't say he'd felt embarrassed—he hadn't known anyone. Mostly, he'd felt like he didn't fit in. He'd wound up just doing his own thing. It hadn't much mattered, since the bulk of his time revolved around training and competing anyway.

But this is different.

Because he wanted Posie to like him.

In preparation, he'd gone to the toy store on his way home from coaching and bought a set of large Lego blocks —the same ones Ruby had liked so much. Only, Posie didn't have even the slightest interest in them.

As soon as the front door had closed, Poise ran into her mom's closet and rooted around through a drawer. She'd pulled out a little container of glitter and asked him to put it on her cheeks and eyelids.

He sure as hell wasn't going to put anything around her eyes, but he'd made her happy by dabbing some of the sticky stuff in a circle around her wrists, like bracelets. Then, she'd strapped on her fairy wings and went flying around the house. For the first fifteen minutes, he'd tried to find a way to play with her, but she didn't need him. She'd just kept flying around, talking to herself.

Now, thirty-five minutes into his hour of Child Watch, she was on the floor of her bedroom playing with her fairy dolls. He sat with her, wondering if he was supposed to insert himself or what. His phone had been blowing up, and he hoped like hell it wasn't Jimmy with a problem—because he needed this situation to work out— but he'd have to check his messages later. He would never be like his mom, distracted and disinterested.

Weirdly, as much as he'd wanted to run with the bulls, he found himself far more fascinated with watching his daughter struggle to put a dress on a plastic doll.

In frustration, Posie thrust it at him. "You do it."

Finally, my moment to shine. "Sure." His big fingers had

a hard time gripping the thin fabric, but he managed to yank it over the doll's hips. *Cool. Almost done.* Now, he just had to get the arms into the sleeves…yeah, not a fucking chance. Was the dress even made for this doll?

Why's it so tight?

Shouldn't the arms bend?

Fuck.

The dress didn't fit. No way.

And why was he getting worked up over this?

Because it's important. His daughter needed him, and he didn't want to fail. He had to get this right.

He pulled the top part of the dress out as far as it could go without ripping it and stabbed the hand into the sleeve. The fingers got caught up in the fabric, though, and he couldn't make it work.

If he bent the arm anymore, it might snap. *Not gonna try. Are you kidding?* And be remembered as the asshole who broke her doll? Nope. He'd figure it out and be her hero.

That's what I want. The truth resonated deep within.

I want to be this little girl's hero.

He stopped stretching and tugging and gave the matter some thought.

And then it struck him. He yanked the dress off, slid it over the doll's head, and jammed the arms right into the holes.

See? Just calm down, and you'll figure this shit out.

He Velcroed the back of the dress closed. Not a chance in hell could his fingers get that little elastic loop around the tiny button, so he handed it back and hoped Posie wouldn't notice.

But she didn't take it. She was involved in setting up some kind of camper and picnic table thing.

He shook the doll. *Here.*

But she ignored him.

He couldn't believe it. While he'd broken out in a sweat over the damn dress, she'd moved onto something else. He set it down, leaned back against the bed, and closed his eyes. It had been easy with Ari. She'd have spent her every waking moment following him around. She'd adored him.

But his daughter wasn't impressed. She barely knew him. So, he'd have to try harder.

"She has to go potty." Posie held a doll out to him.

He took it. *Challenge accepted.* Except...how did he handle this one? Did he bend her at the waist and make peeing sounds? Or did he literally take her to the toilet? "Okay. Let's do this." He got up and took the doll to the bathroom. Pulling out his phone, he started to call his dad —but what did his dad know about playing with a child? Neither of his parents had done the kid thing.

Then, he thought of Will.

Will would get it. He found his friend's contact and called, stressed because he had to get back out there but really needing some advice. The phone rang a couple of times. *Come on, man. Answer.*

"Beckett?"

"Hey." Relieved, he glanced out the doorway to see if Posie was listening. Nope. Totally absorbed in her play.

"What's up?"

"I have to babysit, so I went to the store—"

"I'm going to interrupt you right there. Is she your daughter?"

"Yes, I told you—"

"Then, don't call it babysitting. It implies you're doing the mother a favor. You're not. You're taking care of your daughter. Might not sound meaningful but trust me, it is. So, go ahead. You went to the store?"

"Actually, that's a good point. Thank you for that." *See?* Already he'd gotten good information. "Yeah, so, I bought those blocks you had for Ruby, but Posie hasn't even looked at them. I got her a bunch of puzzles, because the clerk said five-year-olds were into them. I bought some cool Nerf guns, thought we could run around the house and shoot each other." He and Ari had done that countless times. They'd both loved it. "But she's not into any of it. She just wants to play with her dolls." He peered out again —it was like she hadn't even noticed he'd left the room.

Will chuckled. "I'm guessing this is your first time alone with her?"

"Yes. I don't know what I'm supposed to do. She's not interacting with me."

"You pictured building blanket forts and playing hide-and-go-seek?"

"I don't know that I pictured anything, but I figured she'd want my attention." Ari always had. "Am I supposed to play dolls with her?"

"Ruby's not into that, so I can't help you there." He sounded like he was fighting back laughter. "You couldn't pay her to wear a dress, and the one doll she got as a birthday present from my mom is still in the packaging. But your point is that you're looking for a way to interact with her?"

"I don't know if she *wants* me to. Am I supposed to pick up a doll and start talking in a funny voice, like elbow my way in? Or just leave her alone and catch up on some emails?"

"Well, I wouldn't do that. Bonding doesn't come when you're each doing your own thing. I'd hang in there, pick up on her clues...find ways to engage. Look, I get it. When Ruby first came to live here, I had no idea what to do with her."

"That's where I am right now." *And I want to jump ahead to where Will is—I want to know her.*

I want her to love me.

He sat with that for a second. Let it sink in, spread through him.

The idea that this little fairy girl could come to love him triggered a whole lot of fear, but underneath that—if he could just reach it—was a sense of pride that far surpassed anything he'd felt when they'd put the medal around his neck.

So, yeah. That's what he wanted.

"The only thing I can tell you is nothing happens overnight. The bonding comes over time. It comes because you're there every day, feeding her and giving her baths, reading her books at night before bed. You learn her, and she learns you. And, after a while, she comes to trust you with her life."

It was like a hammer striking his spinal cord, the sizzle traveling throughout his body.

No child should trust me with her life.

That familiar image of Ari flashed inside his mind. Her pale complexion, the dark blue snowsuit against the fresh, white snow.

But he forced himself out of the darkness and into the here and now. Onto Posie. On earning her trust. "Makes sense."

"I made a lot of mistakes with Ruby, but I think that's where the bonding happens. You care enough to work through things. You sit with her through tantrums and find what makes her laugh. I know that's not what you want to hear. You want an answer right now, but I think it's like any relationship. It takes time to build trust and to get to know each other."

"Time's the one thing I don't have."

"Well, then, maybe it won't ever be different than it is right now. Maybe every time you come to visit, she's going to do her own thing, and you're going to wonder what you can do to get her attention."

He didn't like that at all. He'd pictured coming to town and having her all over him, asking questions about his travels, marveling over the gifts he'd bought her...

Wow. Had he actually thought Posie would admire his lifestyle?

She'll resent me.

But even worse, I'll hurt her. Deeply.

He imagined a closet stuffed with the presents he'd bought her over the years.

"She's not going to love you because you gave her your DNA," Will said. "She's going to love you because you sat with her while she played dolls, figured out how she likes her eggs, and let her sleep in your bed after she's had a nightmare."

He'd wanted a quick answer. Instead, this conversation had shaken him. He could only stare at himself in the mirror and wonder how the fuck he'd thought one summer would be enough to get a handle on this situation. "I hear you. I have to get back to work in a few weeks, but I'll come back." Of course he would. "And I'll keep at it."

"Again, I'll tell you, it's like with any relationship, every time you come back, you'll be starting over. Relationships need consistency, maintenance. For now, I'd say just hang out with her. When she wants something, she'll let you know. When she needs you, she won't hesitate to ask. And, every time you show up for her, that's bonding. It's really as simple as that. Just be there."

He watched her talking to herself, providing the dialogue for her dolls, and his heart squeezed. "I don't know what's best for her."

"Like I said, you'll figure it out the more time you spend with her."

"No, I mean, is it worse to have a dad who shows up a couple times a year?" Because they hadn't told Posie yet. It wasn't too late to choose a different path. "Or should I bow out and let Coco find a more traditional guy who'll be a good father?"

"But *you're* her father. Unless you're going to lie to her, she'll know that Coco's husband is her stepdad."

The idea of Coco marrying someone else made him sick.

But the image of Posie grabbing some other man's hand and dragging him to the kitchen table to get her toy to work scared the shit out of him.

"So, I don't see how you'll *save her* by taking off. I think the real question, though, is can *you* live with that choice? Can you go back to your life knowing you've got a daughter out there?"

"No." But he'd already known that. He could never go back to his old life as if nothing had changed. He didn't want to. His heart ached with emotion…he cared about her.

He was just scared.

Scared of a five-year-old he didn't know how to relate to.

I'm not going to figure it out by hiding in the bathroom talking to Will.

"I think the only reason this is troubling you is because you already know your priorities. You're a good man, Beckett. You'll figure it out as you go along. There's no textbook that'll tell you what to do. Every family is different, and yours will find its normal."

Family.

Me, Coco, and Posie.

We're a family.

He'd been seeing the three of them as separate entities. His relationship with Coco felt different than the one he was building with Posie.

But one simple word merged them together.

"Where are you, Beckett?" And, after that revelation, her sweet little voice unmanned him.

"Coming." He flushed the toilet.

"Did you call me from the shitter?" Will sounded horrified.

He burst out laughing. "No. She told me her doll needed to go potty. That's why I called in the first place. I didn't know what to do."

"Don't be too hard on yourself. I would've just made a shushing sound, like she's pissing, and then handed the doll back."

Beckett laughed. "That's because you're a crass bastard."

"I'll let you go. I'm around if you want to get the girls together for a play date."

Those were the last words Beckett ever expected to hear coming out of Will Bowie's mouth. He didn't even know how to respond.

Will burst out laughing. "Gotcha." And then he disconnected.

Chapter Fifteen

STOWING HIS PHONE IN THE BACK POCKET OF HIS jeans, Beckett returned to Posie's campground and handed her the doll.

She snatched it and set it down roughly against her white nightstand. "*You* can't play with us."

Her tone caught his attention. He wanted to ask what had happened, but he hesitated to interrupt her. Maybe she worked through her problems with dolls?

"I can so play with you." This voice was different voice, challenging.

Okay, she was definitely working something out. He'd stay quiet and see where she went with the conversation.

She whipped her doll around and said, "You're mean, Jessie, and you can't play with us."

"I can play with you." She'd gone back to the "boy" voice. "I can play with anybody I want."

She flew her doll closer to the boy. "Well, you can't play with me. If you do, I'm going to make Ollie chase you until you fall down and pee in your pants. And then we're all going to laugh at you and call you Peepee Boy."

Posie didn't watch much TV, and the movies she did get to see were animated, so he didn't think this scenario came from media. "Hey, Posie, is there a boy named Jessie at your school?"

Pulled from her fantasy world, she cut a wary glance at him. "Yes."

"Is he giving you trouble?"

She shrugged, clearly uneasy.

Maybe he'd take the focus off her. "I remember Charlie Monroe from kindergarten. Mean as a snake."

"Did he make you feel bad?"

"He made lots of people feel bad. He used to yank on my backpack strap so hard I'd fall down. He tore up people's pictures." *Whatever happened to that kid?* He'd have to look him up. "Does Jessie make you feel bad?"

She shot him a wounded look. "He hurts my feelings."

"What kinds of things does he say?"

"He says fairies aren't real. He says I look dumb flying around because people can't fly. He says I'm stupid if I think I can fly."

"Ah, okay, so he's one of those people with no imagination. Got it."

Her bottom lip wobbled. "He broke my fairy bracelets that you gave me."

"What? How did that happen?"

"I was flying around the room, and he chased me, and he pulled really hard, and I fell down, and it hurt. But I didn't want to cry, so I got back up even though my hands hurt really bad." She shoved her palm in his face. "He hurt me."

He could see the faint rug-burn on the heel. "What he did is not okay, Posie. Did you tell the teacher?"

"No. I went to the bathroom and cried because he

pulled the ribbons off, and now I can't wear them 'cause the magic's gone."

"I can get you new ones."

"But you got them from far away. From someplace special. I don't want you to go back there."

"I don't mind going back there if it'll make you happy."

She shook her head.

"You want the bracelets, though."

"But I don't want you to leave."

Ah. Damn. And here he'd thought she hadn't needed him.

She's not Ari. She's not Ruby.

Will was exactly right. He needed the time to get to know her. "Tell you what, my dad can get the bracelets." Beckett had bought them at the Denver airport. "I'll have him go to the special place and he can bring them when he comes for a visit. How about that?"

"Okay." She nodded. "Is he coming tomorrow?"

"No, not tomorrow. But we really need to talk about Jessie, because he doesn't get to make school difficult for you. First of all, his opinion about fairies doesn't matter, and secondly, he doesn't get to tell you whether you can fly. He just doesn't have that power over you or anyone else. Do you understand what I'm saying?"

She nodded, but there was a vagueness in her eyes that led him to believe she didn't get it at all. "Can I tell your mom about this?"

"Don't tell Mommy." She looked down at her doll, making it do the splits.

"Why not?"

"Because she'll get mad."

"At you?"

"No, at Jessie."

"Well, aren't you angry at Jessie?"

"Yes."

He needed to be careful here. He didn't want to give the wrong advice. "So, what can we do to make sure Jessie understands he doesn't have any power over you? That you get to wear your fairy clothes and fly around the room?"

She hunched a shoulder.

"Seems to me, if we don't do anything about it, he'll think it's okay. And it's not, Posie. None of this is okay. Not calling you names, not chasing you, and definitely not yanking your ribbons. Have you told him to knock it off?"

"I have." Anger glinted in her eyes. "I told him I can fly if I want to. But he just goes like this." She got up on her knees, put her nose right in his face, and started chanting, "Na na na na na na na na."

"That would make me really angry. What did you do?"

"I pushed him away."

"Okay." He got up. "Come here."

"Why?" But she got to her feet anyway.

"Jessie's a bully, and that's not okay. And if you're not willing to tell your mom or your teacher, then we're going to have to figure out some new ways to handle him." He reached for one of her headbands. It barely fit his head, but he made a big show of brushing the ribbons off his shoulders.

She giggled and tried to grab it.

"Nope. I'm Posie."

"You're not Posie. I am." Laughter glittered in her eyes.

"I'm pretending to be you. And you pretend to be Jessie."

"What do I do?"

"I'm going to fly around the room, and you're going to

be Jessie. Ready?" Beckett flapped his arms but stayed in place. "Wait. I need wings."

She pulled off her wings and gave them to him. The elastic didn't stretch far enough to fit across his shoulders, so he let it dangle off one. Then, he went prancing around the room, waving his arms.

Posie covered her giggle with a hand.

"So, that's what Jessie does? He watches you and laughs?" he asked in a teasing tone.

Laughing, she darted out to him, but he skirted around her.

"Come on, be Jessie. What would he say to me right now?"

After a moment, she got a mean expression. "You can't fly, stupid head. Fairies aren't real. You look stupid running around like that."

Beckett stopped flying and sat back down. "Okay, I think I have an idea. Who are your closest friends in school?"

"Margot and Olivia and Samuel and Brie and Lyla."

"What if we made all of them bracelets with ribbons? Would they want to fly around the room with you?"

"Yes. Everyone wants my bracelets."

"Then, let's do that. Let's go to the store and buy elastic and ribbons and lace and make them for your friends. I don't think Jessie will bother you if half the class is doing it."

"Can we go right now?"

"Let's wait for your mom to get home. We can tell her what we want to do. Okay?"

She nodded.

"Cool. So, that's one thing we can try. If that doesn't

work, we'll come up with some other ideas." He pulled off the wings and the headband.

"Can you read to me now?"

"Sure thing."

She skipped off to her bookcase and scrutinized the spines, setting the books she wanted in a pile next to her. Finished, she gathered them up in her arms and dumped them on the mattress. After scrambling onto her bed, she leaned against the headboard like a little princess.

He collapsed next to her, and she slapped a book onto his lap. "Read."

As soon as he started, she cuddled up against him. It was a book about an elephant family, and they seemed to be British, so he used an accent, lowering his voice for the dad and raising it for the kid.

She grinned up at him, her arm going across his stomach for a hug. "I like you, Beckett. I really, really like you."

Oh, shit.

Oh, hell.

Emotion reared up and towered over him. He could smell the baby shampoo in her hair, feel the heat of her body tucked up against him. That little hand pressed flat to his stomach was so delicate, the nails painted a sparkly pink.

She seemed so fragile. And with fuckers like Jessie in the world she needed protection. She needed....

She needs a father.

No, she's got one of those.

She needs a dad.

She needs me.

He stroked her hair. "I like you, too."

But he was lying.

Because he loved her.

He'd fallen in love with his daughter.

"Anybody home?" Coco shut the door, dropped her purse on the dining room table, and listened. That familiar deep voice coming from upstairs sent a rush of pleasure through her.

Ooh, she liked this too much. Coming home to Beckett and Posie. It almost felt like a real family. As she climbed the stairs, smiling when she heard the different voices he used to read a story, her sister's comment lingered in her mind.

If he's The One, then you've got to give it everything you have. You just have to.

She had to reach for the banister and stop for a minute to get her bearings. Because he was. She'd known it all along. Her sister was right about something else. Coco had fallen for *Beckett*, and that meant she had to let him be everything he was. Adjusting to a new normal was part of the deal when two people came together.

Nothing made her happier than seeing his sleep-softened face at the breakfast table, his big hands lathering the shampoo in Posie's hair... And the evenings, when she had her tea, she really, really liked sharing that quiet time with him. Loved those moments when he'd show her images Jimmy had uploaded or tell her a story about that day's coaching.

Posie's giggle lured her the rest of the way up the stairs. Reaching her daughter's bedroom, she came to an abrupt stop when she saw them cuddled in bed together. Posie had her arm slung across his waist, her hand gently patting him, and Ollie lay stretched out across the foot of the bed, his legs straight out in front of him like he was flying.

She got hit with that same tug of fear—of growing attached to a man who'd leave. He might be her person, but that didn't mean he'd stay.

Leaning against the doorway, she watched them, but the moment Ollie noticed her, his tail started thumping on the duvet, nabbing Posie's attention.

"Mommy." She scrambled off the bed and made a run for her. Coco had just enough time to drop to a crouch to catch her daughter in her arms.

Ollie leapt off the bed, barely able to contain his enthusiasm, licking both their faces.

"Hi, baby." She hugged her. Catching Beckett watching, she smiled and mouthed, *Thank you.*

He closed the book and got off the bed. "You have a nice time?"

"Yep." As much as she loved seeing her sister, she would have loved to be part of this family moment. "Who's hungry for dinner?"

"I am. Beckett made lasna, but he said I couldn't eat it until you got home."

"You made lasagna?" she asked him.

He gave a little shrug. "Figured you wouldn't want to come home and start cooking."

"I'm starving, Mommy." Posie tore out of her arms and raced out of the room.

"You wouldn't be so hungry if you ate your lunch at school." They headed down the hall and down the stairs, Ollie keeping pace with them.

"How did you know I didn't eat my lunch?"

Like she'd ever reveal her daughter's tells. If Posie had

eaten her sandwich, she left the crusts in a baggie in the lunch box. If she didn't, she tossed the bag in the garbage.

Once in the kitchen, Beckett gestured to the counter. "I made a salad, too. You guys can get started on that while I let Ollie out."

"I'll do it." Posie charged toward the mud room. "I want to do it, Beckett. Can I take him out?"

"You can, but you know what that means right?" he asked.

"If he makes a poopy I have to pick it up. I don't care. I want to take him outside. Can I throw the ball to him?"

"He'd like that."

While Coco got plates out of the cabinet and silverware from the drawer, Beckett opened the back door, and the dog scampered out. He handed Posie a new tennis ball, and she gazed up at him as if he'd given her real fairy wings.

It was such a simple moment, and yet it filled Coco with so much happiness. She'd given up on finding Beckett years ago, along with the dream of a father figure for Posie after Ethan had moved away.

So, to see the two of them together...him, tall and easy-going, her, tiny and spirited...it just made her so damn happy.

As soon as Posie hit the lawn, Beckett left the door open so they could keep an eye on her in the fenced yard and met Coco at the sink. He leaned in, tipped her chin, and kissed her. "Missed you."

Setting the plates down, she wound her arms around his neck. "Missed you, too." She gazed into his eyes.

Is this real?

Do you feel this, too?

He broke into a little smile. *Yeah.* And then he tilted

his head and opened his mouth over hers. And damn this man could kiss. Slow, lazy swirls of his tongue, the easy caress of his palms on her back, sliding lower…and lower….

The anticipation killed her, and she jerked her hips forward, pressing hard against him. She deepened the kiss, wanting so much more of him.

He grabbed her ass, giving her a good squeeze. "You're gonna get it tonight."

"Promises, promises." She pulled away from him, glancing out the door to see her daughter sitting cross-legged on the lawn, petting Ollie's head as he chomped on a dog toy.

Grabbing her, Beckett lifted her onto the counter. Pushing her legs open, he stepped between them and gave her a deep, wild kiss, one she'd remember the rest of her life. Her body went hot, and her hands wanted all of him at once.

But just as she pulled up his shirt, he batted her hand away. "That was the teaser. You're going to have to wait for the good stuff." Picking up the plates, he set them on the table. "Is lasagna okay?"

"You want me to talk about dinner right now?" She fanned herself. "Fine. It's perfect." She brought the silverware over and set it down. "It's a real treat not to have to cook. Thank you."

"You're welcome. I was going to make my famous quinoa dish, but I wasn't sure she'd eat it."

"Spoiler alert: she won't."

"The way I make it? She'll love it. I'll even put my money where my mouth is."

"Oh, no, no. You leave that mouth alone. I've got plans for it. But if you're looking for a wager….hm, what should we put on the line?" As she got the salad dressing out of the fridge, she remembered what Gigi had said about self-reliance. If she had a hope in hell of developing something real with Beckett, she had to do this. "Babysitting. You pick her up from school, and instead of taking her to my mom's, you hang out with her."

He straightened as if he'd been goosed. "You'd trust me with her for a whole day?"

She set the food on the counter and faced him. "Yeah. I do." He'd been nothing but good with Posie, through all her moods. "And, even though I hired an event organizer, I'm feeling a little overwhelmed with the festival, so I could use a little extra time."

Looking troubled, his fingers tapped on the counter, and he swung a look at the backyard. "I have to tell you something."

Her heart started pounding. "Did something happen while I was gone?"

He watched out the back door, where they could see Posie flying around the lawn, Ollie chasing and leaping after her. "She told me something. She asked me not to tell you, but she's five, and I think you should know."

"I promise not to let her know you said anything, but you should always tell me. What did she say?"

"There's some boy in her class, Jessie, who's messing with her."

Damn that kid. "I know him. Messing how?"

Grinning, he came closer to her, cupping her chin and looking at her with affection. "Coco Cavanaugh in warrior mode is hot."

"Thank you. Now, tell me what that fucker's doing to my daughter."

"He's telling her she's not a fairy, that people can't fly.

281

And then, sometime this week, he chased her, yanked on the ribbons from those bracelets I bought her, and ripped them."

"What? She loves those bracelets. Why didn't she tell me?"

"She said you'd get mad."

"I am mad. That's the same kid who blew out the candles on her birthday cake before she finished making her wish."

As he pulled the lasagna out of the oven, she reached for a trivet and set it on the table. "This looks great." And it smelled good, too.

"So, what're we going to do about Jessie?"

Her heart missed a beat, and she looked away.

He grasped her wrist and turned her toward him. "What did I say?"

With tears clouding her vision, she blinked. "You said we."

He cocked his head. *Huh?*

"This is the first time you've included yourself in our little family unit. It's silly, and I'm being dumb, but she's never had a father, you know? It just…it's nice that you're here for her."

"I love her." His voice cracked. This confident, powerful man had never looked so vulnerable. He swallowed, biting his bottom lip. Color spread across his cheeks. "I do. I love her." He sounded like he couldn't believe it.

"I'm so glad. I've always wanted that for her."

"You say it like you're outside of it, that it's about me and Posie, but you're not. You're the center of everything, Coco. It's about us, this family. I'm not just falling for Posie. I'm falling for you, too."

For him to say something like that…*God. Is this happening? Is this real?* She quickly turned away from him. "You're the worst." She flipped on the faucet and rinsed her hands.

He tugged on her shoulder, forcing her to turn around and face him. "What'd I do?"

Winding her arms around his waist, she hugged him. "I just really needed to hear that."

"So…you're in this with me?"

You have no idea. But when she glanced up, she saw how much he needed to hear it. "I'm in this with you." Her whisper hung suspended, caught in the thick tension between them. He was going to kiss her. She just knew it.

But then Ollie came bounding back into the kitchen, followed by a sweaty little girl. "I'm hungry, Mommy."

Coco pulled away from Beckett, discretely wiping her eyes on a dish towel. "Okay, let's eat."

"Can I have some milk?" Posie asked Beckett.

"Sure." He went right into action, so eager to meet his daughter's needs.

It made Coco smile. "Tomorrow, Beckett's going to make us his famous quinoa." She kicked the step stool over to the sink. "Come on. Wash those slobbery hands."

Posie climbed on, as Coco ran the water and squirted soap onto her hands. "What's kee-wah?"

Beckett reached for a plastic cup. "It's like rice."

"I don't like rice."

"It's like pasta." He poured the milk.

"I don't like pasta."

"Since when don't you like pasta?" Coco asked. "What do you think macaroni and cheese is?"

"I like macaroni and cheese. I don't like pasta."

Handing her a dish towel, he waited for her to dry her

283

hands before handing off the milk. "Quinoa's like ice cream."

"It is? I love ice cream."

Coco rolled her eyes. "What do you say to Beckett?"

She chugged the milk, like a frat boy at a kegger. "Thank you, Beckett."

"Sure." After putting the milk back in the refrigerator, he pulled open the top drawer. "Look at all these vegetables. Perfect for my quinoa."

"You're putting vegetables in my ice cream?" Posie sounded appalled.

"Sweetie, he was kidding. Quinoa doesn't actually taste like ice cream. It's like rice, only he puts special flavors in it."

"I don't want any."

Coco cut Beckett a look. "The fun part is that I didn't say how long I'd need the babysitting. My parents have this cabin, and I've been dying for some alone-time."

On his way to the cabinet, he passed her, leaning in close. "Have I ever shown you my gold medals? I have *five* of them. Know how I got them? By not quitting. That's right. Champions aren't quitters."

"Well, this isn't snowboarding, and your tricks won't work on a five-year-old, so unless you put actual ice cream in your kee-wah, you'll have to pry her jaw open and spoon it in if you're going to win this bet."

Posie sat at the table. Up on her knees, she reached for a crayon from the cup and started drawing on the butcher block paper spread across it. Coco pulled a spatula out of the drawer and started for the table.

Beckett caught up to her. "What do you think about the Jessie situation? Do we leave it alone, and let her handle it? Or do we do something?"

"What did you say to her?"

"First, I asked if she wanted to tell you or her teacher. She said no. Then we play-acted. I pretended I was Posie, and she was Jessie."

"Seriously? That's so cool. What happened?"

"I told her we'd make fairy bracelets for her friends, so that they could all fly around the room with her. Jessie can't bully her if she's got backup."

"That's pretty clever. I would never have thought of that. I just hope the other kids don't reject the bracelets and join in on ridiculing her."

"I hadn't thought of that. Did I just make things worse?"

"You know, there's no right or wrong answers to any of these situations. We just have to wing it. Why don't I talk to their parents first, tell them we're making the bracelets and ask if their kids want them? That way, we're not giving them out randomly to kids who might join forces with Jessie. And then, if it happens again, I'll talk to the teacher."

"*We'll* talk to her." His expression said, *We're in this together, remember?*

And it was the damnedest thing because she was starting to believe him.

Hope sizzled in her chest.

He might just stay.

Chapter Sixteen

CARRYING HER TEA TO THE LIVING ROOM, COCO warmed at the sight of Beckett's big body sprawled on her couch. This late into July, nightfall didn't come until after eight, so they hadn't turned on any lamps yet. The light from his phone lit up his features, revealing a rare troubled expression.

She curled up in a corner. "Everything all right?"

He tugged on his scruff. She wasn't used to having such a masculine presence in her home, and she loved it. Loved the pop of his biceps, the hairy, muscular thighs, and bare man-feet.

"It's my mom."

"I thought you haven't talked to her in seventeen years?"

"I haven't. But she's been reaching out."

"What does she want?" she asked quietly.

"No idea."

Smiling, she nudged him with a foot. *Talk to me.* "What was your last conversation with her?"

"You really want to know?"

While she didn't think she could bear to hear how that woman had hurt Beckett, she nodded solemnly. She very much wanted to know.

"The last time I talked to my mom, I was twelve and a half. My dad and I were eating pizza at the kitchen table. It had been six months since Ari died, and I hadn't gone back to the academy. I'd wanted to be with my family. For some stupid reason, I'd thought Ari's death would pull us together."

"But that didn't happen."

"Ha. No. Basically, I stayed in my room, Dad had the living room with the TV on all the time, and my mom... she went on more trips than ever. I can't even tell you where she went, but we hardly saw her, and when we did, she ignored us."

"I know you said she disappeared, but didn't she take the time to talk to you? Just to make sure you were okay?"

"No. So, at that six month point my dad decided we were going to do family dinners. He told my mom and me he was ordering pizza and to be in the dining room at seven. She, of course, didn't show up, so it was just me and Dad silently eating. Swear to God, that pizza tasted like cardboard. I just wanted to go to my room. All of a sudden, my mom comes downstairs carrying a suitcase." He closed his eyes, and she could see the memory play across his features as if he were watching a movie. "Nothing unusual, right? She was always taking trips."

Setting her tea down, she moved closer to him, resting her head on his chest.

"Only this time, she wasn't coming back."

She pressed a hand to his thigh, wishing so much he'd put his arm around her. Just so she knew he didn't feel alone.

But he stayed still. "She said, 'Every time I look at you two I see Ari, and I can't do it anymore. I just can't stand to see your faces.' And she walked out the door."

No. How could a mother say something like that?

She could see that little boy at the table, forcing down a mouthful of pizza, while his mom cut out his heart. Reduced him to a wad of gum stuck to the bottom of her shoe.

Coco hated that woman.

Hated her.

"That was the last time my mother talked to me."

Hit with shock, disgust, and compassion for that twelve-year-old boy, Coco couldn't hold it in another second. "That's the most selfish thing I've ever heard. I am *so* sorry."

"Not long after that, I went back to the academy." He shrugged. "Life went on."

"What your mother did is inexcusable."

"Right. And now she wants to talk."

"Do you know why?" Cancer sprang to mind. The woman was dying and wanted to make peace? But she kept it to herself.

"My dad thinks she wants to make amends."

"What do her emails say?"

"They're short. The first one said, *Hey, can we talk*?" He chuffed. "After seventeen years of radio silence."

"Did you answer her?"

"Nah."

During that first conversation in Vegas six years ago, he'd blamed his rootlessness on his need to break free from the regimented life of a professional athlete. But now, she had no doubt he was on the run from emotional attachments. Because, for him, they hurt.

That's all he's ever known. A mom who didn't love him, a dad who wasn't there for him, and a sister—that he loved with all his heart—who died.

Her heart ached to give him love, to welcome him into the comfort of her family.

Would he ever be able to trust people again? After a childhood like that? "Do you have any good memories of your mom?"

"Sure, I do. She was fun as hell. She didn't make dinner, but we could eat ice cream out of the carton. She didn't follow rules, so we could stay up as late as we wanted."

"Memories of her. *With* her."

He seemed to give it some thought, before breaking out in a soft smile. "Every time she came back from a trip, she'd tell us stories. It was the only time I saw her happy. Most of the time, I had no idea what she was talking about, but those were the only times I got her attention."

"Well, I can see why you wouldn't want to hear her out, but I'm kind of curious what she wants after all these years."

"The thing is…there's nothing she could tell me that would change anything. I've had a lot of time to think about it, how I'd feel if she said, 'I'm sorry. I did a shitty thing, and I regret it.'"

"And? How would you feel?"

He shrugged. "I don't care. She didn't put in the effort when I was a kid, so…the attachment just isn't there." Under those long lashes, he flicked his gaze over to her. "Maybe I'm a callous ass, but I don't care about her excuses."

"No, you're not. I've seen you with Posie." *I know how you are with me.* "You're anything but callous."

He tipped his head back and closed his eyes, features tensing. "Part of the problem with my lifestyle is the way it'll hurt Posie." He straightened. "I remember what it felt like when my mom was away. I knew she wanted to be anywhere but home with me. And I don't want Posie to feel that, not for one minute of her life. That's why I'm not pushing to tell her I'm her dad."

"Except in this situation, it will never be that you don't want to be with her. It's different. She'll know you do."

Wait, am I telling him his lifestyle's okay?

I think I am.

"I don't want her to sit on a couch with someone when she's twenty-nine and have this same conversation about her father. 'He didn't put in the effort when I was a kid, so the attachment just isn't there.'" He looked so damn lost.

Oh, God. She reached for his hand, clasped it, and brought it to her mouth for a kiss. "That won't happen. You're nothing like your mom. Nothing. You're a passionate, deeply caring man."

He eyed her warily.

"I see you with Posie. Come on, the way you are with me?" *That's passion.* "With a mom like that, you could've become a serial killer. But you didn't. You went back to the academy and became a champion."

"I didn't go back because of some passion for boarding."

"You wanted to make Ari proud?"

He nodded, scraping his palm across his scruffy jaw. "After my mom left, my dad made sure to sit down with me for dinner. And then one night we were talking, and he told me he didn't know what happened when people died, but that he had a hard time believing our minds, our psyches, just disappear. And that meant, in some way, Ari's spirit was still around, and it would kill her to see us living such sad lives. He said nothing would thrill her more than to know I was on the slopes, doing the tricks that used to make her so damn happy and winning competitions. Between that and the comment my aunt made…"

"Oh, wow. I can't think of anything more motivating than that."

"Yeah, it worked. I was back within a week. About a year or two later, my coach said he'd never worked with an athlete as driven as I was." He gave her a sweet, adoring look and sifted his fingers through her hair. "I did it for Ari."

"She would've been so proud, watching you win all those medals." She squeezed his hand.

"Before a ride, we're supposed to visualize our runs. That's what we're doing at the starting gate, visualizing. But, for me, I was thinking about Ari. Pretending she was there in the crowd, imagining her screaming and pumping her fist. So that's why I won. Because I was picturing her face when they announced my score." As he quietly stroked her hair, she couldn't help wondering what he was feeling.

"You're nothing like your mom."

"I'm not so sure about that. But, honestly? She's the last thing on my mind right now. Her emails just annoy me. The only thing I can think about is you and Posie. I want to do right by both of you. And I don't think I know how."

Standing in the mud room, the late day sun warming his back, Beckett took Chris's call. "Hey, man, what's up?"

"Hey. We need to have a conversation."

This doesn't sound good. "Okay. Shoot." He glanced over when he heard Coco laugh, and he breathed in the scents of laundry detergent and baking bread.

"Look, we know you've got a lot on your plate. You've been walloped with some pretty big news, but we've only got one shot at this business. It either takes off, or we're screwed."

"I know that. And Jimmy's doing a great job." They couldn't possibly have an issue with his friend. "He's up for anything we throw at him, I've talked to my contacts, and they only have good things to say about him…he really wants to do this with us."

"It's not about Jimmy. It's about our growth. Did you get the data we sent?"

"Yeah."

"Look at when sales flattened out. It was right when you decided to take time off."

"I haven't missed a single event. The only blip we had was Willow, but I got Jimmy in there right away, and we haven't missed a beat."

"Beckett, man, you're missing the point. When you disappeared from our online presence, sales growth flattened. *You're* our partner. *You're* the face people expect to see. They're not seeing you, they're not as interested in watching people jump off mountains. Nothing against Jimmy, but he's not you. So, you've got to get back out there, and you've got to do it now."

Dammit. He hated this power they had over him. "I disagree. I've been doing some research." Specifically, he'd looked at the competition. "What we need are more guys in the field covering more events. That flattening comes because we only have so much content. We get three of us out there, and that curve's going to start climbing again."

"We can't afford to hire more people."

And I can't afford time away from my girls. So, he had to sell his plan. "We knew at some point we'd need equity to grow. That's the way it works."

"Hell, no. Private equity's going to take over, and you know it. We'll go from being owners to employees. That's what we're trying to avoid. Come on, man. The facts are in the data. We don't know why growth has flattened, we only know it coincides with you taking the summer off." His friend went quiet, and Beckett tensed. He had an uneasy feeling he knew what was coming.

They were going to call him out on nonperformance. And, as long as he sat on his ass in Calamity, they'd have a right to do that.

Fuck. He'd worked so damn hard on this. He'd worked countless hours to bring his vision to fruition.

He couldn't walk away from it.

But I'm not going half-ass on my relationship with Coco and Posie, either.

He honestly didn't think he could stand to be away from them for most of the year. *Then, what're you going to do about it?* "You don't want private equity, then I'll pay someone out of my own pocket. Because more content is what's going to gain us new subscribers. For the next three months, I'll put my money where my mouth is. If the numbers go up, they'll join our team, and we'll reassess. Okay?"

Chris let out a breath. "I'll talk to Dave about it. Listen, you know how much we respect you. This concept was yours, and we appreciate the opportunity you gave us to work with you on it. But we also know, without a doubt, that if the situation were reversed, if I were the one who'd found out I had a kid, and I'd had to take time off a couple months into our launch and our growth had flattened, you'd be having this same conversation with me."

Before he'd found his girls…yeah, he probably would have. But the world had changed for him. "I'll talk to a few guys I know and, if they're on board, I'll run them by you."

"Sounds good." Chris disconnected.

Reeling from the call, he pressed his forehead to the cool windowpane and let it sink in.

The idea that they'd boot him out of the business he'd spent the last six years building ground through him.

It wasn't just the money—though, he'd sunk a good amount of his savings into it. This was his career. He didn't have anything else.

It's my life. This was my vision, my concept.

He *needed* to see it through.

Sounds from the kitchen worked their way through his mental battle, and he listened to Posie chattering aimlessly, while her mom added comments here and there.

He wanted his business *and* his family, but the two lifestyles weren't compatible.

So, what do I do?

Until they saw real growth, he had to get back out there. Even if he hired someone, he still had to meet his contractual obligations.

Would FaceTime and text messages enable him to stay close while he traveled? If he came home after every trip, would that be enough?

Coco turned up the music, and a chair scraped back.

He stepped forward to watch as mother and daughter shook their bottoms to a Taylor Swift song.

Happiness curled around him. And it was the strangest damn thing to feel this way when nothing exceptional was happening. He'd always chased excitement, thought contentment came from a thrilling life. But, now, just cooking beside Coco or folding laundry while she worked at the kitchen table...those quiet moments...*that's where the joy lives.*

Even before Ari died, his home life had felt...unsafe. He'd had a roof over his head and two parents, and yet he'd gone hungry, dirty...uncared for.

Countless nights he'd gone to sleep with the covers drawn up to his nose, terrified of something he couldn't name.

Most nights, he'd lie in bed feeling uneasy.

Lost.

And that's it, right there.

For the first time in his life, he felt safe. Under this roof, with his daughter and Coco, it felt like home.

He pocketed his phone and came into the kitchen. In black leggings and a hot pink T-shirt, Coco spun around. He caught her around the waist and yanked her towards him. Watching, Posie hurled herself at him. Laughing, she lifted her arms, and he scooped her up, hitching her onto his hip.

This moment—the three of them connected, dancing in the sunny kitchen on a warm July day—was perfect.

He'd never felt so full. So complete.

Impulsively, he kissed Coco on the mouth. Emotion spiked, making his heart race. Posie's hand tightened around his neck, the three of them moving closer towards each other, until they stopped dancing, and just stood in the kitchen, barely aware of the change in rhythm when a new song came on.

No one said a word, and no one moved a muscle. Their scents merged—baby shampoo and Coco's subtle mix of vanilla and something floral—and he swore this moment would be imprinted on him for the rest of his life.

Sighing, Posie patted the back of his neck. "I love you, Beckett."

His heart stopped beating. Time came to a screeching halt.

Her words hung in the air, heavy as a rain cloud ready to break.

"I wish you could stay here forever."

Thunder clapped inside his chest, and hot, sticky emotion rained over him. His limbs shook, his knees wobbled. He swallowed.

And then he looked at his daughter and said, "I love you, too, Posie." *So damn much*. It shouldn't hurt to say those words. It should be a relief, right?

Except they seemed to tear through his flesh like a splinter dug out of a wound. They echoed in his mind, the sound waves merging with an ancient memory of when he'd said the same words to Ari.

His memories crashed into reality.

God, he'd loved Ari. With all his heart.

And he knew, standing there in the kitchen, with this perfect little girl in his arms, that he hadn't loved a single soul since she'd died.

Until now.

Before he could check them, tears erupted, spilled over, and he tucked his face into her neck. Coco hugged him tighter, lowering her cheek to his shoulder.

They stayed like that, awash in love, warmth, *family*.

The most perfect moment in his life.

And right then Beckett knew his priorities had shifted irrevocably.

Which meant he finally had his answer.

Posie was quiet on the ride home from school. Her dolls sat neglected on the seat beside her.

As soon as they walked into the house, she handed off her backpack to Beckett and hurried away.

He and Coco stood watching her. Normally, she'd dig through it and hand them permission slips, art work, and her lunch box.

As Beckett hung the strap over the peg, Coco started moving. "I better go talk to her."

But he couldn't help wondering if it had to do with Jessie, the fairy killer. "Can I?"

She stopped, held his gaze, and seemed to wrestle with her answer. She took a calming breath. "Of course. Yes."

Hurrying across the kitchen, he found Posie heading up the stairs. "I'm going to take Ollie on a walk. Want to come with me?"

She shook her head and continued up.

He watched her go, noticing the way she clutched the back of her fairy dress. "Posie?"

She reached for the banister before turning around to look at him. When she released her hold on the fabric, he saw the top layer of tulle was torn and a couple of the pale pink ribbons were missing.

"How are things going with Jessie?"

She looked away, her hand immediately going to the back of her dress. "He's mean. I don't like him."

"Has he bothered you?"

She gave him a yearning look, and he hoped like hell she'd confide in him. He was relieved when she said, "I was flying today, and he grabbed me and tore my dress." She tipped her chin. "I cried." She sounded ashamed, and it enraged him.

Bounding up the stairs, he cupped her face with both of his hands "You can cry. He upset you and ripped your dress, you can absolutely cry."

Big, fat tears spilled down her cheek, and she gazed up at him with a wounded expression. "It's my favorite dress. Ethan gave it to me, and he's gone now, and it's a *real* fairy dress."

"What's going on?" Coco stood at the bottom of the stairs, wiping her hands on a towel. She kept her voice calm, but Beckett had come to know her well enough to know she was restraining her anger.

Picking up his daughter, he carried her over to the couch, perching her on his lap.

Coco sat close beside them, smoothing the hair off Posie's forehead. "What happened, sweetheart?"

Posie looked at Beckett, and he hoped she saw his encouragement.

Finally, his little girl broke down. "Jessie's so mean, Mommy. He tore my dress, and this is my favorite, and he broke the special bracelets Beckett gave me, and now I can never get them again."

"Oh, baby. I'm so sorry."

It was killing him. Jesus, he wanted to grab his sword and fight off the entire world for his little girl.

"Well, the good news is that we bought all that material and ribbons so we could make new bracelets for you and your friends." Coco got up. "Which means I can fix your dress. I'll be right back. I'm going to get my sewing box." Before leaving the room, she gave him a sharp look over their daughter's head.

He gave a terse nod. *Enough.*

Time to take action.

Chapter Seventeen

Stopped at a traffic light, Coco waited for Beckett to finish typing furiously on his phone, before she asked, "Is everything all right?"

His anger leaked out as though she'd pricked him with a pin, and he gave a defeated sigh. "My partners are talking about kicking me out."

What? "It's your app. I thought you invited them to work with you."

"I did, but we're equal partners. I get it."

"Just because Willow didn't jump off a bridge? I thought your friend Jimmy was doing a good job." The car behind her honked, and she quickly hit the accelerator, driving across the intersection.

"For the first six months, we saw ridiculous growth, but it started to flatten as soon as I stopped traveling."

"Well, maybe the novelty wore off. Maybe, instead of firing you, you need to come up with something new, a fresh idea. Maybe you guys need to market to a new audience."

He gave her a smile. "I like the way you think. I told

them instead of booting my ass out, we need to hire more people to cover more events. More content, but you're right. We need to hire someone to market the app."

"Well, one morning I'll take you to the diner, and you can meet the Cooters. They're a group of retirees who meet there every day, and let me tell you, you won't believe the careers these people have had. I can almost guarantee we'll find a marketing whiz."

"I like that."

"In any event, you leave for France next week, so it'll be business as usual."

"It's never going to be business as usual. Everything's changed."

Her fingers tightened around the steering wheel, as she turned down Hangman's Lane. "What does that mean?" *Dammit.* Her heart was pounding. His answer meant everything.

Please don't bail. Please, please, please don't bail on your daughter.

Don't bail on me.

"I'm thinking about buying a house here."

Energy flooded her system, making her jittery.

Why am I getting so worked up over this? Even if he sold his shares and bought a house here tomorrow, it still wouldn't last. He'd grow restless, and then he'd leave.

That's his nature.

And yet…she pressed for more. "Buying a house and…?"

He rubbed his scruff, staring out the window, his gaze unfocused. "If this is my home base, then I'd come here after every trip. I'd make the trips shorter. Just until we've sold the app, and then I'd live here full-time. Maybe coach." He didn't sound excited about that prospect.

"Maybe a lawyer could take a look at the contract?"

"No, I know what it says. We very deliberately wrote it this way. I foresaw this exact situation—only I figured it would happen to one of them. They'd get married, have a kid, the wife would start making demands—" He cut her a look. "Legitimately."

"Don't include me in that. I'm not a wife, nor would I ever make demands. I don't need you to stay." *Ugh. Yes, I hear myself.* "I mean, you're welcome to stay. Obviously. Posie already told you that, but we'd never give you an ultimatum. We understand this is your job. Your career. You have to earn a living."

"I want to stay." The vulnerability in his tone plucked a chord in her soul.

And shook the walls until they collapsed. "I want you to stay, too." At the stop sign, she reached for him, and they clasped hands tightly. "So much. And that might be the hardest thing I've ever said. Because, to tell you the truth, there's a huge part of me that knows my world can't compare to running with the bulls and jumping off a cliff in a wingsuit. That there's no comparison. Why would you ever choose me and Posie over your exciting, wild life?"

Wrapping a hand around her neck, he pulled her close and kissed her mouth. "Because I'm crazy about you. And the three-minute thrill of flying off a cliff's got nothing on the way I feel just sitting in a car, talking to you. You get that, right?"

"I'm starting to." She wanted to climb onto his lap and thank him for the kindest words ever spoken to her, but they had an appointment, and they couldn't be late. After sewing the torn dress, Coco had called the school and spoken to Posie's teacher, who'd agreed to meet with them while the kids were in art.

She pulled away, checked in both directions, and continued the final block to Posie's school. "So, what will you do?"

"I pitched the job to a friend of mine, Shep, and he's down to do it. But I really like your suggestion about marketing, so I'll get on that, too. I think…I'm not ready to leave you—not yet—so I'm going to get Jimmy to cover France for me."

What is happening right now? It took everything she had to keep her emotions in check. "I thought everyone needs to be a gold medalist?"

"He's got one. But, so they can't get me for nonperformance…" He broke into a breathtaking smile. "I'm going to cover Calamity."

"I like the way you think." Her spirits soared. "Given the terrain, we've obviously got plenty of extreme adventures here. Not just heli skiing, but we've got a V-plus white water rafting trip that'll blow your mind. And, no, I haven't done it. But you can bet the Bowies have."

"I'll talk to them when I get to work today."

"Was it your plan to do every single event on the globe by yourself?" She slowed as she neared the school and eased her tires over the speed bump. "That could fill every day of your calendar for the rest of your life."

"Pretty much, yeah." He lifted their joined hands and pressed a kiss on the back of hers. "That was before I had something else in my life."

"Something, huh?" She cracked a sarcastic grin. "Well, that's better than nothing."

"It's better than anything."

Joy exploded in her chest, as she turned into the parking lot. *Better than anything.* God, no one had ever made her feel this way. He was the first person to ever make her feel exceptional just for being who she was.

Could she trust that it would last? That he could actually stay here?

Or were they just words issued in the heat of the moment? *This is all new to him.* He could just be getting carried away.

And that's an answer only time could give.

She found a spot, killed the engine, and reached for her purse.

"Wait." He caught her wrist. "From the minute I retired, I've blown off rules and restrictions. I've lived free as a bird."

"I *know*. And I don't want you to feel trapped by us. I never want you to resent us. I'm not asking for anything from you."

"That's what I'm getting to. That's my point. I don't feel 'trapped.' I thought freedom meant no ties, but loving Posie, loving *you*, is the greatest sense of freedom I've ever felt."

Loving me?

Did he just say he loves me?

"I guess…it wasn't training that made me feel trapped. It's fear."

Holy cow. What a revelation. God, she admired this man. He faced such hard truths about himself.

"You know what I realized last night after turning into a sap just from dancing with my girls? I haven't loved a single person since Ari died. Not one. Until you. I *love* you, Coco."

She opened her mouth to say it back, but fear caught love from behind and slammed it to the ground.

"You're the most beautiful woman I've ever seen." He

reached for a lock of her hair and rubbed it between two fingers. "I felt it the first time I saw you in Vegas, this pull, this…recognition. And, through all these years, you've lived inside me like this hot, little piece of coal. Every now and then I'd feel it, and it'd make me think about you, and I'd get this tug. Like, *her. That one.*"

She couldn't speak through the jumble of emotions hitting her all at once.

"Now, after spending the summer with you, I get it. There's no one like you. There never will be. I'm programmed for you. I'm trying to hold onto my business, but the idea of walking away from you and Posie…it's not going to happen. We'll figure it out, I promise. I *will* travel, that's my job, but I'm going to hire other people so I won't be away nearly as much. And I'm going to talk to you first. Ask what Posie has coming up. Because her recitals and seeing her get ready for the prom…all of that comes before my *job.*"

"I can't believe I'm hearing this."

"I can't believe I'm saying it. But I mean it. I missed five years, and I don't want to miss a minute more."

She wanted to trust him—with everything in her—she did. But…it was just so damn hard for her to do. "We need to get in there."

Oh, dammit. His expression. He'd just opened his heart to her, and she shut him down like it hadn't meant anything to her.

I'm scared.

I'm just so scared of believing him.

"She's waiting for us."

As they headed into the one-story building, he reached for her hand. She could see it in his eyes, *Hey, I'm here. We're in this together.* So, she slowed down.

He's not the only one who's been ruled by fears. I have, too.

If she wanted to ensure he didn't stay, holding herself back emotionally would absolutely do it.

This is what I do to keep myself safe.

He'd cut himself open for her, and if she didn't do the same, these roots he was planting would never take hold.

He pulled the door open, letting her pass through. She turned into the office and smiled at the school secretary. "Morning, Gina." She wrote down their information in the guest log. "We've got an appointment to see Mrs. Thompson." She scribbled their names on badges, ripped the backing of his, and slapped it on his chest.

He grabbed her hand before she could pull away.

She gazed up at him. "Nice reflexes."

He grinned, and her heart flipped over. There was nothing on this earth as powerful as Beckett O'Neill's smile. Like the best song, it held the power to change her mood.

She smoothed her badge on and turned to go. "Thanks, Gina. Have a great day."

They walked quietly down the hall. As they passed each open door, they could hear children chattering, music playing, or the gentle voice of a teacher.

Be brave.

This man's worth it.

Outside Posie's classroom, she touched his arm. "Giving you my heart is by far the scariest thing I've ever done. But I don't want you to think I'm not in it with you. I am." She needed to find the right words. This moment felt big. Probably the biggest of all. "It's true that I don't need you to help with bills or take out the trash, although I could use some help getting Posie to wear pants every now and then. But what I feel for you...I've never felt this for anyone before. And I'm terrified of how much I need to see you walk in the door every morning. I'm scared of how badly I need you to touch me and kiss me. My *heart* needs you, and that's the scariest thing of all."

He leaned in to press a soft kiss to her mouth. "I won't take your gift lightly. I promise to take care of your heart." He stepped back and gave a chin nod to the door. *Is this it?*

She nodded. Opening it, they walked in to find the teacher in a closet. "Mrs. Thompson?"

The woman turned around, carrying a plastic box of crayons. "Oh, hey. Come in, come in." As she headed over, she extended her hand to Beckett. "Hello, I'm Carol Thompson."

"Beckett O'Neill." He gave her a smile and a firm shake.

"He's..." In her moment of hesitation, she could see Beckett tense up. "He's the one Posie's been confiding in."

As the teacher went to sit down at a small table, Beckett cut Coco a look. *What was that?* But it wasn't like she'd tell the teacher before revealing it to Posie.

"Please, sit down." Mrs. Thompson gestured to the other chairs. "Tell me what concerns you."

Coco dropped into a chair made for short, little legs. "You know about Posie's obsession with fairies." She was ready to launch into the long, convoluted story.

But Beckett jumped right in. "You've got a kid named Jessie, who's bullying her about it."

The teacher's eyes flared at the accusation, so Coco gave some history. "I saw a hint of it at Posie's birthday party several weeks ago, when he blew out the candles on her cake. It wasn't a big deal, so I didn't think much of it."

"But Posie doesn't want anyone to know what he's

been doing to her, so she's kept it all to herself." Beckett sounded tough, firm. "She told me he makes fun of her, calls her 'stupid' and tells her fairies aren't real. Which is fine. Kids do that. But he chased her and tore the ribbons off her fairy bracelets."

When she saw the teacher's hint of a smile, Coco added, "And then, yesterday, he tore her dress."

The teacher sighed. "I know."

Beckett sat forward. "You knew he was bullying her?"

"No, of course, not. And I wouldn't call it bullying. Posie's a force to be reckoned with. Believe me, no one bullies her."

"And yet he's damaged her clothing," Beckett said.

"And made her cry," Coco said. "She's having a very hard time with this."

"What I meant was…" She used her placating tone, and it irritated the crap out of Coco. "I'm aware of his interest in her. I've seen him chasing her, and you can bet I've talked to him about it. Of course, I had no idea Posie was upset. She hasn't cried or come to me. From what I can see, she's handling it well on her own. That's why I haven't seen a reason to get involved."

The words hit like missing a step, filling her with cold dread.

She's handling it well on her own.

Of course Posie's not asking for help. She's five years old, and she's already learned to do everything on her own.

Because God forbid she ask for help and someone lets her down.

I did this to her.

"I'm sure you know how boys get when they have crushes," Mrs. Thompson continued. "They poke and tease—"

Beckett's eyes narrowed. "Don't. Don't even go there. Nobody gets a pass for hurting someone—not for any reason. And don't give that line to Posie. I don't want my daughter going through life thinking it's okay for a guy to show his interest in her through cruelty."

In the stark quiet after he finished talking, Coco could see the teacher processing his words. But the two words that mattered most pulsed like a living thing.

My daughter.

And she couldn't even be angry that he'd said them out loud.

Because this man was a fierce father, and it wasn't something she could—or wanted—to suppress.

"You're right," Mrs. Thompson finally said. "That was lazy of me. I'm sorry. I care very much for Posie, and I will pay closer attention to the situation. I didn't know she was upset. She doesn't show it."

"She doesn't need to show it," Beckett said. "It's your job to pay attention to how the kids are treating each other, and if you see Jessie showing his 'interest' in a negative way, you need to step in and teach him the right way to express it."

Mrs. Thompson's features flushed. "You're right." She looked down at her fingertips. "I'm sorry, and I'll do better."

"Thank you," Beckett said.

Coco loved not just how he'd stood up for Posie, but that he'd backed off the moment the teacher apologized.

He's a good man.

A really good man.

The moment they got back in the car, she said, "Thank you for that. I would've had a totally different approach. I would've gone easy on her, but you were right. You didn't put up with her tired excuse." She started the engine but didn't back out. "I've been focused on the part of you that's a flight risk. And that's been my mistake. If I had to choose the best father in the world for my little girl, it would be you. Hands down, every day of the week." She pulled away from the curb. "It would be you."

"Thank you. That…means the world to me."

"And you know what else? Fuck my fears."

His eyebrows shot up.

"They not only hold me back, but I've passed them on to my daughter. She doesn't come to anyone for help with a damn bully?" She shook her head. "That changes right now."

Chapter Eighteen

DONE WITH COACHING, BECKETT HEADED FOR THE office to catch up with the Bowies. If he wanted to keep his company, he needed to post about Calamity.

Funny, though, how badly he wanted to head to the parking lot. He couldn't think of a time in his life when going home held more appeal than working—packing for a trip, heading to the airport, checking into a hotel—all of it used to get him pumped up.

Now, though, he wanted to be home with his girls. He wanted to be with Coco all the damn time.

On his way to the main building, he pulled out his phone to check in with her. With the chocolate festival coming up the day after tomorrow, she'd been working crazy hours. Between greeting the chocolatiers and getting them situated and handling last minute issues, she was a one-woman show of efficiency and organization.

Beckett: Heading home in a few minutes. You need anything?

Coco: I'm good, thanks. Tables being delivered right now.

He couldn't help feeling disappointed. But just before he opened the door, his phone buzzed again.

Coco: I did it again, didn't I? Let's start over. Hey, I sure could use some help.

He grinned.

Beckett: Anything.

Coco: The printer screwed up—delivered the wine tasting posters to me, and the chocolate festival ones to the winery, which means the event organizer had to go all the way to Idaho Falls to swap. Now, I'm alone in the ballroom trying to figure out her drawings, so the guys know where to set up the tables. Do you speak schematics?

Beckett: Like a second language. On my way.

It was a lie, of course. What did he know about setting up for a festival? But he'd sure as hell give it his best shot.

Coco: How'd I do?

He grinned, knowing how hard it had been for her to ask for help. He was glad she'd done it anyway.

Beckett: You did great. Did it hurt to ask?

Coco: Little bit.

And now she's being cute. Grinning outside the office door, he knocked before heading in.

"Hey, man." Fin sat at his desk.

Brodie leaned against the wall, Gray slouched in a chair, and Will leaned over Fin's shoulder, pointing at something on the computer screen. The guys looked over and said, "Hey."

"Am I interrupting something?"

Will straightened. "Fin wants to get married on the glacier."

"He's taking your spot launching our wedding business," Brodie said.

"Cool, right?" Fin grinned.

Will shook his head in disgust. "For you. You think Callie wants to get married on a sheet of ice?"

"Callie runs the museum in town," Gray said. "She's an artist. She's not into boarding." His expression said, *Can you believe it?*

"Just because she's artsy doesn't mean she can't shred." Fin scowled at his brother. "She boards with me all the time." He turned his attention to Beckett. "Forget these assholes. You're not interrupting anything." He tipped his chin. *Talk.*

"Got an issue with Danny."

Their easy expressions turned hard with concern. "What's going on?" Fin asked.

"He's freezing up. I think Katie's injury last year's freaking him out. He could use some sessions with a sports psychologist."

"Yeah, makes sense," Gray said. "He was there when it happened. Saw the whole thing."

"It was gruesome." Brodie shook his head. "Tough break. She worked her ass off to make the team." His promising career had ended with an injury, too, so Brodie got it.

"Yeah, so I think he needs to talk to someone." He knew these guys would take care of the boy.

"I'll get on that," Fin said. "Thanks for bringing it up."

"You bet."

"You off?" Brodie asked.

"Yeah, I've got to help Coco set up for the festival." He was so eager to see her, he'd almost forgotten his second reason for stopping by. "Oh. I'm going to include Jackson Hole on my app. Figured you guys could hook me up with all the good things to do."

"Sure," Fin said. "Be happy to."

"Or you could hit up some of the outfitters in town." Gray turned around in his chair. "They'd have a comprehensive list of things to do."

"Most of them just set up hunting and fishing trips," Brodie said. "Which is why I want to have a full-service kind of place in the resort, offering everything from guided hikes to heli skiing. I'm thinking of setting up an office in the lobby that'll arrange trips like that."

"It's a good idea," Fin said. "And I can think of ten people off the top of my head who'd want to run that for you."

I could do that.

Actually, he'd love to do it.

"Okay, I gotta go. Coco needs me, but let's meet tomorrow and see if you've got any good extreme adventures for me."

"Oh, we've got a few," Fin said with a mischievous grin.

As he left, he thought about running an outfitter company, being part of the Bowie world. He'd never had brothers, obviously, but they sure made it look fun.

Maybe, after he and his partners sold the app, he could come here and do that.

Of course, the company would be well-established by then, and they wouldn't need him. But the idea had opened up possibilities that didn't include him wearing a suit and heading off to the bank each morning.

With hot water sluicing down her skin and the fragrant scent of the hotel's body wash filling her senses, Coco tipped her chin down, closed her eyes, and gave in to the soothing massage.

"Your skin's so soft." Beckett's deep voice, nearly a growl, was filled with hunger. Like what he really wanted was to get his hands full of her.

She'd set an entire day aside to set up the ballroom, but thanks to her family, some friends, Beckett, and the Cooters, they'd finished early. Which meant...she was totally ready for the festival tomorrow.

After a whole year of planning, the day had finally come.

She could hardly believe it.

"I loved watching you work today," he said. "Bossing Tyler Cavanaugh around? Hot."

As much as she wanted to turn in his arms and kiss that sexy mouth, she needed the pressure of his kneading thumbs. Between the heavy labor of yesterday's tables and today's banners, tablecloths, and signage, her muscles ached. Beckett had set Posie up on a playdate and booked them a room in the resort so they could relax, order in, and just take a few hours to themselves.

Steam swirled around them in the glass-enclosed shower stall. His big, strong hands, slick with body wash, felt so good on her neck and shoulders. Was it possible to be relaxed and excited at the same time?

Because, come on. She had Beckett O'Neill naked in the shower with her.

"It's taking every ounce of restraint and respect I have for you to not fuck you from behind, you know that, right?"

And the things he said. *God.* Leaning against his chest, she arched her back. "And I appreciate that *so* much." Cupping her soapy breasts, she pushed them together and

ERIKA KELLY

squeezed. "That's the last thing I want right now. *Obviously.*"

He practically growled, and she loved teasing him.

"You know all I can see is my cock between those fuck-hot tits, right?" His hands slid down her back, until he cupped her ass. Bending his knees, he slid his hard length between her cheeks and pumped.

"Mm." The insistent pulsing between her legs drove her wild.

His mouth opened just below her ear, and he pressed wet, hungry kisses along her jaw. "The last thing, huh? You sure about that?"

She turned towards him, pressing a hand against his cheek to guide him to her mouth. God, she wanted him. She was ravenous for his kiss, the possessive grip of his hands. "The only thing I'm sure of is that I want you." It was her turn to whisper in his ear. "And you can have me anyway you want."

Lifting her, he pressed her against the warm tile. His passionate kisses turned her blood hot, melting her bones. The softness, the heat and wet of his mouth, it just undid her. She clung to him, desperate to feel him everywhere.

Never breaking their connection, he carried her to the stone bench, out of the spray, and set her down. He dropped to his knees, spreading her legs wide, and licking into her wet, throbbing center.

She cried out, her fingers scraping across his scalp, pushing his wet hair off his face, so she could see everything. He loved bringing her pleasure. It was etched in the skin around his eyes, evident in the lusty strokes of his tongue.

Draping her legs over his shoulders, she tilted her hips and reveled in the sensations racing through her. He

316

cupped her ass, holding her against his face, as he stroked her clit and lavished it with the kind of attention that made her shoulders hit the glass wall and her back arch.

Glittering heat raced through her veins, and desire spun so fast she lifted right out of her body, lost in sensation, and racing for her climax. As it gripped her, her toes curled, her fingers fisted in his hair. "Beckett." Pleasure spiked so hard and fast it was almost painful, and she rode one wave after another, until her body, spent, slouched back on the bench.

He looked up at her, alert, straining, and pressed a kiss to her mouth. "Get over here."

She slung her arms around his neck, and he carried her back under the shower head, rinsing the soap off her skin. Kicking the door open, he grabbed a towel and bundled her up, before leading her to the bedroom.

She fell onto the mattress, her body still humming. The way he looked at her, all intense and urgent, made her pull the towel open and bare herself to him.

His nostrils flared, the muscle in his jaw ticked, and his gaze blazed a path from her mouth to her breasts to the patch of hair between her legs. "You. Are. Mine."

Beckett had never been harder in his life. This woman— Jesus, her wet hair all tousled, her plump breasts bouncing as she shifted restlessly on the bed. "Back in Vegas…" His fingertips circled her nipple. Goosebumps burst, pebbling her skin. "I wish we'd exchanged numbers."

"You weren't ready for me then."

"I'm not ready for you now."

She stilled.

He leaned over her, planting his hands on either side of her head. "If you were anybody else, I'd be gone already. But it's you. And what I feel for you is so much more than want, more than need. My love for you is more powerful than my demons."

Her features softened, and she reached for him.

Yeah. She's mine.

For the first time, he saw that those ties he'd avoided connected him to something bigger than himself, something deeper, way more important and powerful than anything he'd ever experienced.

And living for himself felt small and inconsequential in comparison.

I love her like I've never loved anyone in my life.

"I need to be inside you."

"Yes."

"Bare." He knew she was on the pill. "I've only ever used a condom."

She nodded. "Do it. I want it, too."

Kneeing her legs wider, he settled between them. He kissed her neck, licked her nipple and sucked it into his mouth, his tongue circling and flicking. When she arched into him, he grasped his cock and slowly entered her slick heat. *Oh, fuck.* He took his time, savoring every flash of sensation as he pushed into her.

Nothing had ever felt so good. Her hands on his ass pulled him deeper, and he breathed in the scent of body wash rising off her heated skin. His cock ached for friction. He was going to fuck her so hard.

Once fully inside her, he lowered his face into her neck and just savored the moment. Her hips rocked, her hands squeezed, but he forced himself to start a slow, easy rhythm. Jesus, it was so intense, so fucking hot between them.

She sighed in his ear. "You feel so good."

As pressure built at the base of his spine, as his cock ached for release, he got up on his arms to watch as he drove into her. Her half-lidded eyes, that pretty pout of a mouth, and those jiggling breasts, sent him out of his mind with lust.

"Have to have you. Have to—*fuck*." Hands gripping her hips, he sealed their bodies together as he sat back on his heels. Her arms went over her head, her hands flat against the headboard as he pounded into her, his cock glistening with her arousal.

He never wanted this to end.

It doesn't have to.

I can hire people to take all the trips.

And then I can have this every day.

She cried out, her head tipping back. All that dark hair spread out around her, gleaming in the lamplight.

Lust, passion, Jesus, it swept him away, until he was nothing but sensation. Want, need, all of it burning out of control. Jesus, he was going to come so fucking hard.

But he didn't want to. Not yet.

Pulling out, he leaned forward and cupped her breasts, giving them a squeeze. "Turn over. Want to see that peach of an ass."

Getting up on her knees and elbows, she looked at him over her shoulder, that tousled hair half-covering her eyes, her mouth swollen from kisses, and she gave him a grin so seductive he didn't think he could hold back.

He lifted her ass higher and slid back inside her slick heat. Fuck, she felt so good, so tight. The hourglass shape of her torso was so beautifully feminine it turned him into an animal. As he pounded into her, her cries and moans, the slap of their bodies, filled the room.

"God, Beckett."

His blood quickened, his skin tightened, until the pressure grew unbearable.

"I love it when you fuck me. Love it so much."

The shock of those words coming out of her mouth—this beautiful mother, businesswoman, daughter, and friend...shattered his restraint.

He fucked her hard, swiveling his hips every time he slammed into her. He fucked her and he fucked her, until her moans turned to cries. He'd already made her come tonight, so to see the tension gripping her spine and shoulders, to feel her body tighten, grow slicker, it just turned him into a beast.

He grabbed a fistful of her hair and tugged her head back. "Want to see you come." He needed to see the tension break and euphoria hit.

And that was all it took. Her body seized with a climax, twisting and writhing.

It was the hottest thing he'd ever seen in his life. He couldn't take another second. Slamming hard up against her, he pumped in short, tight thrusts until he came so hard it blinded him.

Collapsing beside her, he shut his eyes and let his breathing come under control.

He loved her.

Loved his daughter.

And there wasn't a damn thing that would keep him from them.

· · ·

While Beckett flipped the French toast, Posie sat on the floor with her dolls. Beside them, Ollie ate his breakfast. He smiled when he realized that the soundtrack of his life had become the crunch of kibble and the rambling dialogue of his daughter and her dolls.

"Come give Mommy a hug." Coco breezed into the kitchen, looking gorgeous in a wine-red dress that accentuated the sexy flare of her hips.

"I want to go with you." Posie got up. "You said I could."

"And you are. Grandma's going to bring you by later today."

"Why can't I go with you and Beckett right now?"

Good question. Oddly, they still hadn't fully embraced the idea of him parenting. In spite of how close they'd all become, he still took on the role of guest more than father.

When he thought of being alone with her—being fully responsible for her—his muscles clenched.

But he could do this. He'd *been* doing it.

Sliding the spatula under the toast, he dropped it onto a plate. On his way to the table, he said, "Come on and eat."

Abandoning her dolls on the floor, Posie hoisted herself onto the bench seat.

He squirted syrup on it. "I was going to help your mom out, but how about I stay home with you this morning, and then we can both go over there this afternoon?" He cut a look to Coco to see how she felt about the idea.

He loved the moment her hesitation broke into a slow, blossoming grin. She trusted him with her daughter. His confidence wavered, but he wouldn't succumb. He wouldn't fall into that dark hole.

I got this.

"I could do that?" Posie sounded like it was some great treat.

"Absolutely."

"Yay." She stood up on the seat and flung herself into his arms. "Mommy, mommy, I get to be with Beckett today."

Her enthusiasm snagged Ollie's attention, so the kitchen was filled with the sounds of barking and shouting, and it all filled him up with an unspeakable joy.

"Okay, my little fairy princess. It's you and me today."

Coco stood off to the side, just a few yards from the ballroom entrance, and took in her festival.

The room was packed, and the scent of warm chocolate from the fountain in the center filled the air. Each chocolatier had gone all-out in creating an attention-drawing booth, resulting in a brisk business. She watched as they engaged with the guests, explaining their processes and offering samples. Everyone had prettily wrapped bags for sale.

"There you are." Gigi rushed over and wrapped her in her arms. "I can't believe you did this. It's amazing."

"It is. I'm so happy right now."

She pulled away. "Where's Posie and Beckett?"

"They went for a bike ride, so they won't be here till a little later." She sounded calm and rational, but only because if she shared her concerns she'd flip out. And she wasn't going to do that in the middle of her chocolate festival.

"Is this his first time alone with her?"

Leave it to Gigi to read her so well. "He's been alone with her at home, but he's never taken her out of the house." Posie could be stubborn and impulsive. If she heard the ice cream truck cruising around the town green, she might go racing after it, darting out into the street.

"You're not used to relying on anybody." Gigi rubbed her arm. "It's just a bike ride. Everything's going to be fine."

Chapter Nineteen

"I WANT ICE CREAM."

Beckett lowered the kickstand and swung a leg over his bike. His daughter gazed up at him with an assessing look. She was clever, this one. Liked to push him, see how much she could get away with.

Yeah, well, I might be new to this, but I'm not stupid. "With all the chocolate you're going to have at the festival, I'd rather we just get a drink." *Which is why we stopped here in the first place.*

He'd been surprised to learn she didn't have a bike, so he'd gone ahead and bought her one. Since her mom didn't have one either, he'd bought a set of three.

He hoped Coco wouldn't mind. He almost always checked with her first, but he wasn't about to bother her during the festival. Besides, a bike was pretty harmless.

"But I want ice cream."

"Well, which do you want more? Ice cream right now or chocolate at the festival?"

She didn't look happy, but she conceded. "Chocolate."

And I was worried about this parenting gig.

I got this.

It's much easier than I thought.

The rumble of wheels on concrete sent a signal of alarm racing down his spine. A group of skateboarders whizzed by, so close he felt the breeze. He grabbed Posie's arm, yanking her out of their way. "Watch it," he barked, while lifting her up. *Jesus.* They could've mowed her down. "You okay, sweetheart?"

She looked shaken. "They're bad boys. Very, very bad."

A woman rushed out of the coffee shop wearing a Calamity Joe's apron. "That was a close call. You okay, Posie?"

His little girl nodded, tightening her hold on his neck.

"They shut down the skate park this summer to make some improvements," the woman said. "So, those kids are everywhere. The mayor's barred them from public spaces, but they don't pay attention to anything."

"Good to know. We were going to stop for a drink, but I think we'll just head home. We've got to get to the festival anyhow."

"Oh, come on in," the woman said. "She's had a scare. I'll whip up her favorite vanilla frappé."

"Can I, Beckett? Please?"

When her eyes sparkled like that, he couldn't refuse her anything. "Yeah, okay. Sure."

The woman smiled and headed back inside.

Posie wriggled to get free. With the skate boarders gone, he set her down.

"Take this off." She tugged at the strap of her helmet.

He'd had a hell of a time getting her to wear it since it "scrunched" her fairy headband.

Pinching the buckle, he pulled it off and set it on her handlebar. "Come on." He reached for her hand, and the feel of it sent a rush of protectiveness through him. This kid made him a mess of emotions.

"Can I have chocolate milk?"

"You're cute, but I wasn't born a grown man. I was five once, too. The answer's no Miss Chocolate Pants."

"I'm not wearing pants."

"That nice lady's making you a vanilla frappé, so that's what you're getting." He reached for the door.

With a look of horror, she patted the top of her head. "My crown." She yanked her hand out of his and took off running.

"Posie." Right then, he heard the gravelly sound of wheels on pavement. The skateboarders were back. He bolted after her, but it was too late because the pack of boys swarmed the sidewalk and swallowed his little girl up.

He'd lost sight of her.

Fuck. He pushed through just as one of the teens fell down hard, his skateboard shooting out and slamming into a garbage can.

In the chaos of his thundering heart and the punishing white noise in his brain, he found Posie laying on the ground. Wide-eyed, she blinked at him, confused, terrified.

He knelt beside her. "You okay, sweetheart?" Without looking up from her, he said, "Call nine-one-one. Now."

"Already did," someone said. "On their way."

She's okay. She's just stunned. But he wouldn't move her, just in case she'd hurt her back, neck…brain.

No. She's going to be fine.

My daughter will be fine.

In that moment of not knowing if his daughter would be all right, he became acutely aware of everything. Oddly, he smelled coffee, the hot sun baking concrete, and the rubber soles of sneakers.

Those frail shoulders lifted off the sidewalk, as she tried to get up.

She's okay.

He let out a harsh breath. *Thank Christ.*

She got knocked down. No big deal. "Hang tight, sweetheart. I want to make sure you're okay."

But she didn't listen. Just as she sat up, her eyes rolled back in her head, and her body went limp. In an instant, her skull smacked against the pavement.

His heart stopped beating. "Posie? Honey?"

Nothing. She lay so still, those delicate eyelids shut.

Jesus Christ. Posie.

I lost her.

She's gone.

Pain engulfed him, the harrowing loss amplified by the memory of his sister laying in this exact position.

His perfect little girl…gone.

A siren split the air, bright lights spun, and then paramedics came. With a flurry of brisk, efficient movement they strapped a neck brace on her, laid her out on a clean, white stretcher, and loaded her into the back of the ambulance.

"You coming?" a paramedic asked.

Beckett stood there, locked in pure, raw pain.

"Sir, you coming?"

"Yes. Of course." He forced himself to follow the young woman, climb into the back, and reach for Posie's delicate, lifeless hand.

The door slammed shut, the ambulance took off.

What have I done?

. . .

The curtain whipped closed, and the doctor entered the small, dark cubicle.

Beckett's pulse spiked. "Is she going to be okay?"

He didn't miss the way the doctor looked at him, like she was worried about his mental health, but he didn't care what he sounded like. He needed answers.

"She looks good to me." The doctor sounded cheerful. "I don't see signs of a concussion." She smiled, pulling a pen out of the top pocket of her lab coat. "I think she just got rattled." Edging between Beckett and the hospital bed, she reached for Posie's hand. "How you feeling, sweetheart?"

His daughter—*fuck*—she couldn't speak. She lay there spooked, like her mind was trapped in an uncooperative body.

This girl who normally talked all the damn time couldn't string words together.

The pen turned out to be a flashlight, and the doctor checked Posie's eyes. "You hit your head pretty hard, huh?" Sliding it back into her pocket, she moved to the end of the bed. "Everything looks great, but we're going to keep her here a few more hours, so we can monitor her. If you can just sit tight a few minutes, we'll get her transferred to her own room."

A shudder rocked through him. "It's cold in here. Do you have a thicker blanket?"

Again, that fucking look. Like the doctor was wondering if he was going to lose his shit. "Sure, we can get her another blanket. I'll take care of that right now." She lifted the curtain, ready to take off.

"Hang on. Why isn't she talking? What's wrong with her?"

"Oh, I think she's had a scare. Being knocked down by

those big boys, the neck brace, the ambulance ride…" She smiled at Posie. "Your mommy's on her way, okay?" And then she disappeared.

Beckett drew the lone chair closer and reached for Posie's hand. She barely acknowledged him. *This isn't my daughter.* She looked so weak, like her spirt had left her body.

He knew there was more going on here than being "rattled." Holding her limp hand, he lowered his forehead to the bed. Fear made him wired and hyperalert, but he needed to calm down.

Please bring her back to me.

Please.

I can't lose her.

Please.

I'll do anything if you'll just bring her back.

"Dammit, dammit, dammit." How had this happened?

When he closed his eyes, he went dizzy, the room tilted, and he didn't know whether he was twelve or twenty-nine. The blanket smelled the same, the little hand was the same size, shape, and weight, and the panic holding him hostage…

He'd felt exactly like this waiting for Ari to wake up from her coma.

But she never had.

She'd died.

His sister had fucking died.

Please don't take my daughter. I swear to God, I will be a better man.

The idea that he'd struggled to make a decision between his career and this perfect little girl…that he could be so fucking selfish…disgusted him.

I'm just like my mother.

"I'm looking for my daughter. Posie Cavanaugh?" He heard Coco's voice down the hallway. "This one? Okay, thank you."

He lifted his head at the same moment she whisked into the room. "Posie, baby."

"Murmma." For the first time since landing on the pavement, the little girl grew animated but didn't lift her arms.

She remained inert.

Something's wrong.

"Hey, baby," Coco pressed a kiss to her forehead. "Mommy's here. I heard you hit your head."

Posie just stared at her mom, eyes filled with fear. It was as if, with her mom present, she was allowed to fall apart.

Coco smiled at her, radiating a calm confidence. *Everything's one-hundred-percent all right.* She smoothed the hair off Posie's forehead. "I heard you got a couple of stitches, my beautiful, brave girl. Do they hurt?"

Posie's eyes welled with tears, but she shook her head, *No.*

"That's good, baby. Mommy's here now, and I'm going to take care of everything." Coco kissed her again, her lips lingering at her daughter's temple. Touching his hand to get his attention, she took a few steps away from the bed. "How is she?" She whispered it, like they were in this together.

He was so disgusted with himself, he just looked away. How could he face her? In her five years on this earth, Posie hadn't had a single accident. Not once had she gone to the hospital.

Until me.

"Oh, come here." She wrapped her arms around his waist.

But he remained stiff. Couldn't tolerate her comfort. He wanted to be anywhere but here.

She let go of him and took a step back, and he ignored the hurt in her eyes. "What did the doctor say?"

"That she's fine. Just rattled." Each word came out like he'd pried it out of his throat.

"Well, that's great news." She said it to Posie, moving back to her side. "How do you feel, baby?"

"Hur, Murmma." His little girl tried to speak but only jibberish came out.

Beckett swiped the perspiration off his forehead, and then dragged his palm down his shorts. The doctor hadn't known Posie before this, so she didn't understand that something was very wrong.

She should be scheduling tests. MRI, X-rays...she needed to do something more than a couple stitches to the back of Posie's head, dammit. Jesus, he was climbing out of his skin. He swept out of the room, glancing right. Nothing but an empty hallway and curtain-covered cubicles. He turned left and spotted the doctor at the nurse's station. He took off. "Excuse me. Doctor Anand."

She flicked a gaze at him, before finishing her conversation with the nurse. As he neared, she turned to him with a smile meant to appease. "What can I do for you, Mr. O'Neill?" She stepped away from the desk.

"What you saw in there isn't normal. That girl's full of life, always talking. When her mom came in just now, Posie tried to talk to her, but she's not making sense."

"I know it's upsetting, but she doesn't have a concussion, and the good news is that she got a hit to the back of her head, not the side. Trust me, though, it's perfectly normal. Every child goes flat for about thirty to forty minutes after banging her head, so sit tight and she'll be back to normal soon."

"And if not? Could she have permanent brain damage?"

"Given the nature of the accident, the answer is no. But we'll keep an eye on her for changes in her behavior, okay? All she needs right now is to rest and be loved by her parents."

She was wrong, but he thanked her and headed back to his daughter. When he lifted the curtain, he saw Coco carrying on a one-sided conversation—handling her daughter a thousand times better than he had—and he let it fall.

Coco's got this.

They don't need me.

His head spun with images of the teenagers overtaking Posie, of her laying on that sidewalk, the fear in her eyes as she lay in a hospital bed not speaking.

What if she's like this forever?

Fear spread like a cold, sickly fluid.

I'm not cut out for this. I'm just not.

I'm a fucking menace.

He couldn't get the sound of the skateboards out of his head. The blaze of panic as he'd broken into a run.

And once again that memory dropped into his head, Ari in her navy blue snowsuit against the white snow. Her eyes closed, her skin so pale he could see tiny blue veins just beneath the surface. The image merged with Posie on the concrete.

He lowered his head, going dizzy.

What had he done?

What the fuck have I done?

. . .

Half an hour later, Beckett leaned against the window in Posie's private room, watching Coco chat quietly with her. Just as the doctor promised, the little girl had returned to her normal self within twenty minutes.

But he couldn't seem to feel anything. Not even relief. It was like his body was in the room, but his mind was hovering near the ceiling. "I'm going to let everyone know she's all right."

He had to get out of there. Anxiety was driving him out of his mind.

Heading toward the waiting room, he watched as Tyler and Joss Cavanaugh, Cassian, Gigi...the whole family got up from the couches and stared at him in anticipation.

"She's good. She's talking."

"Oh, thank God," Joss said.

As one, they moved past him down the hallway toward Posie's room.

He felt like he was inside a fishbowl looking out. His chest ached, and it hurt to draw a full breath.

His phone vibrated, and when he pulled it out of his pocket, he nearly dropped it because his hands were shaking.

Jimmy: This is so messed up, but I twisted my ankle. Wish I could say I did it parachuting or some wild shit like that, but it happened on the stairs. Dumbest damn thing. I'll be okay in a few weeks, but I can't go to France. Which sucks cuz...wingsuit.

Beckett stared at the screen, electricity pulsing under his skin.

Beckett: Sorry to hear that.

Jimmy: I can get Shep to do it. He won the FIS World Cup.

Purpose came rushing back in. His head cleared. He felt like himself again. Finally.

Beckett: No. I got it.

Jimmy: Thought you couldn't get away?

He glanced down the hallway, watched the Cavanaugh family turn into Posie's room.

She's got more than enough people who love her and take care of her.

Posie didn't need him. He'd been the one to bring her here, and she hadn't once acknowledged him.

Because it happened on my watch. Kids were smart. They knew who to trust. Who looked out for them.

Come on…anyone can see.

I'm not cut out for this.

Besides, he'd only be gone for a week.

That's right. That made him feel better about leaving, less of an asshole.

If I don't take this trip, they can get me for nonperformance. Yeah, so he had to go.

This is my job.

I'm not Tyler. I can't retire at twenty-nine.

Beckett: If I want to keep my job, I've got to hit the road. Take care of that ankle.

If he left right now, he could catch the last flight out of Idaho Falls to Kennedy Airport.

Beckett checked one more time and found the nurse shooing the Cavanaughs out of Posie's room. It was almost like a scene in a sitcom. Between her mom, grandparents, and three aunts, Posie was going to be fine.

And, anyway, he'd be back soon. He'd visit all the time.

I can do this.

What parent didn't have to balance work and family?

And then he hightailed it to the elevator like the building was on fire.

"Has anyone seen Beckett?" Coco hadn't seen him in a while, and she was getting worried.

Her mom kept stroking Posie's hair in a soothing gesture. "Not since he came out to give us an update."

Her dad glanced out into the hallway, looked both ways, and then shook his head.

The nurse had let her family back into the room during Visiting Hours, so now everyone gathered around her daughter. Posie had her color back, her words…she was just fine.

Thank God.

She'd never been more scared in her life than when she'd gotten that call from Beckett telling her they were on their way to the emergency room. And, then, seeing Posie's little body on the hospital bed…*God.*

"All right," her mom said. "We should get out of here. Do you need to get back to the festival? We can bring her home, get her in her jammies, give her dinner…?"

"Oh, God, no. I'm not leaving her side. I'm going to snuggle with her all night long. We'll probably watch a movie and eat leftover meatloaf. I'm so glad I hired an event organizer. I'd only wanted to learn from them, but now I can rely on them to make sure the rest of it goes smoothly."

"Make me a list, and we'll grab some things at the store before we come over in the morning," her mom said.

"Thanks, Mom. But Beckett can do it."

Will he, though?

Where is he?

He'd been gone too long. She'd understood his panic in the ER, and while she hadn't liked the way he'd gone all stony and cold, she'd assumed, once he saw that Posie was going to be all right, he'd come back to her.

But he hadn't, and now she was scared.

Scared he'll ghost me.

But that was stupid. His daughter—who he *loved*—was in the hospital.

"He looked pretty shaken," her dad said.

He'd been more than shaken, though. It was like he'd left his body, like she was talking to a mannequin dressed in his clothes.

Her mom gave her a hug. "Glad she's all right."

"God, I know."

Her dad enveloped her in his strong arms and gave her a bear hug. "Love you, sweetheart."

"Love you, too, Dad." She watched them go, and then turned to her little girl. "As soon as the doctor comes back and checks you one last time, we can go home."

"Where's Beckett?"

I don't know. But she refused to project her insecurities on Posie ever again. "Maybe he went to find the doctor? The sooner she comes, the sooner we can get you home." She heard the edge in her voice, though, and knew she wasn't kidding anybody, not even her daughter.

Maybe, instead of pushing her fears aside and suppressing them, she should face them.

I'm terrified he's left Posie. It's going to hurt her. Damage her.

I'll be heartbroken if he's left me.

Because I love him. I love him so much, and I never told him.

And she would never forgive herself if she'd driven him away because she hadn't told him.

Tell him now. His sister died in a hospital, he has to be a wreck.

He needs me.

She had to do this. She had to put herself out there. Grabbing her purse from the space inside the nightstand, she pulled out her phone and thumbed the screen to scan through messages. Nothing from Beckett

Coco: Are you okay? I'm worried about you.

When he didn't answer, she fought her impulse to tell him she was taking Posie home, that she was fine. That they'd be perfectly fine without him.

Because that wouldn't be anywhere close to the truth.

So, she told him what he really needed to hear.

Coco: I love you.

And then…the hardest thing of all.

Coco: I need you. Please come back.

Chapter Twenty

The moment Coco opened the door, Ollie rushed at them, barking and dancing with excitement. She carried her daughter into the house, and the dog followed, smacking the cabinets with his tail.

She hadn't seen Beckett's truck, and that pretty much killed her last, remaining hope. The house felt empty, his presence gone.

"Let me grab a nightgown from the dryer, and you can change. Then, I want you to park your little butt on the couch, while I take Ollie out." Setting her daughter down, she pulled the lavender one out and handed it over. Her daughter, who insisted on doing everything herself, stood there listlessly.

She blinked back tears, not wanting Posie to see her fall apart.

But she *was* falling apart. An ambulance had taken her precious little girl to the emergency room. She couldn't stand it. Just couldn't stand it.

She didn't want to be alone. She needed someone.

She needed Beckett.

Needed him. "Here, baby. Lift your arms." She pulled off the dress and tossed it in the washing machine. She wanted to throw it out. Wanted no reminders of seeing her little girl in the hospital.

She carried Posie to the couch, pulled the throw from the back of it, and tucked her daughter in nice and snug. Turning on the TV, she noticed the way her hand was shaking and hoped Posie didn't sense her distress.

Ollie jumped onto the couch, settling right next to his favorite person in the world, his chin on her thigh.

"I'll be right back, and then we can watch any movie you want."

"I want Barbie's Fairy Secret."

"You got it. Okay, Ollie, come on." She patted her leg. "Let's go." But he didn't come. He let out a snuffle and licked Posie's hand. "You've been inside all day. Let's go out really quick, and then you can come right back here." He didn't budge. "Come *on*." She reached for his collar and tugged him, but the big oaf wouldn't leave Posie's side.

She just wanted to change. She wanted to have all her chores over with, so she could cuddle her daughter. "Ollie, dammit. Come *on*."

Her daughter pushed off the blanket and stood up on the couch. She lifted her arms, and Coco leaned in. "It's all right, Mommy. I feel better. My head doesn't hurt. Not even a little."

Coco exhaled, though it sounded suspiciously like a cry. "You're right. Everything's fine. I can let him out later." She kissed her on the cheek. "You're the most amazing person I know, Posie Cavanaugh." She straightened, tucking her back in. "You want cocoa and popcorn?"

"Yes, please."

"Okay. Give me five minutes." Wiping her eyes, she headed back into the kitchen. She glanced over to the carriage house. *Where are you, Beckett?*

If you hurt my daughter, I will hunt you down.

She pulled out the air popper and a saucepan, but before she got the milk from the refrigerator, Posie appeared in the doorway in her purple fairy nightgown.

"Mommy? What's this? I found it on the table."

Grabbing the piece of paper, she recognized Beckett's handwriting. Her stomach bottomed out.

Coco,

If I don't go to France, my partners can take my company from me. I saw that Posie's fine, got her whole family with her, so raced to the airport to catch a flight. Will call when I land in NYC.

He left.

He'd actually left.

What kind of heartless bastard took off when his daughter was in the *hospital?*

Her body tightened, squeezing out the hurt, leaving her nothing but fierce resolve. Because, unlike Beckett, she wasn't a coward. Coco dropped to a crouch. "It's from Beckett. He says he had to go on a trip."

Posie's eyes went round, glistening with tears.

"I'm sorry. It was fun to have him visit, but…" She couldn't get the words out. *He'll be back.* Because she honestly didn't know.

He'd sworn he wouldn't be an absentee father who dropped into town once or twice a year, but…*here you go.*

Tears spilled down her daughter's cheeks. *She's devastated.*

This is exactly what I wanted to spare her.
Imagine if we'd told her he was her dad.
Thank God we didn't.

"Ah, sweetheart. I'm sure he'll keep in touch." Because she knew he wouldn't disappear. Maybe he couldn't handle emotional attachments, but at his core he was a good man.

Just not someone I'll ever trust again. From now on, when he came to town, he could stay in a hotel. She tried to hug her daughter but got pushed away.

"Mommy." Posie went rigid, as she often did when she felt misunderstood. "My crown."

"Your what?"

"Beckett got me a bicycle, and he made me wear a stupid helmet, and I told him I couldn't wear it because of my crown, and he said I couldn't ride my new bike without one." Her lower lip wobbled. "And when he was going to get me a drink, I took it off. He put it on my bike, and I forgot that my crown was stuck inside the helmet."

"Okay, so the helmet's still with the bike?"

She nodded, spilling more tears.

"And where's the bike?"

"Where I got hurt." She sounded impatient. "I want my crown. I need my crown."

Laughter bubbling out of her, Coco fell to her ass on the kitchen floor.

"It's not funny." And now Posie was shrieking.

"Okay, calm down. It's all right. I promise I'm not laughing at you." *I'm laughing at me.*

Because I did it again. I got myself all worked up and transferred all my fears onto my daughter.

Will I ever learn? "Don't worry. We'll get your crown. I'll ask Grandpa to drive into town with his truck and pick up your bike and helmet, okay? It's fine, sweetheart."

"What if somebody took it?"

"I'm not going to worry about that unless it actually happens." She got up and hit her dad's speed dial. "Here. Tell Grandpa what you need while I finish the cocoa and popcorn."

As her daughter relayed the story to her grandpa and begged for his help, Coco turned back to the stove.

I'm a damn mess.

But she'd pull herself together for Posie.

It was her fault for falling in love with a man who wasn't cut out for this kind of life.

She'd go back to focusing on the only two things that mattered, taking care of her daughter and building her business.

And she was perfectly all right with that.

Later that night, after Posie had fallen asleep, Coco set the book on the floor. A shaft of moonlight spilled across Posie's face, accentuating her rosy, plump cheeks, her lips parted as she breathed steadily.

Her heart filled to bursting with love for her little fairy girl.

Coco kissed her temple.

She loved her little girl with all her heart.

Heading across the hallway to her bedroom, her phone lit up. *Beckett.* Her initial reaction was to ignore him, but she knew it was only to punish him. To say, *I don't need you.*

But this isn't about me. It's about Posie. So, she'd have to rise above her own broken heart and be on good terms with him. For her daughter's sake.

Powering it down, she set it on her nightstand and got ready for bed.

Tomorrow, she'd be an adult.

Tonight…she'd give him the finger.

Joy.

Happiness.

My sister.

Icy, clean, fresh air. The wind rocking the chairlift.

"You're the best snowboarder in the whole world." Ari hadn't stopped talking the whole ride.

And he loved it. "Not hardly."

"Yes, you are. I've seen you. I told everyone in my school you're the best, and Jessie said I was a liar. I said, My brother goes to the academy, and he's going to win gold medals one day."

"Don't listen to fatheads like Jessie. Does he know anything about me?"

"No."

"Then screw him. No one gets to take your power away."

The platform approached, and since this was Ari's first time on a chairlift, he needed her to pay attention. "We're getting off, but it's going to keep moving. So, hold my hand and don't let go, okay?"

"What about my poles?"

"I got them. I got everything." As they slowed, he gripped her hand, tightening when she hesitated to get off a moving ride. Her boots hit the landing, and she stumbled.

But he caught her.

She gazed up at him with an adoring look, like he was her hero. She made him feel like he could do no wrong.

Since Ari had never skied before, he'd make it an easy, short run. They stood side by side at the top of the slope. "You ready for this?"

She nodded but didn't move.

"Go on. I'll be right behind you."

"I want to go with you."

"You have to go ahead of me, so I can watch. I want to see what you learned in class."

"But I want to do what you do."

"Ah, come on. Let me see you in action. I want to see your moves."

She grinned at him, and he didn't think anyone had ever made him feel better than his little sister. He felt like, with her belief in him, he could win an Olympic gold medal.

And that was why, even though his fingers and toes were numb from a long day on the slopes, he didn't care. He'd go all night if it meant he got to see the adoration in Ari's eyes.

"You ready, runt?"

"Ready. Let's go." Ari pushed off, fearless, eager.

And Beckett kept pace behind her, watching.

Love.

I love my sister.

If his parents saw her right now, they'd probably talk about getting her in the academy, too. Then, they'd have no kids to bother with. But he wouldn't let them do that to her. Not yet. Not until she figured out what she wanted to do in life—besides be like me.

He kept pace with her, just a ski length behind, so he could catch her if she fell, but she looked strong, confident.

From his peripheral vision, a blur of royal blue streaked by from an intersecting path. He turned to find a man who'd *lost control of his snowboard, arms pinwheeling. And the trajectory of their paths—*

"Ari!" There was nothing he could do but watch as the man slammed into her, mowing her down. Beckett was at his sister's side instantly. Blood pounded in his veins, and noise roared in his head.

His sister lay motionless on a white carpet of snow.

Horror.

Devastation.

She's not moving.

She's so pale.

Boots crunching, people shouting.

The red parkas. Medics.

Fear like nothing he'd ever known squeezed him like a fist, crushing him, until he couldn't breathe.

A hospital bed. Tubes, machines. Beckett stood against the wall, watching, observing, anxiety a constant, thrumming tension stringing him so tight he thought, if someone touched him, he might shatter.

The nurse gave him a sad smile before leaving the room.

Finally, he could be alone with his sister.

He held her limp hand. "I'm sorry, Ari. Please wake up. I'll do anything if you'll just wake up. I'll give up snowboarding, I'll move back home. Just please, please wake up."

He lowered his head onto the thin blanket, inhaling that sickening hospital scent, and waiting—as he did every day— for her fingers to flicker.

Waiting for her to sigh in exasperation and say, "Get up, Becks. I want ice cream. Can we get some ice cream?"

Ice cream.

The ache went so deep it sank into his bones, weakening them.

And then, finally, he felt it. A twitch. His head snapped up, and he looked into her eyes.

Only, it wasn't Ari.

It was Posie.

Beckett jerked awake, his legs and arms kicking out.

What the fuck?

Where am I? What time is it?

An announcement on the PA system for a delayed flight placed him at the airport. He tuned into the noise around him...news on overhead televisions, the clatter of wheels, and a mother soothing an overtired child.

The last image—the one that had awakened him—dropped into his mind like a photograph. Posie, lying so still and pale in a hospital bed. The shock of it blasted through him.

He sat forward, dragging his feet underneath the chair, and glanced out the plate-glass window. *Nighttime.*

After a long day of travel, he was about to catch the red-eye to Geneva. He caught the time on the electronic display board. Ten, which meant it was eight in Calamity. She should be home now. Bathed, hair smelling like baby shampoo. Coco was probably snuggling with her.

She'll probably sleep with her tonight.

Not that he'd find out. Other than the two texts he'd gotten from the hospital, he hadn't heard from Coco. He'd tried calling. She hadn't answered.

Because she's taking care of her daughter.

Seeing Posie laid out on the pavement like that? He would never forget the moment she'd reared back, eyes rolling back in her head.

In that moment, he'd known what it felt like for Posie to die.

And he just couldn't do it.

I don't have it in me.

Needing to get out of his head, he nabbed his phone and pulled up the calendar. *Focus on business.* It had always helped. From now until December, other than a weekend here and there, he was booked. Next year, too, most of the dates were already blocked off.

The hit of satisfaction he got from his full schedule faded, though.

Guilt plucked at his conscience.

He'd told Coco she could count on him, that he wouldn't be that dad who sent postcards from the road and showed up twice a year loaded with weird things he'd picked up at gift shops around the world.

But he couldn't give up his app...*I'm not giving up my career.*

It's all I have.

And it was too new. *This is a critical time—make or break.*

His phone vibrated with a text. *Coco?* No.

What do you expect? You left her while her daughter was in the hospital.

Ann: I guess I'm not going to hear from you, so I'll just have to throw this stuff out.

Wait—throw what out?

Beckett: What are you talking about?

Ann: Hey, I've been trying to reach you. I have a box of your things.

So, his mother wasn't trying to make amends?

Beckett: What's in it?

Ann: Stuff from your childhood.

Beckett: Ari's, too?

Ann: Both. There's some of her things.

Beckett: I want anything that was Ari's. Just hold onto it until I'm back in the States.

Ann: I've been trying to reach you for weeks. I'm out of time. Can you come in the next couple of days?

Beckett: I'm at the airport, boarding in twenty minutes.

Ann: Give me your address. I'll mail it.

He thought about Ari's stuffed dog, Boscoe.

Beckett: Do you have pictures of her?

Ann: A few.

Dammit. The last thing he wanted to do was visit his mom but like hell he'd trust her or the mail with the only remaining photographs of his sister.

Beckett: I'll be there tomorrow.

If he put off his travel by twenty-four hours, he could still make it in time for his event.

But he'd be cutting it close.

Chapter Twenty-One

"YOUR DESTINATION IS ON THE LEFT."

Pulling his rental car alongside the curb, Beckett thumbed off the GPS and leaned forward to check out the building. The nondescript two-story garden apartment sat on a busy street in Columbus, Ohio.

So, this is where she lives.

Cutting the engine, he checked his email for the apartment number, and then got out of the car and stretched. Unease kept him dawdling, but he didn't have time. His flight took off in four hours.

He only wanted Boscoe and the photographs. Both would fit easily in his duffle bag. Climbing the stairs at the side of the building, he breathed in the smell of newly stained wood and the damp earth from freshly watered planters. At the landing, he raised his fist to knock but got hit with a flurry of emotions. Fear, anxiety, even a flash of anger.

No, it's not a flash. Don't diminish it.

His mom had done a selfish, unforgivable thing by

abandoning him. Like everything else, she'd made Ari's death about her.

Yeah, he was angry. He had every right to be.

No, dammit. He turned away from the door, hardly seeing the patch of grass dividing one apartment building from the next. If he wanted to be a good dad to Posie, he needed to cut the cord to his past. He had to face the truth, sink into it.

It wasn't anger. His mom had *hurt* him. And it had started long before she'd walked out that door.

His entire life with her, she'd ignored him. Brushed past him in the hallway like they were strangers in a hotel. She'd never liked him.

That's it right there. She didn't like me.

He could feel it, the shudder that passed through him when she'd make eye contact and quickly look away, as if he repulsed her.

As he stood in the August heat, the sun hot on his face, he felt himself shriveling down to the boy who'd watched his mom walk out the door.

Every time I look at you two I see Ari, and I can't do it anymore. I just can't stand to see your faces.

The memory felt as fresh right then as it had seventeen years ago.

How could his mom have walked away? He'd just lost his sister, for Christ's sake.

So, yeah, he wanted Ari's dog and pictures, but he needed an apology.

Let's get this over with. Turning, he knocked on the door.

It opened right away, releasing the scent of spices and cooked meat. His mom stood there in cargo capris, a black tank top, and bare feet. Her chin-length hair had streaks of gray, and her face was make-up-free. Her weathered skin had more wrinkles than his dad and Marcia, though they were all the same age.

She scanned him from his hair down to his boots. "Look at you, all grown up." Her smile didn't reach her eyes. "Come in."

He stepped into her apartment, the tan carpet worn, the tables uncluttered. On the wall, he noticed some framed photographs, and he wondered if he and Ari were up there.

Funny how the first thing he wanted to say was, *I have a daughter. Posie. She's amazing.*

But he wouldn't. Not yet. He'd see how things went.

"You're so big. Bigger than your father. I've tried to find you on social media."

"I'm only on there for my business."

"Oh, yeah. I follow your Xtreme Adventures page." She brightened. "I'm green with envy. You're living exactly the life I always wanted."

What did that mean? "You've traveled the world."

"Sure, but you get to earn a living doing it. I have to work for months to save up enough money to take a vacation. If I could be on the road as much as you...and get paid for it?" She blew out a breath.

"It's been good. The app's doing well." He didn't want to be rude, but...he really needed to get to the airport. "So...?"

"Right. Well, let me get us some drinks. You want a pop? Some water? Juice?"

"Nothing, thanks. I'm good."

She gestured to the couch. "So, how does it work? Do you have a home base or something? Where're you living these days?"

As he started to sit down, he got a blast from the past. "Is this from the San Antonio house?"

"It is. I didn't ask for much in the divorce, but I did need some furniture. A couch, a bed, the dining room set. Everything I own…you're looking at it. I travel light." Her expression looked encouraging, like, *You do too, right?*

But somehow it edged him out to agree with her, even if it was true. "You said you can't hold onto the box any longer. Are you moving?"

"Yep." She grinned and clapped her hands. "You know the Portal Trail in Utah? I'm doing it. So damn excited."

"Have you been training? That's some of the harshest terrain I've ever ridden." *Three mountain bikers have died on it.*

"Hell, yeah. I'm older now, so I have to be real careful with my body. The last thing I need is to get hurt and stuck in the dead-end life of a worker bee. Can you imagine me in a suit and briefcase, heading off to the bank every morning?"

Time warped, and he could actually hear himself saying the same words out loud to his friends, to Coco, to anyone who would listen. Because that had been his refrain from the time he was a kid.

All this time, he'd just been regurgitating her words.

His mom didn't notice his reaction, though. She kept on talking. "I'm riding my bike out there, so I'm taking off three months. I don't want to pay for storage, so I'm leaving the furniture behind for the next tenant and getting rid of everything else. Come on. Let me show you this box I've been hauling around." She headed into the dark, shadowed kitchen.

He followed her, noticing it appeared unused. "Still don't cook, huh?"

It had always been a point of pride. She'd loved to say, "Oh, I can't even boil an egg." *Hahahaha.*

She waved a hand. "I've got way better things to do with my time."

He remembered the bucket list she'd tacked to the refrigerator with a magnet. "Did you ever climb Kilimanjaro?"

"You bet I did. I try to take three vacations a year, a big one, and then two smaller road trips. I wanted to hit every single continent—that was a big thing for me—and I've done that. Climbed to the top of every mountain on my list."

He gave her a curt nod. What could he say? *Glad abandoning your family helped you reach your dreams?*

"Last year, I did a dive in Truk Lagoon. You should do that, by the way. Amazing. And a microlight flight off the coast of Durban, South Africa. Got to see sea lions playing. Blew my mind. That's another one you should do."

And then it struck him. Hadn't he just abandoned his family to realize his dreams? He grew clammy, queasy, as if she'd just spun around and sucker-punched him. Reaching for the counter, he lowered his chin, hit with the realization he'd become the one person he least respected.

I'm no different from my mother.

She lived for these experiences. *So do I.* Like her, he'd placed a higher value on travel than relationships. For some reason, he needed to see the photographs she'd taken the time to frame and mount on her walls. He returned to the living room. "How long have you lived in Columbus?"

"Only about a year. I'm a medical transcriber, so I can live anywhere. Before this, I was living in Alaska. You probably remember how I used to go on and on about that place. It was on my bucket list. And I loved it for the first few months, but the weather wears thin real fast. I met this guy…we hit it off…I moved here…"

"Oh, you live with someone?" He scanned the pictures—his mom in goggles, standing beside a helicopter. Another of her riding a camel. Another with her hair straight up in the air, arms spread wide as she parachuted out of plane. Grinning big in each one.

"No, it didn't work out."

Her life just felt…sad.

This is my future. A life of one extreme adventure after another—without Posie. Without Coco.

Suddenly lightheaded, he dropped to a crouch, hid his face in his hands.

What have I done?

The world went quiet, muffled, like he'd just put on a headset. His vision tunneled, until the only thing he could see was Posie flying around her bedroom in her fairy dress and Coco smiling at him with a look that said, *We made her.*

"You okay there?"

It's not too late. I don't have to wind up like her. "You know why I travel the way I do?"

"Of course I do. We've only got one life, and what's the point of owning things and pushing papers when we can see the world and experience all it has to offer?"

"That's exactly right. Because I drank your Kool-Aid." And it was all fine and dandy until he found Coco and met his daughter. "You made it sound like there was nothing better than living out of a suitcase and seeing whale sharks, rafting the Inga Rapids, and caving in Mexico."

The gleam in her eyes dimmed.

"But none of that comes close to seeing my daughter's face light up when I pour sprinkles on her peanut butter. And the way she plasters herself to me when I read her a book? Beats reaching the summit any day of the week."

"You have a daughter?"

"I'd give back every one of my medals if it meant I could've been there for Posie's birth. Forget that. If I could've been there when Coco found out she was pregnant." *Coco.* He couldn't believe what he'd done. The moment she'd finally come to rely on him, he'd walked away. "Nothing I've ever done comes close to the simple act of sitting on the couch next to the woman I love more than any-fucking-thing on this earth."

What am I doing, standing here talking to this woman who will never get it?

Gratitude roared through him. Posie and Coco had saved him from winding up like his mother.

All he wanted was to scrape off this feeling of loneliness and emptiness and get back to the two people who gave his life meaning. The only people in the world he truly, deeply loved. "I've got a flight to catch, so let me see the box."

"Sure." She patted the top of a small moving box. "It's right here."

He opened it to find a baseball glove. Anger burbled under his skin. "Why've you been carting this around?"

She shrugged. "It's yours. I didn't know if it meant something to you."

"It doesn't. I've never used it." He pulled out video games for an outdated machine. Underneath those, he found a bunch of pristine teddy bears. "What are these?"

"When you were born, everybody sent stuffed animals. They were in your room."

"Where's Ari's dog?" He dug through all the crap. When he saw the tattered brown ear, joy swept through him. Finally, he had a piece of her. Carefully, he lifted it out.

His mom frowned. "What's that?"

He didn't bother answering. "What about the photos? You said you had some of Ari."

"They should be in there somewhere."

He pulled out all the crap until he got to the bottom, where he found a gallon-size freezer bag filled with maybe a dozen pictures. The first one he saw was of the Grand Canyon. He'd forgotten about that road trip they'd taken. He'd been eight, Ari two. On the right side of the frame, the photographer had unintentionally captured the siblings standing side by side. Beckett had an arm slung around her shoulder, hugging her tightly to his body. "I don't remember this." Seemed a dangerous place for a two-year-old to stand.

"You were always looking out for her."

That's because you weren't.

Holy shit. It all became clear. Posie hadn't talked to him in the ER because he didn't represent comfort and security. Coco did. She'd earned that place of honor by being there for Posie every single day.

And what did I do? He'd left her in someone else's care. Just like his mother, he'd placed the higher value on jumping off a cliff in a wingsuit over taking care of his daughter. The only thing Posie needed was to sit with him on the couch—sandwiched between her parents—so she could feel safe again.

"I have to go. Have to get back to the airport." At the door, he turned to her. "Take care."

He'd come wondering if her apology might give him some insights into himself.

But it was the glimpse into his future that had set him free.

When he pulled into the driveway and didn't see the green Jeep, Beckett crashed. Adrenaline, coffee, and a couple protein bars had gotten him from Columbus back home.

Yeah, that's right. Home. He finally had one.

Idling, he glanced at the dark windows. Had Coco moved him out of the carriage house? Replaced the furniture with the boxes?

More importantly, would she ever let him alone with Posie again? He couldn't blame her if she didn't. But he'd spend the rest of his life proving he'd do a better job of taking care of her.

He glanced at the dashboard clock. Where would she be at two in the morning?

Jesus, was something wrong with Posie? Had there been complications? Maybe a blood clot?

He thunked his head on the steering wheel. *Slow down.* She might've just gone to stay at her parents for the night. He couldn't ask, because she still wasn't responding to his texts.

Parking, he got out and headed to his place, but before he could insert the key, he dropped his duffle bag outside the door and headed to the main house.

Climbing the porch steps, he let himself in, flicking on the light switch and heading into the kitchen. A coffee mug in the drying rack and the hint of roasted beans lingering in the air made him think they hadn't left that long ago.

On the table, he found a hair elastic and a drawing Posie had made with her glitter markers. Two adults, a child, and a dog.

I want that.

He had to talk to Coco, let her know he'd never leave her again.

Because he wanted to give her and Posie the same sense of *home* they'd given him.

On the kitchen table, he found Posie's crown—a sharp reminder of the accident. He'd never forget the twist of her hand in his, the way she'd darted off toward her bike. The skateboarders swallowing her up, surrounding her, knocking her down. Her body still on the sidewalk.

His little girl lying in a hospital bed.

She needed me, and I got in the car and drove to the airport.

I'm an asshole.

But I'm here now, and I'm not going to screw up again.

He headed up the stairs and treaded quietly down the hallway. At her doorway, he leaned in. Moonlight pooled onto the unmade bed. A pile of clothes Coco had left out —jeans, sneakers, long sleeve T-shirts—lay discarded on the floor.

He smiled. His little girl was fierce and full of energy, and he was going to love watching her grow into a woman as strong and kind and lovely as her mom.

And that was when he knew she hadn't gone to her parent's house. Coco Cavanaugh hadn't bawled her eyes out after finding his note. She hadn't fall apart.

She'd taken action.

And so would he.

Chapter Twenty-Two

WHEN HE SAW THE JEEP, HE WANTED TO ABANDON his truck and make a run for the house. Bust down the door and get to his girls. His heart was so damn full he could hardly stand it.

It had taken a lot of pleading to get Tyler Cavanaugh to give up his daughter's location, but thankfully Beckett had convinced the man of his absolute sincerity.

He was here to stay. He wouldn't miss another moment in Posie and Coco's lives.

He pulled into the driveway, his tires crunching over pine needles, and took in what Tyler had described as their "little cabin in the woods." *Ha*. That would describe his place in Boulder. This one looked like a fancy lodge.

Killing the engine, he got out and breathed in the clean, pine-scented air. From inside, he could hear Ollie barking like crazy, and he got a hit of sadness that he'd abandoned his good boy.

The front door opened, and the love of his life stepped out. In black leggings and an oversize blue and white-striped T-shirt, she stood there like a queen addressing her kingdom. "What're you doing here?"

He'd prepared himself for that attitude, so he kept walking toward her.

"How did you know where we were?" She made an expression of disgust and shook her head. "I'm going to kill my dad. He told you, didn't he?"

Reaching the porch steps, he stuffed his keys in his pocket.

"Don't bother putting them away. You won't be here long."

He gazed up at her. "You're the most beautiful, fierce woman I've ever known. I can't believe I took you for granted. I'll never do it again. Not even for one minute out of a day." He climbed one step, saw the way her eyes flared, and stopped right there. "I hurt you, and I hate myself for that."

Her features softened.

Hope sizzled and snapped. Maybe she'd forgive him. He hadn't been gone that long. Not even forty-eight hours. "I love you."

"Okay." All business, she came down the stairs, stopping at the one above his, so they were eye level. "I know seeing Posie in the hospital freaked you out, and you ran. It was too much like Ari. I get it. I really am sorry for all you've gone through, but we're not doing this." She flicked a hand between them. "My heart isn't a yo-yo that you get to play with, reeling me in when you feel safe and tossing me out when you don't."

"I panicked. I won't do it again."

"Those are words I have no intention of testing out."

"No, it's different. I'm different. I didn't go to France. I went to see my mom. Those texts she's been sending me?

She didn't want to make amends. She wanted to get rid of Boscoe."

"Ari's stuffed dog?"

Love like he'd never felt crashed over him. He blew out a breath of disbelief. "I can't believe I walked away from you."

"Same."

"But I'm so damn glad I did, because if I hadn't visited her, I wouldn't be free of my past. I would've spent the rest of my life chasing her twisted version of happiness. She's got all these framed photographs on her walls. You know how you have your whole family in your office and your home? Every minute of Posie's life from the time she was born? My mom's pictures came as part of a package. If you jump out of a plane, they give you a USB disc filled with them. She frames one from each trip."

Coco drew in a breath, the lines around her eyes creasing. She got it.

"You know what I realized? All this time, I've been living her lifestyle so I could figure out why it was so much more important to her than I was. I kept going because I had nothing to compare it to. Now I do." He took a moment to gather his thoughts. No matter how many times he'd gone over what he'd say, it felt different standing right in front of her.

The weight of his words scared him—if he said the wrong ones, he might never win back her trust.

"Standing in my mother's apartment, I was looking at my future. Coco, I don't want to be her. I want to be Posie's dad. And, one day, I want to be your husband. I've already talked to my partners, and we've come up with a plan for them to buy out my shares. I want to live here with you and Posie. I'm going to be here for both of you every single day, so that next time she gets hurt, she'll look at me the way she did at you when you walked into the ER. I want to be her daddy, the one who loves her and reads to her and protects her. I want to be the person you lean on and confide in. I want to sleep with you every night and wake up to your face every morning. More than anything I've ever wanted in my life, I want us to be a family."

She gave him a sad smile. "You're doing it again. Only thinking about what you want. That picture you painted sounds lovely, but it's never going to happen. You're welcome to be in Posie's life as much as you want, but you and I...we're never going to happen. I'm not going to spend the rest of my life wondering whether you're going to take off again. I'm just not going to do it." She twisted around to check the house. "I don't mean to run you off, but I don't want Posie to know you're here. We've had a relaxing couple of days, and if she sees you, she's not going to want you to go. I do, though. I want you to go." She drew in a breath. "Give me the rest of this week to feel sorry for myself, and I promise when I get back, we'll be on good terms, and you'll have full access to your daughter." She turned and started back up the stairs. "Goodbye, Beckett.

Coco had lied. A relaxing week? *Please.* It had been pure hell trying so hard to be a good mom, when all she wanted was to stay up late watching romantic comedies, eat Oreos and ice cream in bed, and cry her heart out.

I mean, seriously, could Beckett have been any sweeter? Any more sincere?

Could he have said more perfect words?

No. No, he could not.

And what had she done? She'd kicked him out. Slammed the door on the future she wanted with a desperation that bordered on pathetic.

I want that man. The one who'd stood on the bottom step of her parents' cabin? Yeah, that one. *I want him.*

I want him forever and ever.

Instead of telling him she wasn't going to spend the rest of her life wondering whether he'd take off again, she should've said, "We've both got fears. Why don't we spend the rest of our lives helping each other work through them?"

Because that's what he'd done. He'd gone to visit the big, bad wolf. He'd faced the woman who'd abandoned him. And it had set him free.

He'd given her all the words she'd longed to hear—only he'd said them far more eloquently and sincerely than she ever could have dreamed. And instead of accepting them, her fears had given him a good, swift kick in the ass.

"I want to go home, Mommy." Posie hadn't played with her dolls since they'd gotten in the car.

That's because she picks up on everything.

Maybe it's time to stop trying to be so damn perfect and just let her see what it's like to be a real woman. A woman who gets knocked down, nurses her bruises, and comes back swinging. "Me, too." She eyed her daughter in the rearview mirror. Lord, did she look unhappy.

"Ollie has to go pee pee."

The dog's tail started thumping at the sound of his name. He'd relieved himself not even an hour ago, so she knew Posie just wanted to get out of her car seat and back to her familiar world.

"We're almost home." She pointed toward the town center. "See?"

"I'm hungry."

"How about I make you ~~make~~ mac and cheese?"

Her daughter didn't answer. Maybe she, too, was worried what she'd find when they got home. Was Beckett still staying in the carriage house? Or had he taken her seriously enough to move on?

Of all the times for Beckett to respect her wishes, now was not one of them.

She wanted to see his truck parked out front, hear the back door open and his boots tread on her hardwood floor. She wanted to listen to him read to Posie on the couch, while she worked on her laptop at the kitchen table.

She needed his kisses and his hugs. She needed the way he looked at her as if she hung the moon.

Ever since she'd hit the highway and gotten cell reception, her phone had been buzzing with incoming messages. She'd catch up when she got home.

She turned onto Main Street, happy to see her pretty little town so busy. She loved it here. Nobody wore suits, and no one was rushing to catch a cab. Instead of Prada bags, people carried backpacks. Instead of make-up, they wore sunscreen.

Tourists, business owners, families…all of them had the common interests of loving the outdoors and preferring small town life over a big city. As she passed Coco's Chocolates, she got a hit of pride. Her pretty little store was filled with customers.

She'd made a good life for herself, and if she and Beckett could work things out, she wouldn't want for anything else the rest of her life.

Well, maybe one thing. Another baby with his crystal blue eyes would be nice. She'd love to give Posie a brother or sister.

When she turned onto her street, she found several cars and trucks parked around her house. *What in the world?*

She could just see her mom initiating some project to cheer her up. Her mom was sweet, but Coco didn't need new curtains or a new couch. Then again, one of the trucks had lumber in the back. *Oh, no.*

Please tell me my parents aren't putting an addition on my house. She didn't want it or need it.

The only thing I need is my family of three. She'd fallen in love with Beckett, and no home renovation project could ever make up for what she'd just thrown away.

There were so many cars, she had to park a few houses down.

"*Mommy.*" Posie kicked the seat. "We don't live here."

"Our driveway's blocked, sweetie. Come on. Let's go home."

She got the bags out of the trunk first and left them on the grass. Then, she snapped on Ollie's leash and let him out of the car. Finally, she pulled Posie from her car seat, and together they started for home.

"Grandpa's here." Posie wrenched her hand free and dashed across the lawn.

"*Posie.* Wait." Ollie jerked on the leash, wanting to run after her, so Coco dropped her bags and took off after her daughter. What if someone backed out of the driveway? No one knew they were home. "Posie."

But her daughter had stopped on their yard in front of the mountain willow and stared at the base of the tree with an expression of awe.

"What is it?" Coco reached her side and couldn't believe what she was seeing. Someone had created a fairy world. A carved door painted red, a sawdust walkway lined with pebbles, and little hanging lanterns.

Tears sprang to her eyes. She had the most amazing parents in the world. To come up with such a beautiful distraction for her daughter...*this blows me away*.

Except...neither of her parents were crafty. *Gigi?* Like she'd know what a glue gun even looked like.

"Mommy." Her daughter screeched so loudly, Ollie bounded over. "*Look.*"

In the shrubs beneath the bay window, someone had created an entire fairy habitat, complete with rope ladders, doors made of twigs, and paths formed out of gravel. Something pink and glittery caught her attention, and Coco crouched to find a tiny pair of shoes outside a door. "Oh, my God."

"My shoes." Posie sounded breathless. "The fairies wear shoes just like mine."

A drill whined, and Posie's eyes went wide. She took off across the lawn and down the driveway.

"Posie, hang on. Wait for me." Coco ran until she hit the backyard and then came to an abrupt stop.

A whole team of friends and family worked busily to construct a wooden playhouse.

Her grip slackened, and Ollie broke free.

"Beckett," Posie shrieked.

Coco watched her daughter fly into the man's big, strong arms. He knelt and caught her, holding her tightly against his chest. His eyes closed, and she could see the stark relief on his features.

Posie wriggled free, jumping up and down and talking

a mile a minute, the dog wagging his tail and nosing Beckett for attention.

Right then, that handsome man glanced up and saw her, his features slowly relaxing with something that looked a lot like love.

The world narrowed to his face, the only one she ever wanted to kiss goodnight and good morning and every moment in between.

He picked up Posie and made his way over to her. Her heart pounded with anticipation.

The moment he reached her, he wrapped an arm around her and hauled her to him.

"Beckett's back, Mommy. I *told* you." She rolled her eyes. "Mommy said she didn't know when you were coming back, 'cause you had to work, but I *told* her you'd be back."

He pressed a kiss to Posie's forehead. "And I'm staying. I'm going to start the Outfitter business for Brodie's resort."

"You...what?" Coco asked.

"That's right. I'm done traveling. There's only one place I want to be, and that's here with my forever girls."

"Posie?" her dad called, opening his arms.

"Grandpa." She squirmed, and Beckett set her down. She took off like a shot.

Grabbing her hand, Beckett led her to the house, and they quickly climbed the stairs, entering the cool mud room. He opened his mouth to speak, but she cut him off.

"It was you. You created that whole fairy world."

"Come look what else." He tugged her across the living room and up the stairs, leading her straight to Posie's bookcase.

"Oh, my God." She took in the fairy houses he'd inserted between books. They had lights and tiny furniture and windows and….and everything. "This is the most amazing thing I've ever seen." She turned to find him watching her, hands on his hips, legs braced, as if he had something to say. She stood up and faced him so she could hear it.

"I did a terrible, unforgivable thing. I saw Posie lying in that hospital bed, and I thought…I told myself she was better off without me. She'd made it five years without any injuries, and then I come along and—"

"She fell off the bed."

"What?"

"That scar?" She touched her cheek. "I ran out of diapers, and I went to the hall closet to see if I had any left, and I heard this terrible thunk. She rolled off the bed and cut her cheek on the heel of my shoe. There was so much blood. I didn't know…I'd never seen anything like it. So, I took her to Urgent Care, and they gave her one stitch." He looked at her like he wasn't sure what the hell she was talking about. "I'm just saying, accidents happen no matter who's watching them."

His shoulders visibly relaxed. "I'm glad to hear you say that."

"But I know how awful it must've been for you. It had to throw you right back to Ari's accident."

"Yeah, it did. But I need you to know it'll never happen again. I love you. I love Posie. I know I fucked up, but will you give me another chance?"

"Yes." And here was *her* chance. "You see me, Beckett, in a way no one else does. And I see you. And that means we can take care of each other. So, instead of running when we get scared, let's just stick together and give each other unconditional love. Because…" Her body went hot, emotion swelling under her skin. "I really love you, Beckett. You're The One for me."

And, somehow, just by saying the words out loud, she let it go. All the weight she'd put on herself to be perfect, to never rely on anyone…to keep herself from ever being hurt and rejected, just lifted right off her shoulders, and she felt free for the first time in her life.

He still hadn't gotten used to it, this sense of *home*. It filled him to the point he thought he might burst sometimes.

"Posie, honey, come on," Coco called out the back door. "You'll be late for school." She grabbed the car keys and turned back to him with a smile. Early morning sunlight slanted across the treetops and created a pale yellow halo around her head. "I can't get her off that swing set." Her smile faded. "What's wrong?" She brushed her fingers around her mouth. "Do I have food on my face?"

"You're so beautiful."

"Oh." Her cheeks turned pink.

"I want to tell her."

"Right now?"

Right the fuck now. "Yeah. She needs to know who I am, that we're a family."

"Okay. Sure. Let's do it."

They stepped onto the porch and watched Posie launch herself down the slide with her dolls seated in her lap. Once her feet hit the ground, she ran back up the steps and did it again.

Coco's parents, the Bowies and their wives, everyone had come to help him build the playhouse. Designed to look like a fairy castle, it rose two stories with swings in the center and a slide on the side. Gray and his wife had used glitter paint, and it sparkled in the early morning sunlight.

He had more than a family. He had a community. And it was the kind of bone-deep satisfaction and sense of belonging his mother would never know.

He'd come pretty damn close to not knowing it.

"Posie, hon, come here," Coco called.

His little girl flicked a glance over at them. "I'm playing."

"Yeah, but it's time for school. And before we go, we need to tell you something."

"Something important," he said.

That got her attention. Leaving her dolls on the slide, she ran over to them. "Can I have ice cream after school? I want bubblegum this time. Last time they didn't have any, and you said we could go back and get some."

"I did. And we'll do that. But right now, I want you to know…" He paused, not sure if he should be the one to say it. He looked to Coco. *You should do it.*

How would she feel, knowing she had a dad? Would it be as momentous to her, as it had been to him, finding out he had a daughter?

Would she throw herself into his arms, holding his neck tightly? Would she cry, *I've always wanted a daddy.*

Oh, hell.

Daddy.

It didn't have to happen today, but one day, she'd say it. She'd call him daddy. The backs of his eyes stung, and he had to blink.

"What's in your eye?" Posie cupped his jaw. "Let me see. Maybe you got a eyelash in it."

"No, it's fine. I'm fine." He shot Coco a look. *Tell her.*

"Sweetheart, remember I told you that Beckett's my friend?"

She nodded.

"Well, until a couple weeks ago, we hadn't seen each other in six whole years."

Posie looked like she couldn't have cared less.

"And back then, when we knew each other, we were very close. But then we lost touch." Coco crouched. "Posie, sweetie, Beckett's your dad."

"I didn't know that your mom was carrying you in her tummy. If I'd known, I'd have been here sooner."

"But as soon as he found out about you," Coco said. "Well, that's why he stayed with us this summer. Because I was finally able to tell him—"

"About my gift." Beckett touched her cheek. "The best gift I could ever ask for."

Posie looked at them like she had no idea what they were talking about.

He sat on the top step. "I'm your dad." His voice cracked.

Posie peered into his eyes. "Are you crying?" She patted his arm, and then climbed onto his lap. She wrapped her arms around him, just as he'd imagined. "Don't cry. It'll be all right."

"You don't have to call me dad right away. We can take more time to get to know each other, but I want you to know that I lost you and your mom, and now I'm so happy I found you, so we can be a family together. I love you, Posie."

She hugged him. "I love you, too, Beckett." And then she pulled back. "Can we get ice cream now? I want the bubblegum."

Beckett burst out laughing. He swiped the tears from

his eyes. "Not right now, because we're taking you to school. But after, on the way home, we'll get it for you."

"Go get in the car," Coco said.

"Okay." She shot off his lap. "I can't wait to tell Margot I'm getting bubblegum ice cream. She says there isn't an ice cream with gum in it. Mommy, will you take a picture of my cone? I want her to see it."

Beckett watched his daughter open the door of the Jeep and climb inside. "Well, that didn't go how I expected."

"It never does with kids. Maybe it'll hit her later." She locked the door and headed down the stairs.

He stopped her, cupped her chin, and planted a kiss on her mouth. "I love you, Coco. I love you with all my heart." Seized with a punch of affection and gratitude, their sweet kiss turned hot.

Posie called from the car. "Come on. I'm going to be late for school."

If he could, he'd frame this moment and hang it on the wall.

And always remember it as the day he'd found his way home.

Epilogue

WITH THE CAR DOOR OPEN, THE INTERIOR LIGHT shone on Beckett's newborn daughter. His breath caught in his throat, and his heart filled with unspeakable joy. "Look at her."

Images of the future shuffled through his mind. Changing diapers, bathing her, dressing her, feeding her, holding her hand as they crossed streets. All the things he hadn't gotten to do with Posie...he'd get to do it all with Violet.

This time, he'd gotten to be there when Coco read the pregnancy test stick. He'd watched her belly grow, felt his baby kick. He'd held his wife's hand, as she'd given birth to their daughter.

And now...they were bringing her home.

Coco waited patiently beside him. "You want me to show you how to detach the car seat from the base?"

Shit. She'd given birth eighteen hours ago, and he was standing in the driveway like a moron. "No, I got it." He'd practiced in the last few weeks of her pregnancy. "I'm not going to bring it in. I want to hold her." He wanted his child to feel loved and cared for every second of her life. "You go in and lay down."

She gazed up at him with a thoughtful expression. "What're you thinking?"

"That I don't want to mess this up. So many things can go wrong."

He'd have to cut up her chicken into tiny bites because, even at two years old, her esophagus would be no bigger than a straw. And the stairs? He'd install gates at the top and bottom. He'd already added covers to the light sockets.

"It's a miracle that any of us makes it to adulthood." She tugged on his arm, forcing him to turn to her. "But we do, you know? We make it."

He'd lived a reckless life, not sparing a thought to his mortality. With his daughters…holy shit, if they even suggested bungee jumping—

"Hey." Coco cupped his jaw to get his attention. "It's you and me, remember? We got this."

He nodded, but he wasn't convinced he got it at all. It seemed so overwhelming.

"You know how to eat an elephant?"

He looked at her like, *What kind of question is that?*

"One bite at a time. And that's how we raise kids. We take it one step at a time." She got up on her toes and kissed his cheek. "I love you, Beckett. Our girls are so lucky to have you as their daddy."

He drew her closer, a fierce sense of love overwhelming him. "They're lucky because you're their mom. You're the most patient, kind, smart, beautiful woman in the world. And you're mine."

"Yes. I am completely yours. Do you know I wake up every single morning feeling unbelievably grateful that I get to spend my life with you? That we're raising this perfect little family together? You make me so happy."

"That's all I want." And to think, a year ago, he'd lived only for himself, for his adventures. Now, he had no greater purpose than loving and taking care of his three girls.

Violet made a mewling sound, and he turned to make sure her neck hadn't bent over. He'd read it could cut off her breathing. "All right, sweetheart. Time to bring you home." He reached for the buckle.

And stalled out once again. The nurse had shown him how to hold an infant, but Jesus...she was so damn fragile.

"You want me to do it?" she asked.

"No. I can do it." He slid his hands under her warm, swaddled body. "Come on, sweet pea." He cradled her against his chest. She was so tiny. And practically boneless —he had to be careful with her neck.

Coco closed the door and locked the car, and together they headed across the lawn to the house. It was a chilly night, the smell of snow in the air—a big storm was coming, not all that unusual for April in the mountains— and he wanted to get Violet inside, where she'd be safe and warm.

The moment they stepped into the mudroom, they heard the usual Cavanaugh boisterous conversation, punctuated with bursts of laughter. He couldn't believe how easily he'd fit into this family, how readily they'd all welcomed him, especially after bailing on Coco when Posie was still in the hospital last summer. Even the Bowies had come to feel like brothers.

They entered the living room, and everyone got up and surrounded them.

"Let me see all that cuteness," Joss said.

"She's kind of squished, no?" Cassian asked.

"I can't believe how much she looks like Posie did when she was born," Tyler said.

While the others fawned over the infant, he noticed Coco pulling her sister aside. "How'd it go?"

Posie had fought like hell to stay at the hospital with them, but a complication had kept them longer than expected, so they'd sent her home with her grandparents and aunts. He wanted to hear how she'd done without them, so he joined them.

Gigi rolled her eyes. "She was livid with us for taking her from you guys. And she fought sleep every step of the way. But she's out now. It's all good." She gave her a soft smile filled with pride. "Happy for you."

"I'm so happy." Coco turned and found his gaze, and he felt a joy so big and wide his knees nearly buckled.

Gigi gave her a gentle hug. "Okay, we'll get out of your hair. You've got to be dying right now."

"Absolutely," her mom said. "We'll go. Do you want us to come back in the morning?"

Itching to check on Posie, he left them to hash out the details of who would do grocery shopping and when they could come back to visit. He appreciated their support—but mostly he liked that they knew when to back off and give them space. The Cavanaughs were good people.

As he climbed the stairs, he reminded himself that, with a new baby in the house, he needed to be careful Posie never felt left out. He would make sure to give her the same amount of attention, even while meeting the needs of a newborn. Like tonight, for the first time, she'd gone to bed without a story from him. Couldn't be helped. They'd needed to keep Violet a little longer to get her bilirubin level down.

He needed to see his little girl. Even if she was asleep, he wanted to whisper the words he said nightly to her. At the top of the stairs, Beckett took in the framed photographs lining the hallway. Lit up by the soft glow of a nightlight, he caught the familiar glimpses of Coco's family and the countless images recording every moment of Posie's life. He'd be sure to chronicle Violet's childhood, too.

He passed the section of Ari's pictures—just a handful capturing a few moments in her short life—but hung in a place of honor over a table. As often as they could, they filled a vase of daffodils, her favorite flowers, right beneath them

When he reached last year's Christmas card, he stopped. Shifting his daughter to a football hold, he touched the glass, warmth spreading through him.

Coco had already been five months pregnant, so really all four of them were in this shot. She sat beside him, with Posie straddling their laps. Beckett's hands spanned both their waists, as if he was holding them all together.

And for the first time in his life he understood his purpose.

This is what Brodie and Will meant. Tasked with loving three women, making them feel beautiful just for being the powerful, strong, intelligent and perfect humans they were…*this is what I'm put on this earth to do.*

He continued on to his daughter's bedroom, smiling when he saw her sprawled across the mattress—evidence she'd fought sleep with all her formidable might. Entering quietly, he leaned in and whispered, "Good night, sweet dreams, see you in the morning…Daddy loves you."

His daughter shifted and said sleepily, "I love you, Daddy."

Tears burned, and he didn't blink them away. Not tonight. Not when he had his two little blessings right here.

Damn, he loved his girls. He would protect them with his life.

As he headed out, his heart so full of love he could practically hear it sloshing around inside him, he found Coco waiting for him in the doorway.

"She asleep?"

"Out like a light." He pressed a kiss to his wife's mouth. "You get ready for bed. I'll make your tea."

"Perfect."

He kissed her again. "Thank you."

"For what?"

"For letting me take this wild ride with you. Hands down, it's the most thrilling thing I've ever done."

Thank you for reading CAN'T HELP FALLING IN LOVE! Up next is WHOLE LOTTA LOVE, where a quiet, introverted chef finally lives her life out loud with a hot, sexy quarterback.

Do you subscribe to my newsletter? Get on that right now, because I've got an EXCLUSIVE novella for my readers in 2021! You'll get 2 chapters a month of this super sexy, fun romance! #oppositesattract #onenightstand #surprisebaby

Are you dying for the youngest Cavanaugh sister's story? YOU'RE STILL THE ONE is finally on its way June 2021! When she's hired as a wedding planner, Stella comes home to Calamity to find the love of her life is the guardian of a troubled teenager. Stella can't help herself, of course, from trying to fix the boy's problems. But if she wants to win Griffin back, she can't be so impulsive, so over-the-top with her ideas...and yet isn't that what the broody, inked, motorcycle-riding hottie loves about her? Second chance romance, redemption...this book has everything!

Need more Calamity Falls, where the people are wild at heart?

KEEP ON LOVING YOU
WE BELONG TOGETHER
THE VERY THOUGHT OF YOU
JUST THE WAY YOU ARE
IT WAS ALWAYS YOU
CAN'T HELP FALING IN LOVE
COME AWAY WITH ME
WHOLE LOTTA LOVE

Have you read the Rock Star Romance series? Come meet the sexy rockers of Blue Fire:

YOU REALLY GOT ME
I WANT YOU TO WANT ME
TAKE ME HOME TONIGHT
MORE THAN A FEELING

Look for YOU'RE STILL THE ONE in June 2021! Grab a FREE copy of PLANES, TRAINS, AND HEAD OVER

HEELS. And come hang out with me on Facebook, Twitter, Instagram, Goodreads, and Pinterest or in my private reader group.

WHOLE LOTTA LOVE Coming February 2021.

Whole Lotta Love

Winter Sophomore Year

HER FIANCÉ BURST INTO LAUGHTER, AND LULU Cavanaugh turned to watch him across the crowded restaurant. Surrounded by her dad and his football buddies, he was totally in his element.

Happiness spread through her in a dizzying rush, and she had to cover her mouth to hide a huge, dopey smile. That tall, gorgeous, life-of-the-party man had chosen *her* to spend his life with. And she didn't know how she'd gotten so lucky.

I'll never be alone again.

The thought came out of nowhere, delivering a stark relief that nearly buckled her knees. She thought about all those New Year's Eves when her sisters—gorgeous and glittering—would race out the door with their boyfriends, leaving her home alone. The countless Valentine's Days when her roommates would dress up for romantic evenings, leaving her alone in a cloud of perfume.

She'd never feel that painful loneliness again.

Because tomorrow she'd marry Trace Heller.

Look at him.

How in the world did I get a guy like that? Starting linebacker for Penn State, big man on campus, he was genuinely nice, smart, and funny. Everybody liked him—professors, students…the cafeteria staff had a smoothie ready for him every morning at six AM—and it wasn't even on the menu. He was the golden boy.

And he's mine.

An arm wrapped around her shoulder and tugged her in close. "I don't think I've ever seen you so happy."

Lulu tucked her face into the crook of her older sister's neck. *I am happy.* She clasped Gigi's wrist. "Thank you for being here."

Gigi released her. "What kind of thing is that to say? Of course I'm here." The lead singer for an all-girl pop band, her oldest sister was in the middle of a world tour. She had virtually no control over her life—down to how she dressed and the color of her hair—so it really was a big deal. "You excited for tomorrow? Actually, knowing you, you're probably more excited about the honeymoon."

Joy bubbled through her at the thought of Tokyo, where she got to spend time in the kitchens of Michelin-starred chefs. Yet another reason to love her future husband—he didn't mind her cooking on three of their vacation nights.

"I just want to get the production over with." Lulu preferred a small, intimate wedding, but Trace and his family had fought her hard on that—they had hundreds of people they absolutely could not "snub."

Her fiancé came by his outgoing nature honestly—his parents and siblings were all big-time extroverts. They lived on a cul-de-sac in Iowa that threw weekly block parties all summer long, and their house was party central during football season.

She'd conceded, of course. Lots of people found her quiet intensity a turn-off, so if he accepted her, she could absolutely respect his big personality—even when it meant she didn't have his full attention when they went out together.

When it meant she had to walk down the aisle with three hundred and fifty people watching her.

Trace lifted his arms, executing a sexy swivel of his hips, as if dancing to a Snoop Dog song. *He's the brightest light in any room.* His welcoming grin served as an invitation. *Come party with me. We'll have a blast.*

A red dress in her peripheral vision grabbed her attention, and she spotted her younger sister in a heated conversation.

As Stella drained a champagne flute, her boyfriend's big hand closed around her wrist and tried to pull the glass away from her mouth. Nobody tamed the gorgeous, wild eighteen-year old, though, so she twirled out of his reach. Stella wobbled on those ridiculously high heels, but Griffin grabbed her, wrapped an arm around her waist and hauled her up hard against him. He lowered his mouth to her ear, and her expression turned sultry, wicked, before she elbowed him in the stomach and freed herself. Just as he started to walk away in anger, Stella fisted his dress shirt and jerked him back, cupping his neck and kissing him like they were alone in her bedroom.

God, they were a fiery, passionate couple.

"She's drunk," Gigi said.

"I know, and it's so weird." Normally, Stella would be right by her side. Her best friend and fiercest protector, her sister made sure to stay close in social situations so Lulu didn't wind up standing alone in a corner. Nobody got her like Stella did. "Why would she do this at my rehearsal dinner?"

"Oh, come on. She's afraid of losing you."

That's ridiculous. Lulu had always needed Stella—not the other way around. "She knows better than that." Unlike her sister, Lulu didn't have a million acquaintances. She had Trace, her family, and a few close friends. And she was fiercely loyal to them all. "But she's going to feel like crap tomorrow." *When I'll need her with me.*

She's my maid of honor.

"Let me go talk to her." But before Gigi could go, Stella caught them staring and broke away from her boyfriend.

Her hair a sexy tousle of chestnut waves, she rushed up to them. "The tank is full, and my car's right out front. Say the word…" With that devilish glint in her eyes—anyone would take Stella's comment as light and jovial.

But not Lulu. She knew Stella down to her very soul, and her sister wasn't joking. She'd been against Trace from the very first time Lulu had brought him home. "Nope. Not going anywhere." And then she looked her sister right in the eyes, so she'd finally hear her. "I love him, Stella. I *want* to marry him."

Any pretense of joking flatlined, and Stella's expression grew desperate. Grabbing Lulu's arm, she forced her to face her fiancé. "Look at him. Why's he hanging around dad's friends and not you? It's your rehearsal dinner. Shouldn't he be by your side?"

"We don't have that kind of relationship." *Which is why it works.*

"What does that even mean? You're going to spend your life with this man."

"That's right. And we work *because* we're so different. What guy would put up with spending three nights of our honeymoon apart from me? Trace loves my passion for food, and he likes that we're not joined at the hip. It means he can go out and party and do his thing without having to take care of a clingy girlfriend. Do you know how freeing it is to do what I love without worrying that I'm leaving him alone too much? Stella, he sees me. And he likes what he sees." It felt good to say it out loud. It empowered her.

Trace is the right man for me.

He chose *me.*

Stella leaned forward, reeking of wine. "If he likes you so much, then why does he flirt with *me?*"

God.

No one can hurt you worse than the people who know you best.

Lulu fought back the rising swell of humiliation and fear. She pressed her trembling hands to her stomach. *Don't let her ruin this night for you.* "He flirts with everyone. That's just who he is."

"You're drunk, Stella," Gigi said. "Not a good look for the maid of honor."

"Why are you defending him, when you know I'm right?" Stella grew frantic. "You're all out of your mind to let her go through with this wedding." She grabbed Lulu's hands. "I want you to be happy—you know I do—I *love* you—but this guy is not who you think he is."

"Stop it." Gigi's voice was low, threatening.

"No, I'm not going to stop." Stella grabbed her hands and squeezed. "This is *me*. You have to know I would never hurt you. I'm trying to *save* you. He's not who you want him to be. He's just not."

Lulu was shaking, but it wasn't from fear. "I know exactly who he is. He *flirts,* but he doesn't act on it. And you, of all people, should know that because he's just like you. He's the life of the party, but he's also loyal and just as protective of me as you are."

"God, Lulu." Stella practically shouted. "You're only seeing what you want—"

"No." Wrenching her hands free, Lulu took a step back. "Your job as maid of honor—as my *sister*—isn't to tell me what's right or wrong for me. Your job is to stand beside me, and if things go sideways, you can hand me a pint of cookies and cream ice cream, two spoons, and a box of Kleenex. But I'm telling you right now, if you can't support me, then you won't be at my side at the altar tomorrow."

Lulu turned away from them, making a beeline for the kitchen.

"What is your problem?" she heard Gigi say.

"How can you stand here and let her make the biggest mistake of her life?" Stella said. "Why is everyone acting like this wedding is okay?"

The back of her neck prickled, as though the eyes of everyone in the restaurant were on her, pitying her. As if they all knew something she didn't about Trace.

But it wasn't true. She did know him.

He'd grown up in a family obsessed with football—of course he was starstruck around her dad and his friends. What was wrong with that? She *wanted* him to be close to her family.

And he flirted with everybody—the bus driver for away games, the security guard at the mall. *That's just who he is.*

Unused to high heels and tight dresses, she grew self-conscious and wished like hell she'd been born with a tenth of Stella's confidence and style.

But she hadn't been, so she sought the comfort of the one place on earth she felt like her best self. Pushing through the doors, the heat hit her first, followed by the scents of grilled meat and chopped herbs. Nothing soothed her like being in the beating heart of a restaurant, with the steam rising, oil sizzling, and everyone busy at their stations.

Here, she felt competent and in control. She felt beautiful in the only way that mattered to her—she created dishes that made people sigh with delight.

Jonny Lee James, the owner and chef de cuisine, spotted her. A big grin cracked his rugged features. Wiping his hands on a dish towel, he opened his arms and came towards her. "My sweet girl."

She fell against him, breathing in the scents of caramelized onions and sautéed garlic embedded in his chef's jacket.

"You come to boss me around?" Tipping his head, he grinned. "Make my béchamel sublime?"

But she didn't feel like joking, so she nestled in against him, comforted by those big, strong hands on her back. He got the message and held her instead of talking.

She should be happy. She should be on top of the world.

But she didn't think she could do that without Stella's support. Because, until Trace, her sister had always been the one Lulu relied on. In fifth grade, when Lulu had a crush on Danny Keene, Stella had invited him over for a playdate. Stella had been *eight years old*.

When Lulu didn't have a date for the junior prom, Stella had surprised her with a weekend in Seattle. They'd had an absolute blast, posting pictures on social media, so everyone would think she couldn't make the dance because of a trip with her mom and sister—not because no one had asked her.

So, for Stella to not like Trace—to not *trust* him—it meant something. She didn't want to choose between her husband and her sister. She shouldn't have to. But if Stella couldn't accept this marriage, this relationship…how would that work? Every time her sister and Trace were in the same room, would Stella accuse Trace of hitting on her? Would she start avoiding them?

Lulu needed her sister. Couldn't bear the thought of them growing apart.

"There she is." Her mom's voice rose above the kitchen noises. "I knew I'd find you here."

Chef Jonny pulled away to greet the tall, slender, and beautiful Joss Montalbano, a former Eighties supermodel who'd passed her poise and confidence on to all of her daughters, except one. *Me.*

"One day, she's going to get this place a Michelin star." Her mom beamed at her with so much pride, Lulu almost felt guilty for choosing Penn State over Le Cordon Bleu, as everyone had expected.

She probably should've gone to Paris, but she'd wanted so badly to be normal. To have fun and party and go wild. Unfortunately, it hadn't even taken one semester to accept that she just wasn't that person.

But she'd found Trace, and that had made attending a big university worthwhile.

"Trust me, she'll do much bigger and better things than The Homesteader Inn." Chef Jonny squeezed her shoulder.

Lulu shook her head. "If Michelin covered Wyoming, you'd have a star. No question." People came from all around the world to stay at the romantic inn nestled in the woods of the Teton Mountain Range. A twelve-course meal prepared by Chef Jonny was a treat—they were booked a year in advance.

"Well, come on, sweetie, we're about to do toasts," her mom said.

"Excellent." Chef Jonny untied his apron. "Let me find my wife, so she can open the champagne."

As her mom hooked an arm through hers and led her out of the kitchen, Lulu glanced back over her shoulder and found Chef watching her with a concerned expression. That same awful longing welled up again, to stay in the kitchen, in the only world where she felt like her best self.

But that'll change tomorrow, when I get married. And then I'll never feel this loneliness again. No matter where I am, no matter what I'm doing, I'll know there's someone at home waiting for me.

They made their way to the head table, where her dad talked with his buddies.

Her mom leaned in. "Where's Trace?"

"No idea." She'd ask her dad. "Do you know where Trace went?"

He spun around with a big smile. Everyone loved Tyler Cavanaugh, not because he was one of the best quarterbacks who'd ever played, but because he listened to their stories. He cared. He was such a good guy. "Uh…he was here a minute ago." Reaching for Lulu, he enfolded her in his big, strong arms. "Before we do toasts, I just want to say something. Tomorrow, I'm symbolically giving you away, but you'll always be my little girl. You know that, right?"

She nodded against his chest. When he was about to pull away, she looked up at him. "Do you think I'm making a mistake marrying Trace?"

He grew instantly alert, as though hearing a burglar in the house. "We've talked about this before." He searched her eyes. "You know my concerns, but you said you loved him and wanted to be with him. Why are you bringing it up now, the night before the wedding?" His sincere expression drew a sting of tears to the backs of her eyes. "If you're having second thoughts, tell me now. I don't care how far along it's gotten, we'll call it off, no problem."

"No, no. I'm not calling anything off. I just want to know...never mind." He was right. Multiple times over the past eighteen months, he'd suggested Trace was spending way too much time with him, and Lulu had told him she liked that he fit in so well, that it gave her the freedom to cook and the comfort to know they'd always live close to her family—not his.

"You sure?" Her dad looked concerned.

"Positive."

He gave her a nod, trusting her, and then reached for a knife, tapping it against his water glass. "Can everyone take a seat, please? Champagne's coming around, so grab a glass."

Chairs scraped, and the conversation grew even louder as people looked for their tables.

"Has anyone seen Trace?" her mom asked.

One of her dad's football buddies, cupped his mouth and called, "Trace? Where's the groom?"

A server with a pewter tray brought glasses filled with bubbly to the head table, and Lulu grabbed hers. Excitement started to roll in, as she pushed aside her doubts and focused on the moment.

"Oh, good," she heard her mom say. "You're here."

She turned, eager to have Trace close, needing his reassurance. He always knew how to make her feel special.

But it wasn't him. It was Gigi. "You're giving the first toast," her mom said.

Nodding, Gigi reached for a glass. She took a sip, eyeing Lulu over the top of the flute with a saucy shrug of her platinum eyebrows.

I should've chosen Gigi as my maid of honor.

"Should I text him?" Lulu asked.

Gigi shook her head. "Why bother? He's not paying attention to his phone right now. Not with all his buddies here to party with him."

Searching the room, her dad cupped his hands at either side of his mouth and called, "Trace!"

But between the shadows created by the low lighting, the potted plants, and the wait staff setting bread baskets on the tables, it was hard to make out individual faces.

Any minute now, he'd pop his head out from a big group of people—probably at the bar—and he'd jog across the restaurant, bumping fists and slapping palms on his way to the head table.

"I'm starting without him." Her dad faced the room. "Can I get everyone to sit down?" His commanding presence had people quieting down. "Thank you all for coming tonight. It's great to see faces we haven't seen in a while." He shoved a hand into the pocket of his dress slacks. "Lulu came out of the womb with a spatula in one hand and a sprig of parsley in the other." He paused for the titter of laughter. "And her first word was, 'kitchen,' breaking her mother's heart."

Laughter erupted, and her dad continued talking. But noise filled her brain. There were only a few people still standing, and Trace wasn't with them.

"Right, sweetheart?" Her dad wrapped an arm around her shoulder and drew her up against him. She'd missed that last sentence, but the guests were laughing, so she didn't have to answer. She just stood there and smiled.

And that's when her gaze snagged on a red dress.

She did a double-take.

Because at the back of the restaurant, behind the fronds of a potted plant, right where the tiny, white fairy lights dripped down the stucco walls, Stella was making out with someone that wasn't Griffin.

Lulu went rigid. She had to take a moment to make sense of what she was seeing because her mind was tricking her into seeing Trace.

Lots of men wore crisp blue suits. Lots of them had neatly trimmed blonde hair.

But none of them wore a neon yellow silicone wristband signifying the Penn State football team's annual fundraiser for The Children's House.

"Now," her dad said. "I'm going to hand the mic over to Gigi, who's got a little story to tell."

But time had stopped. A clammy chill gripped her skin.

"Lu?" Her dad squeezed her shoulder. "What's going on?"

Clothing swished and chairs screeched on the hardwood floor, as everyone followed Lulu's gaze to the back of the room. Trace's hands clutched Stella's ass, squeezing, as he ground his hips against her.

"That fucker." Coco charged across the room. "I'm going to cut his dick off."

"Is that Trace?" her mom asked. "Who is he…is that *Stella*?"

"Oh, my God," someone called.

In the flurry of activity—her sister racing across the room, people jumping out of their seats—Lulu set her flute down on the table. A commotion broke out when one of Trace's friends pulled him off Stella.

Quietly, Lulu headed around the table. Eyes on the bright red exit sign, her legs moved, and it was all she could do to stay upright, as the weight of a hundred suns bore down on her.

Two years ago, Stella had stolen Griffin right out from her.

Tonight, her sister had stolen her future.

And this time, there was no going back.

About the Author

Award-winning author Erika Kelly writes sexy and emotional small town romance. Married to the love of her life and raising four children, she lives in the southwest, drinks a lot of tea, and is always waiting for her cats to get off her keyboard.

https://www.erikakellybooks.com/

facebook.com/erikakellybooks

twitter.com/ErikaKellyBooks

instagram.com/erikakellyauthor

goodreads.com/Erika_Kelly

pinterest.com/erikakellybooks

amazon.com/Erika-Kelly

bookbub.com/authors/erika-kelly